Lost Melody

Roz Lee

DEDICATION

For Terrell.
You make my heart sing.

ACKNOWLEDGMENTS

I conceived this story while driving down the interstate, all alone in my daughters old Taurus that just happened to have a kick-ass stereo. I don't remember the exact song that triggered the idea, but it featured a drum solo that made me forget for a moment that long-haul truckers were buzzing past me at dizzying speeds. So, first I have to thank Sarah for the opportunity to drive her car that day. I doubt I would have come up with the storyline under any other circumstances.

Since I know nothing about music or the recording industry, writing about a musician was problematic. For this, I turned to my cousin Rodney Wall who is a musician and songwriter. He was gracious with his time and his knowledge, and I suspect he rolled his eyes at my ridiculous questions a time or two. Thanks to email, I was spared knowing this and choose to think it only happened sparingly.

Over the years, I entered the

manuscript in a few contests and I can't thank the judges enough for their honest feedback. As THE KEY OF LOVE, it came in second in the Celtic Romance Writers Golden Claddaugh Contest, and as LOST MELODY it won the Contemporary Romance category of the Music City Romance Writers Melody of Love contest.

Without a doubt, this story would never have seen the light of day without the input from my friend, fellow writer, and cover artist, Talina Perkins. Many people read my original manuscript, but Talina, God bless her, took time out of her insanely busy life to critique for me. Her insight prompted a complete rewrite that I am satisfied now is ready for the world to see.

Many thanks to my editor, Laura Garland. Every time I receive an edited manuscript back from Laura, I am reminded that I am nothing more than a storyteller. She is the brains behind my grammar, punctuation, and sentence structure. Any errors in those areas are either intentional on my part or completely my fault.

Lost Melody

Lastly, I must thank my family for indulging me in my storytelling career. Without their support and encouragement, I would never have the courage to pursue my dream.

Roz Lee

Lost Melody

CHAPTER ONE

Mel pumped a nickel into the antique parking meter in front of The Donut Hole and went inside. She paused to savor the intoxicating medley of aromas that never failed to jump-start her system—even after a near-sleepless night. Fatigue rolled off her shoulders. She smiled and greeted a few familiar faces with a wave over the crowded shop.

She took her place in line and thanked goodness for the owner's hot chocolate making skills. In the few months she had been in Willowbrook, a cup of Cathy's concoction had become her morning addiction. It was rich and decadent enough to inspire her to give her new life another chance.

At last, her turn at the counter arrived. Cathy smiled warmly at her. Gratitude for her friendship filled Mel with contentment.

"Morning, sunshine," Cathy said, taking in Mel's appearance and coming to the correct conclusion. Nothing got by her. "Another bad night?"

"So so. I think I'm getting better," she lied. She'd hoped moving to a new place, one far away in both distance and demeanor, would be the magic cure for her sleepless nights, but it hadn't proven to be the case. It seemed her problems were destined to follow her wherever she went.

"I don't get it, girlfriend. There's nothing in Willowbrook to keep a person awake in daylight, much less at night."

"I know. It's not the town. It's me. I just don't sleep well. Maybe I'm part vampire," she joked, knowing it wasn't the undead keeping her awake.

Lost Melody

"I read something about an herbal remedy…Melatonin, I think it was called. The name reminded me of you. Mel…Melatonin. Get it?"

She smiled at the well-meant help. At least her new friend cared enough to offer whatever she could. "Yeah, I get it. Thanks, but I've tried it. Didn't work."

"Oh well." Cathy shrugged. "What will it be today, the usual?"

"I've got an interview, so two hot chocolates, and pick out half a dozen doughnuts for me. Anything will do, but make sure at least one has chocolate on it."

Cathy filled the order and passed it over the counter. "I'll put it on your tab."

"Thanks. Remind me to settle up at the end of the week."

"Oh, don't you worry! Go on, I've got customers waiting."

Mel held the door open for the group of silver-haired ladies who met at The Donut Hole every morning to gossip over pastries and coffee.

She'd love to write an article about them one day. They probably had a million stories to tell about the town, and every one of them would be good. The last one through the door thanked her, and Mel headed to her Jeep. She tossed the doughnut bag onto the passenger seat, stowed the two steaming cups in the built-in cup holders, and went in search of her interviewee.

She pulled to the curb in front of 755 Pecan Street and cut the engine. The house looked like all its neighbors, except for the rioting scarlet azaleas in bloom along the base of the raised porch. She peered through the open front door behind the rusty screen. Seeing no one inside, she rapped her knuckles against the screen door sending it clattering against the jamb.

"Mr. Travis? Anyone home?"

She stepped back, taking a moment to admire the neat yard and well kept flowerbeds. The next-door neighbor tended her rose bushes, wearing a broad brimmed straw hat and rubber gardening clogs. The woman turned, revealing a sleeping infant in one of those backpack things hanging from her shoulders. Mel squashed the ping of envy that inevitably came when she saw a mother with her kids. Maybe one day….

No. It was a dream she'd let go of a long time ago, along with the one about finding a guy who didn't mind her being a fugitive from her own life.

A bee buzzed around her head and zeroed in on the bright spring buds surrounding the porch. She closed her eyes and breathed in the morning air tinged with the intoxicating sweetness of roses and the fresh clean scent of wet earth. Aromatherapy at its best. If peace had a scent, this she thought, was it. As tempting as it was, she couldn't stand on the porch all day. She had a job to do.

She knocked again, and getting no answer she turned to leave.

"Just go on in," the woman next door spoke, halting Mel halfway down the steps. "Henry is in there somewhere. He won't mind."

"Thanks. I'll do that. He is expecting me."

She wiggled her fingers at the neighbor—the best she could do with her hands full—and backtracked up the steps. Life in Willowbrook, and in rural north Texas, was different than anything she had ever experienced. Few people locked their doors, and everyone knew everyone else's business. In a few short months, she had grown to love the lifestyle. At first, the similarities between her busybody neighbors and the paparazzi had shaken her, but it hadn't taken long to figure out the difference. Folks in Willowbrook took care of each other—like a family.

She juggled her offering of doughnuts and hot chocolate and tried the screen door. It was unlocked. No surprise.

She stepped cautiously into the

living room. The furniture was dated but not worn out. Morning light through the front window illuminated a faded floral rug over a hardwood floor. Other than a novel resting on a small table next to an overstuffed recliner, the room appeared little used.

"Hello! Anyone home?"

Silence.

She moved with caution, announcing her presence as she went. She could just see tomorrow's headline—*Reporter Frightens Elderly Resident to Death*. Or another possibility—*Elderly Resident Mistakes Reporter for Burglar and Opens Fire*. Neither one held any appeal.

She passed the tiny dining room and kitchen. They were both empty, which left only the short hallway and the bedrooms to explore. She entered the passage on trembling legs. Her imagination conjured every terrifyingly possible scenario. Poor Mr. Travis might be incapacitated on the bathroom floor…or worse.

Only three doors opened off the hall. Two bedrooms and one bath, she surmised—much like her own house a few streets over. She peeked around the first door and breathed a sigh of relief. The tiny bathroom was empty.

She leaned against the wall and closed her eyes. Her heart beat a wild rhythm in her throat and a pent-up breath rushed past her lips. She took a moment to gather her courage and checked the next room. A bedroom. It, too, was scrupulously clean and empty.

"Thank heavens," she muttered.

A faint rustling of papers drew her attention to the final door. Adrenaline flowed and her heart raced even faster. Fearing the worst, she sucked in a steadying breath and stepped into the open doorway.

She gasped.

Oh, Lord!

The man seated at the antique secretary didn't fit the house.

Literally. He overwhelmed the small bedroom-turned-office. Long, denim clad legs stretched across the room. His feet, encased in canvas sneakers, tapped a silent rhythm. An overweight black Labrador Retriever slept on the floor next to his chair. The useless watchdog rolled her brown eyes at Mel but didn't move from her position.

"Hello," she called. Neither one stirred. The dog was either very well trained or the laziest canine on the planet. She couldn't imagine what the man's excuse was. Then she noticed the thin wire snaking across his chest from his shirt pocket to the tiny earbud headphones he wore. She shrugged and leaned against the doorframe. No wonder he hadn't heard her. He probably had the volume so high he wouldn't hear a freight train bearing down on him.

If this was Mr. Travis, he was younger than she expected—perhaps thirty. Certainly no more than thirty-five. His sandy hair was cut in a familiar style. Willowbrook had one barbershop and one barber, Judd Spencer. Her first week on the job she had been asked to write an article on the aging barber who had been doling out the same haircut to any and all comers for the last forty years.

She noted the man's strong, cleanly shaved jaw. He wore surprisingly stylish reading glasses, Ralph Lauren if she knew her logos, and she did. The sleeves of his starched dress shirt were rolled to reveal the corded muscles of his forearms. He held a sheaf of papers in long fingers.

He looked like he should be in a magazine ad for…something. Men's cologne, a sexy watch perhaps. Whatever. He was too sexy to be in this house—or in Willowbrook for that matter.

He ran a finger down the page, his focus complete. Her skin tingled. *Lucky piece of paper.* What it would feel like to have him study her with the same intensity, and oh Lord, to have those hands explore every inch of her body?

She licked her lips and swallowed hard past the lump in her throat. She had never seen a sexier man. Just watching him made things itch and ache that shouldn't be itching and aching—not for someone she was supposed to interview. It wasn't professional.

She mentally kicked herself. She had a job to do.

She took another step into the room and waved a quickly cooling cup of hot chocolate into his line of vision. "Hello."

Mr. Travis jumped to his feet, pulling the headphones and glasses off in the same motion. Summer green eyes framed by long lashes took stock of her in a brisk head to toe sweep. He dropped the papers and reading glasses to the desk. The earbuds swung on thin wires from his pocket, and the distinct chords of "Melody" by RavensBlood filled the air. The lump in her throat threatened to cut off her air supply, and those earlier tingles turned to icy shivers of dread. Memories battered at her defenses and threatened her hold on reality. She took a step back—as if distance could lessen the impact.

She forced the memories into the neat little box she had assigned them and mentally shoved it into the cellar where it belonged.

You can do this.

The job. Willowbrook. It was a new beginning, a chance to put the painful memories behind her. She *would not* blow it because the man had that song on his player. Hell, everyone on the planet had that song. It was something she had to learn to live with.

She took a deep breath and squared her shoulders. "I-I'm looking for Henry Travis." She nodded down the hallway in the direction of the front door. "I knocked several times. Y- your neighbor said I should come on in." Another more welcome idea blossomed in her chest. Perhaps he wasn't the man she'd come to interview. *Please, God. Let it be someone else, anyone else.* Just not a man with the ability to make her tingle, and long to run away at the same time. "Is Henry home?"

"Which Henry Travis are you looking for?"

His voice, like hot chocolate with an edge, coated the icy points of her nerve endings and brought back that tingly feeling. Insanity. It was the only explanation. "Um, I don't know exactly. Is there more than one?"

"Yes. I'm Henry Travis, Jr., but everyone calls me Hank. Henry is my dad." The dog roused from her stupor and stood next to him. He rubbed her head, earning the dog's adoration. "This is Betty Boop. She's harmless."

"Obviously." She spared a glance at the dog and returned her gaze to the man who most decidedly was not harmless—at least not to her, not with that infernal song still playing from the earbuds dangling from his pocket. She entertained the idea of asking him to turn it off but doing so would only invite questions she didn't want to answer. "Do you live here?"

He flashed a quirky half-smile that weakened her knees. "This is my dad's house. I have a farm outside of town. The Chilcote place. Maybe you know it."

She shook her head. "No, I don't think I do. I'm sort of new around here." Her legs wobbled under his scrutiny. Damn. She needed to get a grip, and fast. The way his eyes raked her from head to toe made her conscious of the way her silk blouse draped over her breasts, and judging by the way his gaze lingered there, he had noticed, too. So much for the professional appearance she'd been going for when she'd selected her wardrobe this morning.

"What have you got there?" He nodded toward her hands.

"Oh. I brought doughnuts and hot chocolate." She raised the bag as evidence.

Lost Melody

His eyebrows shot up. "Okaaay. Why don't we go to the kitchen, and you can tell me why you're here."

She heard his low whistle when she turned and led the way. With each step, she silently cursed her other wardrobe choice, a sleek cotton and spandex blend pencil skirt that molded to her curves but allowed her hips to move when she walked. Heavy footsteps lagged behind—far enough to get the full effect. She placed her burden on the vintage oak kitchen table and turned. He stopped just inside the doorway, his face unreadable as he lounged against the doorframe with his arms crossed over his chest and his hips cocked to one side in a casual yet wary stance. The interview was not going well. Not at all. If she didn't get this back on track, she would walk out of here with nothing—and that just wouldn't do.

She pasted a smile on her face. "Maybe I should start over." She extended her right hand. "I'm Mel Harper from the Willowbrook

Gazette."

Betty Boop ambled past her master and sniffed the doughnut bag. She plunked her rear end down and turned pleading eyes on the man in the doorway. Hank ignored the dog and Mel's outstretched hand.

"Well, Ms. Harper. I don't do interviews, doughnuts or no doughnuts."

His tone cut her bravado off at the knees. She dropped her hand to her side. "But I have an appointment at nine-thirty to interview you about your donation to the Willowbrook High School Band program."

He straightened, dwarfing the kitchen as he had the small office. Gulliver in Lilliput, and she was definitely a Lilliputian. She gripped a chair back to steady herself. The earbuds swung from his shirt pocket, but thankfully, he had turned the music off. He was close enough she could smell his aftershave— something woodsy with expensive undertones. Sexy.

Lost Melody

He cocked his hips to one side and buried his left hand in the front pocket of his jeans while he studied the pattern in the old linoleum. His right hand rubbed along the back of his neck. She gripped the chair tighter to steady herself and to keep from touching him.

With a long sigh, he dropped his hand. He raised his eyes to hers and her heart did a somersault. In a matter of minutes, his appraisal had gone from hot to arctic to a gentle spring breeze—cool with a promise of genuine warmth. Wow! His mood changed faster than the Texas weather.

"I'm sorry, Ms. Harper. You must be looking for Dad. I wasn't aware he made a donation to the band. But I'm not surprised. It sounds like something he would do." He held his hand out, palm up. "He must have lost track of the time. He eats breakfast every day down at the fire station. I'm sure he got wrapped up in a domino game and forgot."

As if on cue, the screen door slammed and a smaller, older version of Hank Travis stormed the kitchen. "I'm sorry. I forgot the time."

She liked the newcomer instantly. Beneath heavy eyebrows, his blue eyes twinkled with merriment and spunk. Smile lines bracketed his mouth identical to his son's. Yes, this was the solid block from which the younger man had been carved. Time had smoothed the rough edges on one but had a ways to go with the other.

She glanced at Hank. He flashed another smile and raised an eyebrow as if to say, "I told you so." Clearly, he loved his father, quirks and all. Her heart softened toward him just a little.

"Chester tried to pull a fast one and got caught," the older man continued, "so we started the game over." He extended a hand lined with age.

She shook his hand. "Mel Harper. I just met Hank." A look passed between father and son.

"I hope he wasn't rude," Henry said, absently petting the dog who had wandered over, tail wagging, for some attention. "He doesn't care too much for reporters."

If that wasn't the understatement of the century, she didn't know what was, but she was a professional. Kill them with kindness was her motto. "No, sir. He's been quite the gentleman." She dared Hank to deny it. There it was again, a quick, shared glance between them filled with unspoken communication. "I brought doughnuts and hot chocolate. Would you like some?"

"Why, thanks! That was mighty thoughtful of you." Henry took a plate from the cupboard and emptied the bag onto it, exclaiming over the pastries as if she'd brought French delicacies.

"Son, why don't you heat her hot chocolate in the microwave? You can have my cup. I'm a coffee man myself," he said apologetically, "and

I'm already over my limit for the morning." He took a paper napkin from the holder and selected a glazed doughnut from the plate. "But I never turn down a doughnut." He took a generous bite and tore off a smaller piece. He tossed it up. Betty Boop made an athletic leap and caught the treat in mid-air. Encouraged by her success, she plopped at his feet.

The older man pulled out a chair for Mel and settled himself across from her. Hank placed a warmed cup at her elbow and excused himself. She watched him go. Mood swings and lack of social skills aside, the man had it going on. Threadbare denim had never looked as good as it did hugging his slim hips, firm ass, and long legs. She forced her mind back to the reason she was here.

"I'm afraid I got off to a bad start with your son. I hope I didn't overstep by coming here."

"No, no, don't mind him. He's always short with reporters. He'll come around," he said. "Now…about the interview."

"Why? I mean, what does he have against reporters?"

"Oh, nothing. He had a bad experience a few years ago. Don't think anything of it."

"Well, okay." She was more than a little curious, but she had a deadline to meet. Though she couldn't blame him for that particular dislike, she had her own reasons to dislike certain members of her profession, Hank Travis and his problems were none of her business. She pulled a mini-recorder from her purse and set it on the table between them. "Do you mind if I record our interview?"

"That's fine as long as I don't have to listen to myself on it. Does anyone like the way they sound on a recording?"

Her gut clenched. She forced a smile to her face. "I suppose some do. But you're right, most people don't recognize their own voices on a recording."

He rubbed his chin. "I sure don't. Nope, I'm always surprised at the way I sound." He waved his hand at the recorder. "Go ahead. Turn it on."

She pressed the record button. "I understand you're making a large donation to the Willowbrook High School Band. Can you tell me what motivated you?"

"Sure. They need new instruments and uniforms." He laughed, deep and rich. "I can see what you're thinking, young lady. Don't be worrying I'm giving my life savings away to a bunch of ungrateful teenagers. I'm doing all right, and they need the money more than I do. They've been doing car washes and selling candy bars all year and they've hardly made a dent in the bill, so I thought I would help them out. They're a good bunch of kids, and I have a soft spot where the band is concerned."

He paused, his eyes focused on something only he could see. He drew himself up. "Anyway, every time there's a budget cut, it hits the music program first. I don't think its right, so I help them out every now and then."

"But Mr. Travis, twenty-five thousand dollars is a lot of money."

He looked her square in the eye. "I can afford it."

She backed off. "Well, then. Okay. You say you have a soft spot for the band. Why?"

His face softened, and a gentle smile curved his lips. "The band and the music program were good to my boy, Hank, and his mother, Gloria. My late wife taught music at the high school for twenty years before she passed on."

She instantly regretted her earlier skepticism.

Familiar footsteps sounded behind her. "Dad? Sorry to interrupt," Hank said. Shivers ran along her spine when she heard the smooth voice. "I made some notes for you on those papers. I'm going out to the farm. Are you coming for dinner tonight?"

"Yeah. How's six o'clock?"

"Perfect. I'll see you at six." Hank

snapped his fingers, and Betty Boop stretched and followed her master as he left without so much as a goodbye.

Rude. She asked a few more questions, thanked Henry for his generous donation and his time, and rose to leave. He followed her to the front door. "You should ask Hank a few questions, too."

She didn't want to bring up how inhospitable his son had been, but she couldn't forget the sudden bolt of desire she'd felt when she first saw him. Personally, she wanted to do a lot more than ask him questions, but professionally he'd made it clear he didn't want to see her again.

"I don't think it would be such a good idea. I'm a reporter, remember? Besides, I only have until this afternoon to finish the article for tomorrow's edition."

His face fell like a kicked puppy. She scrambled to think of something she could do or say to put a smile back on his face. Then, like his son, his mood abruptly shifted. He snapped his fingers. "Hey! Why don't you come out to the farm with me this evening for dinner? You might get a second article if you play your cards right."

She couldn't imagine what kind of article she could write about a farmer, but she genuinely liked Henry and didn't want to disappoint him. "I don't know," she hedged.

"Trust me, Ms. Harper. Meet me there around six. It's the place out on Route 544. The one with the black bird wings painted on the barn."

She knew the place. She'd wondered about the giant black wings but decided it was just coincidence and better left alone.

He waited for her answer, expectation written all over his expressive face. She really didn't want to go, but she didn't want to hurt his feelings either.

"Well, if you think it will be all right." Her body warmed at the memory of the sexy denim-clad Hank

Travis. She could make a dinner out of him, but as tasty as he appeared on the outside, she had no doubt he was pure vinegar on the inside.

"Oh, he won't mind. I bring friends out all the time," he said.

Agreeing to dinner at Hank's house was so not a good idea, but she couldn't bring herself to say no to his father—not with him standing there with a hopeful expression on his face.

"Well, okay, but I have to turn in the article before I can go, so I'd better get a move on."

"Run along, then." He held the screen door for her. "Six o'clock. Don't be late."

She climbed into her Jeep and pulled away from the curb. She had often wondered about her sanity but there was no doubt. She was insane. Completely bonkers to let Henry talk her into dinner at his son's house.

CHAPTER TWO

Hank leaned back in his desk chair. A stack of invoices awaited his attention but images of Mel Harper eclipsed everything. She had stepped into his line of sight and somehow lodged herself into his consciousness, refusing to go away.

He could still see her rose-petal lips telling him she was new in town. Even though he had been on tour for most of the last six months, the information had not been news. He had lived in Willowbrook his entire life. If Mel Harper had been here for long, he would have remembered her. Just like he would never forget the first moment he saw her.

He had been so absorbed in the song he was listening to and trying to concentrate on his dad's tax returns, he hadn't noticed her at first. Something had caught his eye, and he'd glanced up. There she'd stood in the doorway, clutching a greasy bag in a white knuckled grip while she balanced two paper hot-cups in her other hand. Large, sky-blue eyes framed by long lashes had taken his measure, and he'd gladly returned the favor.

At that point, if she had turned out to be a stalker he wouldn't have cared. Talk about visions coming to life. She was the subject of every wet dream he'd ever had—small, perky, and sexy as hell with those curves of hers. Dressed in her stylish business attire, a lurid fantasy involving a secretary, a desk, and a fair amount of sexual harassment had instantly popped into his head.

He'd managed to shake the fantasy out of his head, but he couldn't shake her image. The fact she was a reporter didn't seem to matter much to his body even though a small portion of his brain still urged caution where the species was concerned. What would it hurt to indulge his libido a little bit? It wasn't like he was going to see her again anytime soon. Willowbrook was small, but he didn't spend much time in town when he was at home, and few people came to the farm. Avoiding her would be easy enough.

He closed his eyes and let the image take shape in his mind.

She couldn't have been more than five-foot-two, petite, but not fragile. Her dark hair fell in soft waves over her shoulders, and her skin reminded him of warm milk, creamy and smooth.

At first, he'd thought she had to be a fan—perhaps a crazy one. Being the drummer for the rock band BlackWing, he'd had his share of pushy fans. It wouldn't have been the first time one had tracked him down, but he'd never had one walk right in without invitation and bring breakfast, too. Crazy fan or not, she'd been about the sexiest thing he had ever seen. His hormones had snapped to attention faster than he could get his feet under him. When she'd turned and he'd seen her ass and the way the rose-colored fabric molded itself to her curves as she walked…. Well, there'd been no stopping the fantasies at that point.

Then she'd introduced herself, and his desire had hit a brick wall. Worse than a fan. Worse even than a stalker.

The wet dream was a reporter.

The revelation should have killed his interest, and it had for a few minutes. He shouldn't be thinking about her, not in any way, shape, or form. But here he sat trying to concentrate on work, and there she was, front and center in his thoughts. Sexy. She sure as hell didn't shop locally. Those were big city clothes— understated, sophisticated, classy. And either she didn't know who he was or she was a very good actress as well as a reporter.

He acknowledged the improbability, but with reporters, you never knew. Some would go to any length to get a story. He needed to steer clear of her, avoid further contact, keep temptation at arm's length. He had plenty to do. Enough to keep him busy and far away from town for the next few months. He didn't have to see her. He didn't have to talk to her.

He wrestled his runaway libido under control and turned his attention to the blinking light on his message machine. He listened to two messages from his publicist, one from his agent, and one from his father indicating he would bring a friend along for dinner. The last and most important message was from Sir Jonathan Youngblood in London.

He mentally calculated the time difference between Texas and London. The RavensBlood cover album held top priority, so he made the overseas call. He left yet another voice mail for Sir Jonathan.

Frustrated with his lack of success, he traded his office for a soundproof rehearsal room.

Hours later, he noticed the yellow light on the control panel next to the door blinking, signaling he had company. He glanced at his watch. Damn. Hopefully, his dad already had the steaks on. His stomach sent up its own audible signal. He'd done it again, lost himself in the music, and forgotten about everything else. Oh well. It wasn't the first time, and it wouldn't be the last either.

He shut off the equipment, stretched stiff muscles, and urged Betty Boop to her feet. As he stepped from the barn, the smell of mesquite and grilling beef greeted him. He locked the pedestrian door and stretched again.

Endless Texas sky, azure blue in the late afternoon light, was a welcome sight. No matter how hectic his life got he always had this to come back to. The farm, and the acres of planted fields, grounded him. He loved the rambling old farmhouse he'd inherited from his maternal grandparents. The house was solidly rooted in family history, and the farm predictable in its seasonal routines. Solid and predictable were good things as far as he was concerned. But above all else, Willowbrook was where he lived his life. It was home.

He paused, inhaling the warm, humid air. The smell of turned earth and cut grass was as familiar and comforting as his worn jeans. He surveyed the expanse of young cotton plants growing in the fertile black soil, and peace settled over him. The weight of the world could be on his shoulders and a stroll through these fields would make it all go away. His grandfather had taught him the value of a good long walk to organize his thoughts and calm his soul.

After his mother died, he'd worn a new path through the fields, watering the plants with his tears as he went.

Some might think farm life was isolating, but he knew better. In the fields, he felt part of something big, bigger than he could fathom.

The land comforted, but he longed for another kind of comfort—the kind that came from sharing his life with another. He would never leave the farm, but he hoped to one day find someone who loved it as much as he did, maybe have some kids he could pass the farm down to, but until that happened, he'd continue on his present path. He had the best of two worlds, and there was absolutely nothing wrong with that.

His stomach growled again, urging him to follow his nose to the source of the heavenly smell. He headed toward the patio and grill beneath the ancient oak tree, hoping his dad and whomever he'd brought with him had saved him a Lone Star.

Henry waved a greasy spatula at him in greeting. "It's about time you got out here. We've been waiting for you. The steaks are almost done."

Thanks to the girth of the old oak, supposedly planted by his great-grandfather over one hundred years ago, he couldn't see the 'we' his dad spoke of. He rounded the tree and stopped cold in his tracks. He caught a glimpse of leg and his blood pressure skyrocketed. The guest wasn't one of his dad's domino playing buddies. That leg belonged to a female. A young, shapely female. One who painted her toenails candy-apple red.

No. He wouldn't do this to me. Not my own father. Hank licked his dry lips and closed the distance. What had she told his father in order to finagle an invitation to dinner? It must have been good to get him to go along with it. *Dad knows how I feel about reporters.*

He stalked past his father. Mel Harper occupied his favorite lawn chair. She stood as he approached. Holding a sweating glass of white wine in one hand, she tucked the fingers of her free hand in the pocket of her shorts. Lord help him if he thought she'd looked good in her fancy business clothes. That was nothing compared to how shorts and a tank top showed off her curves. He'd never get her out of his mind. Not after tonight. A bead of perspiration clung to her hairline and his fingers itched to sweep it away for her. Better yet, if he put his lips there…

"It's good to see you again, Hank," she said with an innocent smile that didn't fool him one bit.

What remained of his good mood vanished faster than biscuits at a church supper. "What are you doing here?"

Her smile disappeared. A flash of anger crossed her face, and as quickly as it appeared was replaced by a cold mask of civility.

"Your father invited me." Fury backed her clipped words. "But I made a mistake in accepting his invitation." She stood toe to toe with him, a petite Amazon. "If you'll step aside, I'll be on my way."

He held his ground, trying his best to ignore her scent—roses with a hint of something earthy. Her breasts rose and fell beneath the scoop neck of her top. He shifted his stance, straightening, anything to put distance between them without seeming to back down. "Why are you here?" he repeated.

Her gaze met his boldly. "I told you, I was invited." Her voice matched his in cordiality. She stepped around him, set her wineglass on the picnic table, and retrieved her purse. Slinging the strap over her shoulder, she turned to his dad.

"Thanks for the invitation, Mr. Travis, but I've overstayed my welcome." She stretched to her toes and placed a kiss on Henry's cheek.

"Stay, please?" his dad implored.

She spoke to his dad as if they were old friends saying goodbye after a tea party. "I'd better go. I appreciate the invitation, but coming out here wasn't such a good idea." She patted his arm. "Let's have dinner in town one day soon. My treat."

She turned back to Hank. "It was nice to see you again, Mr. Travis." Her voice had more ice than a Blue Norther.

Betty Boop raised her head from her grassy pillow, saw Mel walking across the lawn, and like the kiss-up she was, took out after her. Henry watched their progress across the lawn and around the corner of the house. When they were out of sight, he shifted his gaze to his son.

Damn. Hank had seen the expression before. When he'd been a kid, he would have given anything for an old-fashioned spanking instead of receiving that look from his dad.

He caved under the disapproval in his father's eyes. Before Henry could lay into him about his manners, his long legs strode after her. "Ms. Harper," he called as he rounded the corner of the house. "Wait."

He caught up to her just as she was about to get in her Jeep. Guaranteed, she was made of better steel than her car door, but she used it as a shield, nonetheless.

"What do you want?" she asked.

"I'm sorry," he said, trying to catch his breath.

She glared at him through the open window frame. It wouldn't be easy to convince her to stay, not after he'd acted like such an ass.

"Look, Dad invited you, and anyone he invites is welcome in my home. It works both ways between us. Please accept my apology and stay for dinner." Betty Boop nudged his hand with her wet nose. He glanced down, rubbed her head to placate her, and shifted his attention back to the woman who made his blood boil—in every way possible. "If you don't stay, Dad will probably take a hickory switch to me."

He flashed her a smile that usually made the groupies scream but for some reason had no effect at all on

Mel Harper. Her gaze continued to drill through his skull with laser precision.

He had never had any trouble convincing a woman to stay with him before—well, not since high school. He should let her go and suffer the consequences. His dad would be mad for a day or two, but he'd get over it. Either way, stay or go, Ms. Mel Harper, reporter, spelled nothing but trouble.

She studied him through narrowed eyes.

Shit. He tried again. "Dad wanted you to come tonight, and that's good enough for me. I'm sorry. I shouldn't have spoken to you the way I did."

Her gaze darted between his face and the road. She had made up her mind. With a sigh, she shook her head and slid her right foot beneath the steering wheel.

Suddenly, keeping her here wasn't about what his dad wanted. It was about what he wanted. He didn't want her to go.

"Stay," he said, grabbing her arm through the open window. Electricity shot up his arm and raced south to his groin. Her eyes went wide, and she jerked her arm out of his grasp.

"Are you sure you want me here?" she asked as her right foot rejoined her left on the gravel drive.

Oh, I'm sure I want you. Here. There. Damned near anywhere. "I'm sure," he said, stepping back, giving her room to make her decision.

She nodded. "Okay. Okay." She hoisted her purse strap to her shoulder. "Apology accepted. You and I get along like oil and water, but I like your dad. He's a good man. And from what I heard today, your mother was a saint. I'll reserve judgment on you tonight, and I'll stay for dinner."

The vise squeezing his chest let go and he took a full breath. She slammed her car door and swept past him in the direction of his backyard. He'd experienced this feeling before—usually as a result of conquering stage fright. Relief.

As he watched her shapely backside sway across his yard he was pretty sure his relief would be short-lived.

**

Hank took over the grilling duties from his father and, true to his word, behaved himself for the remainder of the evening. Henry was an excellent host. He entertained her with dozens of stories, enough she almost forgot about her earlier tiff with his son. One thing she would never forget, though, was the spark of electricity that shot through her when Hank touched her. She had never felt anything like it before. She had been a lousy science student, but she'd read her share of sappy romances—enough to know what the spark meant. Attraction. But it didn't mean she needed to act on it. Really, she could hardly stand the man. Hank Travis was rude, arrogant, overbearing, and confusing.

A trip to the ladies room gave her a glimpse inside his home. The back door opened into the spacious kitchen, which at first glance appeared to be typical 1950s era construction. Its perfection gave away the secret. Behind the vintage façade lurked state of the art appliances. She had seen similar kitchens in home design magazines. The clever disguise didn't come cheap. Someone had gone to a lot of trouble and spent a ton of money on the renovation. She knew virtually nothing about farming, but she'd been in Willowbrook long enough to figure out it wasn't a high-income profession. Her curiosity shifted into high gear.

The two Henry Travises were a mystery. Henry dressed in typical Willowbrook fashion—JC Penney all the way. The solitary department store was as much a staple in town as Judd Spencer and his haircuts.

Hank, however, was a walking

contradiction. His faded Levi's appeared to be authentic, worn threadbare from years of use and abuse in contrast to the holey jeans city slickers paid hundreds of dollars for. His crisp white dress shirt came from Brooks Brothers, the nearest store being in Dallas, several hours away yet he sported a ten-dollar Judd Spencer haircut. He made no mention of what he'd been doing in the barn before she arrived, and given their tenuous truce, she wasn't inclined to ask.

She had been in Willowbrook for six months and hadn't seen Hank Travis until today. It would be hard to live unnoticed in such a small town, and if she *had* seen Hank Travis, she wouldn't have forgotten him. He would stand out in a crowd.

So, where had he been for six months? What did he do for a living? He wasn't a farmer—not the legal kind anyway.

She returned to their alfresco dinner with more questions than she had answers.

"Your home is lovely, Hank, what I saw of it anyway. I would have pegged you as a more modern type," she said.

"Really? Why?"

"Nothing specific. It's just a feeling."

"You couldn't be more wrong, Ms. Harper. I'm a simple man. I inherited the house and farm from my grandparents. I haven't changed much. I like it the way it is."

"I loved all the family photos in the hallway."

"My favorite is my grandparents' wedding photo," he said.

"Why?"

"They were so happy in the photo, but they still looked happy fifty years later. It's a reminder that some things endure. It gives me hope."

"Hope? For what?"

He shrugged. "You know. That I'll find someone, too."

"It shouldn't be too difficult," she said. "I would think a simple life would appeal to a lot of women."

Hank poked a long fork into a steak. "You'd be surprised."

She let the comment slide. There was more to Hank Travis than met the eye. He was hiding something. A good-looking guy like him living all by himself in a big old farmhouse? There was money somewhere, but he'd hidden it carefully. Separately, none of her observations were remarkable. But together? Well, in Hank's case, two and two did not make four. Perhaps his father had been right. Maybe she could get another story after all.

"The farm has been in my wife's family for generations," Henry said. "The first Chilcote got it in a land grant for his service in the Army of the Republic."

As Henry recited the history of the Chilcote farm and Willowbrook, Mel snuck glances at his son. With his back mostly turned to them, tending the grill, she had plenty of opportunities to check him out. He moved with grace, as if some inner rhythm guided his movements. Music in motion, she thought as he poked at the steaks with the fork in one hand and using the tongs with the other, flipped them easily. Flames from the charcoal licked above the rack, highlighting the roped muscles in his forearm.

When everything was done, Mel sat across from Hank at the old wooden picnic table that had seen more coats of paint than she had seen years. The food was delicious, steaks and farm fresh vegetables Hank had sliced and cooked on the grill just before the meat was ready. The simple meal was accompanied by slices of white bread, fresh from the wrapped loaf in the center of the table. Not gourmet, but she couldn't remember ever having a better meal in her life.

Henry kept her wine glass filled from a bottle he admitted snatching from his son's wine cooler. She couldn't bring herself to say no to a brownie for dessert, especially when Henry said he had made them himself.

CHAPTER THREE

Hank watched his dad's old truck disappear down the dusty drive. Thankfully, his father's stories had been old ones, nothing touching on the present. It was obvious Mel didn't know who he was…yet. But it was only a matter of time before someone in town said something or she figured it out on her own.

Six months. It must be some kind of record. Gossip usually spread faster than a prairie fire in Willowbrook. In all fairness to the gossip grapevine, he *had* been on tour most of that time. Out of sight, out of mind, they say. He was back, so tongues would wag. He could take that to the bank.

He checked on the grill, making

sure the coals had burned down enough to be safely left alone, and headed for the house. He needed information and that meant tapping into his own personal branch of the gossip grapevine. It wasn't early, but it wasn't late either, so he made the phone calls. He'd known Chris and Randy his entire life and he could count on them for the latest news.

The childhood friends gathered around the red Formica kitchen table in Hank's kitchen, sipping coffee and eating Oreo cookies straight from the bag. Betty Boop sat nearby using her best begging skills to score an occasional illicit treat.

"So, tell us, man. Let us old married guys live vicariously through you for a few minutes," Chris said.

"Yeah," Randy chimed in, "throw us a few crumbs. How about those French women? Are they as uninhibited as everyone says they are?"

Hank groaned. "You both know I don't hook up with the groupies and I wouldn't give you details if I did."

"Ah, man." Randy sat back, adjusting his long legs beneath the table. "We were hoping for some good stories tonight."

Hank raised an eyebrow. "Have I ever told you a good story from one of our tours?"

"Now that I think about it…no." Chris frowned. "So what are we here for?"

"Hey, it's good to see you, too," Hank groused, tossing a sliver of cookie at his lifelong friend.

"Just kidding," Chris said. He licked his index finger and pressed it onto the cookie crumb that had bounced off his chest and landed on the table. He ate the crumb off his fingertip. "But you got to give us something, man. We left our wives and screaming kids at home tonight to come all the way out here."

"Yeah, we made sacrifices," Randy agreed. He popped a whole cookie in his mouth and chewed. How he ate the way he did and remained stick thin, Hank would never know.

"You were both dying for an excuse to get out the house and you know it. But hey, I'm a nice guy, so I'll give you the inside scoop. This hasn't been released to the public yet so don't go spreading it around town. The band's going to do a RavensBlood cover album. If everything goes right, we'll start in a few weeks."

Randy whistled and slapped the table.

Chris let out a whoop. "That's great, man! You've wanted to do one for a long time, haven't you?" He grinned from ear to ear.

He could always count on Chris' support, and as Hank's personal attorney, the new album meant more work for Randy, but his enthusiasm was personal rather than professional. Hank had made no secret about his desire to do the RavensBlood cover album.

"Yeah. The cover album is my

project. The others are onboard, too, but you know how I am about RavensBlood. We've been working on the arrangements for months. It should be finalized soon."

"So, everyone will invade the farm again in a few weeks?" Randy asked.

"Yep. At least, I hope so. Summer is the best time for the guys and their families. If we don't get it done this summer, it may have to wait 'till next year."

Randy grabbed another cookie. "What are you going to do if it doesn't work out?"

"Watch the cotton grow, I guess. I don't have any other plans."

"You've got a good crop this year if that's what you're worried about," Chris was quick to assure him.

"No," Hank said. "I'm sure you have it under control, as always. I don't know what I would do without you to run the farm for me. If it wasn't for you, the place would be grown up in sunflowers and crab grass."

Chris had "done his time", as he

referred to it, at Texas A&M and had come back home as soon as he could to manage his family's farm. Hank had turned his own acreage over to his friend and hadn't regretted it for a moment.

"So, why did you get us out here tonight? Do you need legal advice? The catching up could have waited until the weekend."

Leave it to Randy voice the question they'd been dancing around from the start. Hank shook his head. "No. I don't need my lawyer, I need information." He slouched in his chair. "There's a new reporter at the Gazette. What do you know about her?"

Chris whistled low. "She's a looker, I know that."

Hank scowled. "You're a married man. Should you be noticing other women?"

"Hell, Hank, I'm married, not dead."

Randy laughed. "He's right. She's beautiful. Classy sort, big city girl, I think. Uncle Ralph hired her away from some magazine in Los Angeles. Or maybe it was San Francisco." He ran his fingers through his perpetually disheveled hair. "I don't know for sure, but she's from out there somewhere. He did say she went to college in Virginia. I can't remember the name of it right off hand. I could ask him for you."

"No. Don't bother. She's from L.A.? Are you sure?"

"I'm sure she's from California, beyond that, I couldn't say for sure. The word around town is she paid cash for her bungalow over on Sycamore Street. You know, the one old lady Williams used to live in?"

"Yeah, I know the one. I used to mow Mrs. Williams yard."

"Yeah, I remember that," Randy said.

Chris set his coffee cup down. "Why do you want to know about her?"

Hank sighed, running his fingers through his newly cropped hair. "Dad made a donation to the high school band, and she's doing a story about it for the paper. He invited her out here for dinner tonight. She didn't act as if she knew anything about me. If she's from California, it could be a cover. Some reporters will go to any extreme to get a story."

Randy and Chris looked at each other then at Hank.

"Do you really think she could be up to something?" Randy popped another Oreo.

"I don't know. I don't think so, but after what Karen did, I can't be too careful. It's taken years to clean up my image and people still call me by that ridiculous name."

"At least you found out what she was up to before you married her," Chris said.

"True. It was a narrow escape though. I learned a valuable lesson from the fiasco."

Chris frowned and tapped his finger on the table. "You think Mel Harper took the job here just to get to you? That's a little extreme. No offense, Hank, but it's pretty farfetched. You might be getting a little too full of yourself."

He knew the lengths a reporter would go to in order to get a story. Been there, done that—lesson learned. Only someone who lived in the public eye could really know what the media spotlight was like, and he'd given up trying to explain the experience to his friends long ago. They'd never get it, no matter how many times he tried to make them to understand. To them, getting their name or picture in the local paper was exciting. They couldn't comprehend what it was like to see your photo in the gossip rags every day along with a story fabricated from the flimsiest bit of truth, or more often, no truth at all. Anything to fill column inches.

He ignored Chris's question, seizing on the reprimand for the good-natured set down it was. "I'm full of it huh? Just exactly how do you propose to remedy that?"

Randy and Chris answered in unison, "Pool challenge!"

God, it was good to be home. "When and where, smart ass?" Hank asked.

"Tomorrow night. Eight o'clock at Smitty's," Randy said.

They agreed on the particulars before Hank walked them to the back door.

"Tell the women folk I said hi," he said.

"Will do." Randy slapped him on the back as he stepped out onto the porch. "Glad you're home."

"Yeah, it's good to have you back," Chris said, adding his own back slap and handshake.

"It's good to be here," Hank said. "And it's good to see ya'll. Thanks for coming out tonight. Next time, you'll have to bring the women and the brats."

"Just name the time," Randy said. "You know how much the kids love to run around this place."

"Man, we had some good times out here when we were kids," Chris said.

"Yeah, we did," Hank agreed. "Your kids love it, too."

"They do. I'm glad it's still here for them."

"Me, too," Hank said.

"See you tomorrow night. Don't forget your wallet," Chris said, following Randy down the steps.

"Yeah, right. You better bring *yours*, my friend," Hank countered.

Chris dismissed Hank's comment with a wave of his cowboy hat as he crossed the yard.

"Drive safe," Hank said to their backs.

Their trucks roared to life and disappeared down the drive.

"Come on, Betty, it's time to call it a night." He followed the dog into the kitchen, latched the screened door behind them, but left the real door open to let in the mild night air.

The house was quiet. He wandered through the empty rooms,

turning off lights, remembering the sound of laughter, family sing-a-longs, and noisy boys playing in the big rooms. His grandparents never complained when he brought his rowdy friends to the farm to run wild in the fields or daydream in the hayloft. They had plowed fields, fed cows, and chased chickens through the seasons and loved every minute of it.

Randy and Chris were like brothers to him. As kids, they had been inseparable. Hank had been the creative one, coming up with ideas. Chris had been the wild one, the instigator, urging them to carry out Hank's ideas, and often embellishing them with a daring element Hank would never have thought of. Chris had mellowed after marrying and having kids, but he could still be depended on to come up with a good prank if need be.

Randy had been the voice of sanity when they were kids he was still the most levelheaded person

Hank knew. He'd had no qualms about turning over all his private legal matters to Randy years ago. Without Chris to manage the farm and Randy to manage his financial holdings, he wouldn't be able to live the life he did. Not and stay sane.

The big rambling house was as much home as his parents' small house in town where he grew up. He loved everything about the farmhouse, the creaking wood floors, the clanging water pipes, the drafty windows, and the memories. He loved that his mother grew up in the house, and with any luck, his children would too. Since his career had taken off, the house and farm were his solid foundation. The house had become his sanctuary, and the converted barn, his creative playpen.

He wondered if the old house would ever be home to more than one lonely man again. In his profession, it was nearly impossible to meet women of the settling down kind, and *because* of his profession, no one in Willowbrook would even consider settling down with him. Mel Harper's image insinuated itself on his mind, and he fought it back. He could not, *would not*, get involved with a reporter.

CHAPTER FOUR

Smitty's was packed to the rafters with locals out for a little recreation after a hard week of scraping a living from the black soil of North East Texas. Hank paused inside the door, soaking in the familiar ambiance of stale spilled beer and the lingering stench of cigarette smoke from the days before smoking had been banned in the bar. The jukebox belted out a country ballad. It wasn't his style, but he could tolerate it. Someone shoved a cold Lone Star longneck into his hand as he passed the bar. He took a long swig and sized up the competition in the back room. Chris and Randy waited for the center table to free up. He joined them, leaning against the wall.

"Glad you could make it," Chris greeted him. "The table should be free in a few minutes."

"I'd never miss a chance to whoop the two of you."

"Right." Randy smirked. "Be prepared to put your money where your mouth is. I've been practicing while you've been gallivanting your pansy-ass all over the world."

"I've never needed practice to clean your pockets. How much are you planning to part with tonight?"

They were still haggling over the size of their bets when the hair on the back of his neck stood on end. Hank turned, scanned the room. He was just about to dismiss the feeling as nothing when he saw her. Mel Harper. It took a couple of seconds before her gaze met his, but when they locked, something flared between them, and he couldn't look away.

She wore denim. Expensive, designer denim. The short jacket matched the jeans and parted to reveal a white lace camisole. His gaze skimmed down her long legs to her sexy high heel sandals. Her toenails, painted a soft pink, matched her fingernails. She'd pulled her shoulder length hair into a high ponytail that swung side-to-side every time she moved. She sparkled like a diamond in a box of rocks.

Lord help him, but he wanted her.

He took a step in her direction, his gaze fixated on the patch of skin peeking out from the collar of her jacket. He'd start by tasting her there. A swish of hair crossed his line of sight, drawing his gaze up to troubled blue eyes. She shook her head and turned to leave.

He pounced, crossing the room in three steps and grabbed her by the elbow to halt her retreat. "Wait."

"Let go of me, Hammer."

Hank flinched at the nickname. He loosened his grip on her arm, and she twisted enough to break the contact. The voice of reason whispered in his head, *Let her go,* but instead he said, "Stay a while. We were about to play a game or two."

Her gaze darted around him to Chris and Randy. "No. No, I don't think so."

There was disgust and something else, fear perhaps, in her eyes. She turned, making a beeline to the door. He let her go. What else could he do? He cursed the nickname Karen had given him and the reputation that went along with it. It was shit like the stunt Karen had pulled on him that made celebrities wary of the media.

"What was that all about?" Chris asked when he rejoined his friends in the back. A table became available, and they moved in to claim it.

"Hell if I know." He leaned against the table and stared at the worn floorboards, absently rubbing the back of his neck with one hand. A part of him told him he'd just dodged a bullet, but another insisted she was worth the risk. Which one was right?

"What did you do to her?" Randy

asked. "She high-tailed it out of here with Cathy Anderson. You would have thought there was a skunk chasing them they were moving so fast."

He straightened. "All I did was invite her to play a round of pool with us. I hardly know the woman."

"Didn't look that way from here," Chris said.

Hank grabbed a pool cue and chalked the tip. "She called me Hammer."

Chris racked the balls. "So?"

"So, she knows who I am. I guess she believes everything she reads."

"She's a reporter. She should know better," Randy said, circling the table to give Hank room at the end.

Hank positioned the cue ball and lined up his shot. "I don't want to talk about it. Okay? I came here to play pool. Let's get on with it."

"There is some good news in all of this," Randy persisted.

"You obviously see something I don't, so fill me in," Hank said.

"Well, she knows who you are now, and it's obvious she doesn't want to be anywhere near you, so the chances of her using your dad to get close to you just dipped to zero."

Chris nodded. "He's got a point."

"Will you two stick a sock in it and just play?"

Leave it to those two to point out the flaws in his logic.

His friends were like two dogs with a 'coon in a tree. They wouldn't leave it alone. He lost the first game to Chris, and the second to Randy. He paid up without comment and settled his bar tab. He left his friends to play a winner-takes-all round without him.

Randy was right. She should know better than to believe everything she reads, which begged the question, why was she so upset to find out who he was? And the other question he couldn't shake— why did he care?

**

Mel barreled through the crowded bar and came face to face with Cathy.

"What's up, girlfriend?" Cathy asked.

"Nothing. Let's go. I don't want to be here tonight." She rummaged in her purse for her car keys. "Come on."

Cathy followed. "Why? Where are we going?" she asked, firing unanswered questions at Mel's back. "Can you slow down a little? It's hard to walk in these heels."

Cathy hopped into the passenger side, and Mel jammed her foot down on the accelerator. She sped out of the parking lot in a spew of flying gravel.

The man should not affect me this way. No one else ever has. Farmer? Yeah, right. She should have known. She knew his music. She just didn't know he lived *here*, in *her* town. She never would have come here if she had known. This couldn't be happening. God, he had to be laughing at her. She had to be the only woman on the planet who didn't recognize him on sight. Jeez, she was stupid.

And to think she'd been attracted to the man, even when she thought he might have been growing pot or something in that big barn of his. But this was worse. So much worse. Pot growers could be reformed, but musicians? Not so much. Not at all, in fact.

"Whoa there! Slow down would you? Do you want to tell me what happened back there?"

She eased up on the accelerator. As bad as things were, she had no intention of killing herself, and Cathy didn't deserve to go along for the ride if she did. "Hank Travis is in there."

"And?"

"Isn't that enough?"

"I don't think so, girlfriend. Where are we going anyway?"

She sighed. As she suspected, Cathy wasn't buying it. Her behavior was not going to be easy to explain.

Women all over the world fell at Hank Travis' feet. "I don't know. My place?"

"Okay, but you better come up with two things when we get there. Something decent to drink and an explanation."

"I've got wine," she said. "The explanation is a bit more complicated."

Cathy rubbed her hands together and bounced in her seat. "Oh, this sounds good. I can't wait to hear it."

Mel rolled her eyes. This was not the way she imagined telling her friend, but she hadn't planned to tell her at all. But with Hank Travis in Willowbrook, it was only a matter of time before her secret came out. Maybe Cathy could help her find a way to keep a lid on it.

Cathy followed her through the tiny bungalow to the kitchen, which like Hank's, was decorated in mid-century modern, but unlike his—what you saw was what you got. The appliances were original, except for the small microwave she couldn't live without. She opened a bottle of wine while Cathy selected two crystal wineglasses from the cabinet. A few minutes later, the women curled up on opposite ends of the sofa.

"Do you want to tell me what happened at Smitty's?"

She twirled her wine glass. The golden liquid swirled inside the cut crystal. She had thought about what, if anything, she should tell her friend and come to the only possible conclusion. If in six months Cathy hadn't mentioned Hank Travis lived in her hometown, she likely wasn't going to spill Mel's secrets either. Nevertheless, she felt the need to hear her say it before she told her everything.

"If I tell you something, can I trust you not to tell another living soul?"

"Of course you can. You know I wouldn't talk about you behind your back."

"I know…it's just…." She took a deep breath. "This isn't something I tell everyone. In fact, there's only one other person in Willowbrook who knows what I'm going to tell you."

Cathy sat up, leaning in. "What? What? Now you have to tell me. I'm going to bust if you don't!"

Her hands shook as she placed her wine glass on the coffee table. She had told a few people her secret over the years but only out of necessity. Telling Cathy was different—she didn't need to know. But Mel needed someone to confide in, someone who might understand or at least sympathize with her plight. There was no way her friend could *really* comprehend her dilemma, but perhaps woman-to-woman she might understand where she was coming from.

"Seriously. This is for your ears only. I don't want the whole town to know." *Though they will soon enough.*

Cathy crossed her heart and made a show of zipping her lips and throwing away the key. "Not a word. I promise."

"I'm not who you think I am. My real name is Melody Ravenswood." There, she'd said it out loud and the roof hadn't come crashing down and flash bulbs hadn't gone off. In fact, Cathy appeared confused. Not the reaction she expected—at all.

"Okay. And you are telling me this because…?"

"My father was Hamilton Ravenswood." Still no recognition. She tried again, this time using her father's title and the name he used on stage. "You know…Earl Ravenswood. Lead guitarist for RavensBlood."

Recognition dawned across her friends face. Her jaw dropped, and her eyes became saucers. "You're kidding, right?"

She shook her head. It was a truth she'd hidden her entire life. And she'd come to Willowbrook hoping to bury it, once and for all.

"Okay." Cathy's eyebrows knitted in confusion. "But what does that have to do with Hank?" She didn't seem the least impressed, or worse, curious about her revelation, which eased her mind about telling her.

She wrapped her arms around her bent knees. "I don't know. It just…does. Up until today, I thought he was a farmer, or to be more specific, I thought he might be growing pot in his barn. I searched the newspaper archives, figuring if he was growing pot, maybe he'd been in trouble before. I couldn't believe what I found. It was too close to home, you know? Anyway, I was still reeling when I got to Smitty's, and instead of finding you there, I found Hank." She reached for her wine and took a fortifying sip. "He wanted me to stay and play pool with him and his buddies."

Cathy nodded. "Randy and Chris. The three of them play a lot of pool at Smitty's." She paused to drink her wine. "Does he know who you are?"

"I don't think so. After the way I acted, he probably thinks I'm some kind of psycho. Maybe that's a good thing."

"What makes you think so? Lord, woman, Hank Travis is a prime, Grade A catch."

"Not for me he isn't. The last thing in the world I want is to be involved with someone like him."

Cathy smiled. "There isn't an unattached woman in the county who doesn't want to be involved with Hank, the Hammer, Travis, even if it's only for one night. Judging by your reaction, I'd say you aren't immune to him either."

She couldn't control the heat creeping from her chest to her face. Denying her attraction would only confirm Cathy's suspicions, and as she had pointed out, a person would have to be dead not to see Hank's appeal. She wasn't dead, but she wasn't like other people either. There were things she needed to consider.

"He's a famous musician. I've avoided them my entire life. I came to Willowbrook because I thought I could lead a normal life here…away from the paparazzi. If I'd known he lived here, I never would have come."

"Anyone in town could have told you, but as a rule, we don't talk about it much. He's just Henry Jr. to most of us. When he's not on tour, he keeps a pretty low profile out at his grandparent's farm. Since he detests reporters…." She grimaced and Mel waved off her concerns. "Sorry. Anyway, not too many reporters hunt him up here, so it's easy to forget he's anybody other than Knobby Knees Hank."

She laughed. "Knobby Knees? You really call him that?"

"Sure. He played basketball in junior high. He had the biggest knees and the skinniest legs you ever saw. He was in my graduating class. We teased him about it for years. I think it may have been the deciding factor in him giving up sports to join the band. Anyway, it seems to have worked out for him. He wasn't any good at basketball anyway."

"At least it explains the donation

his father made to the band program."

"Yeah. Good article, by the way."

"I can't believe I interviewed all those people, and not one even hinted they knew Hank, or the real reason behind Henry's donation. Just goes to show what kind of ace reporter I am." She shook her head in disgust.

"Don't be so hard on yourself. Like I said, Willowbrook doesn't drool over celebrities, especially if they're one of us." She topped off their wine glasses. "So, why couldn't we have a drink at Smitty's?"

"I know this sounds stupid. We didn't exactly hit it off. Like you said, he doesn't much like reporters. But I agree, he's a fine specimen. I thought so even when I was convinced he was a criminal." She shrugged. "I'll admit to thinking he was hot, and I guess deep down I thought maybe…well, that flew out the window as soon as I figured out who he was." She sighed, remembering the rush of feelings when she saw him standing in the back of the room. He fit in seamlessly, but all the same, she'd picked him out instantly, and he had done the same with her.

She hated everything he represented to her, but when his blatant gaze had gulped her down like a cold beer on a hot day, she'd almost forgotten her strictest rule in life—stay away from musicians. It had been an easy rule to live by…up until she met Hank Travis. When he'd touched her, the same zing of awareness she had felt the night before jolted her back to sanity. She had run before she'd done something stupid.

Cathy deserved an explanation, and even though she had just confided her deepest, darkest secret to her, she couldn't bring herself to tell her friend how her body tingled when Hank turned his gaze on her, or how his touch short-circuited her brain. She settled on a partial truth—

the one that really mattered. "I just couldn't stay in there with him. I couldn't exactly explain to him why I was so mad, not without telling him who I was. Besides, I don't socialize with musicians, especially famous ones."

"Why not? He still has knobby knees and skinny legs. He's just as human as the rest of us. Other than the leg thing, he's a prime male specimen, one of the few single ones in town."

A bone deep chill slid along her spine. "I can't be involved with someone in the music business. I saw what that kind of life did to our family. All the traveling, the paparazzi, the fans." She waved her hand in an all-encompassing wave. "My mother couldn't take it anymore, so she left my father and took me with her. My father wouldn't give up the business."

She inhaled deeply. The scars from her emotional wound still had the power to topple her if she let them. "The traveling eventually killed him."

Cathy scooted across the sofa and took Mel's hand in hers. She waited for the pity, but what she got was sympathy and genuine concern instead. "I'm sorry. Your father died in a plane crash didn't he? Somewhere in Colorado?"

She nodded, fighting back the tears she only shed in private as she filled in the blanks for her friend. "They were doing a concert in Denver. It was my tenth birthday and he promised to come to my party. He chartered a small plane, so he could leave right after a concert." She took a shuddering breath. "His plane went down in the Rockies. It was just him and the pilot. They both died."

"I'm so sorry." Cathy squeezed her hand.

"There's more." She had never told anyone about that day, but Cathy's quiet concern made her feel at ease.

"It's okay, you can tell me."

Maybe talking about it would make the memories less volatile. Keeping her thoughts bottled up inside, sometimes she felt like she might explode. Maybe if she pulled the cork on the bottle and let everything out it would be less deadly.

"Everything started out fine. I loved tea parties, so Mom made High Tea for me and my friends." She closed her eyes, remembering the party decorations, the pile of brightly colored wrapping paper torn from gifts, the laughter. Everyone wore pretty dresses with hats and gloves borrowed from their mothers for the celebration. "He was supposed to be there before the party started, but he wasn't. Mom told me he was running late.

"'He's always late,' she said. Mom never missed an opportunity to remind me how unpredictable my father's schedule was. Anyway, the party went on as planned. She didn't tell me the truth until all my friends had gone home. I laughed and played games while my father was dying on the side of a mountain."

Mel sucked in a fortifying breath. "I've never really forgiven her."

"Oh, honey," Cathy cried, pulling her into a bear hug. "It must have been awful for you."

"Pretty much." She reached for the tissue box on the end table behind her. After yanking a few out for herself, she offered the box to Cathy, who did the same. "Well, that's my story. You can see why I have a rule against getting involved with musicians." It was a damned good rule, one she had every intention of living by, no matter what. If she had learned anything from her parents' marriage, it was that musicians would break your heart.

Cathy dried her eyes and settled back on her end of the sofa, pulling her bare feet under her. They sat in silence for a few minutes. Mel finished her wine, refilled her glass, and topped off Cathy's while she waited for her to figure out which of her million questions she should ask first.

"So, why, exactly did you move here? I mean, why didn't you stay where you were?"

Her heart raced as memories of the incident in San Diego came flooding back. Thanks to a casual comment from the building's security guard, she and her mother had managed to escape out a rear exit and avoid the paparazzi waiting in the lobby. Just like when she was a child, on those rare occasions she went out in public with her father, the vultures circled their prey. She knew it was only a matter of time before someone added up all the clues and came up with the correct conclusion—Mel Harper and Melody Ravenswood were the same person.

"I had a close call with the paparazzi in San Diego. My inheritance came to me last year when I turned twenty-five. Before that, my life wasn't of much interest to the media. My inheriting, coupled with the fifteenth anniversary of the plane crash…. Well, it spurred a lot of interest. Suddenly, everyone wanted to know what Melody Ravenswood had been up to, what she was going to do with the money."

"I remember seeing a few stories on TV."

She nodded. "Well, they almost found her. Someone tipped them off that Melody would be visiting her lawyer to sign some papers. They almost caught up to us as we were leaving his office downtown. It took some doing, but we managed to avoid them long enough for me to get out of town and come up with a new plan for my life."

"You came here."

"I was tired of living like a fugitive, always wondering when they'd catch up with me. I wanted to live in a place where I could walk the streets without worrying someone would pop out of the bushes with a camera at any minute. I thought Willowbrook was that place."

Cathy twirled her glass by the stem. "It is."

"It was," Mel corrected. "You don't know the paparazzi. One celebrity will bring them here, Hank Travis. And they'll turn the town upside down. It won't take them long to figure out Melody is here, too, especially if everyone in town finds out who I am."

CHAPTER FIVE

Hank booted up his computer and typed Mel's name in the search engine. Dozens of sites popped up. It was a common name. He checked out several social networking links before he noticed the link to a popular Ravenswood fan site. He clicked on it.

A photo filled the screen. He recognized the man holding a small girl in his arms. His head spun as he read the caption beneath the photo. Sinking low in his chair, he studied the girl.

A fan had posted the picture along with assurances the girl in the photo lived in San Diego and currently went by the name Mel Harper.

Could it be? No. Melody

Ravenswood couldn't be in Willowbrook, Texas—the middle of nowhere, USA. What he was thinking wasn't possible. He had to be mistaken.

A half hour later, he knew he had stumbled upon the truth. Melody's mother, Diane Harper, had been a backup singer with RavensBlood until she became pregnant, married Hamilton Earl Ravenswood, and left the life behind—apparently—to raise her daughter in San Diego. There were no photos of Melody beyond the age of ten when she was photographed standing beside her father's casket at the family cemetery on his estate, Ravenswood, north of London. Earl had been more than a nickname. Hamilton Ravenswood had been the Earl of Ravenswood. His title passed to a cousin, but Melody had received a sizeable inheritance, which included the family estate and her father's extensive music library. One article listed her godfather, Sir Jonathan Youngblood, as the executor of the estate until Melody turned twenty-five. The milestone had passed last year.

His desk chair creaked as he leaned back, absorbing what he had learned in the last few minutes. It was almost too much to take in. She was Hamilton Ravenswood's daughter. *Incredible*.

He had been fifteen years old when Ravenswood died. His death and "Melody", the masterpiece he left behind, were the reasons Hank had chosen to be a musician. It was as though Ravenswood had translated Hank's thoughts and feelings into music notes and lyrics. "Melody" had been his theme song ever since.

He pulled up the cemetery photo again, arranging it on a split screen with the earlier one. What must it have been like for her? Had she been close to her father? Judging from the one where Ravenswood held his daughter in his arms, the answer was yes. You couldn't mistake a love like that. He held her protectively against what must have been a barrage of photographers while Melody clung to his neck. Hank didn't know much about kids, but he figured she was around five years old in the photograph.

He couldn't imagine growing up in the public eye, but as he searched for pictures, he realized, perhaps she hadn't. There were a few photos of them together when she was really young, but after the one when she was five…nothing. Nevertheless, the expression on her face at the cemetery told another story. Melody had loved her father.

His heart ached for her. He knew what it was like to lose a parent. But to have to lay a beloved parent to rest with the eyes of the world on you? He couldn't imagine how difficult it had been for her. He tried to sleep, but every time he closed his eyes, he saw a little girl holding tight to her mother's hand, her eyes and nose red from crying. He dressed in sweats and the old tennis shoes he kept on the back porch for the dirtier jobs around the place, and left the house.

He walked the rows of young cotton plants, formulating his thoughts. Betty Boop kept him company until the sun painted the eastern sky with broad streaks of pink, purple, and gold.

He wasn't a big believer in fate, but something, or someone, had a hand in the way they met. Why was Melody Ravenswood in Willowbrook? He dismissed the idea that she had known he lived here. Judging from the disgust on her face when she'd seen him earlier, she wished he *didn't* live here.

As much as he wanted to ignore the fact that she was a reporter, good sense told him not to. From what he had seen of her writing, she knew how to make the most of a story without stooping to yellow journalism. Just the same, he needed to keep a close eye on her. An image of her in Smitty's, looking like an angel in denim, was permanently etched on his brain. Keeping an eye on her wouldn't be a hardship.

He hadn't had much luck in the dating department. Karen had been his only serious relationship, and finding out she used him to get the inside scoop on him and the band, she'd never harbored any real feelings for him had pretty much put him off his feed.

Yeah, he'd been hungry since her betrayal, but not hungry enough. And besides, most women wanted only one version of Hank Travis—either the rock star side or the farmer side, but never both. They couldn't understand how the two balanced themselves out. He needed both, and he wanted someone to share them with.

Mel was perfect. Of all the people on the planet, she, more than anyone else, should understand his crazy life. The seed of an idea took root, and with each step he took, it grew until it blossomed into a full-blown plan…sort of.

First, he needed to find out exactly why she was in Willowbrook. If she wanted a normal, simple life, if she was searching for a place to put down roots, well…the roots on his family tree went deep.

**

Purse in hand, she stormed out of her boss' office before she lost all control. In the parking lot, she debated the wisdom of driving in her state of mind. She needed chocolate and a friendly face. She slung her purse over her shoulder and turned in the direction of The Donut Hole.

Her new assignment was all Hank Travis' doing—she knew it as well as she knew her own face in the mirror. But, why? He'd told her himself he didn't give interviews. She stewed over the dilemma while Cathy worked the line down to her.

"I need a half dozen, assorted, to go." She leaned over the counter, signaling for a more private conversation. When Cathy met her halfway, she asked in a hushed voice, "Do you have any laced with rat poison?"

Cathy raised an amused eyebrow. "Not today, sorry. How about a few artery-cloggers, instead? It's slower, but it'll still get the job done."

She straightened, deflated in the face of her friend's cheery attitude. "They'll have to do. Load me up. Make sure there's some chocolate in there, too."

"Who's the unlucky interviewee today?"

She glanced over her shoulder to make sure no one was close enough to hear. "Hank Travis."

"Oooh. No wonder you're in such a good mood. What did he do, donate a new school?"

"Nothing so benevolent. He has deemed himself the savior of my career and granted me his first interview in seven years."

Cathy's eyes lit with interest.

"You're kidding. That *is* a coup. I didn't think you'd dare ask him though, not after what you told me last night."

"I didn't." She rolled her eyes. No matter how she examined the situation, it didn't look good. "He called Ralph this morning and offered to put the Gazette on the map, provided *I* do the interview. And, get this…it's a month-long assignment. Exclusive. I'm supposed to follow him everywhere for the next thirty days, so I can write about the *real* Hank Travis."

Cathy's lips twitched, but she couldn't keep a smile from bursting across her face. "It sounds like something he would do. I know you don't want to hear this, but it could make your career and get you out of this two-horse town."

"But, I don't want out. I like it here, or at least I did until I found out about Hank. I may have to find another place to live since he lives here, too." She lowered her voice and leaned in close. "Sooner or later the rest of the media is going to get wind of the two of us living in the same town and then, watch out Willowbrook. I can't do that to the town. I like all these people." Her arm sweep encompassed the tables full of locals. She'd spent a lot of time thinking about it and had come to a depressing conclusion. "Willowbrook can't handle both of us. I'm the outsider. I'm the one who'll have to go."

"That's nonsense." Cathy slid the filled bag across the counter. "Go on, don't keep him waiting."

**

Hank had put his plan into action. All he had to do was wait and see what she did. Ralph seemed sure he could convince her to go along, but there was a chance she would tell Ralph just what he could do with the assignment and his newspaper. He didn't have a plan B. He was trying to come up with one when the phone rang.

"I hope you know what you're doing, Hank."

"Cathy? What are you talking about?"

"Mel Harper is what I'm talking about. She was just in my store. What are you up to?"

"I've decided to grant an interview with the local paper. Don't you think the citizens of Willowbrook want to know what I do all day?"

"You flatter yourself. We know what you do, and we're not particularly interested in it. So what are you really up to?"

"I don't know. I have a crazy idea she may be worth getting to know. Who knows? Maybe I'll ask her to marry me."

"Seriously?"

"Hey, you never know," he said. "She keeps me awake at night."

"Wow. I take it that's never happened before?"

"Never. I think she may be the

one, but I've got to get close to her to find out, and I couldn't think of any other way."

"I'll say it again—wow. You mean it, don't you?"

"Yeah, I think I do. Why? Are you afraid you've lost your chance to grow old with me? You should have taken me up on my offer back in high school."

"Yeah, right. As I recall, you offered a romp in the back of your pickup. If you'd included a wedding ring with the offer, I might have overlooked the knobby knees and gone for it."

"Ha, ha. Is she on the way out here?"

"Yes. And she is worth getting to know, but you've got your work cut out for you. You know how you are about reporters? Well, she's the same way about musicians. She's likely to shoot you for pulling this stunt. I'd make sure the gun cabinet is locked up tight before she gets there."

"She's mad, huh?" He couldn't care less how mad she was. She was on her way. The next step would be to convince her to hear him out.

"She asked me to put rat poison in your doughnut."

Hank laughed. "I appreciate the warning. I think I'll be okay, but maybe I will check the gun cabinet and make sure the rat poison is out of sight, just in case."

"You do that. Good luck, Hank. You're going to need it. Oh, and by the way? If you hurt her, I'm coming for you."

"Good to know." Yeah, convincing Mel his plan could work wasn't going to be easy, but at least she was on her way. "Thanks for the heads-up, and you take care."

**

Why now? Why me? If Hank wanted publicity, he surely had a publicist who could get him better coverage than the Willowbrook

Gazette.

She should turn around, head back into town, and forget all about Hank Travis. What could Ralph do to her if she refused to interview Hank? Fire her? Thanks to Hank, her time in Willowbrook was limited anyway, so what did it matter if she lost her job? At least she wouldn't have to see him ever again.

Whom was she kidding? The truth was she wanted to see him again. Despite everything, she was still attracted to him, to his rich voice, his quirky smile, his nerdy haircut.

Somewhere around milepost twenty-nine, she had made up her mind to see this assignment through, but her first glimpse of him made her rethink her decision. He held the screen door for her, looking too damned good, too damned sexy, and too damned pleased with himself. He might as well have had a flashing neon sign on his head—Danger! Unreliable, narcissistic heartbreaker ahead!

Lost Melody

She stepped into the kitchen, all too aware of his size as she brushed past him in the narrow doorway. He snared one of the insulated cups from her as she passed. "Is this for me?"

Ignoring him, she popped her hot chocolate into the microwave, her fingers punctuating her mood as she stabbed at the buttons. The dog ambled into the room from parts unknown and sniffed at the back of her leg.

"Leave her alone, Betty." Hank steered his four-legged friend in the other direction.

She opened cabinets until she found a plate and dumped the contents of the bag onto it. The dish made a satisfying *thunk* when she dropped it in the middle of the table. An old-fashioned style doughnut bounced off and rolled to the floor. Betty Boop pounced on it, disappearing with the purloined treat.

"I brought doughnuts." She removed her hot chocolate from the microwave, hyper aware of the man leaning against the refrigerator watching her every move. "Today is the one and only time I'll do it for the duration of our project."

She took a seat and rummaged through her purse for her voice recorder. She slammed it down with enough force to rouse the dog from under the table—probably hoping to catch more flying pastries. Hank took the seat next to hers. She scooted her chair back until her thigh bumped the table leg. "I don't take notes. If you have a problem with being recorded, speak up now."

"You can record anything you want, except my music. I have contractual obligations regarding my creative process. I'm sure you understand, Melody."

She faltered. *Coincidence. A lucky guess. That's all it was.* Her tongue felt like sandpaper, but she managed to force words out. "My name is Mel."

"If you say so, Ms. Ravenswood."

Oh God. Her heart raced. Her

vision blurred, and her throat closed. A black fog swam through her mind, threatening to take her under. She couldn't breathe. She'd had panic attacks before, but that didn't make this one any less frightening. She had to get out, away. Why hadn't she listened to her instincts earlier? She stumbled to her feet. Trembling legs miraculously carried her to the door.

He stood and moved in her direction. As she gripped the doorframe, she raised her hand to fend him off. She sucked in the fresh air wafting through the screen door. Oxygen flooded her system.

"Are you okay?" he asked. "Can I get you anything?"

"Leave. Me. Alone." Beyond the screened door, wide-open spaces promised relief. "I have to go." She flattened her palm against the cool wire mesh.

"Please," he begged. "Don't go. I won't tell anyone. I promise."

All she had to do was push and the screened door would open.

Escape was that close. She gazed longingly at the quiet vista beyond. Her brain told her to run, to get as far away from Hank as she could, but her limbs betrayed her. Telling Cathy had been easy, maybe because it was her decision and she trusted her friend to keep her confidence. But being found out by a virtual stranger was different. It was what she lived in fear of every day—that someone, *everyone,* would discover her secret, and the peace she'd constructed with such care would shatter.

He knew and soon everyone in Willowbrook would know, too. She would have to leave, find another place to live, reinvent herself all over again.

"How did you find out?" she asked, envying the nondescript sparrow pecking at something in the grass outside, able to fly away at the slightest threat.

"I ran an Internet search on your name. If I can do it, anyone can."

She slumped against the

doorframe. He was right. Anyone could do it. The only person she'd been fooling was herself. A quiet life in a small town wouldn't be possible because someone would always figure out her secret. She'd been impossibly stupid and naïve.

"How did you find out about me?" he asked.

"I researched you in the newspaper's archives, and then I searched the Internet."

"I guess that makes us even." He held her chair out. "Come sit down, and we'll talk."

This time, her legs responded. She crossed the room and sank into the chair, her body numb with fear of the havoc his knowing would unleash on her life.

He pushed her hot chocolate closer to her. "Here, have something to drink. You'll feel better." His voice, velvet smooth and laced with concern helped to calm her and the warm liquid easing the tightness in her throat. Her life was out of control, and she was drinking hot chocolate with the man who held the key to her future. *Unbelievable.*

He resumed his seat and slid a chocolate frosted doughnut under her nose. "Eat."

She stared at the confection.

"Can I get you anything else?"

She shook her head and reached for the doughnut. She ate mechanically, tasting nothing. She couldn't look at him. With downcast eyes, she could see his hands, knew he drank his hot chocolate, and selected a sugared doughnut for himself.

Hank tossed the last bite to Betty Boop. He dusted sugar from his hands and crumpled his napkin, throwing it across the room for a perfect two-pointer into the wastebasket. "I'm sorry I blew your cover, Melody."

The chocolate helped, or maybe the numbness and fear were wearing off. She raised her eyes, fixing him with a laser-sharp glare. "Don't call me that. No one calls me that."

He held his hands up, palms out. "Okay, Mel it is." He shifted in his seat. "Look, I'm sorry I sprung it on you like the way I did. I can't tell you what a surprise it was.… Well, it blew my mind when I realized who you were."

"I just bet it did."

"Hey, I understand you want your privacy, and you're entitled to it. If it's any consolation, I didn't find any recent photos of you."

"That's just swell, Hank. I feel so much better. You understand why I want to be left alone, yet you went to the trouble of researching me on the Internet." She shook her head. "I came to Willowbrook to live a quiet life, to be my own person…not the daughter of a ghost. You don't have any idea how much I wanted this new life to work. And it would have, too, if you hadn't been here."

"What have I got to do with it?"

"Think about it. The paparazzi know you're here. They'll come hunting for you, and guess who else they'll find?" She shook her head. "This is just what I was trying to avoid. Ever since I inherited, everyone thinks they have a right to know where I am and what I'm doing. I just want to be left alone. I have to leave, move somewhere else. Some place far away from you." She was on the verge of a breakdown, she could feel it coming, building like a summer storm. She swiped away tears before they could spill over and run down her cheeks.

"You can relax," he said. "I'm not going to tell anyone who you are. You can go on being Mel Harper of the Willowbrook Gazette for the rest of your life if it's what you want."

"Easy for you to say. You aren't the one the paparazzi are hunting."

"What do you mean, hunting?"

"Ever since I turned twenty-five, I've been a wanted woman, so to speak. They almost caught up with me in San Diego. So I left."

"Tell me."

"It was awful." Thinking perhaps he could understand, she told him how she had practically been forced from her home the previous year.

"I'm so sorry. Sometimes reporters don't know when to quit."

"You can say that again." Enough about her. It was time to find out what was really going on. "So, what's the deal with the interview? You don't like reporters any more than I do, so why am I really here?"

He smirked. "You don't see the irony in your situation? You're a reporter who hates reporters."

"I don't hate all reporters, just the ones who don't respect people's privacy. I'm a journalist with a conscience. I only write about people who want to be written about, and since you aren't one of those people, we're back to the original question. Why am I here?"

"It was the only way I knew I could get you to come out here to see me. I'm serious about the interview though. Spend thirty days with me, record whatever you want, with the exception of my music. When the time is up, you're free to do whatever you want with the material. You can write a book, a magazine article, a piece for the Gazette, or nothing at all. I don't care."

This, from a man who avoided reporters like they were plague-carrying vermin? There had to be more he wasn't saying. "If you really want publicity, why not call someone from one of the fan magazines? If I write an article about you, it will bring all kinds of attention to me. Attention I don't want."

"You're good at what you do."

He hasn't heard a work I've said. "Let me be clear. All I want is to live in a quiet little town and write about the everyday lives of the real people who live there. I don't want notoriety. If I wanted recognition, don't you think I could have bought myself a position at a big publication? I could buy my own magazine or newspaper if I wanted." She sneered at him. "I could buy you."

"I read some of your work. You don't need to buy yourself anything. Your writing is clear, concise, and compassionate. People like you. You tell their stories in a way that makes them seem special. Everyone deserves to feel special at some point in their lives, even if they live in the middle of Nowhere, USA."

Smart. Hitting her where it would do the most good—right in her pride. "Thank you," she said, sure he was softening her up for something big.

"You're welcome. Now, for the reason you're here."

Here it comes. She stiffened her spine.

He placed his hand on her arm, anchoring her to her seat.

Oh, this can't be good if he thinks I'm going to run.

"I don't need any publicity. I don't *want* any publicity. I want to get to know you."

She frowned. "Why?"

"I think we should get married."

What? Oh no. No. Not going to happen.

She yanked on her arm, but he tightened his grip—not enough to hurt, but firm enough she wasn't going anywhere until he let her. "You're nuts. No one told me you were nuts."

"Not nuts. Practical."

"Practical?" *Practically insane.* She tugged on her arm again. "Let me go."

"Calm down and just listen to me for a minute." He stroked her arm with his index finger, sending little jolts of current skittering up to her shoulder and down her spine. "I think we could be good for each other. Besides the physical attraction, and don't try to tell me there isn't one, I think I have something you need. And you have something I need."

"I *need* to get out of here."

"Just hear me out. Please? I think we can make a relationship work. You said you wanted a quiet life. I lead a quite life…most of the time.

When I'm on tour, you can stay here, or you can come along. Whatever you want to do."

She stared at him. "You've actually given your scheme some thought? Like, you think it's logical. Sane."

"I know it sounds bizarre, but I've given it a lot of thought, and I think it could work for both of us."

"Bizarre?"

"Okay, insane." He leaned toward her. "All I'm asking is one month of your time. After thirty days, if you can't stand the sight of me, we go our separate ways, no harm, no foul. You'll see. I'm right, and in a few weeks, you'll know it, too." His smile was disarming. He sat back, crossing his arms over his chest.

She snatched her arm away the second he released her. She clamped a hand over the spot where his hand had been. Her skin was still warm, the heat radiating through her body. Her mouth hung open. Her mind raced to digest his words.

"Come on, Mel. What do you have to lose? Give me, give *us*, a chance. I want a wife and kids. If you don't want kids, that might be a deal-breaker."

"I want kids," she heard her other self say—the one that lived in an alternate universe where this conversation was normal.

"See, we have something in common already."

Insanity. That's what we have in common. She mentally tried to pry herself out of the chair, but her alternate-universe self remained fascinated by what he was saying and refused to budge.

"You want to live in obscurity in Willowbrook, and it just so happens, so do I. It's a match made in Heaven." He smiled again. "Turn on your recorder, and I'll tell you my life story. I want you to know exactly what you're getting." He reached across the table and pressed a button on her recorder. "Interview with Henry Barret Travis, Jr."

Lost Melody

He's insane. Or maybe she was because she still sat there while he rambled on about piano lessons, his mother, and the unspeakable pain of losing her to cancer when he was in college. He talked about his father's endless support, whether he was on a basketball court or a stage. He talked about the years he spent at Harvard, and how his band, BlackWing, came into being, how they played frat parties and local clubs to help pay their way through school.

Without missing a beat, he rose, poured them both a tall glass of orange juice, and shoved the glass and another doughnut in front of her.

She tried not to react when he talked about how her father's death had affected him, but his words sounded sincere. He told her how he had grieved, how "Melody" spoke to him. How the song had validated his soul-deep love of music. How he'd decided to pursue a music career because of "Melody."

If it was all an act, it was a good one.

"Do you have another tape? This one is done."

His swift change of subject startled her. "Uh, no."

"Okay. Why don't we take a tour of the farm? Afterward, I'll take you into town for lunch. You can get more tapes, or we can call it a day after lunch."

He led her through the house. She made appropriate comments as he pointed out various things, including the small, upright piano his mother had taught him to play. He told her how he moved it from his dad's house with the help of a couple of friends, and how they almost dropped it trying to get it out of the pickup and into the house.

They moved through the house and out to the barn. The barn was no longer a place to house animals, hay, and farm implements. Presently, it contained a state-of-the-art recording studio, several sound proof rehearsal rooms, and Hank's private office. The recording studio was ultra-modern, but his office could have been beamed straight out of a nineteenth-century gentleman's club. *Or Ravenswood.*

A cozy sitting area boasted a brown leather sofa, two matching chairs, and a coffee table large enough to dance on and, by appearances, sturdy enough to take the abuse.

The open laptop computer and an electronic keyboard seemed out of place. Other than a neat stack of file folders and the computer, the massive carved wood desk was unadorned. Matching bookcases held Grammy and People's Choice awards, as well as framed photos and assorted mementos. Gold and Platinum records covered warm green walls. A deep-pile rug softened the hardwood floor.

Traditional lamps scattered around the room provided low but adequate lighting. As with the rest of the barn, there were no windows.

"Well, what do you think?" he asked.

"It's incredible. I've never seen anything like it." In fact, it all appeared very professional. However, she couldn't help but wonder what really went on here. Wild parties? Drugs? Alcohol? Did the farm and the whole town fill with groupies willing to do anything for the musicians they idolized?

"I had it built after our first CD went Platinum. We've recorded here ever since."

"Why spend so much money on your own studio? Wouldn't it be cheaper to rent space somewhere?"

"Probably, but the guys are away from their families for months at a time. I have the farmhouse. It doubles as a resort of sorts. They all move in here for the duration. It's worked so far."

"They bring their families?" She couldn't keep the skepticism out of her voice.

"Yeah. It's great. You should see it. The house is full of kids. It takes about a month to clean the place up after they leave, but I love having them here."

"Who else comes?"

"Technicians, back-up musicians."

"That's it?"

"Pretty much, why?"

"No reason. I was just wondering." He sounded like he was telling the truth, but it didn't jive with the lifestyle her mother said rock musicians lived. And if anyone should know, it would be her mother, Diane Harper Ravenswood.

CHAPTER SIX

Hank dropped her at her house, promising to have her Jeep delivered later. She collapsed on the sofa, grateful for the peace and quiet. Hank Travis could talk the bark off a tree. Eventually, she got up and made herself a cup of tea.

Thinking back over her day, she was both appalled and intrigued. Appalled at his proposal—if that's what it was—and intrigued by the prospect of writing a book about him.

There were several unauthorized biographies of her father's life, and the estate had been approached countless times over the years with requests to pen an authorized version—complete with interviews with her and her mother. Her mother declined them all, choosing instead to remain out of the public eye. And other than her father's best friend and the executor of his estate, Jonathan Youngblood, they'd had no contact over the years with the people from her father's life.

Anytime the subject came up, Diane would admonish her daughter, "Stay away from musicians. They'll break your heart." She'd heard the mantra her entire life, and her parent's marriage was evidence of the wisdom of the statement.

Late in the afternoon, a couple of farmhands returned her Jeep, along with a note from Hank.

Come for breakfast. Eight a.m.? I'll cook.

H.T. Jr.

Her mother's words echoed in her ears as she turned into his driveway promptly at eight o'clock the next morning. Only twenty-nine days to go, and she would walk away, get the heck out of Dodge. Maybe write a book. She could write anywhere—

use a pseudonym, remain completely off the grid. By the time word got around town that Melody Ravenswood was in Willowbrook, she would have the material she needed and be long gone.

The smell of bacon cooking drew her around to the back of the house where Betty Boop, ever the vigilant watchdog, greeted her enthusiastically on the porch. She followed her nose and found Hank in the kitchen looking nothing like the serious rocker she imagined he was on stage.

He stood in front of the stove juggling a variety of cast iron cookery. Instead of drumsticks, he wielded a greasy spatula. Barefoot, he wore a bib apron adorned with red apples and ruffles trimmed with red crochet work. The apron protected a blue oxford-style shirt and tan chinos.

A smile tugged at her lips. "Hi."

"Oh, hi." He waved the spatula at her. "I didn't hear you drive up."

"I'm not too early, am I?"

"Right on time." He slid two pancakes from the griddle to a plate and poured two more from the bowl of batter on the counter. "Make yourself at home. Breakfast is almost ready."

"Do you cook often?" she asked, admiring the way he made it appear easy. If she'd been cooking that many things at once, guaranteed something, or everything, would be burned.

"When I'm home. It's a drive into town, and I'm sure you've noticed Willowbrook is a little short on eating establishments. I cook enough to get by. Breakfast is my specialty."

He'd already set the table with plates, napkins, utensils, and glasses of orange juice. She sat at one place setting, quietly moving the adjacent setting to the other side of the table.

"I also grill a pretty good steak, and I can stir up a killer pot of chili," he said.

"Good to know, if I ever need to kill anyone with chili."

He laughed. "I'm glad to see you brought your sense of humor today."

He set a platter loaded with pancakes, scrambled eggs, and bacon on the table and sat in the new location without comment. "Dig in."

"I thought I could show you how I work today."

She added pancakes and bacon to her plate, absolutely certain the last thing she wanted to do today was watch him work. But if she went through with his interview plan, she would have to get over her prejudices and fears, sooner rather than later.

Memories floated to the surface. One in particular stood out. She'd been around eight years old. It had been a magical time, spent with her father on one of her summer visits to his estate in England. She could still see her father playing her song on the grand piano in the music room of the ancient manor house. He usually sang her song a cappella, and she loved the times when he would play the accompaniment too.

Another memory slammed into her—one much more recent. "I have to ask you something," she said, cutting into the stack of pancakes she no longer thought she could eat—not with the way her stomach was churning. "The other day when I met you at your dad's house, you were listening to something on your MP3 player. What was it?"

"I don't remember. I have about two thousand songs, and they play in random order. Why?"

"No reason. I was just curious." She forced herself to chew and swallow the pancakes. Did he really not remember, or was he lying because he'd been listening to her father's song—*her* song?

**

"Let's go," he said after the kitchen was once again spotless. "I'll walk you through my day. It's pretty mundane actually, so try not to go to sleep on me."

"I think I can handle it," she said.

He produced a stack of mail from a drawer and paid his household bills. If she wanted to see what his life was really like, well, it didn't get more real than sorting mail and paying bills. She'd soon realize his life was mostly boredom, punctuated by brief periods of creativity.

"Don't you have an accountant?"

"No. I have one for everything related to my business, but I like to take care of my personal expenses. It makes me feel normal. How about you?"

"Same," she answered. "I pay my own personal bills. I don't like the idea of an office full of strangers knowing which stores I shop in, or criticizing how much I spend."

"You can tell me where you buy your panties. I won't tell anyone."

Her cheeks flamed instantly, and she turned her back to him as if studying the awards lining the wall. He returned to his bills, satisfied with the reaction he'd received from the off color remark. He laughed to himself. It was easy to throw her off kilter, and he enjoyed watching her get all hot and bothered.

As fun as it was to tease her, he admired her. It must have been difficult growing up, hiding her identity from her friends. He could understand why her mother made the choice to live quietly, away from public life, but it must have taken a toll on her and her daughter. Coming into his celebrity status as an adult, he'd had more choices in the way he handled it.

He'd almost forgotten their last exchange when she spoke, "I shop at Victoria's Secret. How about you?"

She spoke so softly, still facing the wall, that he wasn't sure he'd heard correctly. He replayed it in his head before responding. Visions of angels in underwear with less substance than clouds invaded his brain. Good Lord, was she flirting with him?

"JC Penney. Want to see them?"

"Tighty-whities?"

Damn. She *was* flirting. Who knew she had it in her? His heart rate skyrocketed. He watched her carefully, hoping she would remain across the room. Most of his blood had rushed to his groin, making him lightheaded, among other things. His mouth was as dry as the Sahara. "I'll show you mine if you show me yours."

She spun around. Her stricken expression made it clear the flirting episode had come to an end. She drew in a deep breath, restoring her outward shell. Bright splotches of color on her cheeks were the only remaining sign of their verbal sparring.

"I'm sorry. That was unprofessional and out of line. It won't happen again."

Disappointment stabbed him in the chest. For a few seconds, he thought perhaps he'd caught a glimpse of Melody Ravenswood, but Mel Harper, reporter had returned.

Lost Melody

He'd enjoyed the exchange. There was a real woman inside the walls she had built around herself. He decided to do whatever it took to bring her out again. He didn't think he had much of a future with Mel, but Melody was another story altogether.

"I don't mind. Just please don't print that. I think my underwear choices could be considered too much information."

"I wouldn't print anything so personal."

"Good. I'm glad we understand each other. I won't tell a soul about Victoria's Secret, or should I say, Mel's secret?"

They lunched on sandwiches in the farmhouse kitchen, and then he led the way to one of the soundproof rehearsal rooms, leaving Betty Boop to sleep off her meal under a shade tree in the backyard.

Mel sat in a plush easy chair in one corner and he took his place behind the elaborate drum kit. He flipped switches on the panel mounted on the wall behind him and picked up a set of headphones.

"Listening to me practice is probably going to be boring for you. All you'll be able to hear will be the drums. I hear the track through the cans." He held up the headphones in explanation. "If it gets too much for you, there are some sound muffling headphones in the drawer next to your chair, or you can slip out. I won't mind. It's boring stuff for most people."

"Do you practice every day?"

"I try to get in an hour or two. The rhythm of every song depends on me keeping the beat. It requires concentration, and like any good athlete, muscle memory. Sometimes I play for my own enjoyment. I've been known to go three or four hours, especially if I have something on my mind I need to work through. The music helps me, it always has."

She scanned the room. Other than the drum kit and sitting area in the opposite corner, there were no other furnishings. A built-in console across the back wall contained a dizzying number of knobs and switches. An industrial style clock and a small control panel next to the door stood out against bare, white walls. She pointed to the buttons on the console beside the door. "What are these for?"

"It's a signal system, similar to what you see in doctor's offices. The green light means all clear. The yellow indicates someone is here to see me, or if it's flashing, I have a phone call on my private line. The red is for emergency use only. It means, get the hell out. *Now*. So far, it's never been used. There's a call panel in the house, in my office, and one in the studio. That's how I knew you and Dad were here the other night. He signaled me from the house."

"It's an impressive system."

"It works for me. I tend to forget about the rest of the world when I'm in here."

"Well, don't mind me. I'm just going to watch."

He played along with the song only he could hear. His fingers held the sticks loosely. His hands flew through the air. The play of muscles in his forearms and wrists fascinated her. The steady beat from the bass drum drew her attention to his muscular thighs as his feet worked the foot pedals. His broad shoulders moved in time with the unheard track. He closed his eyes and kept up the steady backbeat, his body moving in graceful harmony with the music.

She was far from bored. The pulsing beat coursed through her body, mesmerizing her. She opened herself to the rhythm. The tempo changed as he moved into the drum solo. A small crease formed between his brows as he concentrated on the music, pouring his soul into the exciting beat, building to its climatic peak. When the tempo eased back into the slow, sensual beat of the melody, she let her eyelids fall, giving herself over to the erotic message of the music.

He risked a glance at her. He fought his body and mind for control. Only years of practice saved him from missing the beat. He had chosen the song with care, a sort of test to see how it would affect her, if at all. The lyrics told the story of a night filled with intense passion, the beat, slow and sensual, mimicked the rhythm of making love. The drum solo built to a soaring climax, mellowing into the aftermath of passion.

Her hand, pressed over her heart, fisted, clenching her blouse and drawing it tight across her breasts. His body reacted, and he fought the urge to throw down the sticks, cross the room, and take her. She could deny it all she wanted, but music ran hot and passionate through her veins.

The music ended in his headset,

but he continued to play. Tiny movements signaled her growing need, mirroring his. He sighed and eased out of the rhythm until the drums were silent.

She sat up. Her gaze locked with his. Behind the drum kit, he dug his fingernails into his thighs to keep his hands from getting him into trouble. He'd never been wound so tight in his life as he was right this minute. A muscle ticked along his jaw line at the sight of her flushed with passion. What had started as a good idea, he thought, had totally backfired on him. He had to get her out of here before he forgot she wasn't ready for him, might never be.

"I've done enough for today," he said, turning to store his sticks in the cabinet behind him—giving him a few extra seconds to wrestle his libido under control. He spun around, rising and crossing the room to her. "I don't know how you slept through it. You must be desperate for sleep."

He offered his hand. Her skin was

so damned soft, and from the current running between them, he knew sinking inside her would be like inserting a plug into a socket. They'd light up the world. As soon as she was on her feet, she jerked her hand from his and stepped away, nervously straightening her slacks and blouse.

"I'm sorry," she said. "I must have drifted off. I don't sleep well at night."

"What do you mean?"

She glanced up, and her gaze met his. Something inside him shifted at the wariness he saw there.

"Nothing," she said, dismissing her comment. "I didn't sleep well last night, that's all."

That was a damned lie. It was written all over her face. He took a step back, giving her space. Maybe he'd been too harsh, demanding she explain. But damn, if she had dragons after her, he wanted to slay ever last one of them. Except, he couldn't do anything for her until she trusted him enough to tell him what was wrong.

An unfamiliar wave of emotions washed through him. He wanted to protect, to comfort, and to shelter her in a way he'd never experienced before. He wanted to break down the barrier she'd built to shield her heart, to take away any pain, erase any suffering. It was a foreign feeling for him, but another one, more familiar, held sway. His arms ached to wrap around her, to hold her close, to explore every inch of her. It was one emotion he understood.

He stood by while she fidgeted; smoothing non-existent wrinkles from her clothing, brushing her hair away from her face, gathering her bag and notebook. Silently he catalogued every movement. He crammed his hands in his back pockets to keep from touching her. Turning away, he stared at the ceiling, took a deep breath, and let it out. Of all the things he had expected from his pursuit of Melody Ravenswood, a rush of emotion was the last. He'd hoped they could forge some kind of emotional bond, but he'd never expected to feel so much, so quickly.

The sooner he got her out of the barn, out of his sight, the better off he would be. This was so not a part of the plan. He walked her to her car, hoping distance would quiet his rioting emotions.

**

"I didn't hear you drive up." Hank gathered the papers and crammed them in his pocket. At least yesterday hadn't scared her off. She'd come back for another day. He took it for a good sign.

Mel closed the screened door and bent to pet the dog, who came to greet her. "Hi Betty, How are you today?" She gave her an affectionate hug and turned her attention to Hank. "I didn't mean to startle you. What are you working on?"

"Nothing. It's not much yet, just a bunch of disjointed notes. It can wait."

"What's that?" She pointed to a small, round object. About the size of dinner plate, it resembled a toy flying saucer.

"It's a portable electronic drum kit." He drew her closer. "It has a tiny finger pad. It's like finger drumming on the table, except it converts the taps into real-sounding drum beats I hear through the headphones." He held the headphones out to her. "Here, try it."

She secured the earbuds, and he tapped out a beat on the finger pad. She smiled at the brief solo. He took her hand, urging her to try it herself. Timidly, she tapped a one-fingered beat then a more complex one. Her laughter rang out in the room, and he thought he'd never heard anything so beautiful in his life. Her lips curved into the first genuine smile he'd ever seen from her, and for a moment, he wanted to kiss her more than he wanted his next breath. The realization rocked him back on his heels.

She jerked the earbuds loose and held them out to him. "That's fun."

"You can try the real thing if you want."

"No. Uh-uh. I'll leave those to you."

"Well, if you change your mind…"

"I won't. What's for breakfast?"

"French toast?"

"Sounds good to me."

After they ate, they took a walk through the cotton fields to the creek that gave Willowbrook its name. Cottonwoods and weeping willows lined the banks, casting long shadows over the sleepy creek. They sat on the grassy bank, and she brought out her voice recorder. She felt better prepared today and resolved not to let him turn the questions back on her as he'd done the day before. It was time to put an end to the two-way interview.

Unable to sleep the night before, she'd gone over and over the previous days and wondered at how easily he'd drawn her out. She'd never talked about her personal life with anyone the way she did with him. Reluctantly, she admitted he probably understood her life better than anyone else in the world. He'd lived the same life her father had—music, tours, fans, groupies, paparazzi, hotels, planes, busses, and limos. If anyone could understand why she hid herself away in Willowbrook, it would be Hank Travis. However, it didn't explain why she felt she could joke with him about where they bought their underwear. Her face flushed at the memory.

He eyed her curiously. "What are you thinking?"

"Nothing." Touching her fingertips to her cheeks, she added, "I'm just a little warm in the sun." She dropped her hand. "Tell me about growing up in Willowbrook."

He accepted the change of subject, lay back in the dappled shade, and began to talk.

Lost Melody

She placed the recorder in the grass between them and wrapped her arms around her drawn up knees. He told her about his maternal grandparents and about his friends and their exploits. She stiffened when he talked about the girlfriends he had brought to the very spot where they sat.

"Why did you bring them here?"

He sat up. With a gentle finger on her chin, he turned her face. His lips were a whisper away—so close his breath feathered across hers. "For this."

He pressed his lips to hers. One large hand slid into her hair, cradling her head. His tongue traced a hot demand across her mouth, urging her to allow him in. She opened for him, and he swooped in. The kiss changed from soft and gentle to flagrant and needy, igniting her desire into a firestorm. Changing the angle, he drew her across his lap and folded her into his strong arms.

Heated blood rushed through her

veins. Every nerve ending screamed for his touch. His other hand on her back molded her body close to his. She was secure in his embrace, warmed by his possession.

As he eased her onto her back, her heated skin cooled against the soft spring grass. He came over her, grinding his hips into the juncture of her legs. She parted for him, and he settled between her thighs. He moved to an age-old rhythm. Propped on his forearms, his palms bracketed her face; his tongue penetrated her in harmony with the movement of his hips.

She trailed her fingers along his jaw and down the tensed cords of his neck. His strength, his weight bearing down on her, awakened something deep inside. Her body mimicked the drumbeat and she remembered the strain on his face while he'd concentrated on playing "One Night". The erotic rhythm pulsed through her body.

Reality crashed over her as if

they'd tumbled into the cold, rushing waters of the creek. She tore her mouth from his, shoving against his shoulders. "Stop! Hank, please stop!"

Tears streamed across her temples. He brushed them away with his thumbs and rolled off her. He pulled her into his embrace, and her sobs eased to a soft snuffling.

Burying his face in her hair, he kissed the top of her head. "I'm so sorry, Melody."

"Don't call me that."

He tightened his hold on her. "I'm sorry. I shouldn't have kissed you. I thought one kiss would be enough, but I was wrong. I got carried away, and I was arrogant enough to think you wanted it as much as I did. It won't happen again unless you want it to."

His voice rumbled through his chest, the timbre as comforting as the words themselves. Oh God. He was right. She did want him. Lying in his arms, she felt safe, cherished, but he was a musician. Her body yearned for his, but she couldn't fall for him. Her mother's warnings set off alarms in her head. *Musicians. Don't believe their pretty words. They'll just break your heart.*

He could never lead a normal life. There would always be someone wanting a piece of him, and it would eventually kill him. She wouldn't put herself through that again.

She pushed from Hank's embrace and gathered her scattered wits. Better to keep her association with him on a professional level. "I should probably interview some of your friends from school, you know, get their side of the story."

Mel the reporter was back. He'd held Melody in his arms for a brief, intense time. His desire had gotten out of hand, but it wasn't his imagination. For a moment, she'd wanted him, too. Then something had happened, and she'd thrown that damnable brick wall up again.

He glanced at her. The tension in

her shoulders made him think she was holding herself together with nothing more than willpower and determination. It didn't make any sense. There wasn't any way she could deny she enjoyed the kiss, but she wasn't going to let him inside her protective shell for more than a minute.

He tamped down on the frustration boiling beneath the surface. Pushing her too fast wasn't going to work. He needed to slow things down or he would lose her for sure. More than ever, losing her was not an option. What had began as a practical arrangement just a few days ago had quickly become more. He took a deep, calming breath and let it out. He still had three weeks to convince her they would be good together, and he would use every minute of it if necessary.

"How about I throw a backyard party this weekend for the gang?" he offered. "I can invite my entire graduating class, all twenty-five of them and their assorted spouses and children. You can do your own version of grilling them while I grill burgers and hot dogs."

She palmed the dampness from her cheeks. "You don't need to go to so much trouble. I can meet with some of them individually and get plenty of material."

"That would take a lot of time." Time he didn't want her to be away from him. "And you would have to hear the same stories over and over. You can hear them as a group and conduct individual interviews on the side. Believe me, there's no end to the number of embarrassing stories they can come up with."

"Do you think they'll come?"

"Sure. I've known most of them my whole life. They'll come. Of course, I reserve the right to tell my own stories about them. They can't get off Scot-free for embarrassing the life out of me."

"Okay. Let's do it, but I insist on buying the food."

CHAPTER SEVEN

Guests began arriving well before lunch on Saturday. Hank and his father set up makeshift tables under the oak and pecan trees in the backyard while Mel took charge of the paper plates, napkins, and plastic utensils.

Hank's pool-playing buddy, Chris, arrived with his family and a giant galvanized tub they filled with ice and sodas so everyone could help themselves. Despite his insistence they needn't bring anything, no one arrived empty-handed. She had never seen so many varieties of potato salad in her life. The dessert table held enough sweets to put an entire army into a sugar coma. Homemade pies, cakes, cookies of every description, and delectable treats from Cathy's bakery tempted her the entire day.

The men took turns cooking, filling soft springtime air with the mouth-watering aroma of charcoal and flame-grilled meat. People came and went. They arrived after work, following their children's Little League game, or as an excuse to get out of mowing the lawn.

She had never seen anything like it. It was a party, yet it held none of the awkwardness she expected. Though unrelated by blood, they were a family—close-knit by the commonality of growing up together in a small town and sharing a classroom from Kindergarten to high school graduation.

Hank made sure she met every new arrival, snaking his arm around her waist in a possessive way that insured her acceptance as a friend. Everyone seemed eager to talk, and stories flew so fast she scrambled to keep up. She used Hank's office to conduct individual interviews with the people he indicated were particularly close to him. She talked to girls he'd kissed under the cottonwood trees along the creek and guys he'd shared girly magazines with in the back of the school bus. He censored nothing. Knowing what a private person he was, his openness humbled her.

As the last guest waved their farewell, she sank into a lawn chair. Hank fell into the one next to her. They sat for a long time, listening to night music provided by crickets and frogs.

"I'm glad that's over." Hank rolled his head to look at her. "Did you get enough?"

She chuckled. "I have enough stories to write two books. Hank Travis, Boy Wonder, and Hank Travis, Hero of Willowbrook."

Silence stretched between them. After a while, she glanced in his direction. The hard set of his jaw, the thin line of his lips betrayed his feelings. He pushed to his feet and began to gather the stray cups and plates, tossing them into a large trash can with more force than necessary.

"Hank, I'm kidding. Everyone in town thinks you walk on water, but I can sort through the hyperbole to find the truth. It's a credit to your good nature that you let them go on the way they did. A few of them had better watch out. You have a justifiable case of whopper-telling against them."

He paused, paper plate in hand. "I have never in my life heard such blatant lies as I heard today. I should have put a stop to it hours ago." He took his frustration out on the plate, slamming it into the garbage.

She stood. "Yet, you never once stopped them or told them to keep quiet." She took the two steps to bring her face to face with him and placed her hand on his chest. "They're your friends. You wouldn't embarrass them by correcting them in public. You're a good man, Hank

Travis."

"I really did want to pound a few heads today, so I'm not as good as you seem to think."

"Yes, you are, Hank. You wouldn't hurt a fly. I know that, now." She wrapped her arms around his waist. He held her close in the deep shadow of the oak's sweeping branches. She closed her eyes, enjoying the feel of him against her, his strong arms folded around her. She felt safe, protected, in his embrace. His shirt smelled of charcoal and mesquite from the grill, but inhaling deeply she detected the subtle musk, the distinctive scent that was Hank. His heart beat strong beneath her ear, and desire pooled low in her belly. Shocked at her unwanted reaction, she pushed out of his arms. He let her go.

"Let's get this mess cleaned up," she said.

They worked together, collecting scattered debris and carting dirty dishes into the kitchen. It was late when they finished, and he offered to drive her into town.

Not really wanting the evening to end, but knowing it had to, she accepted the ride. They rode in virtual silence, enjoying the night air through open windows.

He walked her to her door. "I'm exhausted," she as she fished her house key from her purse.

"Me, too."

"Do you mind if we take tomorrow off?" she asked. It was getting harder and harder to keep an emotional buffer between them, and after today she wasn't even sure she wanted to anymore. She felt like a planet orbiting his sun, drawing closer and closer with each new thing she learned about him. If she didn't find a way to distance herself soon…

"If it's what you want," he said, pulling her close. He didn't try to kiss her, and a part of her thought that was a good thing while another part prayed he would.

"I think we should."

Lost Melody

He hugged her tight. "Okay. Just remember it was your idea. I'll see you on Monday."

**

She set her voice recorder on the nightstand and snuggled under the handmade quilt she had picked up at the Methodist Church bizarre. She played back the recording from earlier in the week. Her skin tingled just listening to the smooth timbre of his voice. Things had been going so well, and then she'd lost control of yet another interview.

There was a gap on the tape, and her memory filled in the words before she heard them. "*For this*." The tape went silent again, except for the faint rustling of clothing. Tears formed as she remembered the joy of being in his arms, the heat of his body, the feel of his arousal grinding against her.

The bedside phone rang, jolting her from her memories. She grabbed the handset. "Hello."

"I need to see you tomorrow."

"Hank," she protested. "We agreed to take tomorrow off."

"Come to Dallas with me. I'll leave the dog with Dad, and we'll spend the day together. No interviewing allowed."

She was tempted. "Is is possible? I mean, to be out in public?"

"Sure. No one expects to find you in Dallas, and with a haircut like mine, no one will recognize me."

"I've been meaning to ask you about the haircut." She smiled even though he couldn't see her.

"Yeah. It's something isn't it? Judd has been cutting my hair all my life. I'll let it grow out before I go on tour again. When I get back from a tour, the first thing I do is go see Judd. He fixes me right up. Instant disguise. So, will you go with me tomorrow? We'll just be a pretty girl and a nerd out on the town."

"I don't know."

"I'll pick you up at eight. Dress

casual." He hung up before she could argue further.

**

Hank accelerated up the freeway on ramp, and she panicked. "Are you sure no one will recognize us?"

He glanced over his shoulder, moved into the left lane, and shifted his attention to her. "No, I'm not sure no one will recognize me. I do have friends, and there are fans who might pick me out of a crowd, but for the most part, I don't expect to be noticed at all. Have you ever seen someone in a mall or at a ballgame and thought you recognized them but you couldn't place where you knew them from?"

She nodded. "I have. I saw a guy in the grocery store once and I knew I had seen him before. It drove me crazy for days until I saw him on TV. He was the weather guy on one of the local stations."

"Once in a while I get that look,

and sometimes the person will come up to me. If they don't come up with my name, and sometimes even if they do, I just shake my head and say, nah, you have the wrong guy."

"And it works?"

"Ninety-nine percent of the time. But don't worry. I doubt we'll see anyone today who would recognize me, and as long as you don't shout your name out loud, no one will know who you are either."

"You never said where we're going. Am I dressed okay?"

"Shorts are perfect. I thought we would go to the Dallas Arboretum. I saw it on the news the other day. They said the flowers should be in bloom this week."

"I love flowers!"

"So, I did good?"

"You did excellent."

"What else do you like, Mel Harper?"

She discovered they both loved Mexican food, snow skiing, and Willie Nelson, then the conversation moved on to the worst restaurants they'd ever been in, and their favorite movies and books.

They strolled hand-in-hand along the Paseo de Flores at the Arboretum and took pictures of the blooming azaleas, tulips, daffodils, and dogwoods. Hank stopped another couple and asked them to take a photograph of the two of them with his cell phone camera, surrounded by spring blooms.

Later, Hank took her to an inexpensive Mexican restaurant where they stuffed themselves with all their favorite dishes before they headed back to Willowbrook. It had been the most perfect date she had ever been on. Spending time with Hank was like being with a best friend. Conversation came easy and he seemed to enjoy a few minutes of silence to take everything in as much as she did.

"I had a great time, but I'm exhausted. Plus, I ate too much." She yawned. "I need a nap."

"Go ahead. I'll wake you when we get home."

"I'll just close my eyes for a few minutes."

He selected a Willie Nelson CD from his collection and turned the volume down low. He hadn't driven five miles before the music and the droning of tires on pavement lulled her to sleep. She bore more resemblance to the little girl he'd seen in the internet photos when she was sleeping. Her lips parted slightly, and her head rolled to one side. He moved into the far right lane and slowed to well below the speed limit. Getting home at a particular time didn't mean anything, but spending time with her, even if she was asleep, did.

He took the long way back to Willowbrook, and when he cut the engine in front of her house about an hour later than they had anticipated, she didn't stir. Slumped against the passenger side door, her breathing was slow and even. In the light of the street lamp, he could just make out her long lashes feathered over pale cheeks. He watched her sleep until he worried a nosy neighbor might alert the police to a strange vehicle parked in front of Mel's house. It was late, but not too late for someone in the neighborhood to be out walking a dog or coming home after a movie.

He remembered her words the other day, *"I don't sleep well at night."* Well, she was sleeping now, and he hated to disturb her.

Her purse sat on the seat between them. He found her house key and eased out of the truck cab. After unlocking the front door, he returned for his sleeping beauty.

He released the seatbelt and scooped her into his arms. She curled against his chest like a kitten seeking warmth. Lord, it felt good to hold her. There was something about her that made him throw good sense to the wind. He placed a kiss the top of her head. Her hair smelled of roses, and an errant strand tickled his nose.

It took some doing to manage the screen and front door with his bundle, but at last, he settled her onto the bed. By the light spilling in from the hallway, he removed her shoes and covered her with the quilt folded across the foot. She sighed and turned onto her side, pillowing her face onto her hand.

Damn. She was so sweet lying there. He had no idea what kind of things disturbed her sleep, but standing there watching her all curled up and innocently seductive, he had the overwhelming urge to crawl in beside her and hug her tight against him. If demons crept into her dreams, he wanted to be there to slay them. But she wouldn't appreciate his efforts—not yet anyway. So, he placed a gentle kiss on her temple and left before he did something she would never forgive him for.

He drove the few blocks to his father's house and let himself in without knocking. Henry was engrossed in a documentary on the History Channel and barely noted Hank's arrival.

"There's coffee," he said, without taking his eyes off the television.

Hank helped himself to a cup and stretched out on the sofa. Betty Boop ambled over for some attention. He rubbed her behind her ears and she plopped at his feet. He waited for a commercial break before he spoke.

"Dad."

Henry found the remote and muted the television.

"I don't know what to do."

"About what?" his dad asked.

"I think I may be falling in love with Melody Ravenswood."

"I didn't know you knew her."

"Don't give me that crap. You made a donation and arranged for her to write the article about it. I wondered why you had me come over to review your tax returns so early in the morning. It didn't take me long to figure it out, especially when you didn't come home on time."

He shrugged. "I've been found out."

Hank shook his head. His father didn't sound the least bit contrite about meddling in his son's personal life.

"Well, thanks. For once, you may have done me a favor. Did you know who she was before you set me up?"

"Yeah. You know I've always been a fan of RavensBlood. When I heard her name, I thought it sounded familiar, so I did a little digging."

"You researched her on the Internet."

"Yep. It's amazing what you can find there."

Hank groaned. "Well, she doesn't want anything to do with me. She has a lot of baggage, and I don't know if I'm strong enough to carry it all for her."

"Sure you are. She'll come around. I suspect she came here to have a life, a real life. You manage it pretty well, so I figure you can show her how to do it, too.”

"What makes you think she came here so she could have a life? Did it ever cross your mind she may have come here for some other reason?”

“Like, to get an interview with you? You don’t believe that any more than I do.”

“Why doesn’t she move to England? She owns a castle or some-such there.”

“Maybe she wants more than to live like a prisoner, no matter how luxurious the prison. What kind of life would she have there? She’s young. And she must have led a pretty sheltered life to have stayed out of the tabloids all these years. Maybe she just wants to be normal, average.”

“And you think I’m normal and average? I only fit the image when I’m in Willowbrook. I’m Hank the Hammer when I’m on the road, her worst nightmare come to life.” The epiphany hit him square between the eyes, and he sprang from the sofa.

"Oh shit! Nightmares. She has nightmares, Dad."

He paced the small room. He'd never been a demon slayer before, but the instinct was there, and he couldn't ignore it.

"Her father died when she was just a kid. And tragically at that," his dad said.

"Yeah, that would mess with your head, for sure. I remember when it happened, and I didn't even know the man."

"It was all over the news for days."

Hank sat back down, trying his best to remember the details from so long ago. "Tell me what you remember about how Earl Ravenswood died."

**

Mel woke Monday morning in her own bed, wearing the clothes she wore to Dallas the previous day—minus her shoes. She propped against the headboard and tried to piece together her ragged memory of the night before.

She remembered leaving Dallas and telling Hank she needed a nap. After that…nothing. He must have carried her into the house and put her to bed. How else would she have gotten here? She glanced at the clock and realized she had slept for almost twelve hours. It was more sleep than she usually managed in a week. Exhaustion had never been the answer before, so what was different about last night?

She hurried through her shower, already late for her day with Hank. She stopped at The Donut Hole to get a chocolate and sugar infusion, and to see her friend.

"Hi, girl!" Cathy greeted her. "Nice party on Saturday. Thanks for inviting me. It was a great impromptu class reunion."

"All the thanks go to Hank. It was his idea. He thought it would be easier for me to hear all the stories in one place, rather than tracking everyone down. I think it may have backfired somewhat. The stories got more outlandish as the day went on. I'm not sure I believe half of them."

"Smart girl. Some of the folks got a little carried away. I can help you sort through them to get to the real story."

"Thanks. You read my mind. It's not too much of an imposition?"

"Not at all. Just tell me when. By the way, congratulations."

"For what?" She frowned.

"For snagging Hank Travis, of course. He never looked at me the way he looks at you. If he had, I might have accepted his invitation for a roll in the back of his pickup when we were in high school."

"He asked you to…uh, you know?"

Cathy laughed and passed Mel's usual order across the counter. "Don't get your panties in a wad. It was a long time ago, and I turned him down flat. He has knobby knees, remember?"

She told herself it wasn't any of her business what he had done when he was in high school, and the event obviously meant nothing to Cathy. She pasted a smile on her face and quipped, "Knobby knees, I remember. I should have some free time on Sunday. Why don't you come over, and we can go through all the stories and try to sort fact from fiction."

The date was set, and she headed for the farm. Hank was in the utility room when she arrived.

"Do you always do your own laundry?"

He stuffed jeans into the washer, measured liquid detergent into the machine. "I send out my shirts and dress slacks. When I'm at home, I do the rest myself. I also clean my own toilets, and vacuum." He made a face. "Actually, I do all the housework." He sounded pleased with himself.

"Why not hire someone to do it?"

"It goes back to paying my

personal bills. Why invite trouble into my home? I could probably hire someone from Willowbrook, but there's something about a stranger handling my underwear that bothers me."

She smiled. "You're a man of many talents."

She followed him to the kitchen where she'd added a bag of doughnuts and two hot chocolates to his boxes of cereal on the table.

"No fancy breakfast today?" she asked, motioning to the boxes of sugarcoated cereal.

"Just lazy today. I see you brought your own food. Tired of my cooking already?"

"No. I stopped to talk to Cathy, and she assumed I was there for my usual. We can save them for later."

He dumped a giant scoop of kibble into Betty Boop's bowl and brought milk and orange juice to the table. "Frosted Flakes okay with you?"

"You bet. They're my favorite."

Mel fixed a bowl of cereal for herself and passed the box to Hank. Soon, all three of them were crunching away. Mel smiled at the simple domestic scene that felt more comfortable than she could have ever imagined.

"What about you? Do you clean house yourself, or do you have a housekeeper?" Hank asked.

"I do my own for the same reason you do. Privacy. I grew up doing chores around the house, so I don't really mind."

He studied her for a moment then returned to his cereal. "How did you do it? Move to Willowbrook I mean, without anyone finding out who you are?"

She put down her spoon and crossed her arms on the table. "My middle name is a pretty good disguise, like your haircut, and I'm incorporated, MHR investments. I bought the house in cash, through the corporation, sight unseen. I hired a real estate management company to rent it to me, and I pay myself rent every month."

"Clever. I'll have to remember that one. It could come in handy sometime. Does anyone in town, besides me, know about you?"

"My boss does. The IRS wants their share of the pittance he pays me, so unless I wanted to change my name, he had to know. Cathy Anderson knows."

"Did you tell her, or did she find out on her own?"

"I told her. Why?"

"Just wondering. You can add Dad to the list. He knew before I did."

Her stomach clenched. A wave of nausea swept through her. She fought the panic welling in her gut. "How did he find out? Who has he told?"

He put a hand on her arm. "Relax. He hasn't told anyone, I'm sure. He didn't even tell me. He just arranged for us to meet, and rightfully guessed I'd figure it out myself."

"Are you saying he made the

donation just so I would interview him?"

"It's worse. He lured me to his house and conveniently arranged to be late, giving us a chance to meet. I have to tell you, he's pretty pleased with himself."

Cold shivered down her spine, and an overwhelming desire to run as far and fast as she could raced through her system. All her careful planning really had been for nothing. The life she'd envisioned in Willowbrook was nothing more than an illusion.

"Mel, it's okay. He won't tell anyone. He's always been a RavensBlood fan. Your name rang a bell with him, so he did the same thing I did, he ran an Internet search."

She rose on shaky legs and took her cereal bowl to the sink. Dazed, she rinsed it and stowed it in the dishwasher, and turned to him. "What did he hope to accomplish by throwing us together?"

He rose and crossed the room to her. He braced his hands on the counter, trapping her between them. "I think he's hoping to get a couple of grandkids out of it." He brushed his mouth across hers. "What do you think his chances are?" He kissed her again, harder, their lips the only contact.

Her toes curled, and her heart did a somersault. Heat replaced the ice in her veins. His lips were soft, incredibly warm. Her body yearned to answer the invitation his kiss issued, but a small grain of sanity gave her the strength to push against his chest. She couldn't do it, couldn't give in to the things her body wanted. If she did, any hope she might have of building a normal life for herself would be gone. "I think he doesn't have a snowball's chance in hell."

He kept her imprisoned against the counter a moment longer before he stepped back and allowed her to slip away. She closed the cereal boxes and returned them to the pantry. *Normal. If you act normal, you are normal.* She was all too aware of his gaze following her as she took his bowl to the sink and returned the juice to the refrigerator.

"I have work to do," he said. "Are you coming out to the barn with me?"

She froze with her hand on the refrigerator door while she wrestled with her conflicting emotions. It was hopeless. Her life in Willowbrook was a sham. Out of necessity, she'd told one person in town who she really was, and now the number was up to four. Every minute she spent in Willowbrook, and especially every minute she spent in Hank's company increased the chances the whole world would find out who she was. So why wasn't she running?

The answer stood behind her, lounging against the kitchen counter as if he hadn't just kissed her senseless. As if he wasn't a threat to her sanity and her existence. Everything about him intrigued her— from his farm boy attitude to his immense talent and good looks. He'd pulled her into his universe, and she was helpless to break free of his gravitational pull.

"I'm coming," she said, turning to follow him out the door.

CHAPTER EIGHT

He pulled an electronic keyboard next to his desk and retreated into his own world, inaccessible behind a headset connected to the device, which in turn connected to the open laptop computer. Mel kept busy, writing out questions and observations while he worked on his composition. He tried notes on the keyboard, sometimes scribbling furiously on staff paper, sometimes working on the computer. With his reading glasses on, he appeared less like a rock star but still lethally sexy, reminding her of the first time she'd seen him. He seemed oblivious to his sex appeal, which made him even more appealing.

Betty Boop jumped up on the

leather sofa and curled up next to her. She stroked the dog's ears, content to watch Hank work. The man had no idea what he did to women. Amazing. He honestly thought he was a simple man—which proved how much he knew. There was nothing simple or ordinary about Hank Travis.

The room was silent except for the occasional muffled woof from Betty, deep in a doggy dream, or the click of the computer keyboard. He'd been right about one thing. His work was mostly boring—at least from her angle. She stood, thinking it was time for a walk. She spied his MP3 player on the corner of his desk. She had it in-hand when he bolted from his seat and covered her hand with his, stopping her progress. He jerked off his headset, and peeled her fingers away from the player.

"Not that one." He opened a drawer and pulled out another MP3 player, identical in appearance to the one she'd picked up. He held it out to her. "You can listen to this one." The off limits device disappeared into the desk drawer.

Unsure what to make of the encounter, she accepted the replacement and retreated to her side of the room. "Sorry I disturbed you."

"It's okay. The music selection is better on that one. I know hanging around while I work must be excruciating for you, but I won't be much longer." He gestured toward the device she held. "You can keep it if you want. It might help you get through the boring parts of my day."

"Thanks. It was just so quiet in here I thought I might go stir crazy."

"I'm working on something for our next album, and I'm afraid it's a long way from anything I would want anyone to hear."

"I understand," she lied. She secured the earbuds and returned to her list of questions, to which she could add several more.

After lunch, Hank spent several

hours in a rehearsal room, his
computer hooked up to a full-size
electronic keyboard. He donned
headphones, and retreated into his
private world again. She watched,
inexplicably feeling left out. She knew
nothing about composing music, but
she wanted to be a part of his world
in some small way.

They spent the rest of the week
together, yet apart. Whenever she
asked him about the music he was
working on, his reply was the same—
it wasn't ready to share. She chalked
it up to artistic temperament and
amused herself while he worked,
listening to the plethora of taped
conversations, making notes, and
jotting down more questions to ask.

Ever since the scene in the
kitchen on Monday, he had asked no
more questions and hadn't so much
as brushed his arm against hers
when they walked side by side. Their
conversations focused exclusively on
the business at-hand. He allowed her
to ask anything she wanted, and he

answered candidly, even when they crossed the invisible line between personal and professional.

She was more than relieved when, over breakfast Friday morning, he announced he was leaving for New York in the afternoon and wouldn't return until late Monday.

"What's in New York?"

"My agent," he said. "It's a business meeting."

With the weekend free, she stocked up at the local supermarket and headed home for a well-needed rest. She knew sleep would be elusive, but she could relax in her cozy little house, and put aside the Travis tapes until Sunday when Cathy would be over to help her make sense of the childhood stories.

□□

Hank joined the other members of BlackWing at their penthouse apartment in Manhattan. The apartment took up the entire top floor of the high-rise building on the Upper West Side. Against the image carefully created for the media, the band members were surprisingly boring people, preferring their wives and children to the groupies and fans who bought their records. With that in mind, they'd purchased the large New York apartment, so they could accommodate everyone at one time. A throng of excited children and frazzled wives greeted him when he arrived. He exclaimed over gap-tooth smiles, heard about new puppies, and admired the newest arrival, three-month-old Katie Sanders, daughter of bass guitarist Kevin Sanders.

Hank held the tiny bundle in his arms, afraid of dropping her yet thrilled at the precious new life. His chest tightened, envisioning holding a child of his own. An image flashed in his mind of Melody, round with his baby. He fought back the longing, the instant need to make the image a reality. Passing the infant back to her mother, he mumbled something he hoped was appropriate and went in search of the band.

They'd gathered in the conference room. He chuckled. If he didn't know better, he'd think he was meeting a bunch of insurance salesmen. They were an unlikely group to be successful Rock and Roll musicians. If not for the unexpected success of BlackWing, the lot of them would have spent their lives pushing pencils for a living. He shook hands all around.

He grabbed Kevin in a macho guy hug, clapping him on the back. "I saw Katie. Congratulations, she's a keeper."

Kevin's smile covered his entire face. "Stay away from her, Hank. She can do better than you!" he joked.

"Ain't that the truth?" He asked no one in particular, "When is Guy going to be here?"

Stephen Anderson, backup singer and master of several wind and string instruments, shoved a sheaf of papers across the desk to him. "He'll be here soon. He sent the contracts so we could have go over them before he gets here."

Hank snagged a copy. He knew all would be in order. Their agent, Guy Nichols, was a stickler for detail and never sent them anything that hadn't been reviewed by at least half a dozen lawyers. Nevertheless, he would read it before signing. "Is Jonathan Youngblood coming with him?"

A chorus of ignorance sounded around the table. He grunted his acknowledgement, and continued to read. He came to the list of songs specifically enumerated in the contract.

It wasn't there. He read it a second time, hoping he'd missed it somewhere. In his opinion, there wasn't any point in doing the cover album if "Melody" wasn't part of the deal. Belatedly, he noticed the silence surrounding him. He set the contract aside and scanned the faces of his friends. Sympathetic eyes met his.

"Why isn't it here?" he asked, knowing in advance, the brilliant Harvard graduates would plead ignorance.

He threw the contract on the table and growled, "Don't anyone sign this contract until we find out what's going on." He stormed out of the room, knowing he needed to curb his anger before Guy arrived, especially if Sir Jonathan was with him.

An hour later when Guy arrived, alone, Hank had tempered his rage, but like a dormant volcano, it simmered just below the surface. He wasted no time getting to the point.

"Why isn't 'Melody' on the list?"

"You'll have to ask Sir Jonathan," the agent said. "He's agreed to meet with you in the morning to discuss it in private. His driver will pick you up at seven and deliver you to his hotel for breakfast."

"What the hell is going on? You know I've been working on the cover for over a year. I won't do the album if 'Melody' isn't on it. What would be the point? 'Melody' is the single, defining work of Hamilton Ravenswood. Any cover album would be incomplete without it."

An uneasy murmur went around the table. He ignored it, convinced he was right. The rest of the band had spent countless hours working on other songs, and the demo tracks were almost ready for Sir Jonathan's approval. As executor of Hamilton Ravenswood's estate, and co-owner of the songs, Sir Jonathan would have to sign off on the songs before BlackWing could record them. He knew he was being unreasonable and unfair to the rest of the group by taking his all-or-nothing stance.

"Look, Hank, meet him for breakfast tomorrow and find out what's going on. He wouldn't tell me," Guy said, trying to appease him. "He specifically asked which one of you wanted to do the song and asked to meet with him, alone. That's all I know. As many times as you've spoken to him over the phone, I'm surprised the subject hasn't already come up."

Hank drummed his fingers on the table instead of letting loose the string of curses running through his head.

"He hasn't said no. Not yet anyway." The agent glanced around the table. "My advice is to wait until tomorrow, until Hank meets with Youngblood and finds out what's going on. I'll come for lunch tomorrow, I'll even bring the food, and we'll hear what Hank has to say. Then you can decide if you want to scrap the album or sign the contract."

They sat in silence long after Guy left. Hank didn't know what to say to his friends. He knew he was being an ass. He wasn't considering them or their wishes regarding the album.

"I'm with Hank," Chad said, breaking the silence. "If we can't do 'Melody' I don't know what the point of the album would be." He addressed Hank. "You're right. It's his signature song, the legacy of Hamilton Ravenswood."

"I know if Youngblood heard you sing it with the changes you've made, he'd agree to the cover," Kevin chimed in. "Your version is a tribute to the masterpiece. To the master. No one but you could cover that song. We all know it, and he must know it, too."

Mike and Stephen added their support. Hank's anger cooled, his obsession somehow validated by his friends' unwavering loyalty. "Thanks, guys. I appreciate the solidarity. I wish I knew what was going on, but I don't."

"Go have breakfast with Sir Jonathan and find out. We'll decide what to do when you get back," Mike said.

"It seems I have a breakfast date tomorrow." He stood. "I should get some sleep so I don't fall asleep in the scrambled eggs."

Lost Melody

□□

Hank tossed and turned. He put the breakfast meeting aside, no need dwelling on something he had no control over, but he couldn't get Mel out of his head. He missed her. He wanted to hear her voice. He wanted to touch her.

Lying in bed listening to his friends and their families outside his door laughing and planning to spend time together opened a mental portal that allowed Hank to see the empty cavern of his life. His music filled a need, it was an expression of his soul, but it wasn't enough. Not anymore. He needed Mel.

He'd never needed anyone before. As an only child, he'd never really been lonely. His house was always full of neighborhood kids, welcomed by his mother with a batch of cookies or brownies. She was always ready to feed the gang he brought home with him. Living in town, he'd played on the street until the streetlights came on, the universal clock by which all mother's called a halt to the evening's fun.

In high school, he'd been busy with the marching band, and dorky as it had been, he somehow avoided the stigma associated with being a member. His friends had extended to every aspect of the social spectrum at Willowbrook High School. Chris and Randy had been stars on the football team, while he cheered them on from the band section.

In college, he'd made another set of friends. When a few frat brothers started a jam session to cope with the intellectual demands at Harvard, he'd joined in, buying a cheap drum kit from a Boston pawnshop. Of the ten original members, five had stuck it out through the years, picking up small gigs on and off campus. They'd been thrilled to pocket a few dollars for doing something they loved.

Their big break had come their senior year. They'd booked a gig at a Boston country club, a dance for the upper-crust teenage crowd. Guy Nichols was chaperoning his daughter's dance that evening. As a result, none of them had ever worked a day in their chosen professions.

In the penthouse he co-owned, surrounded by people he considered family, he'd never felt so alone. He wanted to call Mel to tell her what he was doing in New York. He wasn't sure she would understand why he hadn't told her about the cover album though. She carried a heavy burden where her father was concerned, and there was a real possibility she would shut him out completely when she found out what he was up to.

Before the stinging letdown of the contract, he'd planned to ask Sir Jonathan about Mel. He probably knew her better than anyone else. He'd been the guardian of her estate for the last fifteen years, and he lived in her home in England, still managing her holdings for her. Everyone knew the legendary band had dissolved in the aftermath of

Ravenswood's death. Most of the members had continued their careers, eventually starting their own bands or launching solo careers. Jonathan Youngblood was the exception. He retired from the business and honored his best friend's wishes by taking care of the daughter he'd left behind.

If anyone knew how to reach her, it was Jonathan Youngblood.

Hank fitted the headphone buds into his ears and turned on the MP3 player he was never without. "Melody" spoke to his soul, quieting his unrest. He slept.

**

The elevator opened directly into the exclusive suite occupied by Sir Jonathan Youngblood. Hank greeted the older man, grateful at last to meet him. He was, after all, the living half of RavensBlood and a legend in his own right. It was hard not to be intimidated in the presence of Rock and Roll royalty, even when said prince was dressed in worn jeans and a faded T-shirt from a long-ago concert. He'd lost none of his charisma in the years since his retirement. His graying hair and wizened features hinted at the hardships he'd endured in his lifetime. However, there was nothing soft or feeble in his handshake. The man was solid as a rock. Whatever else he did in his free time, he stayed in shape.

They exchanged pleasantries, and the older man instantly put him at ease with his casual manner and praise for Hank's work. Uniformed waiters served breakfast then left them alone.

"Being here is surreal," Hank said.

"Why?"

"Me…here…with you. I've been a fan all my life."

"Well, that makes me feel old."

"I didn't mean…"

"No," his host waved away Hank's apology. "I am old. Let me guess, your parent's listened to my music."

Hank felt his face flush with embarrassment. "Yes, Sir. They did. And my dad is still a big fan. Truthfully, I wouldn't be where I am today if not for the music you created with Hamilton Ravenswood."

Waiters came to clear the table and they moved to the living room.

Sir Jonathan twisted his teacup between his hands. "I brought you here for a reason," he said.

Hank waited while Jonathan gathered his thoughts. Judging by the grim expression on his face, whatever he had to say to Hank didn't come easy for him. Hank's stomach churned and he wished he hadn't eaten anything. It couldn't be good news.

"Milton Ravenswood was the best friend I had in this world, and I've done my best the last fifteen or so years to do what I thought he would want me to do for him and for the family he left behind."

"I understand. He was lucky to

have a friend like you."

"No, he wasn't. I was lucky to have a friend like him." He sat forward, resting his elbows on his knees. "What I'm about to say is between you and me, Hank. It isn't to leave this room. Agreed?"

He nodded. "Okay."

"I'd love for you to record 'Melody', and I think Milton would agree, but I can't give you permission to record it."

White-hot rage burned through the lining of Hank's stomach and threatened to explode his skull. He gritted his teeth to keep it all in.

"Before you rip me a new one, let me tell you why."

Hank forced himself to remain seated. Raging against Sir Jonathan would get him nowhere. "I'm listening."

"I don't control the rights to the song. I never have. It's never been part of Ravenswood's library."

Hank played the words over in his mind, trying to make sense of them.

"What do you mean? Ravenswood wrote it. If his estate doesn't own the rights, who does?"

"She does."

He knew he must look like a complete idiot, staring as if the man spoke an alien language, but he had no idea what Sir Jonathan was talking about. "Who, specifically, is *she*?"

The legend smiled a cat-who-got-the-canary smile. "Melody Ravenswood. She owns the rights to her song. She always has, since she was an infant."

Hank's world spun out of control. His universe collapsed in on him as the words took on meaning for him. He shook his head, marveling at his lifelong misunderstanding.

"It's about her, isn't it?" He rose and paced the room, letting the new information sink in. "I feel like a fool. All my life I've loved the song because it described the essence of my love for music, the way it feeds my soul. 'Gently it comes, born of my soul, making me whole,'" he quoted.

"It's a misconception Milton would have understood," Sir Jonathan said. "The song works on several levels. You've discovered two of them. It was so much a part of him. He wrote it the day she was born, you know. He never really talked about it much, even to me, and we were as close as brothers."

Hank collapsed into the nearest chair. "Why was it only recorded once?"

Sir Jonathan hesitated. "Our last concert was a live recording in Denver. Milton added the song at the end as a birthday present for Melody. It was the first and only time he sang it to anyone other than his daughter. He brought the house down." He looked away, focusing on a scene only he could see. "I'll never forget the way the audience reacted to the song. There was complete silence when he finished. No one made a sound in the entire place until he walked away from the piano. I'd never seen anything like it in my life. Still haven't."

He sipped his tea, studying the dregs as if they had answers. "He left the stage and never came back out for the standing ovation. It went on and on. I didn't think the audience was ever going to leave, so we played three encores, trying to get them to calm down."

He paused. Hank saw the strain it took to remember, the tight set in his jaw, the moisture glistening in his eyes.

"I never saw him again. He'd already left for the airport when the rest of us got off stage. He had a copy of the recording with him on the plane."

Sir Jonathan raised his head, locking his gaze with Hank's. "Milton left to go to Melody's tenth birthday party the next day. He never made it. Diane knew, but she let the party go on anyway. She didn't tell Melody her father was dead until after the party was over."

Dear God. Hank nearly doubled over, feeling as if he'd been mule-kicked in the gut. He knew the pain of losing a parent, but the circumstances of her father's death sent him reeling. What must she have gone through? He remembered the photo he'd seen of the stoic little girl standing at her father's graveside, and he remembered the brave woman who'd told him he was nuts.

Sir Jonathan left the room. He returned some time later with the glass of orange juice he shoved under Hank's nose. "Drink this. It'll do you good."

He did as ordered, the alcohol-laced drink scalding away his fugue. "Damn. You could have warned me."

The older man laughed. He took a seat across from Hank. "You're in love with her, aren't you?"

Was he? Hell, yes, he realized. He'd been in love with her from the moment he first saw her, long before he knew who she was. Finding out she was Ravenswood's daughter had only confirmed what he had already known deep inside, they were meant to be together. Being in love with her explained a lot, like the ache in his stomach when he was away from her, his new dragon slaying instincts where she was concerned. How could he not have recognized the signs? And he wrote about love for a living. Lord, he was an idiot.

He wondered how many more surprises Sir Jonathan had for him. "So you know?"

"There isn't much I don't know about Melody. She's as much my daughter as she was Milton's. But don't think I've been spying on her. No, she's on her own in Willowbrook, just as she asked to be."

"Then how do you know about us?"

He shrugged one shoulder. "Your reaction to the story I told you. If you didn't feel so strongly about her, you would have said something like, wow, tough luck, or poor kid. Instead, you felt her pain. She could do worse than you."

He wasn't so sure. He could see where his career would be a major roadblock in winning Melody's love. "What am I going to do?"

"I don't know. Seeing how you feel about her, I need to tell you something else, something no one knows except Melody and her mother."

He braced for another blow. He'd come to breakfast expecting to argue his case for recording a song, and instead his life had been put on a centrifuge, spinning completely out of control.

"Milton called Melody every night of her life, including the night he died, just before he got on the plane, and sang her song to her over the phone."

He thought he was prepared to hear anything. He was wrong. "Oh Jesus!"

Leaning over, he rested his elbows on his knees and buried his head in his hand. Her sleepless nights were rooted in a very real nightmare.

"Christ, Jonathan. What am I supposed to do? How can I compete with the ghost of her father?"

"You can't compete with a ghost. You'll have to find a way to put the ghost to rest, once and for all."

Hank sat motionless, his world slipping away, his dreams crashing and burning as if they'd been on the plane with Hamilton, Earl Ravenswood.

"Record the song."

Had he missed something? "You told me you don't have the right to authorize it. How can I record it?"

"I'm confident you can carry the song. Not many people could. I'm also confident you'll do an excellent cover of it. You've probably been working on it for years. Of course, you may want to rethink it, given your new understanding. Record it. Play it for Melody. Better yet, do it in person, just the two of you. She'll authorize it.

Trust me."

CHAPTER NINE

He had no idea what he was going to tell the others. He arrived at the penthouse and went directly to his room. Moments later, he stood in the shower, hoping the cold water would provide the answers he needed.

Guy arrived with enough take-out to feed half the building. Hank declined. They gathered in the conference room after lunch, eager to hear what he had to say. He took his seat, snagged one of the pens in the center of the table, and asked Guy, "Do you have the contract?"

The agent produced the original contract from his briefcase, and slid it across the table. Hank remembered

Sir Jonathan's words, "Record it," and praying the man knew what he was talking about, he asked, "Where do I sign?"

He scrawled his name in the designated places, offering no explanation to the group for his change of heart. He returned to his room, needing the solitude to sort through his emotions. Hunger forced him to face his friends late that evening.

He helped himself to a plate of leftovers and joined them in the living room. The conversation centered on their families and lives at home, catching up with each other as old friends do. He answered questions about his dad and Willowbrook. They had all spent many months there over the last few years, ever since he turned his barn into a recording studio

"Let's go ahead with the project. I have a few things to work out before we can include 'Melody,' but I'm pretty sure it will make the album. In the meantime, let's concentrate on the other tracks. We'll save 'Melody' for last." He hoped he wasn't lying to his friends. In truth, he didn't have much faith he could convince Mel to let him record the song, and with his new understanding of it, he was already working on a new revision in his head.

Satisfied the project would go forth, the discussion turned to the logistics. They agreed to meet at the farm in two weeks to begin the summer-long recording process.

**

Mel caught up with her household chores, cleaning, doing laundry—all the things she'd neglected while shadowing Hank. She was overjoyed when her Uncle Jonathan called to say he would be coming for a visit in a few weeks. He'd stepped in when her father died, offering his broad shoulders to carry her burden. He was as much a father to her as

Hamilton Ravenswood had been. She still had another two weeks to spend with Hank, and then Jonathan would arrive. His timing couldn't be better.

Cathy came to Mel's on Sunday morning after the early church service, bearing doughnuts and hot chocolate. Mel laughed at the obvious jab at her interviewing style. She and her friend spent the day listening to tapes from the picnic, seeking the truth in the stories. Cathy proved to be knowledgeable as well as grounded, and the work went more quickly than she thought possible. Finishing early, the two women ordered pizza and found a chick-flick on cable. Cathy left shortly after, having to be up long before dawn to open The Donut Hole.

Mel was organizing her notes when the phone rang.

"It's me," Hank said. "I came home early."

His voice warmed her all the way to her toes, but there was something in the way he spoke that worried her—as if he were reaching out for a lifeline. "Did everything go all right?"

"Yes and no. I don't want to talk about it. When can I see you?"

She'd done a credible job of denying how much she missed him, but when she heard the desperation in his voice, she gave in and admitted it to herself. It was beyond foolish, but she really wanted to see him. "Why don't you come over? I'm still up."

She replaced the receiver, wondering what insanity had possessed her to invite him to her home. *I can't get involved with him. He's a musician.* She fisted her hand against her rapidly beating heart. She had the sinking feeling it was too late to worry about getting involved. She had passed *involved* and was well on the way to *hopelessly involved.* If she wasn't careful, she'd end up just like her mother—alone, and pining for a man she couldn't have.

The instant she opened her front

door and saw his face—the pain etched in the set of his jaw, the depth of his gaze—she knew she was a goner. She'd do whatever it took to erase that look.

He stepped inside, closing and locking the door behind him. She took a step back in one last attempt to save herself from doing something really stupid. He reached for her, and without saying a word, folded her into his arms. He held onto her like a drowning man would a life vest, as if his survival depended on her. No one had ever needed her as much as Hank needed her right this minute. She'd never been anyone's lifeline.

She wrapped her arms around his waist, flattening her palms against the solid strength of his back. She pressed her cheek against his chest. His shirt had lost some of its starch in his travels, but it still smelled fresh and felt cool against her skin. Instinctually, she moved her hands over the tight muscles in his back, and slowly he relaxed in her embrace.

"What's wrong, Hank? What happened in New York?"

Everything. Holding her, he could almost believe everything would be all right. He never wanted to let her go, but it was too soon to tell her, so he kept his thoughts to himself. Her gentle caress began to melt the solid block of ice at his core, and the scattered pieces of his sanity slowly slipped into place. Loosening his hold, he gently let her go.

"Nothing. It was just business. The usual." He ran his hands along her arms from shoulder to elbow, loving that he could touch her again. "Thanks for letting me come over. I just needed to see you. Two days was too long to be away from you."

Her eyes held so much compassion and understanding, and she didn't have a clue what had him so worked up. He was lost, beyond saving. Sir Jonathan was right—he was in love with her.

"I missed you, too," she said, her words just a whisper. The compassion he had seen in her eyes vanished, replaced by something he knew well. Desire.

He pulled her to him, one hand at her waist, while the other swooped to her nape. He threaded his fingers through her hair. When their lips met, she rose to her toes and wrapped her arms around his neck, urging him closer. Her lips parted, allowing his tongue to swoop in. She tasted of sweet wine, and when he thrust his tongue deep, she parried and pressed her breasts against his chest.

He groaned and moved his hand lower to caress her bottom. He ground his hips against her belly, making his desire for her clear. She caught his bottom lip between her teeth and wiggled her lower half against his erection.

Without breaking the kiss, he lifted her into his arms and carried her down the hallway leading to the bedrooms. Stopping just inside the first door he came to, he tore his lips from hers. God. He couldn't wait to get his hands on her, assure himself she was okay.

"The next one," she said.

"Huh?"

"This isn't my bedroom," she said. He followed her gaze, taking in the small room outfitted with a desk and little else. He groaned. "You were heading to my bedroom, weren't you?"

"Yes, ma'am, I was."

She tilted her head. "That way."

He wasted no time moving down the hall to the last open door. He paused on the threshold. "Are you sure?"

"I'm sure."

He found the correct room, kicked the door closed behind them, and crossed to the bed.

Somewhere in the back of her mind, Mel understood the catastrophic mistake she was about to make, but Hank needed her tonight, and if she was truthful, she needed him, too. Ever since the first moment when she'd walked into the room in his father's house and saw him sitting there, she had wanted him.

He eased her to her feet and stepped back slightly. He slipped a couple of buttons loose on his shirt then paused. "If you don't want me to make love to you, tell me to stop. I'll go, if you want me to." His voice sounded like it had been dragged across sharp gravel. A muscle ticked in his jaw and she wanted to place her lips there and make the tension go away.

She stared at the sliver of skin showing through the gap in his shirt placket and her mouth watered. It would be wise to end it here but her body had already made the decision for her. She locked eyes with him and reached out. She popped another button free. "Don't go."

The rest of their clothes came off

in a blur of stretched buttonholes and rasping zippers. Hank's talented hands learned every inch of her body, driving any lingering doubts about whether being with him was right or wrong completely out of her head. He knew where to be gentle and where a firmer touch was needed. When he added his lips and tongue to his explorations, Mel lost the ability to think at all.

He reduced her world to touch and sensation…and pleasure. So much pleasure.

Her body responded to each caress with a plea for another and Hank answered every one with a slow thoroughness that robbed the air from her lungs.

When he had worked her to a mindless state of desperation, he took her breast into his mouth and simultaneously pressed two fingers into her. Mel lifted her hips and arched her back in blatant invitation. "Please."

He released her breast and

nibbled his way up to her clavicle and along the vein pulsing erratically in her throat. "God, you're hot and tight, sweetheart." His fingers worked in and out of her body in a constant beat that matched her internal rhythm. He caught her earlobe between his teeth and tugged. She groaned and ground her pelvis against the heel of his hand seeking the glorious something glowing on the horizon.

"That's it, darlin'. Let go. Come apart for me."

She didn't want it to end, but the coil wound tighter with each stroke of his fingers and she was helpless to stop the wave of sensation that ripped through her body when the coil snapped and unwound. She bucked against his arm stretched across her stomach, anchoring her to the mattress. He continued touching her, using every resource at his disposal to prolong her pleasure.

Her world slowly righted. She opened her eyes to find Hank staring intently at her. "I've got to have you," he said.

"Yes," was the only word her lips would form. He'd just given her the most intense orgasm of her life, but it wasn't enough. She wanted more. She needed him inside her. She needed to wind that spring again, with him.

"Hang on, sweetheart." He rolled away, and she shivered at the loss of his heat. A moment later, he was back, covering her, spreading her legs, seeking entrance. He nudged her core. "Wider."

Mel brought her knees up and dropped them to the mattress, at the same time, tilting her hips up to receive him. He filled her in one smooth stroke, forcing the air from her lungs and sending shock waves of pleasure all the way to her fingertips and toes.

"Sweet Jesus," he exclaimed. "You feel so damned good, woman."

If she could have spoken she would have returned the compliment, but she was lost in a world where there was nothing but exquisite bliss. He pulled almost all the way out and slid his turgid length back in. She had nothing to compare the sensation to. She'd managed a couple of hook-ups in college, but none of them had been anything like being with Hank. Having Hank inside her was rockets exploding into space. It was Heaven.

Hank moved with confidence. No tentative questing for the right spot, the perfect tempo. She moved with him, gasping with each delicious stroke. She ran her hands over his body and reveled in the steel strength of his limbs and the solid block of his torso. Where she was soft, he was hard, and every part of him was the perfect match for every part of her.

Every thrust brought her closer to the perfect moment when there was no past and the future was measured in throbbing heartbeats.

Much later, lying awake with

Melody cradled against his chest, "Melody" came to him. He hummed softly so as not to wake her. He knew how he would write it, the slight changes of inflection, the nuances of the notes to alter the song from a father's expression of love, his lullaby to a daughter, to a song between lovers. He wondered if Hamilton Ravenswood had ever imagined the metamorphosis when he wrote the words. Surely, he'd seen the dual meanings of paternal love and musical passion. But, had he foreseen the song from a lover's viewpoint as well?

She stirred beside him in the early dawn light. One word summed up the way he'd felt when he sank into her for the first time. Mine. Watching her sleep, he knew there wasn't another woman in the world he wanted or would ever want. Only her. And thoughts of another man touching her, making love to her, sent shards of ice through his system. No way, no how. *She's mine.*

Lost Melody

He reached for the last foil wrapped condom, glad he'd had the presence of mind to grab a couple and jam them in his pocket before he'd driven to her house the night before—not that he'd had any hope she felt the same way he did, but he'd prayed she would. He sheathed his morning erection and rolled on top of her sleeping form. He entered her slowly, stretching her tight passage to take him fully. Her hips moved, responding to his invasion. He watched her face as she awoke, her eyes going from slumberous to aroused. He moved inside her to an ancient rhythm, slowly pulling out and, with torturous patience, pushing his staff to her core.

Braced on his forearms above her, his palms cradled her face while his thumbs traced a line along her cheekbones down her jaw. His lips followed the same path, leaving tiny kisses in his wake. Her body reacted, heating until she melted for him. She wrapped her legs around his hips, urging him to increase the tempo. He buried deep within and stilled. He pushed to one elbow and brought her nipple to his mouth. His lips closed over the tight bud, startling a gasp from her.

There was no sweeter music than the way her body sang when he touched her. He rolled across her and gave the other one the same attention.

Soon, her body tensed, poised on the brink of shattering.

"That's it," he crooned in her ear. "Come for me, baby."

Her inner muscles clenched around his shaft. "Hank," she breathed.

Lord, he loved to make her come. Loved the way his name sounded on her lips and the way she held onto him like he was her anchor in a storm. He pressed her into the mattress and sought his own release. He buried his hands and face in her hair and increased his tempo to match the beat pounding through his brain. The rhythm built to a crescendo, pounded in his system, and claimed his control. The music they made together seared itself on his mind, to be put on paper another time.

He held her close to his sated body. He wondered if she knew, if she could tell by the way he made love to her how deep his feelings ran. Lying in bed with her, her legs tangled with his, his hand on her naked hip keeping her nestled against his sex, he closed his eyes and let the music wash through him. Every note came to him, a reflection of his love for her. It had become part of him, and committing it to paper, a mere formality.

She slipped into a deep slumber, and he held her until the sun bathed the room in a warm golden glow, mirroring the light within. He slid out of bed, moving carefully so he wouldn't wake her.

Life didn't get any better than waking up in Mel's bed, Hank thought

as he flipped another pancake. Last
night he felt like nothing would ever
be right again, then she walked into
his arms and everything fell into
place. She was his. He loved her and
if she didn't love him, she was
damned close to it.

He hummed the new note
structure that had popped into his
head in the wee hours of the morning
while he held her in his arms. It was
perfect—better than anything he'd
ever written in his life, and as soon
as he got home, he would put it down
on paper. He wasn't in a rush to
leave—the tune wasn't going
anywhere. Once he had it in his
head, it was there to stay, so he
could hang around here as long as
she would let him.

CHAPTER TEN

Mel woke to a sun-filled room. She stretched and rolled over to check the clock on the opposite nightstand. Over-worked muscles reminded her of the night before, and the morning, too. Even if she wanted to forget, and she didn't, the heavy scent of heated bodies and sex hung in the air and clung to the tangled sheets. The delicious smell of bacon cooking wafted through her open bedroom door. She'd never had a man cook her breakfast before. Hank was, and it was enough to make her stop and think about what she'd done. She clutched the sheet in tight fists, remembering. She'd never felt anything as perfect as having Hank inside her. And the way he touched her and cared for her…

Her lips stretched into a smile. Hank's shirt lay discarded on the floor, and her inner thighs protested as she bent to pick it up. She slipped the shirt over her nakedness, loving the feel of it as the hem skimmed across her legs. A vision of him wearing nothing but his open shirt, her clinging to him, her legs wrapped around him, taking him inside herself, heated her skin. Embarrassed by her wicked thoughts and the flush creeping over her body, she tiptoed across the hall to the bathroom and splashed cold water on her face.

She padded on bare feet to the kitchen, coming to a stop in the doorway. He stood at the stove, wearing only his jeans. She admired the broad expanse of his shoulders as he hummed a tune while he cooked. Leaning against the doorjamb, she watched and listened. The melody was familiar, yet different. A horrible realization dawned, painting her vision red and eclipsing everything else.

"Stop."

Hank turned, spatula in hand. *Whoa*. Something was wrong here, and he didn't have a clue what it was. The volcano standing in the doorway was not the same happy and satisfied woman he'd left sleeping in bed a short while ago. This was an angry, distant version he thought he'd seen the last of after what they'd shared last night and again this morning.

"I thought you'd be hungry. I know I am," he said with a smile.

She straightened, her body impossibly rigid. He could almost see the bricks rising up to form a wall between them. "I meant, stop humming that song."

His smile vanished as he realized what he'd been humming. *Her* song—but the way he envisioned it now. "I'm sorry. It just comes out sometimes, unconsciously."

"You've changed it. Why?"

She was quick, he'd give her that. Most people, even trained musicians, probably wouldn't have noticed the subtle changes so quickly or could have identified the song as easily, but of course, it was a part of her.

"It's something I've been toying with. A cover, my interpretation of the song."

"Don't."

The single word was like a bullet to his heart, delivered with cold and deadly accuracy. She turned and hurried down the hall.

"Mel, wait!" He tossed the spatula in the sink and followed after her, reaching the hallway in time to see her slam her bedroom door shut. He stood there, unsure whether he should plead with her to listen or barge in and demand she hear him out.

"Shit," he said, staring at the closed door. He'd really screwed things up, and he didn't have a clue how to fix them. "Mel," he called through the door. "Can't we talk? Please, let me explain."

He held his breath, waiting for an answer. When none came, he sighed and returned to the kitchen. He cleaned the mess he'd made and left what was edible of the breakfast on the counter for her. He approached the bedroom with caution. His shirt and shoes sat on the floor beside the closed door. He picked his shirt up and tapped lightly.

"I'm going, Mel. When you're ready to talk about it, I'll be at the farm."

She huddled against the headboard, the covers pulled up to her chin, trying to staunch the tremors racking her body. She wanted to open the door and fall into his arms. She wanted to beg him to make it all go away, the way it did when he made love to her. In his arms, nothing else mattered. Fear held her back. *They'll break your heart.* Her mother's words echoed in her brain. Wisdom or prophecy? Either way, it was a true statement.

The squeaky hinge on her front door, followed by his truck engine coming to life confirmed his departure. The tears came, soaking her pillow, and carrying her grief and panic into the open.

He'd only changed a few notes, but in doing so, he'd completely altered the essence of the song. Her father had written her a lullaby. Hank had written her a love song. There was no use denying it any longer. She was hopelessly, irrevocably in love with Hank Travis, and in the space of a few hummed bars, he had broken her heart.

**

Hank set out two cereal bowls and juice glasses as he had every day since the night he spent with Melody. An hour later, he placed the unused bowl back in the cabinet. "She isn't coming, Betty."

Lost Melody

The dog wagged her tail and grinned at him, grateful for the scrap of attention from her master. Hank tossed her a treat, insuring she would follow him to the barn. If not for the dog's needs he wouldn't have come out of the barn at all for the last few days. He spent hours at a time in the rehearsal room, and later in the week, he'd moved to the recording studio.

He couldn't bring himself to sing the song in front of anyone, so he managed the rough recording himself, erasing track after track until he had it right. It was raw, just his voice and the piano, but he knew it was good, as good as anything he would ever do.

His hands shook as he spun the dial on the wall safe in his office. Betty Boop stood silently by, offering her support in exchange for treats and a few head rubs. He'd managed to feed her, but he'd had little appetite himself. He'd barely slept in the last five days for thinking of Mel and how he'd hurt her with his carelessness. Her silence told him how much he'd wounded her.

The new version of the song landed on top of his previous version. He slammed the safe door, spun the dial, and replaced the framed platinum record over the safe. It was done. It might never see the light of day, but it was out of his head. He'd done what he had to do, even if no one else ever heard it.

"Let's go, Betty," he said, snapping his fingers to get her attention. "I need some sleep."

**

She spooned the last bit of brown powder out of the can and threw the empty container in her overflowing wastebasket. She'd indulged in the pity party to end all pity parties, and since she'd run out of ice cream, cookies, and hot chocolate, it was time to put her big girl panties on and rejoin the living.

Lost Melody

She owed the Gazette something for all the time she'd spent with Hank, so she decided on a series of articles chronicling his daily life. Thank heavens she had enough material already, so there wasn't any need to continue following him.

Saturday morning she swung by the Gazette, dropped off the first article, and headed to the farm to give Hank an advance copy and say goodbye.

There was no sign of life when she drove up. His truck was in the driveway, and the back door stood open behind the screened door. She called out and knocked to no avail. *He's probably in the barn.*

Grateful she wouldn't have to confront him, she tried the screened door. Finding it unlocked, she stepped into the kitchen and dropped the article on the table—a place he was sure to see it, eventually. As she walked out the back door, Betty Boop sauntered around the house and wagged her tail in welcome.

Mel wrapped her arms around the dog's neck, hugging her tight. "I love him, Betty, but I can't do it. He changed my song for one thing. And there's his job. I've seen it before. Lived it. If I went with him on tour, the paparazzi would be all over us. They'd never leave us alone, so I'd be here all alone while he went on tour for months at a time. All those groupies and fans falling at his feet…and the traveling. Flying." She shook her head. "I'd be a basket case, waiting at home, wondering who he was with, and always expecting the phone call. Just like my mother."

Betty wagged her tail and licked Mel's face.

"I can't do it. I just can't." Mel stood, and with one last head rub for the dog, she said, "Bye, girl. Take care of him for me."

**

Hank sat at the kitchen table

reading the article he'd found when he'd woken up. Too lazy to eat properly, he tossed down handfuls of cereal straight from the box.

Mel had done an excellent job. The information was accurate, the quotations precise, and the story compelling. If it hadn't been about him, he'd be eager to read the next installment. He tossed the papers across the table, wondering what Pandora's Box would be opened by printing it. One of the Dallas papers would pick it up soon. From there, who knew? She couldn't remain anonymous for long.

He faxed the article to his publicist, along with a short explanation and a strongly worded message stating he wouldn't do any follow-up interviews with anyone, for any reason.

Melody was next on his list. He wanted to see her. He needed to see her. He needed to tell her he understood about the song, and maybe she would at least hear him out. If she would just listen to the song, she'd know how much he loved her. She might even give him a chance…or he might never see her again.

CHAPTER ELEVEN

Sunday morning, Mel answered the door to find Hank on her porch with a bag of doughnuts and two paper hot cups, balanced one on top of the other. She thought she was prepared to see him, but the sight of him ignited a flame inside her she was determined to extinguish. "What are you doing here?"

"Can I come in?" He juggled his offering, and she relieved him of the teetering cups as he swept past her as though she'd invited him in.

She closed the door and followed him to her kitchen where he made himself right at home. Clearly, he didn't plan to go anywhere anytime soon. He'd already dumped the doughnuts onto a plate by the time she got there.

She placed the cups on the table and faced him. "You misunderstood the reason I delivered the article, Hank. It wasn't a peace offering. It was a goodbye. Our agreement is off. I've got enough to honor the obligation I made to the Gazette, so I'm through. We're through."

"I know you're mad at me." He held a chair for her. She sighed and sat, wishing she had pretended she wasn't home instead of answering the door. When she was seated, he joined her at the table. "I'm sorry about the song. I should have told you I was working on a cover."

She locked her gaze with his over the plate of pastries. "It's more than the song, and you know it. I've gone to a lot of trouble to invent a life for myself, and there's no room for famous musicians in it."

He selected a doughnut and, pulling it apart, popped a section in his mouth. She watched his lips as he chewed, remembering how they felt moving over hers. He swallowed, breaking her concentration.

"I understand, but I thought I'd proven to you that you don't have to hide to have the kind of life you want. Didn't you see the way I live? No one bothers me here. You can do it, too. We can do it together."

"No, we can't."

"Look, Mel, I thought we had something good together. I know I blew it by not telling you about the song, and I'm sorry. "

"I shouldn't have jumped you about the song. It's just …the song is very personal to me, and…well, there probably isn't a musician on the planet who hasn't wanted to sing it at one time or another. And what you did to it…. That threw me. I wasn't expecting it."

"I can't tell you how sorry I am. I never meant to hurt you." He twirled his cup between his long fingers. "It's a compelling song and one very few people could sing."

"I agree. That's one of the reasons

I've never authorized a cover of it."

"I want you to hear something. Will you come out to the farm with me?"

She gathered their trash and headed to the wastebasket. "If you think I'm going to listen to you sing 'Melody' you've lost your mind."

"Maybe I have, but won't you hear me out? Let me tell you why I want to record your song. Please?"

She leaned against the counter and clamped her hands on the edge to keep from running. She could still hear him humming as he stood right here in her kitchen. He had no idea what he'd done to her. She forced in a deep breath, let it out slowly, willing a calm she didn't think she could find.

"If I listen, will you go away and leave me alone?"

"That depends. I'm hoping you won't want me to go once you hear what I have to say."

"Go ahead. Talk," she said. "But let me be clear. I don't want to hear the song."

Lost Melody

He sighed and shook his head. "Will you at least sit down?"

She crossed to the chair she'd left earlier and folded her hands in her lap. "I'm sitting. Tell me your story and leave."

"Thanks," he said. "I was fifteen when I first heard 'Melody' on the radio. Your father put into words what I couldn't. I listened to his lyrics and heard in them my love of music. It never occurred to me he was singing about anything but his love of music, how it consumed him, made him feel alive. It changed my life. I know Cathy thinks the knobby knees jokes were enough reason for me to give up sports and concentrate more on music, but I couldn't have cared less what the girls, or anyone else, thought about my knees. I listened to 'Melody' and I knew music was in my soul. I knew it was more important to me than anything else in the world."

"So why did you major in business at Harvard? Why not music?"

He laughed and shrugged his

shoulders. "I wasn't sure I could make a living with music. Very few people do, and I'm practical if nothing else. I knew I was more likely to be struck by lightning than to make it big in the music world. So I hedged my bets and got a degree in something I could make a living with. I did minor in music, though." He shrugged again. "BlackWing is nothing but a bunch of over-educated frat boys who got lucky."

He got up and helped himself to orange juice. She waved away his offer to pour her a glass. When he'd replaced the carton in the refrigerator, he returned to his seat. "Anyway, it never occurred to me 'Melody' was about something entirely different, not until I talked to Sir Jonathan."

Wait. You talked to Uncle Jonathan?"

"You say that so easily, Uncle Jonathan. I was so scared I could hardly speak when I first met him, and you talk about him like he's family.”

"He is family as far as I'm concerned. When did you see him?"

"Last weekend. In New York."

Her stomach churned. "Why?"

"I went to sign a contract for our next album. It's a tribute to RavensBlood. All the songs will be covers of their greatest hits. The only one I care about is 'Melody', and Sir Jonathan wanted to explain in person why he couldn't authorize us to record it."

To keep the tremors at bay, she clasped her hands tight and focused on his Adam's apple.

"He told me about the song. I honestly didn't know." His tone was apologetic, laced with pity. Her fingers had gone numb from squeezing them so hard. "I felt like an adolescent fool. Sir Jonathan said just enough to let me figure it out on my own."

She flexed her hands, wiping her damp palms on her pant legs, and fisted them tight again. "What else did he tell you?"

Hank reached for her hands. He forced her fists open and wrapped her chilled fingers in his warmth. "Everything. He told me everything."

She jerked out of his reach. "That's why you came home early? The reason you...the reason we…? That's the reason?"

He tried to recapture her hands, but she moved away from his touch. "That's not what it was, and you know it. I love you, Melody."

She jumped to her feet, toppling her chair in the process. "Don't call me that." She crossed her arms over her stomach and backed away. "I don't want your pity, and you don't love me." Every nerve in her body vibrated, and she clenched her jaw to keep her teeth from chattering.

Hank stood, righted her chair, and held it for her. "Please. Sit down." He placed a strong hand on her shoulder and guided her into the chair. Leaning close, he took her hands in his.

"I feel a lot of things, but pity isn't one of them," he said. "You have to believe me. I've never loved anyone else, and I won't stop loving you. I'm sorry it upsets you so much, and I have to say, your reaction doesn't do much for my ego."

"Please don't love me, Hank. I can't be what you want me to be. I can't be what you *need* me to be."

He leaned in closer. She tried to pull her hands out of his grasp, but he only held them more securely. "You're an amazing woman. I fell in love with you the moment I saw you standing in the doorway at my dad's house. I had no idea who you were, but I knew you were special. It doesn't matter what your name is. I love *you*, not your name."

She lifted her eyes. His mouth was a mere whisper from hers. His eyes sparkled with love, his lips crooked to one side, giving him a rakish look. Her heart flipped, skipping a beat in its acrobatic downfall.

"I can't change the way I feel," he said, "and I don't expect you to return the feeling. Not yet anyway. But I think you feel something for me, or was I imagining things the other night?"

She took a deep breath and extricated her hands. She needed to put distance between them before she did something stupid like tell him she loved him, too. She stood on shaky legs and crossed to the sink. She filled the teakettle and prepared a tray with her favorite wild rose pattern teapot and cups. How had this conversation gotten so out of control? She had to get it back on track, and get him out of her house. Now.

"Go on. Tell me about the song." She opened cabinets and drawers, gathering the makings of proper tea even though she didn't think she could drink a drop.

He followed her movements, glad she'd calmed. His bombshell had blown up in his face. The poet in him had hoped for a more hospitable reaction to his declaration of love, but as he watched her rigid back and stilted actions, he knew she felt something for him. If she didn't, she wouldn't be so upset by his words.

"Okay, if you're sure you still want to hear it."

Her laugh was hollow. "I'm sure I don't want to hear it, but you aren't going to go away until I do, are you?"

He hated to be the cause of her distress, but he'd come here to lay his heart on the line and he was going to do it. "No. I have to tell you everything."

She leaned against the counter, her back to him. "Go ahead. I'm listening."

"I've been working on a cover of 'Melody' for over a year, based on my misguided understanding of the song. After the night we spent together, which I'll remember fondly for the rest of my life, no matter what happens between us," he said. "I knew I had to rewrite it. I heard the new notes in my head while I was holding you in my arms. I know how corny it sounds, but it's true."

China rattled as she poured hot water into the teapot.

"All I'm asking is for you to listen to both versions. Just you and me, in the studio. No one else will ever hear them if you don't want them to."

She turned to face him, and the river of tears streaming down her face almost broke him. He went to her, stopping short of taking her in his arms.

"How can you ask me to do listen to you sing 'Melody'? You said Uncle Jonathan told you everything. Didn't he tell you about the song?"

He gripped her upper arms, sliding his hands down to capture hers. "He did. I wouldn't ask you if it was only about me. But it's not. I owe it to the rest of the band. They'll all be here next week to begin work on the new album. We don't want to do the album without Hamilton

Ravenswood's masterpiece. It wouldn't be right."

He considered it a good sign when she didn't try to pull away from him.

"Has Uncle Jonathan approved the album?"

"Yes. He's coming next week to hear the songs in person and give us his opinion. We're bound by contract to make any changes he deems necessary."

She spun away from him, wiping her tears away with the back of her hand. "And I thought he was coming to see me. I'm such an idiot."

He caressed her shoulders, his thumbs kneading the hard knots along her nape. "You're not an idiot. Make no mistake about it. The man considers you his daughter, and he'll do anything to protect you. I think he's coming here for you. He doesn't have to actually be here to approve the songs."

She closed her eyes, letting his

magic fingers soothe away her common sense. His hips rested against her bottom, close but not intimately so. His voice, slow and melodic, seduced her with its soft Texas drawl, more pronounced when he wanted it to be. The fragrant bergamot of her Earl Grey drifted from the teapot to mingle with the fresh scent of Hank's aftershave. She inhaled deeply, remembering how his skin tasted, salty, utterly delicious.

She forced some semblance of sense into her brain. "Okay. Take your hands off me, and I'll come out tomorrow morning. But don't expect me to approve it."

His hands remained on her shoulders, working their magic as if she hadn't given in to his demands. He shifted, pressing his hips against her bottom, applying enough pressure for her to feel his erection before he slid his hands down her arms and leaned in to kiss her neck, just below her jaw line. Desire tingled down her spine, and he let her go, stepping back.

"Whether you approve it or not, I'd like for you to consider something else."

"What?"

"When the band gets here, I'd like it if you came out to meet them. They're a great bunch of people, and I know you'd love them, and they'll love you. I'll even clear it with them so you can watch us record the album. Maybe you could chronicle it for us. We've never had anyone do that before. It could be fun."

"And what makes you think *I* would want to?"

"I don't know." He shrugged. "Maybe you could do one of those coffee table books, or maybe the Gazette would like some more articles. I know I can get the guys to go along with it."

"How long will it take to record the album?"

"That depends. We've been working on the songs for over a year, so it's just a matter of getting them recorded. We'll probably work twenty-four-seven for most of the summer. It's not an easy process."

"I don't know," she said.

"All the guys are married, except me. They bring their wives and kids, and the house is crazy."

She held the teapot with both hands as she poured herself a cup. The last thing she wanted to do, besides hear him sing "Melody" was hang around while they recorded an album full of songs her father had written. Talk about living a nightmare.

"Think about it. You don't have to make a decision today."

"I'll think about it," she said, "but don't hold your breath."

He paused in the doorway. "All I'm asking is for you to think about it. I want you to see the performance side of my life, too. I think once you do, you'll see it's not as bad as you imagine."

"You're pushing your luck. I said I'd listen to the song, and that's all I'm agreeing to."

He crossed the room to place a kiss on her cheek. "I'll see you tomorrow."

When he was gone, Mel found the old reel-to-reel tape player where she'd hidden it in the back of the closet. The tape was where it had always been—sealed in an airtight container in a fireproof box hidden underneath her bed. She threaded the fragile tape through the maze of wheels and pulleys, and dusted off the professional headset. The headset took a little adjusting to fit her properly, and then she flipped the switch. RavensBlood's final concert came to life once again.

Miraculously, the tape Milton Ravenswood had carried with him, the present for his daughter, survived the crash. She had played it once before when she was in college and trying to understand why her mother had forbidden her to listen to her father's music.

She sat on the floor and leaned against her bed, letting the music carry her to a different place and time. She knew the voices—Uncle Jonathan, Archer and Nathan, and her father. There were backup singers, too. Women chosen for their excellent singing voices to fill in the back tracks. Her mother had been one of the chosen few until she became pregnant with Milton Ravenswood's child.

She pushed away the unnecessary issue and concentrated on the concert. The crowd was enthusiastic, and it was easy to tell the band members fed off their energy. A long pause filled with Uncle Jonathan's voice signaled a change on stage. She closed her eyes and imagined the scene.

Stagehands would be moving the grand piano, adjusting microphones and running wires. She had seen photos from the concert, knew her father had worn black jeans, a dark RavensBlood T-shirt, and a black suit jacket. It was the same outfit he'd worn in every concert photo she'd ever seen.

The stage would be empty except for the piano in the center. Her father emerged from the darkness amid respectful applause, taking his place in the vortex of the triple spotlights. He shifted on the bench, adjusted the microphone, and stilled. Quiet descended.

He began to play.

She could envision his fingers moving across the keyboard, coaxing the wires and hammers inside the instrument to do his bidding. His voice joined the melody, a silken thread strung across the expanse of the concert hall, clear and seductive. The crowd was silent. She imagined the audience, mesmerized by the beautiful music, by the man exposing his soul on stage.

The last note vibrated through the instrument, and she heard the faint scrape of the piano bench against the stage. Her father's retreating footsteps had been edited out of the recording issued publicly after his death, but they remained on her uncut version. Heartbeats passed before a single person in the audience began to clap, the sound releasing the others from their trance. She could hear the swell as they rose to their feet, shouting and demanding more, more, as if the man had any more to give.

It was the last song Hamilton Earl Ravenswood would ever sing, but the audience didn't know it at the time. The unedited tape continued for a few minutes more as Jonathan returned to the stage and tried to quiet the crowd, waving the band back on stage to play an encore, one of their hits, without Ravenswood on lead guitar.

She dropped the headset to the floor and switched off the tape player. She closed her eyes. *Oh God! Why did I tell Hank I would listen to his version? What have I gotten myself into?*

CHAPTER TWELVE

She had talked herself out of coming more than once since Hank had left her house with her promise to hear the song, but each time she remembered the sincerity in his voice when he talked about what the song meant to him, and she caved. So, on top of her misgivings about what she was doing, she was angry with herself for not sticking to her guns.

He waited on his back porch for her. She frowned up at him. "Let's get this over with."

He led the way to the barn where she climbed on the stool he indicated in the control room and waited silently as he flipped switches. The studio came to life beyond the plate-glass window. Soft light highlighted the piano, front and center. She tore her eyes away from the instrument, instead focusing on the sparse accoutrements scattered around the studio.

She braced against the memories flooding back. She could still see her father in his recording studio, much like this one. She had been eight, visiting her father at Ravenswood for the summer. RavensBlood had been recording their tenth or eleventh album—she couldn't remember which one, but she did remember sitting in a big upholstered chair while her father played guitar along with Jonathan, Archer, and Nathan. It had been a special summer, and she'd spent countless hours in the studio with her daddy. Somewhere, she supposed at Ravenswood, there was a recording of her voice, singing along with him as they sat side by side—him playing a silly child's song, her matching his cultured British voice with her girlish prattle.

Hank pointed out a button on the

console. "If you want to talk to me, press this button," he said. "Otherwise, I can't hear you."

"Okay," she said, clenching her fists in her lap.

He turned to leave but paused in the doorway. "Are you sure? I thought about this meeting all night, and I don't think it's fair to ask you to listen to my versions of 'Melody'. The guys will get over it if we can't include the song. I can explain it without compromising your privacy. They'll understand."

She lifted her chin. "Just play the song. I'll decide for myself." One thing she was certain of, besides the fact she didn't want to hear the song at all, was that she *needed* to hear it. She needed to face up to reality, make a decision, and move on.

The first notes startled her even though she could see his fingers on the keyboard. Tears stung her eyes. She blinked them away, determined to face the memories and get past her obsession with the song. Hank's voice, smooth as molten chocolate, joined the melody. She noted the subtle changes, the inflections, the way he emphasized different words to change the song. It was no longer a lullaby. Hank had made it a love song. Those few, almost imperceptible changes altered the song to show a boy's love of music, a love that empowered, stirred his soul.

Tears spilled unchecked down her cheeks. This version was what fifteen-year-old Hank had heard in his heart when he listened to the song. It was the same, yet so different. Had her father intended this interpretation as well?

The last string ceased to vibrate and silence descended on the control room. Hank dropped his hands from the keyboard, his head bent. Mel fumbled with the switch, and finding her voice, said through the microphone, "Play the other one."

Her heartbeat filled the silent control room and Hank raised his hands to the keys once again. His eyelids dropped, and he began to play. Once again, his voice filled the small room, the words stirring her in new ways. Passion poured from the instrument—a lover's passion. The melody sent tingles down her spine and his voice stroked her soul. The words were the same, the melody the same, but his arrangement implied a physical and emotional intimacy between lovers completely absent in her father's version.

The small confines of the control room closed in on her, stealing the oxygen from her lungs. The panic attacks had become infrequent, but she recognized the signs immediately. She needed to get out.

She pushed through the barn door, and warm, humid air rushed into her lungs. Pressed against the outside wall, she gulped in the air, rushing much needed oxygen through her system. When her legs stopped trembling enough for her to walk, she crossed to the oak and dropped into one of the lawn chairs scattered under its broad limbs. Betty Boop roused from her place next to the back porch and joined her, nudging her hand with a cold nose. She petted the dog's smooth head, taking comfort in the unconditional love offered.

She closed her eyes and let the tears fall. She'd known hearing the song would be hard, but she'd truly had no idea what she'd agreed to. It was so much more than she'd imagined it would be, and so beautifully done. Her father would love it. He'd understand Hank's interpretation. But the question was, could she live with it if it was out there, on the radio every day?

No way. Her father's version was bad enough, but Hank's? It was much too personal, too intimate. It wasn't simply a love song, it was a lover's song.

**

Hank opened his eyes, expecting

to see his soul bleeding across the gleaming expanse of the grand piano. Only the glare of the overhead lights reflecting off the polished surface greeted him. His hands fell to the bench, and clutching the edge in a white-knuckled grip, he waited for her pronouncement. With bowed head and clenched jaw, he waited.

Nothing.

He squeezed his eyes shut, and without moving, found the courage to speak. "Mel?"

Silence.

He turned to the control room window. Empty. She was gone.

"Melody." Her name fell from his lips, a soft benediction.

He took his time closing the studio. In his office, he opened the wall safe and removed both copies of "Melody". She'd made her decision, and as agreed, he would turn the only existing recordings as well as the sheet music over to her. For a moment, he stood in his office, holding the two manila envelopes, waiting for the pain to come. His music was so much a part of him—it should hurt like hell to surrender the two works knowing no one would ever hear them, but that wasn't what was killing him. It wasn't losing the music. It was because he'd hurt her. *Christ, what was I thinking?*

When he left the building, he was surprised to find her waiting for him. She was pale, and her eyes were red from recent tears. Guilt gnawed at his gut. He laid the envelopes in her lap and sat in a lawn chair facing her.

"Those are the only copies in existence. Only the band has heard the first one. No one other than you and I has heard the other. They're yours to do with as you please. The sheet music is there, too."

She picked up the envelopes, reading the handwritten labels on each one.

"I'm so sorry. I should have known how hard it would be for you. I shouldn't have put you through that."

With a steady hand, she extended

one envelope to him. "Record this one."

He took it, his original version, and nodded his acceptance. "Are you sure? I don't have to record it. I won't if you don't want me to."

She raised blood shot eyes to him. "It's different enough. I think anyone with a love of music will understand it. You haven't changed the lyrics, only a few notes. I can live with that."

He admired her courage, but still knew how much it must hurt for her to give her consent. "If you're sure, I'll go ahead with it. I promise, you can change your mind anytime before it goes into mass production. All you have to do is say so, and I'll pull it."

"I won't change my mind. I'll call Uncle Jonathan and have him bring the contract with him next week. Record it, Hank. It's your song."

She rose, stopping next to his chair. Focusing on the distant cotton fields, she said, "It never occurred to me until today someone else would have an entirely different interpretation of the song. Thank you for showing me."

He sat in the shade of the stately old oak, listening to the soft hum of her car engine fade in the distance. Somehow, she'd managed to assuage his guilt with a few words. His love for her carried him into the barn, where he lost himself in the music.

CHAPTER THIRTEEN

She drove out of sight of the farm and turned down a dusty road running along the creek edging Hank's farm. Under the shade of a cottonwood, she let her head fall back on the headrest. His voice filled her mind. He'd forced her to see the song in a new light, and in that, there was a freedom she'd never felt before. He had given her a precious gift. By opening her eyes to other interpretations of the lyrics, he had released the song's hold on her. Maybe in the future, she could listen to it and hear it the way Hank and probably countless others heard it.

His version would be a sensation in its own right—a masterful interpretation brought to life by a man whose skill rivaled her father's.

She traced a finger across the handwriting on the envelope lying on the passenger seat. She was in love with Hank, and he was in love with her. His second version convinced her, as nothing else could have.

It was a beautiful song. It deserved to be recorded.

It could—no *would*—establish him as a superstar in his profession, but she couldn't bear for anyone to hear the deeply personal, even intimate way he sang those words. Once they'd lulled her to sleep, set to the sweet, poignant melody her father had created, but Hank's second version was different. Hank sang his love as eloquently as he made love. He'd altered the melody to suggest a deep and alluring passion, and it was too personal to share, too close to her heart.

Anyone who heard it would know he spoke of her, of them, and it would bring the paparazzi to her doorstep. They would hunt to the ends of the earth to find her. Her heart wasn't strong enough to survive the public scrutiny again. She'd openly displayed her love for her father, sometimes amid the paparazzo's flashing cameras, and despite the security measures Uncle Jonathan had insisted on, the vultures had even been at her father's funeral, snapping photos of her and her mother. Those had been plastered on magazine covers everywhere and still popped up once a year on the anniversary of his death—her birthday. So, no. The song wouldn't see the light of day, not if she had anything to say about it, and luckily, she was the only one who did have a say.

She drove to the bank and placed the envelope in the safety deposit box. After placing the airtight container holding her father's original recording in on top of Hank's envelope, she returned the box to the attendant.

CHAPTER FOURTEEN

Nearly a week had passed since she'd gone to the farm, and Hank hadn't contacted her, nor had she tried to contact him. She longed to see him, to hear his voice, but it was better if she stayed away. *They'll break your heart.* Once, the warning had seemed dramatic, but it seemed her mother had known what she was talking about. Her heart was all ready broken over a man she loved and couldn't have. History repeating itself.

She turned her grocery cart into the next aisle, almost crashing into Hank as he studied the gazillion varieties of cereal available. Their gazes met and held. She didn't know what to say, what to do. A million things went through her mind—things she should say to him, but couldn't.

"Hi, Mel," he said, stepping behind his cart so she could pass.

Her feet were glued to the floor. He looked good. Maybe a little tired around the eyes, but still sexy as hell. "Hank."

He nodded at her full cart. "Getting ready for company?"

She glanced at her load of groceries. "Yes. Uncle Jonathan arrives tomorrow, but of course you know that."

"No. I thought he was coming in on Monday. The band will be here then." He indicated his overflowing cart. "What I have here won't even begin to feed the invading hoard, but it's a start. The wives will take over as soon as they get here anyway. I'm just trying to get a head start."

She unglued her feet and tried to move past him in the aisle. His fingers wrapped around her upper arm, halting her progress. Heat seared her skin from the light touch. She shrugged, jerking her arm from his grip.

"Have you given any more thought to what I said about meeting everyone? You know, chronicling the recording?"

"I don't know. I don't think I can."

"I wish you'd reconsider. Even if you don't write about it, I'd like you to be there." He glanced up and down the aisle, and even though there wasn't anyone in sight, he leaned closer and lowered his voice. "It would mean a lot to me and the band to have you there. You, of all people, deserve to be a part of the recording process."

"Hank," she pleaded, "it's too much."

"It's the first Ravensblood cover album to have 'Melody' on it. Don't you think someone should take notes for the occasion? I still think a coffee table book would be great, and you could write it, easy. Use a pen name so no one knows who you really are."

She once thought Hank was insane, but maybe *she* was the

insane one, because she was seriously considering doing it. It would mean being around him daily for the rest of the summer—something she really shouldn't do, but she had already made up her mind to leave Willowbrook at the end of summer. She'd be taking a big chance on the paparazzi staying away while BlackWing was in town recording, but it would be worth taking the chance to spend more time with Hank. She was going to leave broken hearted anyway. How much more broken could it get?

"Okay, I'll do it," she said before sanity returned.

"Good," he said. "I'll clear it with the guys. They're going to be freaked, really."

"In a good way, I hope."

"Yeah, in a good way."

"Well, I've got to go. When do you want me to come out?"

"How about Wednesday? Everyone will be here, and I'll have had a chance to tell them about you.

Wait. Why don't you bring Sir Jonathan out to the farm on Sunday for lunch? I'll cook, and we can talk about your involvement some more."

Sanity reared its ugly head, telling her to say no, telling her to run, but instead she just said, "Okay."

He smiled. "Around noon? It'll be very casual. Do you think Sir Jonathan would mind if Dad came, too?"

"I think he would love to meet your dad," she answered honestly.

"Great. I'll see you both on Sunday."

**

Mel tried unsuccessfully to get Jonathan to rest, but he insisted on talking first. He wanted to know everything about Willowbrook, and how Mel was getting on in her new home, and he especially wanted to know about Hank Travis.

Sitting in her cozy living room sharing a pot of tea, she told him how she met Hank, how they each found out whom the other was, and how he coerced her into doing the month-long interview.

"Does he love you?"

She closed her eyes, remembering the one magical night of lovemaking, his assurances of his love, the song. "Yes." Of this one thing, she had no doubt.

"Do you love him?"

She crossed to the window, staring into the gathering darkness. "I knew you were going to ask." As the streetlights winked on, one by one, she turned to him, answering as truthfully as she could. "I'm afraid to. I think I could, maybe I do, but it scares the hell out of me."

Jonathan took her hands in his and their gazes locked. "He's a good man, Mel. I know he loves you. He told me so himself. If you love him, don't let him go. You of all people know how short our time can be. Don't let this chance for happiness pass you by."

She threw her arms around him. He wrapped her in his embrace, holding her close. "What if something happens to him? I don't think I could stand to go through that again."

"There aren't any guarantees, luv. Screw up your courage and give the man a chance." He brushed tears from her cheeks. "I think it may be too late to worry about the what ifs. You're already too close to him, aren't you?"

She buried her face against his chest. "Yes," she sobbed.

**

Mel set aside her fears and drove Sir Jonathan drove out to the farm on Sunday. His excitement was almost enough to make her forget the reason he had come to Whispering Springs in the first place.

The Travis men met them on the back porch and introductions were made. Sir Jonathan shook hands with Henry. "Please, call me

Jonathan. The title isn't really me."

"Jonathan it is. I'm Henry."

The two older men talked as if they'd known each other for years instead of minutes. Mel and Hank sat across from them at the picnic table, listening to them discuss everything from gray hair to the world economic situation. After lunch, they toured the house and barn, Hank proudly showing off his recording studio.

Jonathan sat at the piano and easily launched into one of RavensBlood's iconic hits. Henry sang along, never missing a beat, even if he was a little out of tune. Mel followed Hank into the separate drum room. She watched as he changed the drumheads in anticipation of recording later in the week.

"How often do you change the heads?"

"I'll change them daily, sometimes more often, during the recording session. On tour, we change them before each show. I use natural skins for a warmer sound, but they have their drawbacks. On the road, I'm constantly tuning them, finding their sweet spot. Temperature and humidity take their toll. The stage crews can be less than gentle when they handle them sometimes, too."

He quickly and expertly replaced the heads, cleaned, polished, and reassembled the drums. He wiped fingerprints from the cymbals, careful to handle them by their edges only. He greased the foot pedals, wiping away excess.

"I didn't know how much work it was to keep up the equipment. It must be a nightmare on the road."

"It can be, but it's how I make my living, so like any other worker, I have to take care of the tools of my trade. On tour, the stagehands and my drum technician take care of the initial set up. I come in several hours before rehearsal to adjust height and distance. The audience might not notice if something wasn't just right, but I would. I figure they've paid a hefty sum to hear us play, they deserve the best quality sound I can give them.”

“Uncle Jonathan says I should give you a chance,” she blurted.

Hank stilled, polishing cloth in hand, frozen in midair. “He did?”

“Yes. He thinks you’re in love with me.”

He turned to her. “I am.”

“I know.” She fought to control her voice. It was important to make him understand. “I’m not in love, Hank,” she lied. “I don’t know if I can be.”

He sat on the throne, shining the rim of a tom-tom. He set the rag aside. “Are you going to give us a chance? All I’m asking is for you to spend time with me, get to know me.” He lowered his voice to a whisper, even though the older men were still having a ridiculous sing-along in the adjacent room. “I want you. I won’t deny it. I want all of you, but the physical part can wait. I won’t pressure you to sleep with me again.”

Mel glanced over her shoulder, checking, even though Henry and

Jonathan were still singing at the top of their lungs. "I don't know how much I can give you, Hank, emotionally or physically."

"I can wait. I don't want anyone else but you."

She couldn't decide if his words were reassuring or threatening. Either way, she wasn't any closer to making Hank understand he was wasting his time with her. She wasn't going to marry him, so she changed the subject. "We'd better get them out of here. They'll both be hoarse tomorrow if we don't stop them."

CHAPTER FIFTEEN

Monday, Mel showed Jonathan around Willowbrook. They had breakfast at The Donut Hole where Jonathan graciously sipped tea from a cardboard cup and praised Cathy's doughnuts as the best.

After a tour of nearly every store on Main Street, they ended up at Smitty's for lunch where they ate burgers and were serenaded by a RavensBlood mega-hit another diner selected on the jukebox.

Jonathan smiled at Mel across the table. "Cha-ching. Money in your pocket, luv."

Mel, taken aback, asked, "Is that all you think when you hear one of your songs? Has it all come down to money for you?"

"No, not at all. I don't need any more money, and neither do you. To tell the truth, I miss it. Not the touring so much, but the creating, discovering something new. For a good many years after Milton died, I was grateful to be out of the limelight. Taking care of Ravenswood for you and managing the music library was enough. Hank approached me last year, wanting to do a cover album, and I realized how much I've missed the business the last few years."

"You've never said anything to me about wanting to get back into the business. What's stopping you from resuming your career? You're certainly not too old," she teased.

"I've been thinking about it. I've written a few new songs. I thought I might trot them by BlackWing, see what they think of them. I doubt anyone would want to hear an old bloke like me sing, but they'd listen to these youngsters."

Mel laid her hand over his. "Uncle Jonathan, you are not old. I'd love to hear you sing again. I'd be so proud to sit in a booth, munching burgers and listening to you on the jukebox. Don't sell yourself short. The world still loves you. RavensBlood fans would welcome you back with open arms, and a whole new generation would be blown away by you."

"It's kind of you to say, but we'll see," he said, dismissing the subject. "I had a great time yesterday, singing like a fool with Henry. Milton and I used to do that. Of course Milton could carry a tune."

Mel laughed. "Henry was having a good time, too. I think Hank gets his musical talent from his mother."

"He's good for you, Mel."

"Maybe. But could we not talk about him, please?"

**

"We're all settled in here, or at least as settled as it's going to get, so why don't you and Jonathan come out? I'll introduce you both to the gang."

Hank's call wasn't unexpected, but still, Mel hesitated. "Can't this wait?" she asked.

"It can," Hank agreed, "but it's not going to go away. Might as well get it over with."

It was hard to argue with his brand of logic. Mel gave in and once again drove her Uncle out to the farm.

Hank's friends greeted them warmly. Genuine smiles quickly replaced surprised expressions, and soon, the guys wandered off together to the barn, discussing the recording session, leaving Mel behind with the wives and children, who closed ranks around her. Other than at college, she'd never had a wide circle of friends, and she'd never been around so many who knew her identity. To her surprise, they were more interested in her relationship with Hank than anything else.

They sat on the back porch steps, watching the kids play a game of tag with Betty Boop at the center, dodging and darting out of their reach. Tall glasses of ice-cold lemonade were handed out before the women got down to grilling Mel.

"We're so glad to meet you, Mel," Marci jump-started the conversation. "Hank is such a great guy, and we've been hoping he would meet someone special."

"He deserves a family. He's a good guy," Stephen's wife, Stacey, echoed the sentiment. "We all love him."

"You'll be so good for him," Erica, the wife of bass guitarist Kevin Sanders, chimed in. "I felt so sorry for him on the last tour. He spent way too much time alone."

"With your connection to RavensBlood, you're perfect for Hank. It must be fate. How did you two meet?" Chad Winston's wife, Sarah, asked.

Mel spent the next hour answering questions. She was surprised how few after the initial inquisition had to do with her family, or even Hank.

They wanted to know her opinion on everything from the price of groceries to what kind of car she drove and her favorite places to shop.

They talked about their kids, fashion trends, and the latest stupid thing their husbands had done. Mel was entranced. They were a group of women brought together because of their husbands' careers, yet they'd formed their own close friendships. Mel was welcomed into the group, without reservation, because of her association with Hank.

Erica brought little Katie to the porch and nursed her while the women talked. Mel's arms ached to hold a child of her own, but since she'd lost her heart to Hank, the possibility of that happening was more remote than ever. She'd never have a family with Hank, and she didn't want it with anyone else.

Lunch turned out to be a rowdy affair with everyone talking over each other. They acted more like a big, extended family than a Rock band.

They shared parenting duties to the point it was difficult to tell whose kids belonged to whom. Hank chipped in and did his part, wiping grimy hands and faces, refilling empty glasses, and rescuing dropped food before the dog could get it. Even her Uncle Jonathan joined in, amusing the kids with ridiculous stories.

Hank promised to bring Jonathan to her house later in the day, so Mel returned to town alone. Just as she was sitting down to eat, Hank appeared on her doorstep. As promised, he'd brought Jonathan into town but dropped him off at Henry's house instead.

"What are they up to?"

"I don't know. I haven't heard from Dad today, and he didn't mention anything yesterday when I saw him."

"I was about to have dinner. Want to join me?"

"Oh, yeah." He pushed past her and headed toward the kitchen. "I thought you'd never ask."

By the time she caught up he was

already taking plates from the cabinet. "Make yourself at home."

"Don't mind if I do. What are we having anyway?" He opened the oven door and peeked inside. "Looks like chicken casserole," he said, reaching for the potholders she'd left on the counter.

"King Ranch Chicken. Cathy gave me the recipe."

He lifted the hot dish and set it on top of the stove. "One of my favorites. My mom used to make it."

She handed him a serving spoon and he ladled generous servings onto their plates. They moved to the table and sat.

"The casserole looks great. I love all the kids, but every few days, I need a break. I guess it's different when they're your own, or at least you know you can't take a break, so you grin and bear it. Anyway, a quiet meal for two sounds pretty good."

She laughed. "I wondered how long you would last out there. Don't get me wrong, they're a great bunch of kids, but after living out there all alone for months, it must be a shock to the system to have all those people around."

He stopped eating and fixed her with an intense look. "This may sound crazy, but the house is happier with all of them around."

"Oh?"

"It's hard to explain. The house seems more alive when it's full. It feels sad when it's just the dog and me. I don't think we make enough noise, or something."

"Maybe you should move a drum kit into the living room and practice there instead of the barn."

Hank smiled. "Yeah, maybe I should. Or I could get myself a house full of rug rats and cure the problem once and for all."

Mel dug into her meal. "Don't go there," she admonished. Glimpses of the children they could have ghosted through her mind. Longing whispered along her spine. She clenched her fork in one hand and the napkin in her lap in the other. It was a silly dream. A fantasy for normal people. The man sitting across from her wasn't normal people and neither was she, so entertaining fantasies about a happily ever after with Hank was the last thing she needed.

The phone rang, and she jumped to answer it. Anything to take her mind off her dinner companion and the impossible dreams his casual remarks brought to mind.

"That was Uncle Jonathan," she said when she returned. "He said he's going to stay at your dad's place tonight. Do you know someone named Miriam?"

"Miriam Wallingford. She lives next door to Dad. She's a widow, has been for about twenty years. Her husband died young, and she never remarried. Why?"

"They're playing cards at her house tonight. He said Henry would take him out to the farm tomorrow. He said something about there would be room in the car." She frowned.

"Why wouldn't there be?"

"The sound guys are crashing at Dad's house. They should be coming in tonight. It takes dozens of people to get everything just right. We'll have musicians coming in over the next few months too. They all stay at the local motels or in Dallas if they're only here for a day or so. The farmhouse can only hold so many." His eyes twinkled with amusement. "Last time, we had a guy from Austin drive up. He slept in his van out at the farm. He was kind of strange, but he knew his way around a violin."

"You're good for the Willowbrook economy."

He grinned, helping himself to more casserole. "It's all selfish on my part. I'd much rather spend my time and money here than anywhere else. Willowbrook is home."

Mel picked at her food. Even though he was engrossed in his meal, his gaze was on her more than they were his plate. Her skin tingled with awareness of the blatant male attention coming from across the table. Logic told her to feed him and show him the door before he fully swallowed his last bite, but her libido was being anything but logical. Where her brain urged caution, her body yearned for reckless abandon. She couldn't stay in Willowbrook. She couldn't have the life she wanted with a man like Hank, but she was an adult, and these were modern times. She could indulge in a purely physical relationship if she wanted.

Even as her heart called her a liar, she glanced across the table. He'd put his fork down and his crumpled napkin lay beside his plate. Their eyes met, and the smoldering heat in his gaze was like a flash flame stealing the oxygen from the room.

"Hank," she pleaded.

"Don't," he said, reaching for her hand. "You want me to stay. I can see it in your eyes." His thumb swept her wrist, found her pulse. "Your heart is racing. You want this night together as much as I do."

"We shouldn't."

"Why not? There's something between us, Mel. You know it, and I know it. We're good together. Let me stay tonight." He squeezed her hand and tugged it across the table. He leaned in and brushed his lips across her knuckles. "I need to be with you."

Her resolve, already thinner than mist on a summer morning, evaporated.

"I need you, too," she whispered.

"Say that again. Please."

She took a deep breath and when she exhaled, the stale air carried her last bit of sanity with it. "I want you, too."

Hank was out of his chair, sweeping her up in his arms before she completed the sentence. His mouth came down on hers. She wrapped her arms around his neck and parted her lips in invitation.

She didn't resist when he maneuvered her down the hall to her bedroom. The moment the door clicked shut, she reached for his shirt placket. He pulled back to watch her hands. One by one, the buttons came loose. She tugged the fabric from his waistband, continuing until his shirt hung open. He planted his feet, his hands fisted at his sides, and let her explore. She flattened her palms against his stomach, sliding them over his abs, over his chest and flat male nipples to his shoulders, pushing the shirt away, inch by torturous inch until at last her hands skimmed down his arms, sending the shirt to the floor.

She leaned in closer and grazed his chest with her lips. Slowly, she trailed feather light kisses over his body, creeping lower with each pass, until her lips grazed the top of his jeans.

He grabbed her shoulders, pulling her up. "Not yet," he growled, crushing his mouth down on hers.

He seized control. Her T-shirt and shorts hit the floor in record time. He backed her to the bed, following her descent onto the patchwork quilt.

Lost Melody

She wrapped her bare legs around his jean-clad hips, and he raised her slightly, easing her fully onto the bed.

Rough denim abraded the sensitive skin on her inner thigh. Each article of discarded clothing took with it a layer of her hesitance until she wore nothing but her need. She forgot everything when he kissed her, every reason why they shouldn't and couldn't be together. Every reason she couldn't love him.

She thought she might die before he removed his jeans, freeing his bold erection. She closed her fist around him, loving the velvet-covered steel.

CHAPTER SIXTEEN

She needed. Oh, how she needed him. Her body silently urged him to end the torture, moving in invitation.

"Don't move." He leaned over the edge of the bed and snared his jeans. A second later, he knelt between her thighs. He groped through the pockets of his jeans, found what he wanted and tossed them back to the floor. A small string of condoms slipped from his shaking fingers and fluttered onto her stomach. His cock rocketed, and he grinned. She closed her hand around him, forcing a groan past his teeth. Emboldened, she managed to sheath him. When she reached the base, he grabbed her wrist.

"I can't wait any longer," he said,

reaching between them to test her readiness. His fingers slid easily through her moist folds.

"Please," she begged.

Then he was there, pushing into her, claiming her, filling her.

She closed her eyes, concentrating on the fullness between her legs. He played her like a master musician, coaxing her body to sing until every nerve ending screamed for release. He varied the tempo, set the rhythm. His hands stroked along her thighs, finally caressing the point of their union. His thumb found her clitoris, flicking over it in sync with his thrusts, driving her up, up, beyond their world, into a universe where sweet music built to a crescendo. Her fingernails dug into his back as she sought her release. She was so close.

He'd never heard music as beautiful as the soft cries from her lips when she climaxed. He continued to play her sweet body until she relaxed beneath him. He cradled her head between his hands and covered her lips with his. Only then did he seek his own release, driving into her welcoming heat to a rhythm only he could hear.

His physical body expressed the miraculous communion, even as his soul translated it into an ingrained language of notes and melodies that became a part of him. As he poured his essence into her, the music ran hot through his veins, became as much a part of him as Melody had become. Spent, he collapsed on top of her. The notes were there, and there they would stay until he could commit them to paper.

Mel slid her heels down the mattress, bracketing Hank's limbs between hers. His hard body pressed against her, still joined intimately. She managed to raise her arms and press her hands against his slim hips skimming them over his taut buttocks. Slowly, she stroked his sweat-soaked back until her arms curved around his neck. She flicked her tongue out, tasting the skin at his shoulder. Salty and uniquely Hank. A taste she would never tire of.

Hank raised his head and trailed hot kisses along the pulse in her neck. He nipped her and eased the sting with his tongue. She made a small sound, part groan, part purr.

"Don't move," he said, pulling out of her.

Mel pulled the sheet over her nude body, chilled without Hank's heat, and watched the muscles in his firm backside as he padded to the bathroom. She stretched. A few areas would be sore in the morning, but she didn't care. Maybe remorse would come along with the soreness, but watching Hank return to her, his desire for her blatantly obvious, she couldn't think of anything but having him inside her again.

He dove under the sheet and pulled her against him. "Again."

"Yes," she said.

CHAPTER SEVENTEEN

"Good morning," he said, his voice husky with desire.

"Good morning."

And just like that, she went into his arms. He had never felt as much for anyone as he did Mel. Her body seemed made for his, and when he was inside her, he didn't want to be anywhere else ever again.

Much later, as she lay in his arms, the morning sun slanting across their sated bodies, Hank murmured against the top of her head. "Come out to the farm with me."

Her body tensed from head to toe. Silence stretched across a heartbeat. Two. God, he hated the idea of spending time with him was something she had to think about when spending time with her was all he thought about these days.

The words *forget it*, were on the tip of his tongue when she shifted against him.

"Why?"

He tightened his hold on her. "Because I need to know you're there."

It was the truth. He couldn't imagine going through the day without her near, close enough to touch, but he didn't think it would be a good enough reason for her—not yet anyway. She felt the connection between them, he was certain of it, but because of who they were, she refused to acknowledge it. She would. Eventually. He needed to keep her close so he could convince her what they shared could overcome any obstacle in its path.

"You can watch us work," he said. "I talked to the guys, and they agreed to let you write about the band. You could write a book about the recording process from start to finish."

She sat up and pulled the sheet around her. "You don't know what you're asking me to do, Hank."

"Yes, I do." He scooted up so his back was against the headboard. "I'm asking you to confront your past. I know how hard it will be for you. I want to be with you, Mel. I'm a musician. It's who I am, and if you can't learn to accept it, then I'm not sure what kind of future we have together. I want a future for us, and I think you do, too."

He was right. She did want a future with him, but she was enough of a realist to understand it could never be. If she was smart, she'd pack her bags and leave Willowbrook today, but apparently, she was the stupidest person on the planet because she wasn't going anywhere. She wanted more time with Hank, and if she had to confront her past to do it—she would. But it would be on her terms.

"Okay. I'll spend some time at the farm. I can interview the band members and their families, maybe write a few articles for the Gazette, but I can't do it twenty-four-seven. I still have a job, you know."

"Quit the Gazette," he said. "If money is an issue, I'll pay you."

Mel shook her head. "You are paying me, in a roundabout way. Since I own the rights to every song you're recording, I'm going to make a lot of money off this cover album."

"True enough. So quit the Gazette and spend the summer at the farm." He reached out and stroked his index finger along her arm from her shoulder to her elbow. "With me," he added, his voice dropping an octave.

His finger left a ribbon of heat on her skin, a reminder of the way he warmed her from the inside out. *Tell him no.*

"I'll see what I can do, but I'm not going to promise anything."

After Hank left, she took her time, soaking in the tub before dressing and going downtown to the Gazette offices. An hour later, she had officially taken leave of her good sense and a leave of absence from her job. The latter came with a promise to turn in one article each week chronicling the work going on at Hank's farm.

Agreeing to chronicle the recording was stupid and impulsive. But her stupid, impulsive heart wanted to be there. She wanted to see Hank work, even if it meant hearing her father's songs. She ignored the tiny voice of reason in the back of her mind chanting a warning about broken hearts and shattered dreams.

She loaded up on pastries at the Donut Hole and left a standing order for more of the same, twice a week. With a little luck, the bribery would loosen tongues and open doors with the band and crew.

A large truck from a local equipment rental company had pulled into Hank's backyard, and an army of men in coveralls struggled to unload poles, ropes, and canvas. If she didn't know better, she'd swear the circus had come to town. Children cavorted around the workers, excited and eager to see what was going on. Betty Boop sat on the back porch, wisely overseeing the confusion. She spied Hank and his father across the yard, talking to yet another coverall-clad worker.

"Things are a little crazy around here," she said.

Hank turned and graced her with a smile. "Boy, am I glad to see you." He grabbed her in a bear hug. "Let's run off together and leave all these people here to fend for themselves," he whispered in her ear.

"It's too late, I'm afraid." She pushed out of his arms, aware of the speculative looks from the workers. "Hello, Henry," she addressed Hank's father. "I hope Uncle Jonathan wasn't any trouble last night."

"No. Not at all. We had a good time."

"Enough chit-chat," Hank interrupted. "We need to get the tent up before lunch."

He turned back to the worker. "Just put it over there, same as last time."

"What's the tent for?" she asked.

"Everyone takes breaks at the same time, so we came up with the idea of a big tent to accommodate the whole bunch at once. So, rain or shine, we can feed everybody and get back to work."

"You've thought of everything, it seems."

"There will be problems. There always are," he said.

"I brought doughnuts."

Hank smiled. "A woman after my heart."

He dispatched some workers to get the pastry boxes from her car and ushered her into his office. He closed and locked the door before drawing her into his arms. In the space of a heartbeat, his lips were on hers, seeking, taking.

Lord, it was heaven to be in his arms again, and it would be hell when she eventually had to leave. But she would savor the moment and leave the recriminations for later. She kissed him back, wrapping her arms around his neck and pressing her body against his.

He broke the kiss and eased her away. "We can't do this right now. As much as I want to, I have to work." He cradled her head against his chest. "I love you, and I'm so damned glad you're here."

Beneath her cheek, his heart beat out a rapid rhythm matching her own. As good as it felt to be close to him, they needed to be more discreet.

"Work aside, we can't keep doing meeting behind closed doors. People will talk."

"You're right. I'm sorry. It won't happen again, I promise. I know you don't want anyone to know about us, so I'll keep my hands to myself." He stepped back. "So, are you here to stay? Did you quit the Gazette?"

"Yes and no. I'm on a working leave of absence." She told him about the deal she'd made with her boss. "I brought the doughnuts as a bribe for the band and crew."

"They'll appreciate it." Hank, all business now, sat behind his desk, and Mel took a chair in front. She had asked to appear all business around the others, so why did it feel so wrong?

"Tell me what you have in mind for your articles and I'll talk to the guys, see what they're willing to do," he said.

"I'm not sure. Maybe a series of articles featuring each of the band members from a personal standpoint?"

"I'll ask, but I don't think it'll be a problem as long as you don't get too personal." He winked, and she blushed, remembering an earlier conversation on the subject of where they purchased their underwear.

She relaxed. "I promise I won't print anything they aren't willing to share."

"I guess we're all set," he said and started to rise.

"Wait, Hank." Mel halted him with her upraised palm, and he dropped back into his chair. She wrung her hands in her lap. "I'm going to try, but I don't know if I can handle being here. I think I'll be okay with the technical end of the recording, but I don't know if I can stand to hear the music every day. Maybe if it was anything but RavensBlood, it would be different."

"You can do it. You're stronger than you think you are, but if it gets to be too much, you're free to walk away."

She took a deep breath and let it out on a sigh. "Thanks for understanding. I promise I'll try." Her time with Hank was limited to the next few months, and she would do anything to spend as much time with him as possible. When he went on tour again, she would leave Willowbrook. She couldn't stay here alone, wondering, worrying, and waiting.

"So, what happens today?" she asked.

He walked her through the schedule for the week and gave her a quick tour of the activity in the barn. Cords and wires lay everywhere in what appeared to be organized chaos. Workmen crowded every room, and the studio itself was in an uproar as the techs installed microphones and wired them to the control room.

Hank introduced her to Rick, the technician who would be in charge of his drum kit for the duration of the recording. He was young, but watching him tape down the lugs on the kit, he appeared to know what he was doing.

"Why do you do that?" she asked.

"Anything with the potential to rattle is taped down to minimize extraneous noise on the track," Rick said.

"I won't wear my watch, and I'll

empty my pockets before we record," Hank added. "The microphones are sensitive enough to pick up the slightest sound. It doesn't matter so much on stage because the audience can't hear over the music. But in the studio, everything matters. It's Rick's job to make sure the drum heads are replaced, the lugs are tight, and the drums are tuned, and he gets to shake me down before I sit on the throne."

Rick laughed. "Just make sure I get billing on the final album. Babysitting you can be a real pain in the ass. And remember, I get to keep anything that comes out of your pockets."

Mel stepped over coils of wires and peered into the control room where two electricians were hard at work.

"We're upgrading some of the equipment to digital, so we called in the experts to install it," Hank explained. "The installation was supposed to be completed last week, but they ran into a few problems."

Jonathan was in one of the isolation rooms, playing his guitar. Hank opened the door and stuck his head in. "I brought someone to see you."

Mel pushed around Hank and gave Jonathan a hug. "I see you found the only quiet place in the whole building. What are you playing?"

"I'm brushing up on a few oldies. The guys asked me to sit in on few of the tracks. I thought I might need a little practice. It's been a long time since I played for anyone other than myself."

Mel kissed his cheek. "That's wonderful, Uncle Jonathan!" She turned to Hank.

He smiled. "No need to thank me. Our motives were purely self-serving. We got together the other day and were talking about how great it was to have Sir Jonathan here, and how incredible it would be to play with him. The next thing we know, we got the bright idea to ask him to join us. We didn't really think he would, but he said yes. We're all as excited as a bunch of kids with a new puppy." He winked at her.

They left Jonathan to his practice and went to see how the tent was progressing. The canvas covered roof sat in the center of the support poles, ready to be hoisted into place. Workers made final checks before dividing into groups and lifting the heavy roof. The children sat on the back porch under their mothers' watchful eyes, fascinated by the process of erecting the giant tent.

Observing from a shady spot, Hank took Mel's hand in his, lacing their fingers together. "We're having a Karaoke party in the tent tonight for everyone. Crew, electricians, even the kids. We even invited the guys setting up the tent. You should come back for it."

"I don't know…."

"It will be totally G rated. With the kids invited, the music will be everything from The Wiggles to BlackWing. No alcohol, wives' orders."

She should say no. Keeping her association strictly business would be wise, and a lawn party wasn't business.

"Maybe we can sneak out after dark and be alone." He squeezed her hand and she caved to temptation.

"Okay. I'll come, but I won't sing."

A crooked smile lit up his face. "It starts at five. You don't have to bring anything. We hired a caterer."

CHAPTER EIGHTEEN

The sweet smell of barbeque drifted on the late afternoon air. Her mouth watered at the wonderful aroma, and she suddenly couldn't wait to sink her teeth into the promised feast. She located the source of the aroma, a large portable barbeque pit, tended by two men in red aprons and black cowboy hats. Tables covered with red-checkered cloths had been set up along one side. The round banquet tables had been covered in the same cloth, and boasted centerpieces created from old vinyl LP's molded into bowls. Summer flowers added to the cheerful atmosphere.

Hank and his friends, Chris and Randy, worked at a table at the back of the tent trying to figure out which wire went where on the Karaoke machine. She moved closer, watching the men argue over whose idea was the most likely to be correct. Satisfied at last with the placement of the wires, Hank looked up and saw her.

"Ah, our first victim. Come here and try this thing out for us."

She took a step back, shaking her head. "Uh uh. Nope. Not me. You're the singer, you try it."

Hank scanned the play-list and selected a song. He stepped around the table and grabbed her hand, dragging her to a spot where she could see the screen. "It's a duet. Sing with me."

She tried to protest, but the music began, and she recognized the song. It was a fun one, a karaoke favorite. Hank launched into the Kenny Roger's solo, giving it all he had. His voice was smooth and rich, drawing her in until there was only Hank and her. She would never get tired of hearing him sing.

When the chorus came up, he took her hand and their eyes met. Without conscious thought, her voice joined his, and then she was watching the words scroll across the screen and singing Dolly Parton's solo all by herself. When the final chorus came up, Hank wrapped his arm around her waist and their eyes met and held. Their voices blended in the familiar words and, as the last note faded away, his head dipped.

There was nothing in the world but the two of them blending seamlessly, body and soul. The thrill of it ran like hot lava through her veins, and she shifted in order to press herself closer to the man who made her feel more than she ever thought possible.

Applause rained down around them like shattered glass. Startled, Mel jerked away from Hank. A shrill whistle from the porch had her spinning around. The entire band and their wives stood on the porch, applauding. Uncle Jonathan and

Hank's father were with them. She buried her face against Hank's shoulder and silently wished the earth would open up and swallow her. *So much for professionalism.*

"Thank you very much. Now go away," Hank admonished the group.

The screened door slammed a few times, and people resumed what they'd been doing before she'd made a spectacle of herself.

"Come on," he said, taking her hand in his and towing her in the direction of the barn.

He deposited her on the sofa in his office and crossed to the mini fridge. Grabbing a soda from the fridge, he popped the top and shoved it into her trembling hands. As if on autopilot, she sipped the drink and curled her feet under her. She seemed to be staring at a spot across the room, and she hadn't said a word since they'd finished the song. He didn't have a clue what was going through her mind, but his raced with a million questions.

Several minutes passed, and her hands remained unsteady as she sipped at the soda.

"You have a beautiful voice," he said. "Have you taken singing lessons?"

She turned to him, her eyes wide. "Good Heavens, no. Mom wouldn't have ever allowed something like that."

Hank chuckled. "Well, you are your father's daughter. That's for sure. You surprised the hell out of me. And everyone else, too."

Her face flamed, and she turned away.

"You really don't know, do you?"

She sat silent as stone, staring at something across the room. How could she not know?

"You have a stunningly beautiful voice, Mel. But rest assured, no one here will push you to use it. You just took us by surprise. Do you play any instruments?"

When she spoke, her voice was

flat. "No. Mom didn't want me to have anything to do with the business."

He nodded. "I forgot about your mother. I suppose the voice could come through her just as well as from your father."

"Yes. Mom has a beautiful voice." She glanced at Hank. "I used to sing with Daddy when I was little girl."

He doubled over with laughter.

"What's so funny?" she asked.

"Oh, honey, I'm not laughing at you. Well, I guess I am. You call Earl Ravenswood, Daddy? It's cute." He wiped his eyes with the back of his hand. "To me, it's the same as calling Queen Elizabeth, Mumsie. I don't think I'll ever get used to your casual acceptance of something so extraordinary."

She laughed along with him for a moment then quieted. "Hank, that's what he was to me, just Daddy. It's taken me most of my life to understand and accept I have to share his memory with the world. Most children who lose a parent grieve, and then they move on. They never hear his voice again, and the only images they see are the ones *they* have. The photo on the mantel, the family album. But everywhere I go, I'm reminded of my father. People sing his songs, and they feel they have a connection to him even though they never met him."

Hank winced, her remark hitting home. He was one of those people who claimed a part of her father's memory for himself.

"Driving down the road, I hear Daddy's voice on the radio. I can't even have a burger at Smitty's without hearing his voice. *Really* hearing it, not some ghost of a memory. His image shows up in the most unlikely places, with or without my release to use it. Every newspaper and magazine, every television station has a file of photos and film of *my* father, and they drag them out at least once a year. That's what I deal with every day."

He understood. He still missed his

mother every day. How much more difficult would it be if he had to live with the daily reminders Mel did? And she'd been a child when her father died. He admired her ability to function under the circumstances because he wasn't sure he could do half so well if their situations were reversed.

"People like me sing his songs. I'm sorry. I never thought of your loss from your point of view. How do you deal with it?"

She uncurled, planting her feet on the floor, with her elbows planted on her thighs, she rolled the soda can between her hands. "I tried running away from it. I went to a small, little-known college, after that, when things didn't work out in San Diego, I moved to Willowbrook. I thought I could live far enough under the radar the reminders wouldn't be a daily issue. I was wrong."

"I messed that up for you, real good. I don't know what to say, Mel. I love you, but I can't change who I am or what I am."

"I don't want you to change who you are. I would never ask you to. I know I can't run from who I am any longer, but I don't have any kind of plan for going forward either."

"Will you still document the recording session? I think it's important for you to be the one to chronicle our project. It seems right"

"I'll try. I know you and the band want to honor Daddy's music, so I'll try. He'd want me to try."

Hank stood and pulled her to her feet and into his arms where she belonged. "He'd be proud of you, I know he would. I'll be here for you and so will Jonathan. If it gets to be too much, let me know."

"No more singing."

He kissed her lightly on the lips. "No more singing," he agreed. "Come on, let's get some barbeque before it's all gone."

Mel pushed her conversation with Hank to the back of her mind, choosing instead to focus on enjoying the evening. Everyone, it seemed, tried their luck at the karaoke machine, even the kids, who had the most fun of all. Jonathan and Henry excused themselves early to meet up with Henry's friends at the bowling alley. Mel wished them luck at the lanes, shaking her head as they left.

"Uncle Jonathan is having the time of his life," she said to Hank.

"I'm glad. Dad thinks he's great. I can't believe they've gotten on so well. You'd think they'd known each other for years."

People began to leave, and Hank walked Mel to her car. Alone for a brief moment, he trailed a finger along the curve of her jaw to her chin, lifting her face to his. He kissed her, his lips undemanding. "Do you want me to follow you home?"

"No. I'll be fine. I'll bring Jonathan out in the morning. I suppose since you've included him in the recording, he'll be here a lot longer than the week he originally planned."

He continued to stroke her jaw, his fingertip their only contact. He traced the shell of her ear, and down the long column of her neck. Her pulse quickened at his touch. His finger skimmed her collarbone and down across the swell of her breast just under the v-neck of her shirt. All it would take was a word from her and he would stop, but his touch was magic, wrapping her in a warm blanket of sensuality and need that stole her words.

"He'll be here most of the summer. Will it be a problem?" His voice flowed dark and sweet over her senses.

"Um. No." What were they talking about? She had to leave before she did something else she would regret tonight. She forced her feet to move, and his hand dropped away.

"Goodnight, Melody." He leaned in the open window and pressed his lips to hers. The kiss was brief—a simple front-porch goodnight kiss—and he walked away.

She closed her eyes and let her head fall against the headrest. She sat there until her breathing evened out and she remembered her destination.

Warm Texas air blew through the open windows. The occasional passing car reminded her she wasn't totally alone on her journey home. She took several deep breaths in an effort to clear her head. Snippets from the day flashed like a bad movie through her brain.

The walls she had spent years building around her heart were crumbling at an alarming pace, and it was all because of Hank Travis. He'd forced her to confront issues she'd long ago confined to cold storage. It wasn't just the RavensBlood cover album. It was Hank himself. He said he loved her, and she believed him.

No one she had ever known would have dared to laugh at her relationship with her father, but Hank had. His laughter made her realize she had elevated the relationship to more than a simple father-daughter connection. Somehow, over the years it had become more—a fantasy. For years, her father's status overshadowed the simple relationship they'd shared, and she'd lost touch with the more intimate memories.

With his laughter, Hank had reduced the unique circumstance of her birth to its most simplistic terms and given her permission to accept it herself. Yes, Hamilton Earl Ravenswood was her father, but who was she, besides the little girl who had caused his death? No one understood the burden she carried. People blamed her for what happened. How could they not? It was true. She loved her father, and he'd loved her, and because of that love he was dead.

Hank hadn't mentioned it, but he would. Eventually. He just hadn't put it together yet.

CHAPTER NINETEEN

Mel slipped into her favorite nightshirt and, with a cup of chamomile tea, slid under the covers. The day's events had her mind reeling with memories and unanswered questions. One question, always the one she'd wanted to ask but never had the nerve to, lodged in her brain and wouldn't go away.

She tried to find the answer in what she knew of her parents' marriage. To say they had a strained relationship was a gross understatement. Diane and Milton Ravenswood had disagreed on just about everything. The one place they found common ground was in their unconditional love for their daughter.

Lost Melody

They'd married in order to give their child a name, but to her knowledge, they never lived as husband and wife, unless it had been in those few months before she was born. The only thing they'd shared was her.

Mel spent summers in England with her father, and he made infrequent trips to California, usually around the holidays. Her mother had facilitated the nightly phone calls from her father. Those began when she'd been an infant and ended on the eve of her tenth birthday when her father called from Denver to tell her he would be at her party the next day.

Hoping she would find the courage to ask the question she desperately wanted the answer to, she placed a call to her mother.

She exchanged pleasantries, inquiring about her mother's gardening hobby, the weather, and other mundane topics. Before her courage could desert her, Mel blurted out the question nagging at her.

"Mom? Why didn't you tell me about the plane crash when it happened? Why did you let the birthday party go on?"

A cavern of silence gaped across the phone line and she thought she'd gone too far.

"I didn't tell you because I couldn't believe it. I didn't want to believe it. I wanted Milton to come walking through the door, present in hand, and tell me it had all been a mistake."

Her mother sniffed. Could she be crying?

"I didn't really believe he was gone until the party was over. When he didn't call or come to the party, I knew it was true. He wouldn't have disappointed you for any other reason."

For once, she glimpsed the agony her mother had gone through, hoping and praying for her husband to walk through the door. Maybe she didn't really understand her parents' marriage after all. Had they been in love? The pain in her mother's voice indicated a depth of feeling she had never considered. Had her father felt the same about her mother? And if so, why had they lived apart?

**

Mel stumbled into the kitchen in dire need of a caffeine fix. The first rays of sunlight, golden and cheerful, streamed through the window. Jonathan sat at her small breakfast table with a teacup in one hand and a copy of the Gazette in the other. He glanced up when she came in.

"Have a cup of tea, luv. You look like you could use it."

He poured her a cup and slid it across the table where she sat with her forehead propped in her hands.

She sipped the tea and groaned. "Thanks." She savored the bittersweet drink, strong, the way he preferred it. "Why is your tea always better than mine? I swear I make it the same way you do."

"You rush yours. You have to be

patient with tea. Impatience is an American trait, I believe."

Mel rolled her eyes at him. It was an old argument between them—one she knew she would lose. Needing more than tea to get going she fixed a bowl of cereal and returned to the table. She took a few bites before the question running like a train through her head spilled out.

"Did Daddy love my mother?"

"Why do you ask?"

She toyed with her cereal, her eyes downcast. "I was talking to Mom last night and she said something that made me think she was in love with him. I was just wondering if he felt the same way."

"Yes. He loved her until the day he died."

Mel dropped her spoon. "Really?"

"Really. From the minute Milton laid eyes on Diane, she was all there was for him. He would have married her, with or without you coming along. You just rushed it a little."

Jonathan moved closer, covering

her hand with his. "Letting her go, letting her take you away, was the hardest thing he ever did. I thought he was going to come apart at the seams for a while. Eventually, your mother convinced him you would be better off living a normal life, away from the music business. He knew she was right, but it nearly killed him to see you go. We were on the road too much back then. It's different these days. There are more ways to promote, MTV, the Internet, iTunes. It's not necessary to be on the road three hundred sixty days of every year to sell your music."

"Why didn't Mom take me to Ravenswood?"

"Do you really think you could have lived a normal life there? Milton did a good job of keeping the fans and paparazzi away, but they still got through sometimes. Diane wanted you to be a carefree little girl, no celebrity demands on you. Milton wanted that, too."

"So, they lived apart because of

me. They sacrificed their marriage so I could have a 'normal' life?"

"They didn't live under the same roof, but their marriage was as good as it could be under the circumstances. Diane wouldn't live the kind of life Milton needed, and he wouldn't live the kind of life she wanted. But they still found time to be together. Besides you, it's what kept Milton going all those years. Didn't you wonder why they never divorced?"

No.

Shame filled her. Should she have? She had been a child. She hadn't really understood they were still married until her father died and all the funeral decisions had fallen to her mother—his wife. Up until then, all she'd known was her parents lived apart, and in her child's mind that equaled divorced. As an adult, she knew better, but she'd never asked her mother why.

She had little time to dwell on the question though. Jonathan was eager to get to work, so they left as soon as they finished their breakfast. Jonathan chatted like a kid on his first day of school all the way to the farm. She'd never seen him as excited about anything as he was about recording with BlackWing. If she weren't already in love with Hank, she would love him for his kindness to Jonathan alone.

Henry turned into the driveway right behind her, and sound technicians poured out like circus clowns stuffed in a toy car. She opened the back hatch on her Jeep and passed out boxes of Donut Hole pastries to the men as they walked past. Today, the real work would begin.

"You've made yourself a carload of friends." Henry greeted her and Jonathan, wrapping an arm around Mel's shoulders and steering her in the direction of the barn. "The only problem is they'll expect you to feed them every day from now on."

"No problem. I have a standing

order. You two better get in there and grab a doughnut before they're all gone."

Henry and Jonathan took off for the barn at an exaggerated pace, leaving her laughing at their antics. They disappeared through the door, and she headed toward the house. The backdoor was open, and calling out, she let herself in. The wives sat at the kitchen table, coffee in hand.

"Hi, Mel!" Stacy greeted her. "Grab a cup and join us. We're enjoying the quiet before the storm."

She helped herself to a mug and filled it from the carafe. "Thanks. Let me guess, the kids are still asleep and the husbands have gone to work."

A chorus of, "Thank God, yes, and hallelujah," rose from the group.

She joined them at the table, pulling her chair out carefully so as not to disturb the black dog sprawled underneath the table. "Betty must be resting up for another day of chasing kids."

"Yeah. She loves them, but they tire her out," Marci agreed.

"Did Hank talk to you about the interview?" Mel asked.

Marci answered, "Yes. We trust you to write a responsible article, so we'll talk."

Murmurs of agreement went around the table.

"Thanks. I'd like to ask you all a few questions. Maybe I'll come out a little earlier on Thursday, and we can have coffee and talk before things get going."

They finalized the arrangements, and Mel left them to enjoy what was left of their peaceful morning. She paused outside the barn, steeling herself for the emotional battering awaiting her inside. She took a deep breath, and let it out slowly. Sucking up her courage, she opened the door and stepped inside.

The chaos of the previous day was gone. Today was all about business. She found BlackWing and the entire production crew in the studio. Jonathan sat at the piano. The others had scattered around the room on folding chairs or sat cross-legged on the floor. Most still worked on their morning caffeine addiction. Empty Donut Hole boxes sat atop the closed piano. Hank leaned casually against the doorframe of the adjacent drum booth.

She found an out-of-the-way place to observe. Hank glanced over the top of his reading glasses, and their gazes met. His lips lifted slightly on one side, and his eyes flashed with male approval before he returned his attention to the paper in his hand. His gaze, brief as it had been, sent a tingle of awareness along her spine.

Comments flew from all corners as the group discussed the day's chart. She pushed her sudden desire for Hank out of her mind and concentrated on the fascinating process going on in front of her. Suggestions were made, discussed, and acted on as swiftly as in any stuffed-shirt board meeting—without all the corporate trappings.

Instead of a polished conference table and suited executives, these professionals sat amongst dozens of instruments, amplifiers, microphones, and enough wires to rig out a three-mast schooner. They had dressed casually in worn denim and logo T-shirts advertising everything from a favorite beer to an Ivy League college—Harvard, of course. Jonathan's RavensBlood T-shirt had faded almost beyond recognition.

Her gaze wandered across the room to where Hank lounged carelessly, his hips cocked to one side like a Brooks Brother's advertisement. He had chosen his usual attire, washed out jeans and a crisply starched blue oxford button-down, the sleeves rolled to mid-forearm. His farmer-boy haircut, closely shaved jaw, and reading glasses, should have translated into nerd, but on Hank, were inexplicably sexy. He'd left his shirt open at the throat, the small patch of golden skin reminding her of what lay beneath the starched cotton. His only ornamentation was a tasteful watch on a leather wristband.

He held the day's chart in his right hand. His left hand was tucked into the pocket of jeans that hugged his lean body and emphasized long, well-defined muscles, and slim hips. Mel filled in the missing details from memory. Embarrassed by the direction her thoughts had taken, she jerked her gaze away, hoping no one had noticed the way she'd been ogling the man.

By the time the meeting ended, she had regained some semblance of composure. The Recording Engineer, now in charge of the studio, issued orders. Final equipment checks were first on the agenda, followed by a preliminary run through of the first song from start to finish. From there, they would break it down into its essential parts, recording various combinations of instruments and solos as necessary to mix and master the track.

Hank directed her to a high stool in the control room where she would be able to see over the control board. From her perch, she could watch the techs, musicians, and engineers work. Last minute adjustments were made to microphones and acoustical gobos, or go-betweens to absorb sound waves from the individual instruments and make for a cleaner recording. Every connection was checked and rechecked.

As the band fine-tuned their instruments and adjusted volumes, Mel's nerves skittered. At last, they donned headsets through which they would hear the click track—a steady tempo similar to a metronome. Jonathan entered the control room and stood behind her, his strong hands resting on her shoulders. She drew strength and courage from his touch.

Everyone turned to watch Hank through the glass partition separating the drum booth from the studio. He nodded his head in time with the click and launched into the intro. As he bridged to the steady rhythmic beat, the others picked up the melody. The backbeat was seductive, and she closed her eyes, focusing on the melody and blocking out the rush of panic threatening to engulf her.

The song was one of RavensBlood's early hits, penned by her father and Jonathan years before she was born. Her rational mind told her it shouldn't affect her so much, but there wasn't anything rational about her reaction. If not for Jonathan's calming touch, she would have bolted from the room. She'd heard the song countless times. She couldn't turn on the radio without hearing it, and nearly thirty years had passed since the song was recorded. Hearing it live, her heart raced and her lungs struggled with every breath.

"Relax. It's going to be all right," Jonathan whispered in her ear.

His was the voice of sanity she

needed, bringing her back to reality. She opened her eyes. Chad sang the familiar lyrics, not her father. The men in the studio were not RavensBlood. Opening herself to the music, she noted the subtle differences.

Hank's fill bridged the distance from the melody to the chorus. His eyes locked across the room with hers, and she knew she would be all right as long as Hank was there for her. His gaze—filled with love and understanding—warmed her and banished any lingering doubts about her feelings. She was in love with him. Her foolish, foolish heart was totally lost…to a musician.

The song finished on a particularly intricate drum solo to which Hank added his own personal touch. With a final flourish and a dramatic tone from a crash cymbal, the speakers went silent. Time stood still. Mel held her breath, her hands clenched into fists in her lap. At last, a whoop rose up from the crew followed by a joyous celebration consisting of macho handshakes and perfunctory backslapping.

Sir Jonathan entered the room and silence fell, anchoring everyone in a frozen tableau. They all awaited his verdict. Jonathan, even more so than she, held the power to end the recording session. They had authorized a few covers of RavensBlood songs over the years, but all the ones BlackWing had requested were firsts. Mel stood behind Jonathan just inside the door, as anxious as anyone present to hear what he had to say.

"Well done, chaps! I couldn't have done it better myself." Jonathan's British accent floated across the near perfect acoustics in the room.

Chaos erupted. Mel added her praise, speaking individually with the band members. Randy, the Recording Engineer, let out an ear-piercing whistle, bringing the celebration to an abrupt halt. When he had everyone's attention, he listed the technical flaws in the performance and doled out assignments for the day. Everyone dispersed like leaves on the wind. The band members holed up in the rehearsal rooms to try to find *the tone*, that elusive sound signature unique to each guitarist while the technicians went to work correcting the mechanical problems Randy had pointed out.

CHAPTER TWENTY

Hank drew Mel into his office and into his arms. She wrapped her arms around his waist and her soft curves molded to his harder angles as though she'd been made just for him. He had wanted to hold her from the moment she'd walked into the studio and checked him out. Knowing she was so close, only a few feet across the room and he couldn't go to her, hold her and kiss her the way he wanted—no, make that *needed*—had almost driven him crazy. Instead of listening to the discussion, he had concentrated on calculating the mass of the piano in the center of the room. He couldn't remember the formula for the calculation, but the thought process kept blood circulating in his brain where it belonged.

As they played the song, he'd locked eyes with her. He'd gone a little crazy, almost calling a halt to the whole thing rather than put her through another minute of the torture hearing the songs would be for her. Then something had changed and instead of pain, there was something else in her eyes, something he'd been sure she hadn't wanted him to see—love. It was enough to banish some of his concerns and allowed him to finish the song.

She was in his arms where she belonged, and he owed it to her to do whatever he could to help her through the recording.

"Was it as difficult as you thought it would be?" he asked.

"No. It was hard at first. I wasn't sure I could do it, but I did. The song is good. I like the changes you made."

Gently, he turned her face up to his. She was so damned perfect. Beautiful and smart. And she thought she was weak. It boggled his mind. "I knew you could do it. You're so much stronger than you think you are."

"I'm not," she said.

"You are, and I love that about you." He dipped his head, and rising onto her toes, she met him halfway. He teased her lips apart and tasted her sweetness. She pressed herself more fully against him.

He broke the kiss. "I want to stay here with you, but I have to go," he whispered in her ear. "I'll be recording drum tracks the rest of the day."

She dropped her arms and stepped out of his embrace.

He let his hands trail down to rest on her hips, unwilling to let her go until he absolutely had to. "Today's song relies heavily on the drums with the solo at the end. With a little luck, it won't take all day. But knowing Randy, I don't hold out much hope."

She smiled. "He's a task master, for sure. I even heard him telling Uncle Jonathan to get busy rehearsing. He said he wasn't going to cut him any slack because of his past glories."

Hank laughed. "I wouldn't have the nerve to say something like that to him. Randy has engineered all our albums, and he's the best, so we listen to him. It's paid off for us so far." He kissed her on the forehead. "I'm his today, so I better get going before he sends a search party for me. The sooner I get started, the sooner I'll be finished." *And the sooner we can be together.*

Mel spent the next few hours interviewing the band members during their breaks and sitting in the control room watching Hank patiently try to please Randy. She slipped out before lunch and went home.

The schedule allotted one week for each song, with a whole week off for the Fourth of July holiday. It would take the entire summer to complete the album, recording the songs in chronological order. Each week would become more difficult for her as they led up to the final song on the list. "Melody" would be the very last song they recorded. Rightfully so. It was the last song her father sang— as it turned out, less than two hours before his death.

The thought of listening to all those songs sent a shiver of dread along her spine. Even if she found the courage, she wasn't sure she could survive watching them record "Melody." Two weeks had been allotted to track it, and nothing short of perfection would do. Two weeks of painful memories she had spent the last sixteen years trying to avoid.

Hank planned to bring in a host of backup strings and woodwinds for his orchestration, and the final mix would be a masterpiece in its own right. She couldn't deny Hank the chance to record it. She loved him too much. But watching the process, hearing him sing the lyrics, would be her undoing. Scheduled to be the first single released from the album, it

Lost Melody

would be on the radio soon enough.
She wouldn't be able to escape it.

CHAPTER TWENTY-ONE

The first week of tracking passed as quickly as a summer storm, complete with flashes of lightning and furious winds. Mel couldn't believe the level of passion the Ivy League over-achievers brought to the project. On stage, they played as much for their own enjoyment, as for the audience; but in the studio, they pushed themselves and each other for perfection. Tempers flared white-hot but cooled quickly. Randy was skilled at diffusing the tension and keeping them to the schedule. No less of a perfectionist himself, his demands often extended the workday well into the evening.

She saw little of Hank the first week, and as the weeks passed, she saw even less of him. The days fell into a routine. Weekends were supposed to be free time for the production crew, allowing the ones who lived nearby a chance to go home if they chose to, at least for a few hours. Eventually, even the weekends fell under Randy's quest for perfection. Jonathan, working as hard as the rest of the group, had taken to spending his evenings with the sound crew at Henry's house, freeing Mel to come and go as she pleased.

Some days she helped the wives with the monumental task of feeding the crew and entertaining the kids. Living in town, she was the natural choice to bring in supplies, often picking up enormous loads of pastries, cakes, breads, rolls, and whatever else Cathy could produce for them. The local grocer was well versed in the extra demands and arranged a call-in order and delivery system for them.

She occasionally stopped at a

local produce stand to pick up fresh fruit and vegetables. One morning that promised a particularly hot day to come, she spied a trucker unloading his burden of watermelons at the produce stand. She made the first u-turn possible and went back to bargain with the owner of the stand. It didn't take much to persuade him to sell her a pickup load of the fresh melons. She returned in Hank's truck to pick them up within the hour. More cash changed hands, and the melons were covered in ice.

The build-your-own sandwich lunch was topped off with cold, sweet watermelon. The kids held a seed-spitting contest, and not to be outdone, the adults held one of their own. It was messy, fun, and relaxing. Even Betty Boop joined in, playing in the stream from the water hose as they washed down the area afterward.

Sometimes Mel would walk the older kids to the creek and watch them play, carefree and uninhibited in the natural setting. One morning the two oldest, Mike's daughter Allison, and Stephen's son Dane, were pestering their mothers to take them to the studio. They wanted to watch the recording session—a natural enough request at their age. Neither of the women could spare the time to supervise the kids, and letting them go alone was out of the question. Mel offered to escort them, and much to the kids delight, permission was granted.

She ushered them into the control room and found stools for them, so they could see over the control board. They were full of questions she tried her best to answer.

"How do you know so much about recording stuff?" Allison asked.

"My daddy wrote the song your fathers are playing in there. When I was about your age, he let me sit in the studio with him while he was recording. I remember sitting at the piano with him, and once he let me sit in a big, overstuffed chair while he played the guitar. He sang, too. I had to stay in the control room when he was recording vocals."

She'd never spoken about that special summer to anyone, not even her mother. It felt good to share the memory with the kids—kids she realized she shared a bond with.

They peppered her with more questions until Randy silenced them with a look. When the band took a break, she ushered her charges into the studio where they begged and cajoled their parents into letting them remain in the studio through the next tracking.

Hank, having little need of his office, turned it over to her. Several days a week, she retreated to the quiet space to listen to the taped conversations and pen the articles she had promised the Gazette. She realized early on she had far more material than she needed for the articles and began to think about a longer work. She laid out an outline for a book chronicling the recording of the cover album, interspersed with human-interest type sketches of the musicians and their families. The work kept her busy and focused on her writing rather than the recording and the emotional roller coaster she was riding. Every week brought the band a step closer to "Melody", and she still didn't know what she would do when the time came.

In the midst of the controlled chaos, she was alone, and worse, she was lonely. Everyone there was part of some extended group—family, musicians, or crew. As close as she was to the project, she was an outsider. She loved the time she spent with the kids, loved holding little Katie, loved watching the toddlers awkwardly chasing after Betty Boop or their older siblings. She did have the company of the older kids more since they'd been given permission to visit the studio. They often sought her out when they came to the barn. Watching them with their fathers brought back cherished memories of time spent with her own.

What little time she and Hank had together, she didn't have his full attention. He was either too keyed up to sit still, or he was so exhausted he fell asleep the moment he stopped moving. When he could get away in the evening, he came to her. She let him into her bed, content to have him nearby. He was usually too tired in the evening to make love to her, but if he woke early, he reached for her. More often than not, she would shake him awake and hand him his first cup of coffee before his feet hit the floor.

The closer they got to "Melody", the higher and stronger she built the wall around her heart, but she was honest enough with herself to admit it was a futile effort. Hank had found a way in, and bit-by-bit, had taken over. She tried not to think about the time when she would have to leave. Being with him was emotional suicide, but she wanted him, needed more time with him to store up sweet memories to take with her.

The Fourth of July arrived and recording came to a standstill for an entire week. The crewmembers fled to their homes and families, and the band members let themselves relax for the first time in over a month. Chad, Mike, and Stephen took their families to Six Flags in nearby Arlington. Kevin and Marci took little Katie with them to a luxury hotel in Dallas for a week of quiet and pampering at the spa. Jonathan swept Miriam Wallingford off to Las Vegas before Mel had a chance to ask how he'd found time to get to know the woman, much less plan a trip with her. He was happier than she had ever seen him, so she waved them off with a smile and headed out to see Hank.

She pulled into the deserted driveway and cut the engine. Over the last month, she had come to associate the farm with children's laughter and preoccupied adults. The insects in the trees made their own music. She rounded the corner and stopped in her tracks, taking in the peaceful tableau. Hank slept in the dappled shade, relaxed as she hadn't seen him in weeks. The deep lines around his mouth and the creases on his forehead were gone. She approached with soft steps and removed the warm soda can from his lax fingers. Betty Boop opened her eyes and closed them again.

She knelt and stretched a finger up to trace the lines of Hank's parted lips. She stopped short when his breath brushed softly over her fingertip. She drew her hand away, reluctant to disturb his rest.

She let herself into the house and went upstairs to Hank's bedroom. She sighed at the mess. The man really did need a keeper. She made separate piles for the cleaners and the laundry room and filled a trash bag full of discarded candy wrappers and chip bags. Every scrap of paper, no matter how insignificant it appeared, went into a stack on top of his dresser.

She hauled the laundry downstairs and, after checking to see Hank and Betty Boop were still sleeping, continued cleaning. She put in a load of laundry and located a can of furniture polish. Starting upstairs, she cleaned the antique furniture in Hank's bedroom and the hallway, leaving the guest rooms to their inhabitants. Descending the stairs, she shined the oak banister, admiring its craftsmanship as she went. Pausing at the foot of the stairs, she noticed the old upright piano Hank had learned to play on, standing sentinel against the living room wall.

Making her way carefully around the room, she polished the dainty piecrust tables which were obviously sturdier than they appeared, having survived generations of children and continued to hold up under the onslaught of BlackWing's next generation. She lovingly dusted the piano, carefully moving the framed family photos scattered across the top. Setting her dusting tools beside her on the bench, she reverently lifted the keyboard cover.

The ivory-topped keys had yellowed with age. Chips on the corners and along the front edge of some of the keys attested to the many years of frequent use. She imagined a younger Hank and his mother sitting together on the bench as she patiently prodded him through his lessons. He would have protested every step of the way, as a young boy would, but in the end he had turned to music to make his living.

She pressed a well-worn key, and another. Bringing her hands up, she placed her untutored fingers on the keys. Tentatively she experimented with the sound. At first, it was harsh and foreign to her ear, but as her fingers moved across the keyboard, she learned the sounds, and soon the disjointed notes came together into a somewhat pleasing melody.

Hank joined her on the bench and

she jumped in surprise. Jerking her fingers from the keys, she started to pull the cover back in place, but his strong hand clamped around her wrist, staying the movement.

"Don't," he spoke softly, releasing her.

Mel dropped her gaze to her hands, lying limp in her lap. "I'm sorry. I should have asked before I abused your piano."

She sensed his gaze on her, studying her. With a gentle hand on her chin, he lifted her face. Hot tears of embarrassment stung her eyes.

"No need to apologize. You can play it anytime you want."

A tear escaped down her cheek, swept away with the soft brush of his callused thumb. Desire flared to life, hot and wild, doused equally as quickly by his next words.

"I'm confused. You told me you don't play any instruments. Why did you lie to me?"

Her gaze darted to the piano keys and back to his face where his green eyes questioned her. He was kidding, right? He had to be. It was the only explanation because she had only been fooling around with the keys.

She burst out laughing. "Oh Hank! That's good. You had me there for a minute. Thanks, I needed a good laugh."

He wasn't sharing her amusement. His eyes flashed shards of glass. "There's nothing funny about this situation," he said, his words slicing sharp. "You're lying, and I want to know why."

Her heart sank to her toes. He was serious. She rose from the bench, putting the length of it between them. Stung and confused by his accusation, she matched his tone. "I don't know what you're talking about, Hank. I'm not lying. I've never had a lesson of any kind in my whole life. I was just goofing around with the piano. Other than playing chopsticks with Daddy when I was a child, I've never touched a piano until today. We didn't have one at home. I don't know what you think you saw or heard, but you're wrong."

Her whole body vibrated with anger. How dare he accuse her of lying? She had been more honest with him than with anybody she had ever known. Hank covered his face with his hands and scrubbed them up and down. The only sounds in the room were the rhythmic tick from the old mantle clock and the faint rasp of skin across Hank's unshaven jaw. She waited for him to say something, anything to explain his absurd accusation.

A hoarse laugh bubbled up from deep in his chest. "I'm sorry. I should have known better. You wouldn't lie to me." He stood to face her, his hands resting on hips cocked slightly to the side, one leg bent in a casual stance. "I heard the piano from the backyard, and in my sleep, I guess I thought it must be a ghost or something in here playing my mom's old upright. I saw your Jeep in the driveway and knew it had to be you, so I came in. I stood in the doorway and listened to you play for quite a while. I was furious. Convinced you'd lied to me. Every minute you played, I got madder and madder." His eyes pleaded with her in the gloaming light of the living room. "I'm sorry. I really am. You continue to surprise me, that's all."

His words spun through her head like a tornado, whirling, making no sense. She forced her mouth closed. "You're mad all right. Completely insane. What are you saying?"

"How many times have you listened to the CD I gave you?"

The change of subject took her by surprise. "What CD?" An image of the manila envelope containing "Melody" flashed in her mind. "You mean the other version of 'Melody?'"

"Yeah. How many times have you listened to it?"

"I've only heard it the one time you played it for me in the studio. I haven't opened the envelope at all. I put it in my safety deposit box at the bank the same day you gave it to me. Why?"

He sank onto the bench and shook his head. "That's what you were playing."

He spun around to the piano and played the chorus. The notes sang through her system. Her blood ran cold, freezing the air in her lungs, and rendering her legs useless. She collapsed onto the bench beside him, her back to the keyboard. She sucked in a deep breath. The tart freshness of the lemon-scented furniture polish tickled her nose and she chuckled to herself at the absurdity of her observation.

The music faded away. Hank sat motionless beside her.

"I don't know how to play the piano, Hank. I swear I was just toying with the keys, but you're right. I can hear it now."

Hank half turned toward her. "What time did you start playing today?"

Her shoulders slumped. "I don't

know, four-thirty, maybe. Why?"

His voice carried low, tinged with compassion. "Mel, it's nearly six o'clock."

Her gaze darted to the window, and she noticed the soft light of early evening, the deepening shadows in the East-facing room. "Oh God."

He swiveled all the way around on the bench and took her in his arms. "It's all right."

She wished she could believe, but at that moment, it didn't seem like anything would ever be all right again.

CHAPTER TWENTY-TWO

Mel stretched and opened one eye, taking stock of her surroundings. *Morning. Hank's bed. Alone.* Memories flooded back. She closed her eyes, draping one arm across them in an effort to block out reality.

She didn't know what disturbed her more, the realization she could play the piano like some freak of nature, or Hank's distrust and disappointment. He'd thought she'd been lying. He hadn't been convinced even after she swore she'd never taken a lesson in her life. Still, he had held her through the night while she slept.

She bolted upright, her feet hitting the floor as the thought settled in. She had slept, *really* slept. In fact, she had slept like a baby. Her jeans and shirt were draped across the ladder back chair in the corner. She pulled them on and finger combed her hair before going downstairs.

Low voices and the aroma of freshly brewed coffee met her at the bottom of the stairs. She stepped cautiously into the kitchen where Hank and his father sat, a plate of doughnuts on the table between them. Betty Boop was at Henry's knee, her eyes pleading for a handout. As she stepped into the doorway, Hank turned.

"Dad brought your favorite, doughnuts and hot chocolate. Come join us." His voice was smooth as ever, but his eyes were distant, cool, and wary. He'd taken time to pull on jeans and a wrinkled T-shirt, but he hadn't shaved and his feet were bare. He was adorable, and sexy, and pissed.

She decided she didn't want to know how Henry knew she would be here. She took a seat and helped herself to a chocolate-frosted pastry. "Good morning, Henry. Thanks for the doughnuts."

Betty Boop shifted her eyes to Mel. She pinched off a piece of dough without chocolate and tossed it into the air. The dog caught it on the fly.

She popped the lid off the cardboard cup Henry slid in her direction and tested the temperature. It was still reasonably warm, so Henry hadn't been there long. If they could pretend everything was just dandy, so could she. "What's up, guys?"

"I came out to see if there was anything Hank needed done today and to remind him about the parade tomorrow. The high school band will be wearing their new uniforms," Henry stated proudly.

Hank laughed, spinning his coffee cup between his hands. "I'll be there, Dad. You haven't volunteered me to work on anything tomorrow, have you?"

"No, not this year. I figured you have enough to do with the album and all. Why don't you come by the house tomorrow and we can walk downtown together. This year's picnic and fireworks should be pretty good. There's a carnival set up in the high school parking lot, too."

She couldn't contain her excitement. She'd always enjoyed the small town parades when she was a child. She grew up in a small coastal community, and the townspeople were always finding excuses for a parade. "Sounds like fun. Am I included in the invitation?"

"Of course you are." He stood. "I've got to go. Things to do, you know. I'll see the two of you tomorrow around nine-thirty. We should have plenty of time to get a good viewing spot. I wouldn't want to miss any of the floats."

As the sound of Henry's car faded into the distance, Mel spoke. "Did you tell him?"

"About last night? No, I didn't. I

don't want to talk about it." He crossed to the coffeemaker and refilled his cup.

"I didn't lie to you, Hank. I swear. I feel like some kind of freak of nature." Tears filled her eyes. She swiped them away with a napkin and sat up straighter, tamping down on the cold fear threatening to take over.

Hank resumed his seat at the table. "I want to believe you. It's hard though. I've been used before and I was so sure you were different. But first you sang like an angel, and now I find out you can play the piano. It's a lot to believe, Mel."

"I'm sorry, Hank. I don't know who lied to you before, but I'm telling the truth."

"I've heard of people who could play by ear, but I've never met anyone who could. It doesn't mean you aren't one of them. Who taught your father to play?"

"I don't know. I've never thought about it. My mother might know." She jumped up and grabbed her purse from the counter where she'd left it. She found her cell phone and made the call, heedless of the two-hour time difference. She was aware of Hank watching her as she spoke with her mother. She ended the conversation as quickly as she could and turned to him.

"Did you follow that? Mom says he played by ear—at least at first. He did learn to read and write music, but not until he was in college."

Hank sipped his coffee. "Well, it explains a lot. Where did he go to college?"

"Cambridge."

He flashed his crooked grin, and her insides melted.

"It isn't Harvard, but it's an okay place," he teased.

Mel returned the smile. The conversation with her mother explained her obviously inherited talent but disturbed her on another level. She realized how little she knew about her parents and her father in particular. Since his death, her mother had avoided talking about him, and Mel, mired in her own grief and guilt, had been all too willing to let the subject slide. She didn't want to think about it today either.

"Let's fix a picnic and go down to the creek," she said. "We can sit under a shade tree and listen to the water, or take a nap, or whatever." She needed the peace and quiet, and Hank could use a restful day, too.

"Or whatever sounds good to me." He wiggled his eyebrows in a suggestive manner.

"That's not what I meant, and you know it. I was thinking more along the lines of reading or fishing."

"Well, if we can't do *whatever*, I vote for napping. It's the next best thing on your list."

Mel raided the kitchen for suitable picnic fare while he rounded up old quilts and insect repellant. He found a couple of old throw pillows suitable for outdoor use and piled everything into a wagon and they set off for the creek bank.

She kicked off her shoes and stretched out beside Hank on the quilt, curling onto her side so she could watch him. He'd fallen asleep almost as soon as he lay down. A soft breeze wafted through the shade, tempting her to do more than was wise. His jaw and lips were more relaxed than she had seen them in weeks. She brushed a lock of hair from his forehead. He needed to find the time to visit Judd Spencer. She smiled to herself. *I love you.*

She closed her eyes and waited for the panic and doubts to creep in. The drone of summer insects and the leaves whispering on the breeze lulled her. "Melody" filled her mind as it often did, but today, it was Hank's voice crooning the lyrics, weaving a sensuous tapestry that blanketed her. He loved her and she loved him. Drifting into sleep, she wished it could be so simple.

CHAPTER TWENTY-THREE

The Fourth of July dawned hot and humid, but it wasn't enough to deter the citizens of Willowbrook. From her kitchen table, Mel watched the sun blaze its way into the sky. These were the kind of days she had imagined when she chose Willowbrook. Nearly everyone in town would be in the parade or lining the downtown walkways, cheering and waving as the revelers passed by.

She slipped her camera into her shoulder bag. There would be plenty of photos in the paper tomorrow but she wanted to take her own.

Over the last few weeks, everything she knew about herself had been called into question. She had fallen in love with a man she couldn't live with, and she'd ruined any chance she had of staying in Willowbrook by doing so. Despite her inner turmoil, she wanted to spend the day with Hank. She wanted to enjoy the simple pleasures of small-town life with him. All too soon, it would be over, and she would have to leave. Today, she wanted to make memories she could take with her, memories to pull out and savor when the inevitable loneliness overcame her.

Their time together had grown shorter day by day. The recording session was on schedule. Six songs were already in the hands of the mixer, who would reunite the disjointed tracks into the final two tracks for mastering. Seven more were still to be recorded.

She tamped down the panic she felt every time she thought about the final two weeks. Moving in chronological order was like some macabre countdown to reliving the worst nightmare of her life. Each song, each week brought her a step closer.

When Hank knocked on her door, she was ready and waiting for him. In honor of the holiday and bowing to the summer heat, she'd chosen to wear blue denim shorts, a red T-shirt, and white sneakers.

"You could be Uncle Sam's niece," Hank said, pulling her close for a kiss.

"Uncle Sam doesn't have a niece," she said against his lips.

"Yeah? Well, if he did, she'd look like you—cute, and sexy as hell."

"Flatterer." She grabbed his hand and pulled him out the door. "Let's go. I don't want to miss a thing."

They drove the few blocks to Henry's, and the three of them walked the short distance to Main Street. A crowd had already gathered, but they found a place on the sidewalk in front of the Donut Hole to view the parade. Cathy came outside, handing out miniature flags and doughnut holes covered in red, white, and blue sprinkles. Mel snapped her picture—the first of many memories she wanted to document.

The Willowbrook High School Band led off the parade, proudly sweating inside their new uniforms. The School Superintendent trailed behind the band in an open convertible. When he was right in front of The Donut Hole, he jumped from the moving vehicle and snatched Henry from the crowd. The car stopped long enough for the two men to climb in and continued on its way, leaving Hank and Mel laughing on the sidewalk. They waved their flags, clapped, and shouted good-naturedly at the passing entries. She clicked away, taking photos of every float and turning the camera on Hank as often as possible.

As the last group made its way down the parade route, they moved with the crowd to City Park where all the floats would be on display and the picnic festivities would be held. Henry was there, accepting thanks from band members, their parents, and school officials. They left him to his admirers and wandered through the displays. She bought earrings from one booth and a handmade tote bag from another. They ate roasted corn on the cob, barbeque, and ice-cold watermelon. Hank bought two apple pies from the Methodist Church women's group and arranged for them to bake a special batch to be delivered to the farm the following week.

She didn't have a care in the world walking hand-in-hand with Hank, sitting in the shade of the ancient oak with him while sipping lemonade made by the Boy Scouts. This was normal. It was the life she longed for, the one she could never have if the paparazzi found out where she was. And they would find out if she stayed with Hank. There was no way around the inevitable. When she thought about living the rest of her life without Hank, her heart felt like a stone, but she couldn't live with him either. If they had been anyone but who they were....

Hank stopped at nearly every booth or food vendor and was greeted by name. Everyone in town seemed to know him, and to her surprise, he knew them. He asked about their families, jobs, and vacations. She expected someone to ask for his autograph or want his or her picture taken with him, but no one asked. Instead, she handed over her camera several times for his friends to snap a photo of the two of them. He went along with it every time, holding her close for each photo. In one, he even turned his head at the last minute and kissed her as the shutter clicked.

In Willowbrook he was simply Henry Travis, Jr. His worldwide celebrity status didn't mean a thing to the people of his hometown. *Who* he was eclipsed *what* he was in their estimation. Some offered congratulations on his latest Platinum album or the Grammy the band had recently won. Plenty commented on both, sometimes referring to some childhood peccadillo or other, letting him know, at the heart of it all, he was one of them. Hank accepted the praise and the teasing with good humor, as if his youthful escapades were equally as important as the career accolades.

They rested the late afternoon away at Henry's house and retreated to the air-conditioned living room to eat pie and down giant glasses of sweet tea. Hank's dad dozed in his easy chair, so they moved to the kitchen where they could talk without disturbing him.

"Are you having a good time?" he asked.

"Yes, very much so. I know the Willowbrook celebration is corny by big city standards, but I love it. The whole town is involved from the smallest ballerinas at the dance studio, to the little old ladies selling pies for a good cause. It's wonderful."

He smiled. "I love it, too. I've been to many places around the world since I left for college. I've seen lots of cities, big and small. I keep coming back here, though. Willowbrook is home. It's where I want to be, even when I'm not here, if that makes any sense. Not everyone can say as much about the place they grew up."

She envied him. "I know what you mean. The people here may be short on sophistication, but they're long on caring. They care about their town, and they care about each other." She swirled her tea glass, watching the expanding damp circle on the tabletop. "They care about you."

"I suppose they do. I care about them. I've known these people my entire life. I've shopped in their stores, been in their classrooms, played with them, and dated a few of them." He chuckled. "Maybe more than a few. I've even mowed lawns and raked leaves for a bunch of them."

"They treat you like you're just another member of the community. Your celebrity status doesn't seem to impress them much."

"I guess if I was overly impressed with my status, things would be different, but I'm not. When I'm home, I'm just Hank, the kid who did chores for them or who rode his bike through their flowerbed. My job is a little different from most folks in town, but it's what I do, not what I am. They accept it."

A band of longing tightened around her heart. "I don't fit into your world, Hank. As much as I want to, I don't. If they all knew who I was, they'd look at me differently. People always do."

He covered her hand with his and waited until she turned her gaze up at him. "Mel, your Uncle Jonathan has been in town for over a month. You don't honestly think no one has noticed, do you? He's hard to miss, even though he's spent most of his time at the farm." He released her hand, sitting back in his chair. "These people may be small town folk, but they aren't stupid. Most of them have probably figured it out on their own."

Dear God! She gasped for breath as panic threatened to take her under.

"Hold on," he said, reaching for her hand again. "Think about it. Did anyone treat you differently today? Did anyone ask you uncomfortable questions?"

His touch calmed her. "No. No one said anything." She wanted him to be right. She wanted what he had, to be accepted for the person she was, not because of her name. "Well, a few ladies at the pie booth did ask about Uncle Jonathan."

"See, I told you so." He smiled. "Half the town knows where he went and who went with him. You can't hide anything in a town this size. It's the price you pay for all the *caring* you were going on about. Everyone knows everything about you, and worse, they think they have the right to know it." He paused and rolled his shoulders. "You get used to it."

When the sun dipped low in the western sky, taking the temperature and humidity down with it, Hank asked, "Ready to try the carnival?"

"Oh yeah," Mel said.

He kept her close to his side the whole evening. Hank won a giant purple teddy bear by landing dimes on upturned goblets. She noticed a few envious looks, some from small children admiring the prize, others from teenage girls, and a few grown women who openly admired her date. Mel hugged the bear close while Hank explained his winning secret to the gathered crowd.

"It's all in the wrist." He demonstrated the action. "It's just like playing the drums."

She tried her hand at a few games, but couldn't come close to duplicating Hank's success. She consoled herself by feasting on the usual carnival delicacies, cotton candy, snow cones, and greasy burgers with fries. Hank steered her to the Ferris wheel and discreetly bribed the ride operator to stop them at the top when the fireworks started. She loved picking out landmarks among the glimmering lights across town and laughed when the ride spun in a lazy circle leaving her stomach behind. The fireworks exploded in the sky, showering the town in red, white, and blue glitter. The wheel inched to a stop. Dangling on the cusp, their seat rocked a few times and stilled. Mel took in the unprecedented view.

"I've never seen anything more beautiful in my life," she said.

"Neither have I," Hank replied, draping his arm over her shoulder and pulling her close.

**

At his touch, she came into his arms. She smelled of sunshine and fresh air, her lips were as sweet as cotton candy under his. He framed her face in his hands and drew his thumbs softly across her pink tinged cheeks. Exploding fireworks reflected in her bluebonnet eyes captivated him. Love for the woman in his arms filled him. For the first time in ages, he was happy. He liked a parade as much as the next guy, but with Melody by his side, he'd had more fun than he could ever remember.

Standing on the sidewalk earlier, her head tucked under his chin and his hands resting on her hips while she laughed and waved at the passing floats had been one of the best moments. She fit in his arms and his life. She fit in the recording studio. She fit with the band members and their wives. She fit with his friends in Willowbrook. Everywhere they were together, she fit right in.

He could see a future with Melody. She would be by his side in his career as well as here in his home. Maybe one day they'd watch their kids in the Fourth of July parade. He could see it happening with Melody, and only Melody.

He hadn't planned anything beyond a few minutes alone with her to watch the fireworks, but he couldn't stop the words flowing from his heart.

"I love you. I want to spend the rest of my life with you. Will you marry me, Melody Ravenswood?"

So, this is how it ends. Here, on top of the world, Hank's world, after the best day of my life.

Her heart skipped a beat. She'd thought they would have more time together.

His hands framed her face, and sincerity gleamed in his eyes. The truth of his words were written across his face and carried in the depth of feeling in his voice.

They could have a lifetime. It was up to her. The single, affirmative syllable trembled on her lips.

But she couldn't say it, couldn't sentence herself and Hank to the kind of life awaiting them. He was a dreamer, but she had given up on her dreams long ago. The life he envisioned just couldn't be. Not for people like them.

Hot tears spilled from her eyes, brushed away by a tender swipe of his callused thumbs across her cheeks. The shiver began in her hands, loosening her grip on his forearms. It continued across her chest and down her spine until it erupted into an uncontrollable quaking. She forced the air from her lungs, across her vocal cords. "I love you, too, Hank, but I can't marry you."

The moment the words left her lips she wished she could take them back. But she couldn't. It was the right thing to do. The only thing she could do. For Hank. For herself.

He held her for the space of a heartbeat then he dropped his hands from her face and turned in his seat. She hugged the purple bear to her chest, squeezing as tight as she could to still her shaking. Even in the warm night air, a bone-deep chill crept over her.

Where his proposal had been as smooth and warm as silk, his voice was now as cold and sharp as chipped ice. "Can't or won't, Mel? Which is it?"

The one thing she could give him was honesty. "Won't. Hank, don't you see? If we were to marry, everything you see here would change." She swept her arm across the sky showered in gold glitter, to encompass Willowbrook which sprawled like a blanket of twinkle lights below them. "I can't stay here. Eventually, the tabloids will figure out I'm here. Add you into the mix and it will be nothing short of a disaster. I can't do it. I won't do it to you, to us, or to this town."

"You're wrong. But if that's the only reason you can think of, we'll live somewhere else. You're making excuses, Melody."

Fear gripped her, and pain shot

through her heart, a knife twisting for good measure. "You have no idea what it's like living a shadow life, hiding who you are. I do, Hank. I've done it all my life. Living with an alias. Never telling people your real name or talking about your family. Avoiding places where other celebrities will be on the off chance someone might recognize you. It's the way I grew up. My mother constantly drilled it into me, 'Don't do anything to draw attention to yourself or the paparazzi will find you.' Marrying you, you marrying me? It would break every rule of self-preservation I know." She clutched the bear impossibly tighter. "You know as well as I do it wouldn't work."

Fireworks exploded overhead. Multi-colored sparks fizzled and died, raining down like shattered dreams. The seat trembled, and he glanced at Mel. Tears streamed down her cheeks, and she looked as frightened as a child on the deck of a sinking ship, watching in horror as the icy water crept closer and closer.

His anger vanished. He folded her into his arms. His broken heart was nothing compared to the demons she fought every day. He wrapped an arm around her back and cradled her head against his shoulder with his other hand.

"What is it you're afraid they'll find out?"

She startled when a particularly big firework exploded and he wrapped her tighter, shushing her fears with soft, reassuring words.

"You can tell me, Mel."

"They blame me. I know they do. Daddy would still be alive it wasn't for me."

He rubbed his hands up and down her back. "That's not true, Mel. It was an accident, and you were just a child. No one blames you."

"They do because it's true. If they find me, they'll never let it go. They'd drag you down with me. I can't let that happen."

"I don't know how I can change your mind. None of what you say is true, but even if it was, I don't care. I want to be with you. I want to marry you. I want to raise a family with you right here in Willowbrook. You've got to know I'll protect you."

"I know you think you can, but you can't." Her muffled sniffle nearly broke his heart all over again. "Please, take me home."

"Okay. Let's table this discussion for another time. I'll take you home as soon as the fireworks are over."

He held her tight until the wheel came to a stop and the attendant raised the safety bar, all the while trying to make sense of what had gone wrong. She loved him. She'd admitted as much. He loved her, so everything else was immaterial. He'd find another way to make her see what they could have together. She needed more time. He could give it to her. He had waited a long time to find her—he could wait until she saw what he saw.

On the silent walk home, he held her close, matching his stride to her shorter one. At her front door, he kissed her gently, asking nothing in return.

"Will you be all right? I'll stay if you need me to."

She closed the short distance between them, laying her cheek against his chest. "I'm sorry, Hank."

"Don't be. You can't help the way you feel, but the offer stands. We're good together. I'll convince you."

"Oh, Hank, please don't."

He pressed his lips to her hair, holding the contact for a moment before he let her go. "This conversation isn't over. We aren't over."

He forced his feet to move, leaving her there in the open doorway. Alone.

**

Mel indulged in what her college

friends referred to as a massive pity party. She spent the remainder of the week on the sofa, eating ice cream from the carton and watching chick-flicks on cable. The giant purple bear was her only companion. When Jonathan returned on Sunday evening, she pulled herself together.

Hank's proposal made her decision to chronicle the recording session even more difficult—if that was even possible. She would never forget the expression on his face when she'd refused him. She had hurt him, but it was nothing compared to the misery she would bring him if she'd said yes. The stubborn man would eventually see she was right and thank her for saving him. Until he did, she would just have to keep her distance and somehow finish the project she had started.

Her resolve to stay far away from Hank nearly crumbled the moment she stepped inside the barn. He came out of his office, looking good enough to eat, and from the set of his eyes, he either wanted to eat her up or murder her, she couldn't tell which.

She drank him in and squashed the impulse to throw herself into his arms and tell him she had changed her mind. With a curt nod in her direction, he continued along the hall away from her. *Well, what did you expect?*

It was the week from Hell. She was a virtual stranger among a close-knit group of friends and her welcome depended on Hank. She couldn't help but notice the derisive glances directed at her and her questions garnered the shortest possible answers. By the end of the week she'd had enough and cornered Hank in his office.

He was so incredibly handsome, sitting behind his desk with his shirtsleeves rolled up to expose his wrists and muscled forearms. With his reading glasses and his ultra-conservative haircut, he resembled a college math professor more than a rock star.

She closed the door and took a seat in one of the guest chairs in front of his desk. He continued to sort through a stack of mail, completely ignoring her. She couldn't quit staring at his his hands. Desire raced through her veins as she remembered the feel of them on her, stroking, pleasuring. She knew the ecstasy of his skilled hands. With one, he kept her body pulsing to a steady rhythm, while the other coaxed her heart into a sweet melody. By varying the tempo, he kept her writhing in a constant state of need.

She hated the new mask of indifference he wore whenever she was around. Among his friends, he smiled and laughed, but as soon as she approached, the mask slipped into place, closing her out.

He was aware of her from the moment she'd stepped into his office. He'd spent the last week trying to avoid her, trying to keep from touching her. She was like a magnet, drawing him closer with nothing more than her presence. Without raising his head, he could just see her breasts, rising and falling. She was a sickness, he decided. A fever he couldn't shake. An addiction. He needed a twelve-step program.

He wanted her with every fiber of his being, and no matter how hard he tried to stop it, his body reacted every time she came near. He hadn't touched her in over a week. Hell, he had barely spoken to her.

Feigning indifference was killing him. It was affecting his work. He couldn't concentrate on his job because all he could think about was her. Where she was. Who she was talking to. What she was wearing. The way her skin felt like satin. The taste of her lips. The way the two of them fit perfectly together. Her insane denial of their love.

No one had said anything yet, but they had to be thinking about it. If he didn't get his head on straight soon, one of the guys, or all of them, would do it for him.

"Hank, we need to talk."

He tossed another envelope onto the trash-it pile. "About what?"

"Will you stop and look at me? I can't stand your cold shoulder anymore."

The last envelope dropped from his fingertips, and he looked at her for the first time since she'd invaded his office. She wanted a life without him in it. Well, this was what it was like. *Get used to it, Melody.*

"What do you expect from me? I'm not made of stone. I can't act like nothing happened." *I'm not like you.*

"This situation is unbearable, Hank. The wall you put up between us is bad enough, but it's affecting the whole crew. The rest of the guys will hardly speak to me. Might I remind you, the book, me being here, was your idea."

He tossed his reading glasses on the desk. The woman across from him inhabited the same gorgeous body he knew so well, but this woman was cold and distant. Not at all like the woman he'd fallen in love with. He wished she'd jump over the desk, do something, anything to him. He was so far gone, he thought letting her strangle him would be okay as long as she put her hands on him.

His kept his voice steady, controlled. "I'll talk to them. There's no reason for our problems to be theirs, too. Is that all you wanted?"

"I know you don't understand, but refusing to marry you is for your own good. I love you. I love you too much."

He bolted out of his chair. Her calm rationalization of the irrational was a match to the tinder of his banked emotions. Everything he had held in for the last week boiled to the surface as he faced her across the desk.

"I understand a lot more than you think I do. Don't do me any favors,

Mel. Don't throw our love away and tell yourself it's for my own good. I can decide for myself what's in my best interest."

He flattened his palms on the desk so he was eye-to-eye with her. She flinched, but he was through pretending he didn't have any feelings in order to protect hers. It was time for her to face up to a few truths.

"You don't love me too much, Melody. You don't love yourself enough. Everything you said the other night is bullshit. You're using it as an excuse to run away again, just like you ran to Willowbrook. What happened in San Diego?"

He didn't wait for her answer, didn't care what sent her running before. All that mattered was what she was running from now.

"You're hiding. I don't give a shit about who your father was. I don't care if the tabloids follow us to the ends of the earth. I love you, and I want to spend the rest of my life with you. We can make it work. But you have to want a future for yourself, for us, enough to let go of the past."

She opened her mouth to protest, but he cut her off. "The core of the problem isn't your guilt about what happened to your father. No, the real problem is you don't trust me. If you did, you'd know I would never let anyone hurt you."

He rounded the desk and crossed the room in long, angry strides. He had to get away. He had already said too much, and he needed to leave before he said something he didn't really mean.

At the door, he turned back to her. "You're right. You being here is my fault. I brought you into the recording. I won't stand in the way of you doing your job. But hear me, Melody. You're the only one for me. Run and hide all you want. And when you come to your senses, I'll be here waiting for you. As long as it takes."

CHAPTER TWENTY-FOUR

"Hey, Mel. Have you seen Hank?" She spun around at the sound of a man's voice.

"No. Yes. He left, I think." She gathered her wits and stood next to her chair, facing Stephen.

"Where did he go? Is he coming back?"

"I don't know. He didn't say."

"Are you okay? You don't look so well."

Her legs trembled, and she put a hand on the back of the chair to steady herself. "I'm fine," she lied. "I've got to go." She forced her feet to move, pushing past Stephen in the doorway.

She drove home, but as she closed the front door behind her, she couldn't remember a single detail of the drive. Did she stop at the four-way stop at the corner? She closed her eyes and leaned against the door.

"What's wrong, luv?"

She jumped at the sound of Jonathan's voice. "You scared me. I thought you were at the farm."

"I was. Henry dropped me off a few minutes ago. I have to be back later, but no one's going to miss me for a few hours."

"That's good," she said. "You've been working too hard."

"It feels good to be working again." He stood in front of her. "Come on. You look like you could use some rest yourself." He slid an arm around her shoulders and steered her to the sofa. He perched on the coffee table and took her hands in his. "Tell me what's wrong."

She was so tired of being strong. For once, she needed someone to lean on, and Jonathan had strong shoulders. He had always been there for her. Tears welled in her eyes and spilled over, and once they'd begun, there was no stopping them. Jonathan moved to sit beside her and drew her into his arms.

"Here, here now, luv. What's got you so upset?"

The story came out in a rush. Between bouts of tears and hiccups, she told him everything. She told him about playing the piano, about Hank's proposal, about turning him down, and, about his angry verbal attack.

He pushed a box of tissues into her hand. "Dry your tears. I'm going to fix us a pot of tea and we'll talk about you and Hank. Maybe I can help."

She dried her tears, and when he returned, she welcomed the warmth of the mug he placed in her hands.

"Drink up. It'll do you good."

She took a sip. The hot liquid began to thaw the block of ice in her gut, and a maniacal drummer hammered a steady beat against her skull. "Thank you."

Jonathan settled in the chair across from her. "Since you've calmed a bit, let's talk. I understand you being upset about discovering you have some musical talent. That sort of thing would come as quite a shock to anyone, especially a full grown adult who just happens to stumble on it." He paused to sip his tea. "Your father started playing the piano when he was a teenager, I believe. Even being the heir to the Earl, he wasn't exposed to music in the traditional sense, not like I was. We were poor as the proverbial church mice, but my mother made sure I had piano lessons. I was always envious of Milton's ability to hear a tune and play it back, note for note, almost immediately. It was a talent he took for granted, but one I often wished I had."

Mom was right.

"Drink your tea. I'll talk, you listen."

Mel took another sip of tea. "He took enough music classes in college to learn to read and write music. That's when he started putting his compositions down on paper. By that time, he had a whole library of original music in his head."

He drank from his cup. "I would have given just about anything to have his talent, his ability to compose in his head and have the same composition just spill out of the instrument like some sort of magical birth. So now it seems his daughter has inherited his talent."

He shook his head. "Instead of fighting it, you should be embracing it. I bet Hank feels the same way I did about Milton. Envious. Incredulous. Unworthy, even. I'll tell you, it's bloody difficult sometimes to be a lowly mortal around a musical genius. Bloody difficult. You should cut the man some slack. He can't help the way he feels, but he loves you, so he'll come around on that score. He did ask you to marry him, so I'd say he's coping pretty well."

She let her head drop back

against the sofa. She supposed he was right. The talent was obviously there, and it wasn't going to go away. She should embrace it to whatever degree it would manifest itself. She didn't think she had the ability to compose original music, but she could play by ear. It was a good parlor trick, at least.

"Uncle Jonathan, I'm far from being a musical genius." An understatement if there ever was one. "I'll leave the composing to you. Thanks for telling me about Daddy. It does help, and of course the tea helped, too." She set her mug on the coffee table. "I'll be okay. I'm not sure if Hank and I can work out our differences or not, but you shouldn't worry about me."

"I can't help but worry about you. What else is bothering you? You can tell me."

No, she couldn't. Jonathan had never blamed her for her father's death, but she knew in her heart he did. Everyone did. How could they not?

"Nothing. Really, I'm fine." *Liar.*

"For the record, I think you're making a mistake pushing Hank away. He's a good man, and if you love him, you should hold onto him with everything you've got. A love so powerful doesn't come along every day you know. Take me for example. I've been searching for it all my life, and believe me, when I find it I won't let it go without a fight."

**

Hank stood in the doorway to his office, watching her work. Her dark hair fell from a high ponytail, exposing the creamy curve of her neck as she bent over the computer keyboard. His fingertips itched to touch her, to trace the graceful lines of her curves, to feel her satin skin.

"Hi."

She glanced up with wide eyes. The ponytail swung down her back. "I'm sorry to disturb you, but I thought you should know Guy arranged for a photographer and a video crew to come out next week. They'll be here off and on until we're through recording."

"Why?"

"For the cover shoot. We've asked Jonathan to be in it. He said he would be honored. Can you imagine? *Honored.* We're the ones who are honored." He shook his head. "Anyway, the video crew will tape some of the recording sessions. Pieces of it will be used during the tour and to promote the CD when it's released."

"Don't sell yourself short. I think Uncle Jonathan would recommend you all for Knighthood if he could."

"He's the best. I don't think we could have done made the album without him."

"What about me? I mean, in regards to the photographer and video crew."

What about you? You're gorgeous, smart, stubborn, and I'd

give anything to touch you right this minute. "If you don't want them to know who you are, they won't. We'll keep your secret."

"Okay. I'd appreciate it. I'll keep a low profile, just in case."

He nodded. *Whatever you want.* "I'll talk to everyone and let them know." He turned to go.

"Thanks. I'm almost through anyway. I'll be spending less time here over the next few weeks. I can work on the last articles and the book at home."

With a silent nod of acknowledgment, he left. Nothing had changed. She was still bent on running and hiding.

She stared at the empty doorway long after he was gone. He hadn't argued with her about her choice to remain out of the public eye. Not like before. After all the times she had tried to get him to understand her reasoning, he did. He wasn't going to push her to come out of hiding.

She should be happy she had won him over to her way of thinking, but instead, all she felt was…lost. And alone in an empty prison of her own making.

He loved her enough to let her live the life she saw for herself. He wouldn't try to force her into one she didn't want.

It was as if she'd turned a page in a book and there it was—the truth. He had tried to make her see it. The only thing standing between her and a lifetime of happiness were her own hang-ups.

I love him. He loves me.

The hopeless paralysis that had engulfed her for so long vanished. She wasn't free, but she *wanted* to be free, and it made all the difference. Hank was right. The choice was hers to make. Happiness or miserable loneliness.

I choose happiness. I choose Hank.

But it wasn't so simple. Making the decision to be happy was the easy part. Actually achieving happiness would require a lot of hard work. She'd lost her way a long time ago, and she needed time to find it again.

I have to find out who I am before I can be who I want to be.

Her head spun with images, flashes of what could be. She saw her life with Hank, the children they would have. That was the life she wanted. That was the life she would have.

His words came back to her. "When you come to your senses, I'll be here waiting for you."

Wait for me, Hank. Please, wait for me.

CHAPTER TWENTY-FIVE

She had a plan, and as soon as the photography crews hit town, she made herself scarce. She spent her days with her laptop in her home office and finished the promised articles for the Gazette. She dropped them off before they were due and handed in her resignation at the same time.

She polished her book outline and wrote several chapters. It took days to research literary agents online and compile a list to query. She had to stop and take calming breaths before she took the next step toward claiming her life. With trembling hands, she typed her name on the bottom of the first query letter. *Melody Harper Ravenswood.*

It was shocking to see it in print. Even her high school and college diplomas didn't have her full name on them. She checked the paper tray on her new printer and bit her bottom lip as she hit the print button.

She practiced her signature a few times on a notepad before affixing it to the letters. Just for fun, she tried writing Melody Travis a few times. It looked good. Really good. But before she could be Melody Travis, she needed to learn to be Melody Ravenswood.

She stared at the strange signature for a moment before folding the letters and sealing them in the appropriate envelopes. She drove to the post office and tossed them into the drive thru drop box before she lost her nerve. Trembling, she pulled to the curb until she was calm enough to continue.

It was done. The letters were signed, sealed, and delivered. No going back.

She pulled into a parking space as

close to the Donut Hole as she could find. She pasted a smile on her face and went inside. Cathy spotted her immediately and waved her to the side.

"Mel, you're shaking. What's the matter? Come in the back and tell me what's wrong." Cathy led her around the counter to her office. She pushed her into a chair. "Wait here."

Cathy returned with two hot chocolates and a plate of doughnuts. "Here, eat, then tell me what's got you in such a state."

Her hands trembled too hard to hold a mug, and she didn't think she could keep anything down the way her stomach was churning. "Thanks. I shouldn't have come here. You're busy. I should go."

"You aren't going anywhere. I'm not so busy I can't take a few minutes for a friend, so tell me what happened."

She took a deep breath and told her about the letters she'd written. "I guess I needed to tell somebody what I'd done." Calmer, she sipped the chocolate and bit into a glazed doughnut. "Thanks for listening. And for the sugar, too."

Cathy whistled low. "Wow! So, you're going public?"

"Yep."

"I think that's fantastic, but why now?"

"It hit me a few days ago. I love Hank. I want a life with him, and the only way I'm going to have one, is to get my act together. He accused me of running and hiding. He said I was making excuses not to be with him. It took me a while to see it, but he was right. I've been Mel Harper for so long I lost track of who Melody Ravenswood is. I have to find her again. That's the first step. You can't even imagine how strange it was to see my own signature." She laughed at herself. "I even had to practice before I signed the letters. Imagine. A woman my age having to practice her name like a kid in grade school."

"Have another doughnut. Your

return to the real world is cause for celebration if I ever heard it." They ate in silence for a few minutes. "What's next?"

"I'm going to finish the book I started on Hank and BlackWing. It would be great if I could sell it, but if I can't...." She shrugged. "I'm going to write my dad's biography."

Cathy froze, her cup of chocolate midway to her lips. "Are you sure you're ready to do that?"

"I think I have to do it. I've given it a lot of thought. Writing the book will help me come to terms with what happened, so I can get on with my life. I need to ask the questions I was too young to ask when he died. I hope, once I have the answers, I'll be able to move on. Either way, I have to learn to live with being Melody Ravenswood, and everything that means. Hank says he can live with it. But I'm not sure I can."

"What do you mean?"

"I grew up in fear of being discovered by the paparazzi, and to hear my mother tell it, musicians will break your heart. If I'm to use her life as an example, and I have, then she makes a good case. But, being around Hank and the other band members, I've learned some things, and I can't help but question the way I was brought up. My mother is going to have a cow if she starts seeing my name in the papers, but it's what I have to do. I have to find out who I am and deal with it."

Cathy offered Melody another doughnut and took another one for herself, too. "What do you expect to find?"

"I know what happened to my dad, and there's no way around the fact he was coming to see me when his plane crashed. I'm just wondering why our family was in that situation in the first place. You know, my parents never divorced, don't you?"

"I think I remember hearing that."

"Yeah, well, I, for one, want to understand why. Maybe if I dig into my father's life I can figure out why my mother and I lived the way we did. It was almost as if we were in the witness protection program or something. I didn't know any better when I was a kid. As an adult, I can see it wasn't normal. I need to know why."

"What if you put yourself through all this soul searching and heartache and you still can't face a life with Hank? What will you do?"

Mel swallowed hard, trying to force a bite of doughnut past the lump in her throat. There was too much on the line. Failure was not an option.

"I don't know. But it's past time for me to confront my mother, and even Uncle Jonathan about what happened. Hiding from it all these years hasn't done me any good. It's time for me to confront it, head-on."

Cathy placed a reassuring hand on her arm. "I'll be her for you. Just tell me how I can help."

She squared her shoulders. "You can call me Melody for starters. It's my name, and I'm going to start using it. Only two people have ever called me by my name. One of them is gone, and I pushed the other one away. I'm going to get to know the first one, and I'm going to get the other one back."

Cathy embraced her. "Oh, Melody, I'm so happy for you. You're going to be all right, I can see it. You and Hank are going to be so happy." She sat back. "You aren't going to drag him off to England to live, are you? I want you both to stay here in Willowbrook."

Melody laughed. "No. I plan to fill his big old farmhouse with kids. Lots of them. Hank thinks we can live here without too much media attention. I hope he's right."

"I'm sure he is. So, how are you going about this return to the living?"

"I quit my job at the Gazette the other day. I'm going to Boston to interview some people about BlackWing, and I'm going to finish the book. It's almost done. After that,

I'm going to confront my mother and Uncle Jonathan. I'll interview everyone else I can think of who knew Daddy. I'll probably spend quite a bit of time at Ravenswood, getting to know who he was, interviewing people he knew there. I may even stay there and write for a while."

"What about Hank? Where does he fit into your plan?"

"I can't be with him right now. I have to get my head on straight first. If I don't do it while I've got the courage, I probably never will. He's got to finish the album, and they're going on tour soon. In January or February, I think."

Cathy's eyebrows shot up. "So soon? He just got back."

"Yeah. I don't know how they're going to get the CD out so quick, but that's what they're planning. I think Uncle Jonathan is going to tour with them."

"So, Hank's going to be on the road anyway?"

"Yes. And while he's on tour, I'm

going to find Melody Ravenswood.”
“I wish you all the luck, girlfriend.”

CHAPTER TWENTY-SIX

She waited until late Friday afternoon to seek out Hank, hoping the video crew would be long gone by the time she reached the farm. Telling Hank about her plans would be hard enough. She had no desire to do it with a camera in her face.

Hank let her in—though he didn't appear too happy about it. She followed him into the living room where he muted the television and plopped onto the sofa.

"Where is everybody?" she asked.

"Took the weekend off. It was either that or resort to murdering each other." His weak smile suggested he wasn't kidding. After spending weeks with them, she understood. Tensions sometimes ran high and though ideal in many ways, the close confines of the farm didn't allow for a lot of personal space.

"Sounds like a good idea."

Silence descended between them. Melody glanced around the room. A squashed juice box sat under a chair, and children's books were stacked on every flat surface. Her gaze landed on Hank. He leaned on the arm of the sofa, one ankle crossed over his knee, staring at the silent television.

She wrung her hands. What had she expected, anyway? There was no one here so he had no need to pretend everything was all right between them.

"Hank."

He looked at her. The blank expression on his face almost sent her running. He wasn't going to make this conversation any easier for her. Okay, then.

"I came here to tell you something."

"I'm listening."

"I've been doing a lot of thinking lately, about us, about me…my life. I have no right to ask you to wait for me to get my act together, but I wanted you to know I'm working on it. I've made some changes, and some decisions. I've taken my name back. I'm Melody Ravenswood again. I've changed it on everything. My bank account, my driver's license, everything. And I have a plan."

Silence.

"Do you want to hear my plan?"

"Does it end with you marrying me?"

She wished she could say it was a certainty, but she couldn't. Instead, she opted for honesty. "It's my goal."

He nodded. "Okay. What's your plan?"

The longer she talked, the hotter his blood boiled. He ground his teeth and forced himself to appear calm on the outside. *Hear her out. Don't jump to conclusions.*

"So…that's my plan," she

concluded with a sigh.

Seriously? She calls that a plan? He stared at her and silently counted to ten. Exploding in a fit of rage wouldn't get him anywhere.

He cleared his throat and willed his voice to a conversational tone. "What about us? I didn't hear anything in your plan about us being together while you work through your issues." *Not one single goddamned word.*

"I need to do this by myself, Hank. When we're together, I can't think straight. It would be too easy for me to hide behind our relationship, use it as an excuse to ignore everything else. I can't see anything else when I'm with you."

He stood and paced across the room, keeping his back to her while he tried to rein in his anger. She might as well have taken a kitchen knife to his gut. His stomach cramped and his knees threatened to give out.

What if she didn't come back?

What would he do then?

A band tightened around his chest, and he fought to bring air into his lungs. He had to reach her, make her see what she was doing.

He faced her. "I'm proud of you for taking the steps you have. Taking your name back is big. But please, don't do cut me out of your life. I want to be there for you, but I can't help you if you leave."

She stood, but as if an invisible barrier separated them, she remained across the room, cold and distant.

"I'm sorry. Please don't think you don't matter. You do. More than anything. I love you, and I want to be your wife."

He ran a trembling hand through his hair.

"You're everything to me," she said. "Can't you see? I have to do this for myself, for us. If I can't learn to live with who I am, I'll never be able to live with who you are, who we would be together."

His heart knocked against his ribs. What could he do to convince her to stay? There was only one thing he could think of. Desperate, he laid his last card on the table. "What if I quit? Retire. I can after the 'Melody' tour. I've been thinking about if for a while. I don't need the money. I need you."

She shook her head, and his heart sank.

"You told me once you couldn't change who you were. You can't give up your music any more than you can give up breathing. I won't ask you to try. All I'm asking is you give me some time to figure out who Melody Ravenswood is before I become Melody Travis. I don't want to begin a new life with all my past hanging over my head. I need to understand what happened to my family, what happened to me."

He stared at her, searching for a crack in her veneer. But she'd made up her mind, and nothing he might say was going to change it. He tucked his hands in his pockets in an effort to appear casual, as if she hadn't just gutted him.

"So this is it? You're leaving?"

She took a single step toward him, and he took an answering step back.

"Please try to understand." She held her hands out to him, palm up. "I'll be back, I promise. I love you."

"How long? How long am I supposed to wait? I don't understand why we can't see each other while you get yourself together."

"I'm coming back. I don't know how long it will take me, but I *will* be back. I know I don't have any right to ask you to wait, so I won't ask. But I *will* beg. I'll plead. I'll get on my knees if I have to."

He closed his eyes and took a deep breath. "I told you once, and I'll say it again so you know it still stands. When you're through running and hiding, I'll be waiting."

CHAPTER TWENTY-SEVEN

Hank felt like he was on autopilot. He ate because he had to. He worked because it was all he had. He tried to sleep, but his mind inevitably went back to the last time he saw Melody, and sleep eluded him. He lost count of the number of nights he walked the fields or sat under the big oak in the backyard until the sun painted the eastern sky. One day bled into the next, an endless cycle he could neither speed up nor stop.

Through Jonathan, he learned she had left town, but if her guardian knew where she had gone, he didn't say, and Hank didn't ask. He concentrated all his flagging energy on his work. There were only a handful of tracks still to record. He cursed his decision to record "Melody" last, wishing it had been the first, or sometimes wishing it would go away completely. For years, he had anticipated the day he would record that one song, and now it hung like a crippling stone around his neck, dragging him down into an abyss of loneliness and despair.

In the final week before tracking "Melody," he sequestered himself in his office. Words and notes flowed from his soul, through the electronic keyboard, and to the computer program that transcribed his creation into sheet music. In the past, his music had kept him sane, but these days, he turned to out of desperation, purging the crippling emotions in the only way he knew how.

Two weeks of hell.

Musicians hired for the background work crowded the small studio. Hank studied the daily chart in his hands. Today would be the usual complete run through before breaking the song down into its various parts.

"No. This is wrong," he said, interrupting Randy's read-through. "'Melody' was never meant to be sung this way."

All eyes turned to him. He pushed away from the wall, more sure of his decision since he'd made the first move toward implementing it.

"What do you mean?" Randy asked. "We discussed the process and everyone agreed on the schedule."

"I changed my mind. The original recording was one track, and this one will be, too…at least for the piano and vocals. I want everybody out. I'm going to do the song one time and one time only. You can record whatever you want for the background, but the primary track is a single take only."

"Hank, do you think that's wise?" Randy asked.

Wise? No. "It's the only way I'll do it."

Chad rose from his position on the

floor. "Okay, everybody out except BlackWing, Randy, and Sir Jonathan. Everybody else clear out, take a break."

When the room emptied, he turned to Hank. "Don't we have a say in how we record the song? We have a lot riding on the CD, too, you know. We've been here all summer, working our butts off and putting up with your foul mood for most of it. Where do you get off making these kinds of decisions without us?"

Chad had a point, but "Melody" was Hank's song. He knew he was right—he just needed to make them see it, too.

"Okay, you decide. Let me do it my way. You can stay in the control room and listen. If you don't agree with the first take, I'll do it your way. What have you got to lose? If I get it on the first try, we all get out of here that much sooner, maybe a week instead of two."

Hank waited while they put their heads together and discussed his proposal. When they reached a decision, Chad stepped forward.

"I hope you know what you're doing," he said. "You have one shot to get it right. If it's anything less than perfect, we start over, and you do it until its right. Agreed?"

"Agreed. But if I get it the first time, I'm out of here. I'll leave it up to the rest of you to finish the tracks any way you see fit. I trust your judgment."

Randy sent for the sound technicians who checked and rechecked the mic and equipment.

"Do you want a click track?"

"No. I'll sing it live."

"Okaaay," Randy said, clearly skeptical.

Hank took his place at the piano. He pushed everything but the song from his mind. *One take. One last chance to make her see.*

Randy cued him from the control room. "Ready when you are, we're recording in three, two, one."

He closed his eyes and absorbed

the complete silence for the span of a heartbeat. The melody came to him, sweet and haunting. His love for Melody filled his heart until it overflowed. The piano keys were cool to his touch. Love spilled across the keys and his heart sang.

There was nothing in his world but the music and his love for the woman he had lost. He played as though in a trance. Eyes closed, his fingers flew across the keyboard, bringing the melody to life.

His fingers slipped from the keys, and his shoulders slumped. The piano wires quivered their last, and silence once again filled the room. He opened his eyes and turned to the control room. "Am I done here?"

In that breathless moment, Hank understood the plight of the accused awaiting the jury's verdict. Life or death. Which would it be?

Jonathan's eyes met his through the glass. His lips edged up in a faint smile and delivered his verdict with a nod of his head. A measure of relief flooded his system. Jonathan knew or at least suspected what he had just done. In the poker game of life, he'd just gone all-in.

Randy's voice came through the speaker. "You're done."

Pushing the piano bench back, Hank stood and faced the men on the other side of the glass partition. "The orchestration is on the computer in my office. I'll call in a few weeks."

He left the barn, stopping long enough to pet Betty Boop and kiss her on the head. He climbed into his pickup and drove away. Cool air blew from the dashboard vents, cold against his sweat-soaked skin. He drove along the winding Farm to Market roads of North Texas, and with each passing mile, he breathed a little easier. Finding freedom in action, he turned toward the airport.

Melody wanted time to find herself, and he intended to let her have it, but she couldn't keep shutting him out. His actions today staked his claim. Now it was up to her.

Would the song bring her to him, or was he destined to see her in court when she sued him for breach of contract? Either way, he'd done what he had to do.

**

Melody spent her last few weeks in Willowbrook in a frenzy of activity. She wrote for hours at a time, pausing only to eat so she could continue. She arranged interviews in Boston, and when she should have been sleeping, she laid awake, thinking of Hank. And in the deepest part of the night, she sat at the kitchen table with her laptop and made a list of questions she wanted and needed to ask her mother.

She jumped for joy when an agent in New York called and asked to see her. She scheduled her trip to Boston via New York, turned the house over to Jonathan, and left Willowbrook.

The trip proved even more difficult

than she had imagined. In the small world of New York publishing houses, her name was instantly recognized, and it didn't take long for the tabloid media to find her. Everywhere she went a horde of paparazzi and RavensBlood fans followed her. On the advice of her agent, she moved from her hotel to an apartment owned by the agency in a high-security building on the Upper West Side.

She watched the daily spectacle with cool detachment. She'd done nothing to earn her celebrity status. But by accident of birth—and accident it truly was—she was newsworthy. The fact she'd been virtually off the planet for the last sixteen years added to the insane curiosity surrounding her re-emergence on the world stage.

Her book sold to a publisher quickly—perhaps in part because of her name. But as it turned out, an authorized book on BlackWing, and Hank Travis in particular, was marketable. If millions were willing to buy their music, it followed those same people would buy the book.

She left the details to her agent and snuck out of the city on a commuter train headed for Boston. She took a cab from South Station to her hotel and from there, contacted the people on her list. Having sold the book, she needed to finish it.

She spent the next several weeks interviewing Harvard professors and administrators who remembered BlackWing in their early years. She visited clubs and venues where they appeared, and interviewed other members of the fraternity where they got their start. Boston was unfazed by her celebrity status. No one alerted the media of her presence even though they were aware of the attention she'd drawn in New York. Her face was on every tabloid at every newsstand. If she'd seen it, she knew the people she interviewed had seen it, too.

The last person on her list to

interview was BlackWing's agent and promoter, Guy Nichols, and he was in New York. She caught the midday train to the city. As always, when she stopped working, her thoughts were with Hank.

He would be in the studio tracking "Melody." A flutter of unease tripped through her system, but she fought for control and won. Closing her eyes, she rested her head against the seat back and remembered those panic-filled minutes in the studio months ago when he presented his two versions of the song for her. Her mind played the lover's version over and over. The rolling rhythm of the rails lulled her, and she slept.

She took a cab from Penn Station to the apartment where she greeted the doorman warmly before taking the elevator to her floor. She checked her watch and decided it was still early enough to contact Guy Nichols. To her surprise, he answered the call himself.

"I've been expecting your call.

Hank told me about the project and insisted I cooperate fully," he said. He agreed to meet her at the apartment the following day and asked for her address, which she gave. "You're not in the penthouse?"

She laughed. "I wish! No, I'm in apartment 10D," she reiterated. "Tomorrow at noon. I'll provide lunch for your trouble."

**

"Glad to have you back, Mr. Travis." Jimmy, in his elaborate navy blue doorman's uniform, held the heavy glass door open for Hank and followed him into the lobby. "I figured you'd be coming into town pretty soon."

"Yeah? Why?"

"Word on the street is there's a book coming out about you, and since you have an aversion to reporters, I figured you'd be here soon to put an end to it."

Whoa! Had he missed something?

"How do you know about the book, Jimmy?"

"The author's been in all the papers, Mr. Travis. She blew into town a couple of weeks ago, and next thing you know, the rumor mill has it she's shopping a book around about you. She says you authorized it, even cooperated with her. I wouldn't blame you if you did. She's a looker all right."

"Where did you see her? Did they print her picture?" Warning bells clanged in his head.

"Yeah, she's been in the paper, and she's staying here in the building. She was gone for a week or two, but she came back a few minutes ago."

His heart skipped into an irregular beat. "You didn't let her into the penthouse did you?"

"Oh no, Mr. Travis. No one gets up there except the people on the list, and Ms. Ravenswood isn't on it," he assured Hank.

"Which apartment is Ms.

Ravenswood in?"

"10D."

Hank peeled a hundred dollar bill off the stack of currency in his pocket and, smiling, pressed it into Jimmy's palm. "Thanks for the information. I'd appreciate it if you didn't tell anyone I'm here, especially Ms. Ravenswood."

He received the assurance he expected and headed for the private express elevator that would take him to his apartment. As the cubicle ascended to the top floor, he cursed his luck. He knew Melody had planned a trip to Boston, but he'd never considered she would come to New York.

The elevator door opened into the apartment. He went straight to the telephone and rang Jimmy.

"Is everything okay in your apartment, Mr. Travis?"

"Everything's fine," he assured, "but I need a favor."

"What can I do for you?"

"I need everything you can dig up

for me on Melody Ravenswood since she came to New York. Maybe you could find some old newspapers lying around? There's an extra hundred in it for you, and did I mention I want it all ASAP?"

"No problem, Mr. Travis. I'll get right on it."

Hank took a hasty shower and donned clean clothes from the wardrobe he kept there. Jimmy delivered a stack of papers, promising to bring more as soon as he found time to go through the ones in the basement destined for the recycler.

Later in the evening, he brought up another stack of back issues, and Hank made the grateful doorman another offer. "I'll make it worth your while if you'll keep me informed of the comings and goings from Ms. Ravenswood's apartment. I want to know who comes to see her, when she leaves, where she goes, and how long she's gone. I want to know anything you can find out."

"Sure thing, Mr. Travis," he agreed.

Hank made a mental note to see the doorman received an extra large holiday bonus, including tickets to their next New York concert. He could even throw in a few backstage passes for good measure.

The next day Jimmy called to tell him his agent was on the way to Melody's apartment.

"Did you tell him I was here?"

"No sir, but he asked if I'd seen you today."

"What did you tell him?"

"I didn't exactly lie to him. He asked if I'd seen you today, and I told him I hadn't, which is true. I haven't *seen* you today."

Hank laughed. "Good job, Jimmy. I don't want you to have to lie, but evasion is okay, I guess. If he asks point blank if I'm here, don't lie."

CHAPTER TWENTY-EIGHT

Melody arranged the sandwiches and pasta salad on the dining table and tweaked the flatware into soldier-straight lines while she waited for Guy Nichols. She planned to feed him first—her preferred method of interviewing—and ask questions after his stomach was full.

The doorman called to announce Mr. Nichols was on his way up, so, when he rang the doorbell she was prepared to meet him. She wasn't prepared for the thunderstorm he carried on his shoulders.

"Ms. Ravenswood." His voice was cold, far from the friendly person she'd spoken with less than twenty-four hours earlier. "Where's Hank?"

Her mouth dropped open, and she

stared at the middle-aged man bellowing in the entryway. He was well dressed in a charcoal gray business suit with a striped tie. His thinning hair was cut in a typical boardroom style. If not for the angry flush of his face, he reminded her of Hank in an older sort of way. He could easily pass as Hank's uncle.

"I don't know," she stammered. "Willowbrook, I suppose. Why?"

He took a step closer and wagged his finger at her. "I don't know what you're up to, but if you know where he is, you better tell me. You won't get any interview out of me until I know what's going on."

She edged around him cautiously and closed the door before they drew attention from the neighbors. "I don't know what you're talking about. Hank is supposed to be at the farm tracking 'Melody'. Isn't he there?"

"No, he's not. He left yesterday, and no one knows where he went."

Her heart skipped a beat before it lodged in her throat. "Why did he leave? Where did he go?"

His shoulders slumped, and he seemed to crumple before her eyes. "I'm sorry, Ms. Ravenswood. I thought you would know where he was. Apparently, Hank finished his part of the tracking and just walked away. He said something about calling in a few weeks. I need to find him, make sure he's all right. I don't know what's going on, but I feel responsible for these guys. It worries me he just disappeared like that."

He was right to be worried. It wasn't like ultra-responsible Hank to walk away from the recording, even if he personally, was finished. "Do you have any idea where he went?"

"My first thought was he'd come to the penthouse, but the doorman says he hasn't seen him. He could be anywhere in the world. With that gosh-awful haircut of his and his nerd clothes, he can go anywhere he pleases without anyone giving him a second look."

She smiled. "Don't forget the

reading glasses."

They shared a moment of laughter. "Are you talking about the penthouse in this building? Is that why you asked me yesterday if I was in the penthouse, because Hank owns it?"

"BlackWing owns it. When you gave me the address, I thought he might have let you use the place."

"I didn't know about the penthouse. Hank never mentioned it to me. My apartment belongs to my literary agency. They suggested I use it because the paparazzi have been hounding me since I came to the city."

"I understand. Under the circumstances, I can't stay for lunch. I've got to see if I can find Hank."

She walked with him to the elevator. "Please let me know when you find him."

"I will. Don't worry. I'm sure he's fine. We'll reschedule the interview once I find him."

Guy stepped into the lobby. A delivery boy walked past him and approached the doorman.

"Delivery for Hank Travis."

He changed direction and told the boy, "I'm Hank Travis. How much do I owe you?"

He paid the named amount, plus a generous tip, and turned to the doorman. "Haven't seen him? I hope he ordered enough for two." He headed to the private elevator, turning before he stepped inside. "Don't tell him I'm coming. I want to surprise him."

When the car reached the top, Hank stood waiting in front of the elevator door.

Guy frowned "Damned doorman. I told him not to call you." He brushed past him and headed to the kitchen.

Hank helped himself to the burgers and fries in the bag. "Jimmy is loyal to the almighty dollar. You should have tipped him better than I did." He handed his uninvited guest a burger in a greasy paper wrapper.

"Have one. I was going to eat them both myself, but I can share."

Guy took the offered burger. "It's the least you can do. I turned down lunch with a damned fine looking woman for you. You owe me a lot more than a cold, greasy burger."

Hank took a big bite, chewed and swallowed. "How is Melody?"

"I suppose your damned nosy doorman told you I went to see her. Does he tell you everything that goes on in the building?"

"No. Only what goes on in regard to Melody. So, how is she?"

He took a bite before answering. "As I said, she's a beautiful woman. Is she for real? I mean, she really is his daughter, isn't she?"

Hank wiped his hands on a paper napkin. "Yeah, she is. She calls Sir Jonathan Youngblood, Uncle Jonathan. Can you imagine?"

After lunch, Hank led the way to the family room. Guy settled into the overstuffed sofa. "Why did you leave? Chad called me. They're worried about you."

Hank shifted to sit on the edge of his chair, hands clasped, elbows propped on his knees. "I was finished. I'd done my part. They can wrap it up without me."

"You're missing the point, Hank. Chad told me they were going to finish without you, but you walked out on a recording session and you didn't tell anyone where you were going. It isn't like you. They were concerned. Hell, after Chad's phone call I was ready to put out an APB on you myself."

Hank slumped back into his chair. "I'm sorry. I'll call and let them know I'm okay. I just had to get away for a while."

Guy nodded. "Did you know Melody was in New York?"

"No. I knew she was going to Boston, but it never occurred to me she would be here, much less in our building."

"I think I'll take her to dinner tonight to make up for ditching the lunch interview. Why don't you join us?"

Hank crossed the room to the bank of floor to ceiling windows. Waves of heat made Central Park into a living impressionist painting. "Thanks, but no. I told her she could have as much time as she needs. If I show up tonight she would think I was pushing her."

He thought about the track he'd just recorded. Yeah, he'd be pushing her soon enough as it was. "Hopefully, she'll be in a better frame of mind in January. If not, I'll probably lose her forever."

"What do you mean by that? What's happening in January?"

"I want you to promote the hell out of 'Melody.' The release date is January fifteenth, and it's not negotiable. I want it on every radio station, in every market across the country." He paced the room, thinking out loud. "I mean *every* market, Guy. Big and small. How are the plans coming for the tour?"

After talking business for nearly an hour, Hank walked Guy to the elevator. "Keep an eye on her for me, will you? She says she needs to be alone, but I want to know she has someone to turn to if she needs it."

"I can do that. Wouldn't she call on Sir Jonathan, though?"

"Probably. But just in case, make sure she knows she can trust you, too."

**

Mel's phone rang, startling her. Seeing Guy Nichols on the caller ID, she breathed a sigh of relief.

"Did you find him?"

"Yes, I did," he said. "I'll tell you what I know over dinner tonight. How's that sound?"

As soon as he arrived to pick her up, she peppered him with questions.

"Where is he?" she asked. "Did he say why he left the farm?"

"He didn't say, just said he was fine and wanted a few days off. I guess the house full of people finally got to him. He sounded all right. I wouldn't worry about him."

Thank God.

"I'm glad he checked in with you," she said as they walked to the elevator.

"Me, too." He pushed the elevator call button. "Ms. Ravenswood, I owe you an apology for leaving you in a lurch this afternoon. I should have known he would call me, but I overreacted. I upset you, and I'm truly sorry. Can you forgive me?"

She stepped into the elevator. "There's nothing to forgive, Mr. Nichols. You were worried about someone you love, and I understand that. Hank is lucky to have an agent who cares as much as you do."

"Thank you. Please call me Guy. Mr. Nichols sounds so old."

As the elevator bounced to a stop at the lobby level, she decided she liked Guy Nichols. "And you can call me Melody. I think we're going to get along just fine, Guy."

Lost Melody

She stepped into the lobby. "Where are we going for dinner?"

His private car dropped them at a posh restaurant in the Meat Packing District. The Maitre d' escorted them to a quiet table on the Mezzanine, where Melody could conduct her interview with a degree of privacy. Over a beautiful meal of Lobster Salad and Duck, she asked her questions. An hour later, the waiter removed her empty plate.

"Thank you for the wonderful meal," she said, and sipped the hot chocolate she'd ordered for dessert. "You must come here often to receive such excellent service."

Guy sipped his coffee. "I come here fairly often. Thanks to BlackWing, I enjoy a standard of living I never thought to aspire to. It was a lucky day when I ran across them. Don't get me wrong. From a financial standpoint, I've been more than lucky, but from a personal standpoint, I've been blessed. I love those guys as if they're my own boys.

I've just got the one daughter, and they're like sons to me, every last one of them."

"Can I quote you on that?" she teased.

He sat up and, placing his forearms on the table, he leaned toward her. His face was solemn. "Yes, you can. And I'll do anything to see my boys are happy. Anything. I think you can make Hank happy. If there is anything at all I can do to help you, you just let me know. Anytime, day or night. I'm here for you."

"Thanks, Guy. I want Hank to be happy, too. For the record, I love him. If you talk to him again, you can tell him I haven't forgotten what we talked about and assure him I'm working on it. He'll understand."

He sat back, relaxed once again. "I'm glad to hear that. He's waited a long time to find the right woman. Whatever it is you're working on if I can help in any way, don't hesitate to call."

CHAPTER TWENTY-NINE

Mel arrived in San Diego on a beautiful, early fall day with no marine layer in sight. Her hired limo drove north along the sparkling coastline to the house she had rented on the La Jolla cliffs. After the crowded streets of New York, she looked forward to the quiet of the coast for a few months. Most of the tourists had gone, the gold-flecked beaches would be empty except for the diehard locals and surfers.

The house turned out to be everything the realtor had promised over the phone. The Spanish-style architecture gave a lazy, laid-back feel to the property. Terra cotta roof tiles and beige stucco walls complemented the rugged coastal landscape. Lovely, well-tended gardens surrounded the house on all sides. They filled the yard with vibrant color and soft, sweet floral scents. The vanishing-edge swimming pool appeared to drop off the cliff into the ocean. Steep wooden steps descended the cliff face to the beach below if she wanted a more challenging swim in the cold waters of the Pacific.

She spent her first afternoon unpacking and getting to know the house she planned to call home for the next few months. She ate her dinner on the patio where she could enjoy the sound of the surf and the mild ocean breeze. After the summer of controlled chaos in the recording studio and a few hectic weeks in New York, the solitude was relaxing. She lazed in the garden and watched the seagulls soar against the backdrop of sparkling ocean and the setting sun.

Her mother lived just up the coast in Encinitas in the same house Melody had grown up in. She called her mom to let her know she was fine and she would drive up to see her on the weekend. She wanted a few days to adapt to West Coast time and to establish her new work schedule.

Her time was hers to do with as she pleased. She swam in the pool in the morning, wrote for several hours. After lunch, she walked on the beach before returning to her computer for a few more hours of writing, stopping as the sun began to set on the western horizon. She loved the quiet backyard where she would sit and watch the sunset. After dinner, she returned to work, or if her creativity was low, she simply sat outside and listened to the surf crash against the shore.

The first week passed quickly, and to her surprise, she made remarkable headway with the book. Her only regret was Hank wasn't there to share it with her. She thought of him constantly. Beneath her contentment swirled the ever-present loneliness and heartache of missing him.

As the weekend approached, she dreaded the visit with her mother. She'd always been close to her, growing up in what was for all intents a single-parent home. However, underneath the close bond lurked a festering undercurrent of distrust she needed to come to terms with. Her mother never wanted to discuss her father and never mentioned his death if she could avoid it.

Melody wanted to build a life with Hank. His parents' marriage was by all accounts a model for the perfect life. Hers was anything but. In order to live with Hank in his bi-polar world of rock stardom and small town farmer, she needed to understand the forces driving her fears and lay those fears to rest.

She rented a car and made the short drive up the coast.

Nothing has changed.

The modest family neighborhood existed in its own bubble of reality, where children still played on front lawns and drove Barbie cars along the sidewalks. It was a neighborhood filled with PTA moms, scout leaders, and Sunday school teachers. The residents mowed their own lawns and tended their own flowerbeds. Everyone knew everyone else, and holidays were celebrated with bike parades and potluck dinners in the park around the corner.

Her mother knelt on a foam cushion, spade in hand, weeding the front flowerbed. She dropped the tool and her gloves, rushing to grab Melody in a huge hug. She returned the affection, genuinely happy to see her mother despite the serious reason for her visit.

They eased apart, and her mother took her by the arm, pulling her along behind. "Let's go in and have some tea. I want to hear all about this Hank Travis who wants to marry you. I can't believe you'd get involved with a musician after everything I've been through."

She stiffened at the mention of Hank's proposal. She never should have told her mother about it in the first place. Her mother's reference to her own suffering, with no mention of her daughter's, hadn't gone unnoticed either.

She forced herself to relax and allowed her mother to drag her through the house to the kitchen. She sat at the work island while her mother fixed a pot of tea. Melody hadn't ever thought much of it before, but she realized brewing tea was a skill her mother probably picked up from her father. It was as good a place to start as any, and it might keep her mother away from the subject of Hank.

"Where did you learn to brew tea so well?"

Her mother, Diane Harper Ravenswood, finished pouring the hot water into the teapot before turning to her daughter. Her lips were thin, but she managed a slight smile. "You came here to ask me about your father, didn't you?"

"Yes. I need to know, Mom. Don't

you think I'm old enough to hear the truth?"

Her mother sighed and placed the teapot, cups, and saucers onto a tray. She added a plate of homemade cookies and a crock of honey. "Let's take our tea out on the patio. We'll be more comfortable there."

She held the door for her mother and followed her out. A trellis covered with wine-colored bougainvillea in full bloom shaded the area. Her mom poured the tea as neatly as any lady of the manor.

"Cookie?"

To be polite, she selected a cookie and set it on her plate. *How many tea parties did Mom put on for my friends and me? Hundreds, at least.* The memory brought a genuine smile to her lips.

"You're remembering the tea parties, aren't you? I used to love seeing you with your friends, all dressed up in your frilly dresses, playing at being grown up. Thanks to your summers spent at Ravenswood, you could put on a passable British accent your friends were always trying to mimic. I was sorry when you no longer wanted to have tea parties."

Melody remembered bitterly why she'd quit having the parties. The one on her tenth birthday had been the last. "They were fun for a while."

"Yes they were." She sipped her tea and set the fragile cup back on the saucer. "What do you want to know, Mel?"

"For one, why don't you ever call me Melody?"

"Your father named you. I wanted to name you something normal, but he insisted. When you started school, I knew if you went by your real name, it wouldn't take long for someone to figure out who you were. Once that happened, you'd never have a moment's peace, so I registered you in school as Mel Harper. Of course, the school principal knew who you were from your birth certificate. She didn't want the notoriety for her school, so she agreed to keep it quiet."

She sensed her mother was still holding back. At least she was willing to talk about a few subjects, but clearly, she wasn't going to get much further today.

She rose to leave.

"Wait. I've got something for you." Her mother left, returning a short time later with a stack of scrapbooks. "It's time to pass these on to you. I started keeping clippings about Milton long before I met him. You can learn a lot about him and the kind of life he led by reading these. Don't make the same mistake I did, Mel…Melody."

She stared at the huge stack of scrapbooks, all filled to capacity and bulging with newspaper clippings, magazine articles, and photographs. Stunned, she said the only thing that came to mind. "Thank you. I'll take good care of them and return them to you when I'm through."

Her mom laid a hand on her arm. "They're yours. Keep them."

Mel loaded the binders into the backseat of her car. She pulled to the curb around the corner from the house and sat until she was steady enough to continue back to La Jolla.

Back at home, she sorted the scrapbooks into chronological order. It would probably take a year or more to read them all, she guessed. She changed her daily routine to include an hour or more each evening to pour through the books.

Her mother was thorough in her obsession. Diane Harper had been infatuated with her late husband many years before they met. Some of the clippings dated back to when her mother was in high school, and Hamilton Ravenswood had begun to make a name for himself in the world of Rock and Roll music. She'd saved articles and photos from every kind of print media. There were clippings from *Rolling Stone, Tiger Beat, 16,* and even *Parade,* the magazine insert in the Sunday newspaper. There were glossy, color magazine photos, and grainy tabloid clippings. Melody was overwhelmed with the sheer quantity as well as the fanaticism the collection testified to.

In many of the early photos, her father was in the company of one beautiful woman or another. She recognized many of them as actresses and models popular a few decades ago. Some still maintained a degree of success after all the intervening years. As she read, she jotted down names in the event she might want to interview some of them for the book she was more determined than ever to write.

She studied the photos, seeing her father as a young man just coming into his adult years, fresh out of Cambridge, and thrust onto the world stage. She lined up a few of the better ones in chronological order. It was easy to see the maturing process he'd gone through. From the first, almost shy, candid shots to the posed publicity shots, there was a natural progression of confidence and arrogance as his talent matured along with his celebrity. Undeniably handsome man, it was easy to see how her mother had become infatuated with him early on. How she became his wife was a mystery still to be solved.

One evening, she gathered several of the paparazzi shots of her father with various models and actresses and studied them closely. It took her some time to pinpoint what bothered her about the photos. Then it became clear. In all of them, Hamilton Ravenswood was not touching his partner. The women hung off, or leaned against him. His hands would be in his pockets, wrapped around a drink or anything but his date. The women gazed adoringly up at him, but his eyes were always on something or someone else. She scribbled down a few more names, certain she would interview at least a few of them to learn if what she'd noticed indeed had been going on at the time.

Hank's biography neared completion, and the holidays were fast approaching. Not a day passed she didn't think of him in a way that had nothing at all to do with her writing. She ached to be with him, to hear the sound of his voice, to touch him.

The day after Halloween, BlackWing announced their new tour. It was to begin in New York's Madison Square Garden on Valentine's Day. The six-month long tour would stop in eighteen cities across the country, ending with Dallas in August.

Guy Nichols was doing his job, and doing it well. She couldn't listen to a radio station, watch television, or drive on the freeway without seeing or hearing an advertisement promising tickets would go on sale January sixteenth. She was tempted to call Guy and ask who had chosen the date, the day after her twenty-seventh birthday, and seventeen years and one day after her father's death. She was afraid she knew the answer to whom, and even more, the reason why.

She spent Thanksgiving with her mother, their relationship more strained than it had ever been. Mel dried the last pan her mother handed her and returned it to the cabinet. She leaned against the counter, waiting for the next one. "I'm going to New York next week. I've finished the book, and my editor wants it before Christmas. She asked if I could come and meet with her and some of the people I'll be working with."

Diane continued to scour the pot submerged in the soapy water. "Will you be coming back here? You know I want you to be here for Christmas. I've invited Jonathan to come, too."

It was the first Melody had heard about her mother's plans, and she didn't bother to hide her surprise. "Did he accept?"

"Yes. He said he'd love to come. I

think he may be bringing someone with him. Who do you think it is?"

"I have an idea, but it's probably not who *you* think it is. My guess is he's bringing his new girlfriend, Miriam Wallingford. You'll like her, Mom. I think he's fallen for someone."

"You don't think he'll bring Hank Travis?"

"No, I don't."

"So, what's Miriam like? Tell me everything you know." She handed the clean pot to Melody to dry. "How did they meet?"

It was a safe subject, and she really didn't have much to tell. She had been so wrapped up in her own troubled relationship over the summer she'd hardly noticed what her Uncle Jonathan had been doing.

CHAPTER THIRTY

Hank returned to the farm and filled his time helping with the cotton harvest. He welcomed the dawn-to-drop work schedule that kept him too busy to think about Melody more than a thousand times a day.

He let his hair grow. By February, he would once again be the man his fans paid to see. In the past, the ritual elicited excitement, but lately he could hardly stand the sight of himself in the mirror.

After the harvest, he turned to his music, sequestering himself in the barn for long hours composing and practicing. Plans were under way for the new tour and details requiring his attention poured in daily. Conference calls with the other band members and hours of discussion, compromise and negotiation added to his workload.

In addition, there was the mixing. Since he lived closest to the mixing studio in Dallas, it fell on his shoulders to monitor the progress of the CD. Highest priority was given to mixing "Melody," and he was relieved when he approved the final product. Guy assured him the single would hit the airways across the country on January fifteenth—Melody's birthday.

As the days flew by, each one bringing him closer to the release date, he questioned his decision over and over again.

He spent Thanksgiving with his father and Sir Jonathan, who still resided in Melody's house. They were four at the table. Jonathan brought along Miriam Wallingford, who Hank suspected was the real reason he remained in Willowbrook.

"What are you going to do for Christmas?" Sir Jonathan asked Henry.

"For the last few years we've gone skiing in Colorado. Are we going again this year, son?"

"I bought our tickets, and I reserved the same condo we had last year. I thought it worked out pretty well. You could ski right up to the chair lift from the front door."

"Why don't you two come along," Henry asked the other couple. "There's plenty of room."

Jonathan shook his head. "Thanks for the invitation, but Miriam and I are going to San Diego. Diane asked us to come, and I told her we would."

"Is Melody there?" Hank asked.

"I don't know. Diane didn't say, and Melody hasn't called me in months."

Hank nodded. "I haven't heard from her either. You'll let me know how she's doing if you see her?"

"Sure. She'll be in touch soon," he assured.

"Thanks." He hoped Jonathan was right. Every day Melody didn't call or even email, he felt her slipping further away from him.

**

    Sir Jonathan answered the doorbell. "Hank. It's great to see you." He held the screened door open. "Come in."

    He stepped into Melody's living room. "Thanks. I should have called first," he apologized.

    Jonathan waved him to a chair. "No need. I was just sitting here wondering what to do next. So…what brings you my way today?"

    "I was hoping you could deliver something to Melody for me." He pulled a small box wrapped clumsily in red Christmas paper from his coat pocket. "If she's at her mother's, will you give her something for me?" He passed the gift to Jonathan.

    Jonathan weighed it in the palm of his hand. One eyebrow rose, questioning. "Is there something in here?"

    He smiled. "Yeah. I'd rather not

say what it is, but you won't get arrested at the airport for carrying it."

"Well, that's good." Jonathan laughed. "I'll give it to her." He turned serious. "How are you doing?"

"I'm okay, I guess. Could be better." He leaned forward and rested his forearms on his thighs. "Can I ask you something?"

"Anything."

"I'll understand if you don't want to answer."

Jonathan nodded. "Okay, ask away."

"How did you feel when you retired? What was it like to walk away from the business like you did?"

Jonathan set the present for Melody on the table. "Are you thinking about retiring?"

Hank sat back in his chair. "Yeah. I've been thinking about it for a while. I just don't know if I can do it. What was it like?"

"You have to understand, I didn't walk away by choice. When Milton died, a part of me died, too. We'd been as close as brothers, and his death hit me hard. It hit us all, knocked the wind right out of us. So we walked away. You're talking about walking away in the prime of your career. Do you think Melody will come running if you quit? And if she does, will you be able to live with yourself and your choice?"

"I don't know. Sometimes I think I would do anything to have her in my life, and then I try to imagine what I would do with myself if I quit, and I can't see it. The thing is, I don't know if I can continue performing without her. But on the other hand, I may never have her if I don't walk away from it."

"I can't tell you what to do. You remind me of Milton when he was your age. You have a talent as big, maybe bigger than his. His life was cut short by circumstances beyond his control. But I can tell you this, he had to make a similar choice once, and it nearly ended his career. I watched him struggle with his decision for months, and from his struggle came the best piece of music he ever wrote. Eventually, he came to accept that he'd made the only decision he could, and he lived with the consequences every day after that."

Hank nodded in understanding. "Thanks. I still don't know what I'm going to do, but I appreciate you telling me the story. I don't know about the talent thing, but I'm not stupid enough to argue with Sir Jonathan Youngblood. So, I'll just say thank you for the vote of confidence."

"You're welcome. For what it's worth, I think she'll come around. She loves you. No doubt about it." He paused. "Can I ask you something?"

"Sure."

"She didn't approve that version of 'Melody,' did she?"

"No."

"Has she heard it?"

"I played it for her once. I promised her no one would ever hear it.”

“You’re taking a big risk, son.”

“I know, but it was the only thing I could think of to make her see what she means to me.”

Jonathan shook his head. “I don’t know if you’ve made a wise decision with the song, but it’s a bloody masterpiece, in my opinion. If she sues you over it, I’ll be happy to testify in your defense.”

“There you go again with the flattery, and I may be calling on you to testify, so don’t be surprised.”

“It’s not flattery if it’s true, and I would be surprised if she sues you. She may never speak to you again, but I doubt she’ll take legal action.”

Hank stood and zipped his coat. “I’d rather she sue me than quit speaking to me. At least if she takes me to court, I’ll get to see her. It could take years to sort it out in the court system.”

Jonathan stood, too. “You could probably drag it through the system in two countries if you put your mind to it. It could go on for a lifetime."

Hank smiled. "Good to know. I'll hang onto that happy thought. Thanks again."

CHAPTER THIRTY-ONE

Melody took care of her business in New York then spent a few extra days shopping and enjoying the holiday decorations. She stood in line to glimpse the elaborate window displays at Saks and Macy's. She bought gifts for her friends in Willowbrook and arranged to have them wrapped and shipped. For her mother, she purchased a beautiful jewelry box and a pair of diamond earrings to place inside as an extra surprise.

Strolling in the Chelsea Art District, she found the perfect gift for Hank in the window of a small gallery on W. 25th Street. The oil painting, in the impressionist style, depicted a couple and a black dog walking along a dirt road. Their destination, a small brook, could be seen in the distance. Summer heat all but shimmered off the painting, relieved by the cool blue water hinting at relief from the relentless sun.

A woman exited the gallery and approached her. "Are you okay?"

"Yes, yes, I'm fine." Focusing on the artwork she could see through the window, she asked, "Do you work here?"

"I'm Sunny Sheldon. Sunnyside is my gallery. Would you like to come in?"

She glanced once again at the painting and nodded. "Yes, I would. I want that painting." She pointed to the summer scene.

Inside, she fell in love with several of the artists' works and bought one for herself and the one in the window for Hank. She handed over her credit card and arranged to have the paintings shipped.

"Are you *the* Melody Ravenswood?" She handed the

credit card back and slid the charge slip and a pen across her desk.

Melody froze. Of all the purchases she had made in the last few days, this woman was the first person who had actually noticed the name on her card. "Yes, I am."

"Don't worry, I won't tell. I know what it's like living in the shadow of a legend. My father is Curtis Sheldon, the actor."

Her matter-of-fact speech put Melody at ease. "Oh! I love his movies. I guess you *do* know what it's like. I've just recently gone public. I've been trying to hide for most of my life. Well, my entire life actually. I'm not used to being recognized."

"I've been living with the notoriety since the day I was born. You get used to it, sort of. But there are a few things you can do to minimize the intrusion in your life. I'd be happy to give you some pointers."

"Would you? I need all the help I can get."

"Are you free tonight? I know a

great restaurant…”

**

Melody almost didn't recognize her new friend when she arrived at the small restaurant in Hell's Kitchen. Sunny had changed out of her business suit into jeans, a black turtleneck sweater, and Ugg boots. Her long yellow-blonde hair was hidden under a knit cap. She had transformed from the sophisticated gallery owner to just another busy shopper in Manhattan. She blended in seamlessly.

Sunny talked about what it was like growing up the daughter of a well-known movie star. Her mother wasn't part of the business, much like Melody's, and the women quickly found many areas of common ground. Sunny was two years older than Melody, but had a lifetime of experience dealing with being the offspring of a celebrity.

"I admit, I'm probably not as

newsworthy as you are," Sunny said, "but I've found if you act like a non-celebrity, the world treats you like one. I don't do anything to draw attention to myself...unless I'm in the market for attention, say for a charity event. Otherwise, I dress like everyone else. I keep a low profile, and when there is something newsy going on in my life, I smile for the cameras and let them take all the pictures they want. I go to great pains to make sure I'm as dull as dishwater the rest of the time, and they leave me alone. In other words, I hide in plain sight."

"I don't know how well it would work for me," Melody said.

Sunny shrugged. "You're big news because you just popped back up on the radar. Given what you've told me about the way your father died, there's going to be some interest about you ever so often. My advice? Give them what they want. A few photo ops, release a statement through a publicist, lay low somewhere, and they'll go away. Think about it. It's the same people in the tabloids all the time."

"I guess you're right. There are lots of people you never hear anything about."

"That's because they don't draw attention to themselves, and if someone wants a photo, they smile and let them take one. The tabloid photographers are trying to make a living. Give them something to sell once and awhile, and they'll be a lot nicer to you. Like I said, there are certain times when they might come hunting for you, but if you're proactive, you can manage them to suit you."

"You've given me something to think about," Melody admitted. "I just wish the interest would die down."

"It will. Give it time. But if you just go about your business and smile for a camera once in a while, then when you want some publicity for the book you wrote, the media types will be more likely to give you good press."

Lost Melody

**

Melody scanned the crowd of holiday travelers at San Diego's Lindbergh Field, looking for familiar faces.

"Uncle Jonathan," she cried. "It's so good to see you." She threw her arms around him as he stepped off the escalator.

He returned her hug. "Hello, luv. I've missed you. You remember Miriam don't you?" He reached for the woman accompanying him. She'd been right about Jonathan's traveling companion, and though she hadn't had a chance to get to know Miriam yet, she couldn't be happier for Jonathan. It was about time he found someone who recognized what a wonderful man he was. She only hoped Miriam had the fortitude to stick it out once Jonathan's career got back into full swing. He'd need a strong woman by his side.

Melody smiled at the older

woman. "Sure I do. I'm so glad you could come." She gave her a warm hug. "Let's get your luggage. You'll be staying with me. My house is larger than Mom's, and she's agreed to have Christmas dinner there as well."

While they waited for the luggage at the carousel, Jonathan pulled Miriam close. "Melody, we have a surprise."

"Oh? Am I going to like it?"

"I hope so, luv." He gave his companion a little squeeze. "I asked this lovely lady to marry me, and she said yes!"

Happiness radiated off the couple like the midday sun reflecting off the ocean. Melody embraced them both. "I couldn't be happier! When's the big day? Are you going to have a big wedding? Am I invited?"

"We'll tell you everything." He grabbed their bags off the carousel. "Let's get out of here first."

Later, sitting on the patio sipping champagne, the happy couple regaled Mel with their plans for a fall wedding in Willowbrook. After they were married, they planned to split their time between England and Texas, spending summers at Ravenswood, and winters in Texas.

She was genuinely happy for them, but she secretly wondered if Miriam knew what she was getting herself into. Christmas Eve, she walked alongside the older blonde on the beach, enjoying the sunshine and the soothing sound of the surf. She couldn't contain her curiosity any longer.

"Miriam, are you ready for the kind of public life Uncle Jonathan leads? After the 'Melody' tour, he's going to be in demand as much as he ever was. The paparazzi will be everywhere, even in Willowbrook."

The older woman continued walking as she chose her words. "I appreciate your concern, but I've given it a lot of thought. I love Jonathan more than anything. Being with him means more to me than my privacy does. Besides, the reporters won't be inside our house with us. We aren't going to do one of those daily life reality shows or anything. Jonathan assures me when he's not on tour, he plans to lead a rather quiet life. The paparazzi follow the people who insist on throwing themselves into the limelight. We have no intention of doing that."

"What about the times when you'll be out in the social whirl? Uncle Jonathan said he wanted to get back into the business, which means public appearances and even more tours maybe. How will you deal with all of that?"

Miriam's voice relayed confidence. "We'll handle it together. I'll stand by his side and he'll stand by mine. I won't hold him back, if that's what you're concerned about. He's an incredibly talented musician. If he wants to share his talent with the world, I wouldn't hold him back, but the rest of him is mine and mine alone."

"I wasn't concerned about you holding him back. I don't think you could, even if you tried. He's come out of his self-imposed retirement, and I'm pretty sure he won't be going back anytime soon. I'm really glad he'll have you by his side. I think you'll be good for him. He's been alone for a long time."

"So have I. I was married once, a lifetime ago. We weren't together very long before he was taken from me. We didn't have any children, something I always wanted. That's past both of us, but we'll have each other, and I hope we'll have you, too. I know Jonathan thinks of you as a daughter."

"He's been a father to me for almost seventeen years. I love him with all my heart. That won't ever change." They stopped at the wooden staircase winding up the cliff face to her house. "I'm glad you'll be staying at Ravenswood part of the year. The summers there are beautiful."

Miriam hugged her tight. "Thank you. I can see why Jonathan loves you so much. I'm honored to be part of your family."

Melody's mother joined them for dinner and stayed the night so they could get an early start opening presents the next day. Melody woke to the smell of coffee and bacon. She found her mother and Miriam laughing and working together. Diane regaled Miriam with stories of Jonathan during the years they toured together with RavensBlood.

Melody took a seat at the counter and nibbled fresh fruit from a prepared platter while she listened to the stories, none of which she'd ever heard before. Jonathan joined them. He helped himself to coffee and added his own anecdotes.

She'd never heard her mother speak so openly about her time with RavensBlood. It was a side of her mother she didn't know, and one she desperately needed to understand. She listened attentively, noting the easy way she and Jonathan interacted, the story telling seesawed back and forth between them as they each told their side of the story. Contrary to what she'd always believed, it became clear her mother had enjoyed her time as a backup singer. Why then had she always discouraged her daughter from pursuing music—even to the point of banning her father's music in their home?

She followed the couple to the family room after breakfast to open presents, so she put her questions aside to enjoy the moment. Jonathan handed her a small package.

"Hank sent it," he said.

She carefully unwrapped it. Inside was a folded note and, beneath, a beautiful gold chain and a gold-plated house key. She read the brief note.

The key to my heart.
The key to our home.
Love, Hank.

She looked up to meet Jonathan's sympathetic gaze.

"He asked me to bring it to you."

She closed her fingers around the key. "Thank you. It means everything to me. He's well? You've seen him?"

"I've seen him. He's surviving."

Her heart lurched. *Surviving.* Getting by. Just like she was.

She hung the key around her neck and pressed it close to her heart. "I know it's hard for him. It's hard for me, too, but I have to resolve these issues in my own way. I hope he understands."

Jonathan stood and held his hand out to her. "Let's go for a walk."

She followed him down the steep staircase to the beach and across the sand to the wet surf line.

"The man is crazy about you," he said. "You have to know that."

"I do. I'm just so messed up right now I can't think about being with him the way he needs me to be."

"What's wrong, luv? Can I help you?"

They strolled along the surf for a few minutes before she answered. "I have a lot of things to work out for myself. I've made a decision, and I hope you can help me with it."

"Anything. You know I'll do anything for you."

With Hank's biography at the editor's, she had no reason to put off the next step of her plan any longer. She took a deep breath and let the words flow out with it. "I'm going to write a book about Daddy. A biography."

Jonathan stopped in his tracks. "You don't have to do that."

She took another step and turned back to him. "Yes, I do. Mom has done her best to shelter me from the media, from life. Even to the point of not telling me my own father was dead. I wasn't allowed to listen to his music growing up or take piano lessons. I don't understand any of it, Uncle Jonathan. I need to make sense of it before I can move on. Don't you see? Hank leads the same kind of life you and Daddy did. It scares me because I don't really know anything about his life. I need to. I need to understand why Mom sheltered me so much."

He stared out across the ocean. Melody waited for him to speak.

"Okay. Talk to your mother first. I'll answer all your questions after you talk to her."

"Okay." She nodded. "I'm going to Ravenswood to write it."

"When?"

"I'm going to talk to Mom next week. So, the first week of January maybe. When you see Hank, will you tell him I love the gift, and I understand?"

He gathered her in a fatherly embrace. "I will. Let's go see if we can find a pot of tea in your lovely kitchen."

She clung to him as they walked back the way they'd come, sharing the peaceful solitude of the beach.

CHAPTER THIRTY-TWO

Melody checked the batteries in her voice recorder and threw it along with several extra tapes into her bag. To remind herself why she was delving into the past, she wrapped an unsteady hand around the key hanging from a chain around her neck.

I can do this. I have to do this.

She took a deep breath, hoisted the heavy bag to her shoulder, and grabbed her car keys from the hall table. The most direct and fastest route to her mother's house was by freeway, but she chose the more scenic Highway 101—a small, two-lane road winding along the northern San Diego County coastline, through beach communities and a state park.

She drove with the windows down. The fresh, salty sea air teased her hair and helped clear her head.

Her attitude would set the tone for the interview. She needed to focus and be firm in her commitment to the project. She needed to set her personal issues aside and listen with the ears of a reporter, not the frightened, lonely child still living inside her.

Melody sat at her mother's kitchen table and pulled out her voice recorder and the note pad where she'd written down her list of questions. She tried to put aside the fact she was interviewing her own mother and focused on getting answers.

Her mother sipped her tea and set the fragile china cup back on the saucer. "What do you want to know?"

"Everything." Melody turned on her recorder. "Let's begin with your obsession with Earl Ravenswood when you were in high school."

Her mother's eyes widened and

she paled. For a second, Melody regretted the harsh tone she'd taken. The last thing she wanted to do was insult her and loose her cooperation entirely.

Her mom reached for her tea, raised the cup and set it back down without taking a sip.

"You don't pull any punches, do you?"

"I'm sorry, but you were obsessed. The scrapbooks you gave me are evidence enough."

She nodded. "You're right." She mopped at the counter with her napkin then focused on something across the room.

"I saw Milton on television. RavensBlood had their first hit, and they were big news in the United States. The local television station was at the airport when they landed. That was before they had jet ways. They rolled stairs up to the plane…." She closed her eyes and a smiled. "He stepped out of the plane, and I fell in love with him."

She sighed and looked at Melody. "It was more than a teenage crush. I'd had plenty of those. What I felt for him was different. I knew with every cell in my body he was the man put on this planet for me."

Hours later, her mother's voice was strained, and Melody was on information overload. That it all had to do with her parents only made it harder to comprehend.

"Let's pick up again tomorrow afternoon, Mom. Okay?"

"I suppose," she answered.

Melody shut off the recorder and closed her notebook.

"I love you, Mom. Thanks for talking to me. I know it can't be easy for you."

"I knew I'd have to answer for my decisions some day. I'm glad it's you I'm telling. I know I can trust you to preserve some sort of dignity for me."

Melody smiled at her. "You can count on it, Mom. I won't lie, but I don't have any desire to make you into a pathetic figure. You weren't, you know. Sometimes, we just know when we see someone that they're the one."

Later that evening, Melody went over her mother's words. She had taken one look at Milton Ravenswood when she was sixteen and had known he was the one. It was stupid and impossible for a junior in high school to conceive of ever getting close enough to someone like him, much less hope he would see her in the same way. Nevertheless, she set in motion a plan that would forever change her life—and his.

At seventeen, barely graduated from high school, she'd set out to meet the then twenty-three-year-old musician, using her adequate singing voice to open doors for her. By a stroke of luck, she'd landed a job touring with RavensBlood as a backup singer. Her parents had been devastated and disowned her for publicly embarrassing them.

It hadn't mattered to her mom—or to the object of her obsession.

Hamilton Earl Ravenswood fell as hard for Diane as she had for him. It hadn't been just her mother's obsession talking. Jonathan had confirmed her story months ago.

So, she knew her parents' marriage had been love match, but getting pregnant hadn't been part of the plan.

Melody had hours of tape where her mother had described the whirlwind year she'd spent on the road with the band. She related stories about the roadies, the groupies, and the drugs and alcohol so many used to make it through the demanding schedule of performances and media appearances. She talked about the endless travel, hotel rooms, and constant demands for her husband's time. Their personal time together had whittled down to those few precious hours in the middle of the night after a performance and before the real world awoke. Then he'd done interviews with the local media before the band boarded a plane or bus and headed for the next venue.

She described the man she loved, his sense of humor, his incredible talent, the passion he had for music, his need to perform—to have that connection with an audience. Through her mother's words, Melody came to know her father more as the man he had been, rather than the icon the media portrayed him as.

Sleep eluded her. Images, thoughts, and questions raced through her mind. There was much more to hear, more truths to uncover, more roads to travel on her journey to understanding.

The next day was more exhausting than the one before. Her mother attempted to explain why she'd chosen not to live with her husband and raise their daughter as a real family. Melody tried to comprehend, but as the child who had been denied daily contact with the father she loved, she found her mother's reasoning less than convincing.

"If you were going to let him sing to me every night, why not just live with him? I don't understand. If you loved him as much as you say you did, what was the problem?"

Her mother hesitated. "I couldn't stand it. I hated the traveling. I hated everything about the business. I had a fantasy he would love me enough to give it up. Maybe not music all together, but at least the touring. And we'd go live somewhere, just the two of us. I realize how selfish and childish it was, but I was just barely eighteen when I became pregnant. When I told Milton and he insisted on marriage, I thought he would quit then. But he didn't... wouldn't."

"What did you do?"

"I told him I was leaving, that I wasn't going to raise you on the road. He argued, but he knew I was right. That was no way to raise a child. He let us go. He provided everything we both could possibly need, money, a house...everything. Then, he wrote *that song* and started calling every night to sing to you."

Melody reached for the teapot in the center of the table and refilled her mother's cup and her own. She added a lump of sugar to hers and stirred.

"Why did you help him?" she asked. "It began long before I was able to actively participate."

"I loved him so much, and because of the song, I was able to talk to him every day. He loved me, but I'd become third in line behind you and his music.

"He used to sneak into town when the band was on the West Coast. He'd come to the house after you were in bed and watch you sleep."

"I didn't know...."

"Those summers you went to Ravenswood when you were older? I stayed in a house a few miles away. He still loved me, but he said it would only confuse you if you saw us together."

Did he love you, or did he tolerate

you in order to see me? How much of what you're telling me is your fantasy, and how much is reality?

"What happened the night he died?"

She had never heard her mother's version of the events, and knowing how much her mother had loved Milton Ravenswood, she wondered at the lack of emotion in her mother's voice. The retelling was flat, a practiced recitation of the facts, minus the part where she let her daughter's birthday party continue after she'd received the news of his missing plane.

Had her mother withheld the information in order to protect her daughter or to punish her because her husband had loved Melody more than her? It was an insidious thought, and one that had haunted her for the last seventeen years.

It was me he was coming to see. It's my fault he's dead. Do you hate me for taking him away from you? She couldn't bring herself to ask. Time to change the subject before she found out more than she wanted to know.

"Why didn't I have piano lessons? Why didn't you let me listen to music? Given your own musical background and Daddy's, I would think you would have wanted me to explore my musical talent if I had any."

Her mother surprised her again. "Oh, I knew you had talent. I suppose you've figured it out for yourself."

Melody nodded.

"Music took Milton away from me. I didn't want it to take you, too."

Melody reeled at the bitter and pathetic tone of her mother's voice. A pattern of manipulation for selfish purposes had begun to emerge, and she wondered why she hadn't seen it before.

"I wasn't going anywhere, Mom."

CHAPTER THIRTY-THREE

Ravenswood wasn't the most hospitable of places in the winter, especially for someone who had spent the last few months in the tropical clime of San Diego. The manor house, built in the eighteenth century, was cold and uninviting, but Melody loved it all the same. Except for the few people employed to keep the place from falling down, she had the house all to herself. For six summers she could remember, she had run through the hallways, followed her father like a faithful puppy, and basked in his love and undivided attention.

At night, he had tucked her into bed and sang to her.

She hadn't been back to

Lost Melody

Ravenswood since her father's funeral. Her mother had refused to let her go, even when Jonathan had offered to make the trip to San Diego and accompany Melody. Mired as she had been for so many years in her own guilt, she hadn't argued. Seeing the place through the eyes of an adult, she was capable and ready to understand the man who had loved her so much.

She paused in the music room where she'd spent so much of her time with him. Memories rushed over her, and she crossed to the grand piano and sat on the padded bench. She lifted the cover with trembling hands. The keys gleamed in the light from the chandelier overhead. She tapped one key and another, tentatively testing the instrument. She took a deep breath and let it out. She began to play.

She experimented with random melodies—anything that sprang to mind.

With the music came memories of

summer afternoons spent with her father sitting at the piano. Her small fingers scrambled to keep up with his strong ones. They mostly played children's ditties, but occasionally he encouraged her to try more complex arrangements. She realized they were his own compositions, and she wondered if he had committed them to paper or if they were forever lost.

Her days fell into a rhythm of writing, playing the piano, and exploring the house.

Shortly after her father's death, Jonathan had moved into the house and taken over Milton's office for his own. He had stored all of his friend's personal papers in tightly sealed boxes in the attic. Every day she discovered something new, and in little increments grew to know her father better. By extension, she learned about herself, too.

Hank was never far from her thoughts. Sleep came easier. Dreams of Hank had replaced the nightmares she had experienced since her father's death.

The more she learned about her father the more it became clear why she had fallen in love with Hank. The two men shared many common likes from their love of music to their love of nature, reading, and business.

On a day she couldn't get Hank off her mind, a package arrived at Ravenswood. The small box contained a CD and a slip of paper containing a short note written in Hank's bold handwriting.

Happy Birthday, Melody.
I love you.

No signature. No plea for her to return. It was the first time she'd heard from him since Christmas when he had sent the key with Uncle Jonathan. The CD was probably an early cut of the new album—a polite gift because she had been involved with the recording and nothing more. She turned it over, looking for anything to make it more personal. Nothing. Just a blank jewel case.

For the first time since her return

to Ravenswood, she sought out the small recording studio her father had built in the basement. She located the CD player and put in the disc. The first notes filled the air, and she sank like a stone into the control room chair.

Hank's voice filled the room. She closed her eyes, remembering the spring day when he had played "Melody" for her. She recalled every line of his face—the raw emotion as he sang those words and put his innermost feelings on display. His love wrapped her in a blanket of contentment.

The song ended, and she pressed the play button again. The second time, she forced herself to listen with a degree of detachment. Why had he sent her another CD? She had the only copy, didn't she? Then she noticed the orchestration, the background tracks. The soaring violins, the seductive clarinet, other strings and voices rounded out the recording.

Her heart pounded against her ribs. Her lungs fought for air, and tears formed twin rivers down her cheeks. *How could he? He swore he wouldn't record it. How could he betray me?*

She wrapped her arms around her midsection and rocked back and forth until she had no more tears.

In the cold clear light of morning, she wondered if it was too late to stop him from releasing it. A phone call from Sunny confirmed her worst fears. The song was on every radio station across the country, and the reaction was unanimous. It was a hit.

As the day wore on, she realized she wouldn't be able to fight him. Even her mother had heard it and understood the implied message. It didn't take a genius to figure out to whom the song referred. After many tries, she got a call through to Jonathan.

"Happy Birthday, luv," he said.

"Uncle Jonathan! What is going on? Did you know he recorded this version of 'Melody'?"

"Hank is desperate to get your attention, and yes, I knew about it."

"Did you know about it at Christmas?" She sighed. "Of course you did. He recorded it in August. I can't believe you went along with him. I thought I could trust both of you. I was wrong."

"Have you really listened to it? Even if you don't like being the recipient of the sentiment you have to admit, it's a damned fine piece of work. I didn't think anyone could sing that song better or with more feeling than Milton, but somehow Hank has done it. It's the same song. He didn't change a word, but he changed the meaning entirely. Its bloody genius, is what it is."

"I know. He played it for me months ago, and he promised—no, he *swore* no one would ever hear it if I didn't agree. And I didn't agree, Uncle Jonathan. He lied to me. What we have—*had* between us is ours. It's private. He stands to make a fortune from that song. I don't think I can get past that."

Jonathan explained about the scholarship fund, how the money would to go to help music students pursue their dreams, and that he agreed to match the money with a donation of his own.

"Listen to it again," he said. "Really listen this time. I've never heard a more beautiful love song in all my years. He did it for you. *You* inspired that kind of love. Take it from someone who knows how hard it is to find. Don't let a love like that get away."

"I can't listen to it again. If he really loved me, he wouldn't have lied to me."

Heartbreak manifested itself in the form of headaches severe enough to keep her in bed for days at a time with the drapes drawn against the gray winter light. She hardly ate. Sleep was once again an elusive dream she needed but couldn't find.

Her research came to a standstill.

On the days she managed to get out of bed, she played the piano. She had found stacks of handwritten sheet music in the attic, but she didn't know how to read it, so she simply made up songs to suit her mood, which alternated between rage and melancholy. The piano keys became her therapist. She expressed her deepest emotions and thoughts through the music.

Slowly, she pulled herself together and resumed work. She moved a stack of papers one morning and found the note Hank had sent with the CD. She reread the few short words, crumpled it in her fist, and tossed it into the wastebasket.

Why had he done it when he had given his word? Why hadn't he *tried* to explain?

There was one piercing pain no amount of music would alleviate. He hadn't called.

CHAPTER THIRTY-FOUR

The Chelsea Art District was lively and colorful, and Hank loved it on sight. He'd been to New York countless times, but never to this part of town. Leave it to Melody to discover a gem in a barrel of rocks.

A bitter January wind blew through the tunnel of buildings, and he wished he had thought to grab a heavier coat before he'd ventured out. Huddled against the elements, he studied the gallery window.

The works on display varied from ultra-modern—which he couldn't understand—to beautiful and simplistic realism. Beyond the window, a lovely blonde woman sat at a glass-topped desk near the back of the store. She appeared to be the sole occupant—not surprising considering the holidays were over and the weather inhospitable.

He entered the store, and she stood and stepped around the desk. Smiling, she extended her hand. "I'm Sunny Sheldon. Welcome to my gallery."

He pulled off his glove and took her small, fine-boned hand in his. Her skin was soft, her manicure perfect. Her hair and makeup were flawless, and her suit fit her as if it had been made just for her—and probably had been, he noted. She was a high maintenance woman if he'd ever seen one, and despite her radiant beauty, she wasn't his type at all.

"Hi. I'm Henry. Henry Travis," he said.

Her eyebrows raised slightly, and her hand slipped from his. "Are you in the market for something in particular, Mr.Travis?"

He glanced around the room. "I have a painting by a new artist, and I was hoping you might have some more of her work. It was a gift from my fiancé, and I think she may have purchased it from your gallery."

He named the artist and described the painting. He caught the flash of recognition in her eyes. *For the painting, or does she know who I am?*

"I'm afraid I don't have any of her paintings at this time. She's promised me more in the future."

"Oh well, it was just a thought. I won't take up any more of your time."

"Have a seat, Hank."

He stared at her, allowing her to usher him to a chair facing her desk.

"No need to run off." She returned to her seat. "I promise not to bite. How is Melody? Is the engagement official? I haven't heard from her in days."

What was going on here? "You know Melody?"

She folded her hands on top of her desk. "We met when she came into the gallery last month. The painting she bought for you was in the front window. It struck a chord with her, and she came in to see it. I recognized her name from her credit card, and we found we have a lot in common. Have you talked to her recently? What does she think of the song? It's fabulous by the way. You have an incredible talent."

"Thanks. Uh, no, I haven't talked with her, and no, she hasn't agreed to marry me yet. But she will. I sent her a copy of the song before it was released, but she hasn't acknowledged it." He frowned. "Do you mind telling me what you have in common with Melody? I mean, she's a very private person, so I find it strange she would talk freely with you." At her faintly amused expression, he hastily added, "No offense intended."

She laughed. "None taken. I should have mentioned right away when you didn't recognize my name. My father is Curtis Sheldon, the actor."

It was his turn to smile. "Ah, yes,"

he said, nodding. "Sorry. I guess I'm a little slow today. I've always enjoyed your father's work, by the way."

"I'm glad you didn't recognize me. Like you, I try to remain out of the public eye. Sometimes I succeed, sometimes I don't. Melody and I spent some time discussing how to live under the radar. She's a fantastic person, and I'm glad to call her my friend."

He nodded. "I appreciate you helping her. She needs friends like you. I haven't done a very good job convincing her she can have the life she wants."

"Give her time, Hank. She's come a long way from where she was."

"You're right, she has." He paused.

"Why did you really come here? I don't think you were interested in buying a painting, were you?"

"I don't really know why I came. I just knew she'd been here. I love the painting, but I guess I just wanted to be somewhere I knew she'd been. I know it sounds stupid, but—" He threw up his hands in defeat. "—that's all I've got."

"I wish I could help you," she said. "But I haven't heard from Melody since the day the song was released. I called her as soon as I heard it. I thought she would be over the moon, but I didn't get the impression she was happy about it. In fact, she sounded pissed. Pardon my French."

"Yeah. She's pissed all right. I took a stupid chance, and it backfired on me."

**

Hank wanted Melody back. He could see her, feel her in his dreams. His body ached to hold her. He tried to concentrate on his job, but his heart wasn't in it. What he lacked in spirit he compensated for by taking on additional responsibilities for the upcoming tour.

The days passed slowly. He

hounded Sunny for information about Melody, and he questioned Jonathan until the older man lost his patience.

"Do I look like her bloody babysitter? She's at Ravenswood. Do us all a favor and go talk to her yourself."

"I'm sorry, Jonathan. I just wanted to know if she's okay. She hasn't even acknowledged the song. I thought at the very least she might file suit to stop it, but she hasn't even done that."

"She's not going to sue. It surprised her, and she's bloody mad enough to take your head off. All she can see is that you lied to her. You knew what you were doing when you recorded the song so you've only got yourself to blame."

Hank stood and rubbed the back of his neck. "I know. I thought when she heard it, she would understand how much I love her and come back. Instead, I may have lost her for good. I wish I could go to Ravenswood, but I can't. I promised I would give her time to get her head on straight, and it's *one* promise I intend to keep— even if it kills me."

"If it doesn't kill you, my friend, someone else probably will, and soon, too. You're taking your frustrations out on all of us, and I can tell you, even your friends are ready to push you under a bus."

"You're right. My troubles aren't their fault, and they shouldn't have to suffer along with me." He met Jonathan's gaze. "Thanks for listening and for the kick in the pants. I owe you one."

"You don't owe me anything. Just find a way to straighten things out with Melody."

He had made a major mistake with the recording and there was nothing he could do to fix it after the fact. He'd broken his word to her, and he might have to pay the ultimate price for it. There was a good chance she would never speak to him again.

He worked day and night. As the opening concert at Madison Square

Garden approached, the infinite number of problems, big and small, was more than enough to keep him busy. No detail regarding the tour was too minute to escape his attention. Guy Nichols and his staff were more than capable of handling the details, as were the professional production crews. The stage managers, tour, and production crews were competent people BlackWing had worked with before, and he trusted them to hire the best technicians available.

As the official representative from the band, he met with every group involved in the massive production from the skilled audio and electrical technicians to the catering and wardrobe crews—not that they needed much more than jeans and T-shirts, but someone had to see to it they had clean clothes. When the truckloads of equipment arrived at the venue, he even found time to meet with the truck drivers, who would haul the equipment from city to city, as well as the bus drivers, who would transport the crewmembers and the band on the shorter trips.

They met the security team as a group. It was important for everyone to know the safety routines and cooperate fully with the experts hired to accompany them for the next six months. Occasionally, fans could become overly zealous, or in a few instances, just plain crazy. No one anticipated any sort of violence, but they were all reminded of John Lennon's untimely demise at the hands of a crazed gunman. He hated the idea of a bodyguard but resigned himself to having one for the next few months. Taking chances was not an option.

Jonathan had sent Melody a ticket for one of the VIP Boxes at their opening concert. Hank hoped she would come, but realistically, he didn't believe she would.

He sent front row tickets to Jimmy the doorman and Sunny Sheldon. His dad, as usual, would be in one of the

VIP Boxes, along with the wives and families of the other band members.

It was a short walk from his hotel to the venue. The air was cold and crisp, and the sky shimmered ice blue above the jagged New York skyline. If Hank could have ordered perfect weather for Valentine's Day, this was it.

When he arrived at the Garden, it was alive with activity. The stage manager issued orders worthy of a five-star general. Audio techs and lighties made fine adjustments to their already precisely installed equipment. No wire or bulb went without inspection. The backline roadies were busy cleaning and tuning instruments, and checking plugs, wires, and amps. He stopped to see how Rick was doing, and while he was there, took a moment to sit on the throne so he could adjust height and distance on the kit.

Hank glanced at the day sheet, noting the times he was needed for the sound checks and wardrobe fittings. BlackWing had never been much for costuming, preferring to focus more on their music than on theatrical gimmicks, so the wardrobe fittings for him consisted of making sure his shirt was clean and his fly was zipped. The wardrobe stylists were necessary, however, for the small group of backup singers, who traveled with the band.

He welcomed the opening band, who was on stage preparing for their sound checks. Handpicked for the gig by Guy, they were an eager group and somewhat dazed by the size and scope of the production they were now a part of. Standing in the center of the stage looking out at the empty arena, he understood their nervousness.

BlackWing had started out small but rocketed to the big time under the expert guidance of Guy Nichols. He hoped the young opening act they'd booked for the "Melody" tour was equally as lucky. They were good and would do an excellent job of warming up the crowd.

Hank walked down the side stairs to the floor of the arena and sat a few rows back from the stage. He watched as they went through their sound checks. He always found the hours before a concert to be a special time, where layer by layer, the excitement built, and with it, his anticipation of taking the stage.

Hank sat in the empty arena and for the first time in his professional life felt—nothing. He grimaced, knowing plain and simple his heart wasn't in it.

The giant screen behind the stage came alive with a view of him sitting all alone. He smiled and waved until they switched camera views. They tested the various cameras placed around the arena. With modern technology, everyone would have a close-up view of what happened on stage. From vocals to drums, they wouldn't miss a thing.

He thought back to Blackwing's early days, playing frat parties and country club dances—schlepping their gear from gig to gig in a rusted out Ford Econovan that probably shouldn't have been on the road at all. They'd come a long way in a short period of time, and he didn't regret a single moment of it. His success was a dream come true, an adolescent boy's fantasy come to life. He still believed in the dream, even if it had lost some of the magic.

The opening band completed their sound check and filed off to await their stage call while the backline techs ran through the line checks on BlackWing's instruments. Hank made his way backstage. The rest of the guys would arrive soon, and it would be their turn.

CHAPTER THIRTY-FIVE

Melody checked again to make sure she had the VIP pass and copies of the news articles she wanted to ask Jonathan about. She touched the gold key around her neck. She always thought living like the "normal" people was what she wanted, and she did. She wanted the quiet small town life Hank offered, but like him, there were times like today when she would have to bow to her status. She wanted to slip into New York, attend the concert without Hank knowing she was there, and quietly slip out of town again the following day. The terse note he'd sent with her birthday CD and his silence since told her all she needed to know. He didn't want to see her, and the wound he had inflicted was still too raw to be poked at anyway.

She'd watch the concert because it was Jonathan's return to the stage and *he*, not Hank, had asked her to be there. Afterwards, she would find a few minutes to ask her questions.

She boarded the private jet that would deliver her without fanfare to New York. As the plane left the winter-gray skies of London behind, she powered up her laptop and tried to put into words the tumultuous emotions churning inside her.

Sunny was waiting for her when she cleared customs. "How was the flight?"

"Long. Tiring."

Sunny's car and driver were waiting for them at the curb. Melody slid into the backseat and sighed. In what seemed like no time at all, she was curled up on Sunny's sofa with a steaming mug of hot chocolate.

"Why don't you take a nap?" Sunny asked. "There's plenty of time before we have to leave for the concert."

"I don't think I could sleep a wink. I'm too nervous. What if Hank finds out I'm there? I'm not ready to face him yet."

"He won't. If we follow Sir Jonathan's instructions and arrive after the opening band is on stage, no one will take any notice. He said someone would be waiting for us, right?"

"Yes. He promised his security guard would meet us at the gate and escort us to our seats. He's supposed to stay nearby, just in case someone recognizes me."

"We should be fine. Go. Lie down for a few minutes and rest, at least."

She rested, but couldn't sleep, so she took a shower and dressed for the concert. She chose faded jeans and a black knit turtleneck. She tucked the gold key under the sweater, the cold metal startling against her warm skin. A pair of comfortable boots and a red scarf completed her simple outfit. Nothing about her attire would draw attention among the thousands of fans crowded inside the arena.

Sunny waited for her in the living room, similarly dressed. Melody argued against stopping in mid-town for dinner, but her friend insisted. Too nervous to eat, Melody only pushed the food around on her plate. Jonathan's security detail was right where he was supposed to be, and a few minutes after arriving at Madison Square Garden, they were at the VIP box where Henry and Miriam had already been seated. Melody introduced Sunny over the deafening sound of the enthusiastic warm-up band.

All eyes in the sell-out crowd were trained on the young band on stage. She wondered how their lives would change when the "Melody" tour was over. To open for BlackWing was a singular honor, and according to her research, several other opening bands had gone on to great success.

The set ended, and roadies

scurried to strike the equipment. BlackWing took the stage. A familiar swagger caught her eye and her heart slammed against her ribs.

Hank.

His hair was longer. He'd dressed in his usual style—worn jeans, sneakers, and a button-down shirt in a shade of green to match his eyes. His shirtsleeves were rolled to expose his muscled forearms, and she didn't need to be any closer to recall the texture of his skin, the softness of the hair dusting his strong arms and hands. Her skin tingled, remembering the feel of his hands playing across her body. Her mouth went dry. With practiced ease, he sat on the throne and picked up the sticks lying across the snare.

Sunny elbowed her in the ribs and pointed to the giant screen behind Hank. Four cameras showed a close up of each band member. The crowd screamed their excitement. The band members adjusted their instruments and microphones, and in unspoken agreement, they turned to Hank.

There was an almost imperceptible nod shared among them. Hank raised his sticks to chest level and tapped out the beat. The band launched into one of their more popular hits, and the crowd roared their approval.

Chad stepped to the microphone, and the crowd drowned out his lyrics. She didn't care if she heard Chad or not. Hank was on stage, and nothing else mattered.

Images from the stage cameras flashed across the big screen. Stationary views alternated with ones from the roving handheld cameras moving from one band member to the next, providing the audience close-up views of everything happening on stage.

There were no less than three cameras on Hank all the time. One hung directly above the drum kit, somewhere in the massive rigging holding the lights and speaker system high above the stage.

Another was low and to one side, allowing a view of his lower body and the drum kit. Still another one must have been in the front of the stage rigging and captured his face.

The band was magnetic. They drew the audience into the music, and in turn, fed on the energy coming from them. Spotlights panned the arena, and the stage lights pulsated to the pounding beat of the music, adding to the electric atmosphere.

She was aware of everything happening at once, but all of it was perceived in her peripheral vision. She focused on Hank and Hank alone. She drank him in. He belonged on stage. In the studio, it had been easy to see how much he loved to play, but here on stage, he was at home. The close-up views revealed a light in his eyes and an unmistakable set to his shoulders.

He loved what he was doing. He loved the music, the screaming fans. She could almost hear the blood pounding in his veins across the distance. From the overhead camera, she watched his hands and arms, the muscles of his thighs bunching as he worked the various foot pedals. Energy and excitement radiated off him in waves and danced across the crowd.

He was magnificent. He was brilliant. She understood how the thousands of women in the arena would be attracted to the men on stage, and raw jealousy pulsed through her.

He's mine!

In a flash of insight, she understood a little of her mother's torment. Another generation of women had felt the same rush of desire for her father at one time. She understood why her mother had wanted to distance herself. How difficult it would be to witness the adoration day in and day out. How hard it must have been for her mother to know so many coveted what she claimed as her own. Her mother hadn't been strong enough.

Lost Melody

She walked away from the man she loved.

Her heart ached for her mother, for the loneliness she endured over the years as a result of her decision. Her mother had been faithful to her father, but was the reverse true? Could any man withstand the type of temptation this lifestyle presented—especially when the woman he loved denied him her companionship? Melody doubted it, but she forced the question from her mind. Hank was different. She was different.

BlackWing alternated their hits with the covers from the new CD. The tempo varied along with the instrumentation. Sir Jonathan joined them midway through the concert to a standing ovation. It was long minutes before the crowd settled enough for them to continue. Melody squeezed Miriam's hand as the older woman watched Jonathan on stage for the first time. She knew exactly how she was feeling, and they shared an understanding glance between them. Miriam would be all right. She loved Jonathan, and judging by the expression on her face, she understood how much it meant to him to be back on stage.

He sang the old familiar lyrics, paying homage to his deep friendship with her father. Her heart swelled with love and pride. BlackWing stepped back ever so slightly and gave him the stage. Jonathan rocked the house. He had lost none of his stage presence over his years of his self-imposed retirement, and the crowd reacted with wild enthusiasm.

After his brief solo performance, Jonathan blended seamlessly into the band, and the concert continued. Her gaze rarely strayed from Hank. She noticed when he reached for a water bottle. She saw when Rick handed him a fresh towel or passed him another set of sticks. She made a mental note to thank Rick for watching out for Hank.

The hot lights along with the physical exertion took a toll on him.

She noted the thin lines of fatigue around his mouth and eyes, but he kept him going. Adrenaline was his drug of choice, and it would keep him going, night after night, for the next six months. No wonder he wanted to live on his farm when he wasn't on tour.

She pictured Ravenswood in her mind and knew it was the place her father sought out for redemption following a strenuous tour. Hank would like it there, too.

The crowd showed no signs of mellowing as the evening wore on. If anything, they grew louder and bolder. They stood in front of their seats, dancing, singing, and waving their arms. The sequence of songs was designed to gradually bring the event to a close. Each song decreased in tempo by infinitesimal degrees. Her heart threatened to knock a hole in her ribcage.

The last song would be "Melody."

The band jammed while the roadies pushed the grand piano to

center stage. A wave of anticipation rippled through the audience. Backup singers and a phalanx of string musicians found their way to the stage, almost beneath notice in their subtlety. By infinite degrees, BlackWing masterfully brought the house under their control.

CHAPTER THIRTY-SIX

The spotlights panned around the arena, and Hank's gaze followed them across the crowd. A spark of adrenaline coursed through his veins and a little of the old excitement built. He owed it to the loyal fans that had paid good money to see them play to do the best he could tonight. Wondering if Melody was among them wouldn't help.

He made eye contact with the other four men on stage and one-by-one determined they were ready. With a tiny nod, he listened for the click track to come through his earpiece.

The beat began. He absorbed it for a moment then brought his sticks up to chest height where the others could see them and counted first to himself, *one, two, three, four.* Then with the sticks—*tap, tap, tap, tap.* They simultaneously burst into the melody of their first song of the tour.

He fell into the beat—allowed it to consume him. Energy emanated from the crowd in rolling waves. He felt, as much as heard, the moment the others recognized it, too. Their playing ramped up to meet the level of the crowd's response, and so it went for song after song. He recognized the adrenaline rush for what it was—a powerful drug that gave him strength he didn't possess.

Where earlier he felt nothing, now he knew it had been deceit on his part. He loved the music. He loved performing, and he loved the enthusiasm from the audience. The wilder the crowd became the more heart and soul the band poured into the music. He would be all right if Melody was never his because he still had his music and he still had the audience. Like an addict with a habit he couldn't kick, he craved the adrenaline rush of being on stage. With or without Melody he would still perform. He couldn't walk away from it for any price.

Sir Jonathan took the stage mid-concert. He'd never heard anything like the crowd's response for as long as he'd lived. A Rock and Roll legend was on stage after a long absence, and the audience paid homage to his talent and genius. BlackWing gave him his moment in the spotlight. He held the crowd in thrall, and like he'd done it a million times, he blended seamlessly into the group. Never in his wildest dreams had he ever envisioned sharing the stage with Sir Jonathan Youngblood.

The sequence of songs gradually set up the finale, and as each blended one into another, he steeled himself for his solo performance. It was one thing to hide behind the drum kit with the cameras flashing close-up views of his face and hands on the giant screen behind him. It was another thing entirely to sit at the grand piano, center stage, while every set of eyes in the house focused on him.

The band settled into a jam session. The roadies pushed the piano to center stage and adjusted the microphones. He continued to play, gently easing out of the mix until the drums were silent. The others continued on, easing out one at a time. Hank accepted a water bottle from Rick. He took a long draw from it and exchanged it for a dry towel. He wiped the sweat from his face and hands and tossed the towel back.

The last of the group eased out and the stage and audience went silent. Hank took his place at the piano. A single spotlight lit him from overhead. Darkness cloaked the backup singers and string ensemble who would accompany him.

He shut out the silence in the arena, focused on the notes and lyrics written on his heart. He straightened, adjusted the microphone. Eyes downcast, fingers hovering over the keyboard, he spoke softly into the silence.

"For Melody Harper Ravenswood. My life. My love."

Her heart skipped a beat, and she automatically reached for the key around her neck. Hank faced the VIP box where she stood, like everyone else in the arena too pumped with adrenaline to sit. Two camera images split the giant screen, one a close-up from overhead of his hands on the keyboard, the other a direct close-up of his face.

His fingertips touched the keys. Love, pure in its simplicity, pulsed across the arena. His deep voice melted over the crowd like the smoothest, most intoxicating, chocolate.

She ceased breathing. Every word, every note, fired across her being. As soul-baring as the recording had been it was nothing compared to what was happening on stage. His voice replaced the life giving oxygen in her bloodstream, sustaining her for those suspended moments in time. Swept up by the magic spell he wove, her spirit soared above the crowd and merged with his on another plane of existence.

The last note faded away, and the stage went dark. Melody collapsed to her knees in the aisle. Her lungs fought for oxygen like a diver breaking the surface of the water. She tried to hoist herself up and heard concerned voices in the fog of her confusion. Strong arms lifted and carried her out of the arena.

Cold winter air slapped her in the face, bringing her out of the darkness enveloping her. A limo appeared, and her rescuer scooted her inside. Sunny, Henry, and Miriam joined her.

"I'm sorry. I couldn't catch my breath," she whispered.

Sunny patted her hand. "No need to apologize. Hank Travis is a vortex.

He sucked the oxygen right out of the arena. There wasn't a woman in the place who was breathing, including me."

The car moved forward. "Where are we going?" she asked.

"That depends on you," Henry said. "If you want to go back to Sunny's apartment, we'll take you there. Or anywhere else you want to go."

"Where's Hank?"

"By now, he's on the bus with the rest of the band. They'll be going to the hotel for the after party."

"Take me there."

**

He managed to stand and make his way across the stage to the drum riser. Rick handed him a water bottle and a towel. He went through the encore on autopilot, wishing they'd chosen any other song besides "One Night" to end with. He remembered Melody's innate reaction to the erotic and suggestive beat. Where "Melody" drained him physically and emotionally, "One Night" had the opposite effect. It aroused him almost beyond his ability to endure.

The stage went dark. Rick was at his side, penlight in hand, ushering him off the platform and across the stage to the stairs. He stepped onto the luxury bus, his home away from home for the next few months. Tonight it would take him a few short blocks to the hotel where they would hold the after party. Everyone was invited to the first one of the tour, from the lowliest roadie to the executives from their record label, Madison Square Garden, and even the Mayor.

He collapsed onto one of the sofas and consciously relaxed every muscle in his body. He instantly fell into an exhausted sleep. Rick woke him when they arrived at the hotel and ushered him through the rear door and into the service elevator. Minutes later, he was in the suite of rooms obtained for his use until the tour moved on to Boston the following week.

He braced against the shower wall and allowed the hot water to wash away his fatigue. The adrenaline rush subsided, and with it, his energy. Hunger gnawed at his stomach, and another type of hunger rose anew. Rick would have a room service meal waiting for him when he got out of the shower to appease one of the appetites. Only Melody could appease the other one, and she was in London.

He shut off the hot water valve. Cold water hit him full force and a litany of explicit curses echoed through the small bathroom.

Rick came through for him with a thick steak, medium well, and a baked potato on the side. The ballroom downstairs would have several buffet tables laden with enough food for an army, but it would be hard for the band members to eat there. They would pose for photos with people they didn't know, accept congratulations from nameless individuals, and make nice with the executives who made it possible for BlackWing to exist. And there were the interviews with the few select reporters.

Invited guests would arrive first followed by the roadies, who after securing the stage, would walk over to the hotel only a few blocks from the Garden. Eventually, BlackWing would be expected to make an appearance. Long ago, they'd figured out it was best to trickle in one at a time rather than arrive as a group. He had every intention of being the last to arrive and the first to leave.

CHAPTER THIRTY-SEVEN

Melody made her way along the buffet table more to silence Henry and Miriam than because of any interest she had in eating. Sunny worked the crowd, drawing attention to herself and away from Melody. The older couple however, hadn't left her side since they'd entered the hotel. She questioned Henry and learned Hank had a suite on an upper floor. He would go there first to clean up before joining the party. She considered trying to get to his room, knew with Henry's help she could circumvent the security, but if she did, he probably wouldn't come down to the party at all, and he needed to make an appearance.

She couldn't lose track of the

reason she was there. She needed to see Jonathan tonight to congratulate him on his successful re-emergence on the Rock and Roll stage and to question him about the articles.

Henry knew many of the executive types in attendance, and he introduced her and Miriam to several. Miriam attracted her share of attention as Sir Jonathan's fiancé—a fact attested to by the enormous rock on her ring finger. She accepted the congratulatory remarks with grace no matter the level of surprise accompanying them. Miriam's presence was a godsend as it served to deflect attention away from Melody.

Sir Jonathan arrived in the company of Chad Winston, who adroitly maneuvered them to Miriam's side. He wore his love for her on his face. He was protective and possessive, inquiring if she needed anything, if she wanted to stay longer or go. Her wish was his command. Miriam stood next to him, fingers entwined with his while he accepted his accolades. She need not worry about Jonathan—he had found the right woman.

A disturbance near the ballroom entrance drew her attention. Hank stood in the doorway. She drank him in.

He was magnificent, from his still damp hair to his crisp tan chinos. He gradually made his way deeper into the room, posing for snapshots and signing autographs as he went. Each step brought him closer to her, and she pressed her hand over her chest where the key lay warm against her skin.

Underneath his relaxed, pleasant demeanor ran an undercurrent of tension. She sensed it first before she noticed the evidence in the slight clenching of his jaw and the way his smile never really reached his eyes. He glanced over the heads surrounding him and made eye contact with his father, and then his gaze shifted to the side. To her.

With no pretense of courtesy, he closed the distance between them. His strong fingers clenched around her upper arm, and he half-dragged her to the nearest door. In the service hallway, he pressed her against the wall, and before the door closed behind them, his lips came down to cover hers.

He cradled her face in his hands. His hard body pressed hers against the wall. She didn't try to resist—didn't want to struggle. She had wanted to feel his touch since the moment he stepped on stage.

He smelled of soap and the musky aftershave he favored. He tasted like Heaven. She brought her hands up to the back of his neck and speared her fingers through his hair, pressing him tighter against her lips.

The door behind them burst open. A man dressed in service attire clambered through with a stack of empty trays. His eyes widened in recognition, and he apologized profusely before scurrying along the hallway to the kitchens.

She dropped her hands to her sides, and Hank shifted his from her face to her shoulders.

"Let's get out of here. I have a suite upstairs. No one will disturb us there."

She nodded in agreement, and he took her hand, lacing their fingers together. He pulled her behind him to the kitchens where he stopped the first person he saw.

"Where is the service elevator?" he asked.

The stunned employee pointed, and a few minutes later, they were on an upper floor of the hotel. He fished a key card out of his pocket and slid it into the slot. The LED flashed green, and he pulled her into the room.

He fused his lips with hers once again, stealing what little breath she had. His hands scorched her skin through her thick sweater. She tugged at his shirt, trying to pull it from his waistband. He released her and took a step back.

She stood her ground while he looked his fill. His gaze, darkened with desire, devoured her. His need for her was evident beneath the pleated front of his slacks, and she reveled in her power over him.

"You look wonderful. I've missed you." His voice was hoarse.

"I've missed you, too."

"Were you at the concert?"

"Yes. I was there for all of it. You were fabulous. You had the audience eating out of the palm of your hand."

He took another step back. "Would you like something to drink? I think I have a mini-bar here somewhere or maybe something to eat? I can call room service."

She took a step toward him and was surprised he took another step back from her. "Hank, what's going on?"

He moved past her into the living room. "Don't get me wrong, I want you like the very devil, I always do. But I'm not sure how much of my wanting you is normal, and how much is still the adrenaline rush. I've always passed on the offers of cheap sex after a concert, so tonight is a first for me."

She stiffened. "You think that's what I'm offering, cheap sex? You think that's why I'm here?"

He ran a hand across the back of his neck, his other fisted in his pocket. "No. That came out wrong. All wrong. There's nothing cheap about what we have together. I love you. I'm afraid to touch you. I would be using you for my own selfish needs."

He shifted on his feet and scanned the room, glancing everywhere but at her. When his gaze came back to her, he let his breath out on a long sigh. "I know it's not the Rock Star image, but I've never had sex right after a concert. Not even in college. I want to know…I *need* to know when I take you it won't be because I'm still on some high I got from being on stage.

It wouldn't be fair to you."

She let her shoulders drop. "Do you want to go back downstairs to the party?"

"God, no."

She walked around him, sat on the sofa, and patted the cushion beside her. "Why don't you sit here with me? We don't have to do anything. We'll just sit here together until you feel more like yourself."

He sat next to her, and she clasped his hand in hers, lacing their fingers together once again. She tugged his hand over so it rested on her thigh and traced lazy circles across the back. He closed his eyes and slid down until his head rested against the sofa, his long legs stretched in front of him. She listened to his breathing grow slow and even.

Even in sleep, his grasp on her hand was firm. His steady pulse beat against her wrist, and she counted the beats. Each one was precious, marking a moment spent with him. She wanted him. She wanted to be with him. She wanted to give him as much of herself as he gave to her.

**

Hank woke in the wee hours of the morning. Melody had shifted in the night, and she lay curled on the sofa with her head in his lap, their clasped hands held close to her cheek. It hadn't been a dream.

She opened her eyes, and he stroked her cheek again. Her skin felt like silk beneath his thumb.

She turned her face to his. Her lips tilted up in a warm smile, and he cradled her head with his free hand, and gently lifting her, dipped his head to taste. She sat up and returned the kiss. He cradled her face in his palms and stroking her cheeks softly with his thumbs.

"Feeling better?" she asked in a husky voice.

"Mmm. Much." He kissed her long and slow.

Easing her onto her back on the

sofa, he came over her, pressing himself against her core, gently at first, then with more urgency. She met his thrusts, silently urging him to speed things up. He had waited too long to feel her beneath him again, and he wouldn't be rushed.

He peeled away the layers of her clothing, worshiping every inch of skin as he uncovered it. When he slid her sweater up over her breasts, he paused. The key he had sent her gleamed against her chest. His heart hammered against his ribs.

She was here. She was wearing the key. It had to mean something. He dared to hope it meant she had come to her senses. "You wore it," he breathed.

"Always."

He pressed his lips to the key, and then he kissed his way down to the twin mounds surrounding it. She moaned and writhed against him. Her hands slid across his broad shoulders and down his back to his firm buttocks. "Too many clothes," she said, tugging at his tucked in shirttail.

"Right." He stood and shucked his clothes in a blur. Before she had a chance to admire all of him he had fished a condom from his wallet, sheathed his erection and rejoined her on the sofa. The man had skills.

His hands and mouth were everywhere, making her desperate to feel him inside her. She was on the brink of begging when he plunged deep inside. Arching against him, she moved her hips in timeless rhythm with his thrusts until the shattering release overtook her.

When she quieted, he increased the tempo. Seconds later, he groaned and ground against her. She held him until he collapsed on top of her. She placed a tiny kiss against his shoulder and mouthed soundlessly against his damp skin, "I love you."

He pushed himself up and off the sofa. Cool air raised bumps on her sweat-dampened skin. "Where are you going?" she asked.

He reached for her hand and tugged her off the sofa. "To the bedroom. We're going to do it right this time."

"I thought we did it right that time," she teased. "I guess I have a lot to learn."

The shrill sound of the phone woke them. With the curtains drawn, it was impossible to tell if it was still dark outside, or if the day had dawned. The conversation was short and one-sided.

"Tell him I'll be right there."

He pulled her close. His lips moved against her neck, sending shivers of excitement down her spine. "I wish I could stay here all day with you, but that was Rick. I'm due at the ABC studios in an hour for satellite interviews. Guy made a lot of excuses for me last night, so I have to show for the interviews."

"I don't want you to go, but I understand. How long will you be gone?"

"A couple of hours. I'll be back as soon as I can. Will you be here?"

"I don't know. I planned to return to London as soon as possible. I came here to talk to Uncle Jonathan. I'm going to leave after I speak to him."

He rolled out of bed, and she instantly sensed the change in his demeanor. He turned away and dug through his suitcase. Gone was the tender lover who had given her so much pleasure.

"Do what you have to do." His words sliced at her. "I want you to stay, but I understand if you can't. You have the key. Use it when you're ready."

He crossed the room, naked, magnificent, and angry.

"Hank!"

He slammed the bathroom door. She scrambled out of bed and followed. She placed her hand on the doorknob and froze.

What have I done?

CHAPTER THIRTY-EIGHT

"Hot chocolate." Sunny set a steaming mug in front of her. She pushed a bowl of fresh fruit and a plate with a croissant across the table. "Eat."

Melody nibbled at the food. It smelled wonderful but held little appeal. She should have stuck with her original plan. Things would have been so much simpler if she had.

"How did things go with Hank?" Sunny asked.

"Good," she lied. "He had to do interviews this morning, so I left."

Her friend eyed her suspiciously. "He let you leave?"

"No. I left when he was in the shower."

Her friend remained silent and the

enormity of what she had done sank in. Going to him last night had given him the wrong impression. She should have avoided him altogether or at the very least told him she couldn't stay. Not yet, anyway.

She raised her eyes and met Sunny's disapproval head on. "Honey, you better get yourself together before you lose him."

"I know you're right. I want to. I'm almost there." She speared a strawberry with her fork and contemplated eating it. She laid the fork down. "After hearing him sing the song I've forgiven him for the sneaky way he went about recording it. But I still have questions I need answered. Believe it or not, I think I may have found the key to everything. Perhaps, two keys."

"What are you talking about?"

"It may be nothing. I need to talk to Uncle Jonathan. If anyone can help me make sense of all the things I've discovered, it will be him."

She called the hotel and connected with Miriam in Jonathan's suite. He too was doing satellite interviews, and Miriam didn't know exactly when to expect him back.

"Can it wait?" she asked. "Last night was long, and he had to get up early this morning. I'd like him to get some rest before tonight's concert."

How could she argue with that? Jonathan wasn't a young man any longer. "It can wait. I'm glad he has you to take care of him," she said. "Maybe tomorrow?"

"I'll tell him. I'm sure he'll make time for you soon," Miriam promised.

Over the next few days, she tried several times to see Jonathan, but Miriam always had another excuse. By Wednesday, she was sure Jonathan was avoiding her. He had time to give interviews to every major network morning show as well as every magazine and radio station in New York but he couldn't find ten minutes to see her. Hank, however, found time to dog her every step.

She wasn't sure when he slept, but she knew when he ate because he made sure she was with him when he did. He escorted her to a matinee of *Mama Mia* and took her to lunch at the Central Park Boathouse.

Jonathan was avoiding her, and Miriam was assisting in the scheme. But why? He couldn't possibly know why she wanted to see him. That left only one reason. Hank had put him up to the charade to keep her in town. She shouldn't have told him she would be leaving as soon as she talked to Jonathan.

Two can play at that game.

She sat in the back of the hired limousine parked near the rear entrance to the hotel. She could see the service entrance over her shoulder and the bus waiting to transport the band to Madison Square Garden for the final concert in New York. Thanks to a delivery truck, the bus driver hadn't been able to get as close to the door as usual, so they would have to walk along the sidewalk a few steps to get to the bus. Melody waited until the security team opened the service door before she stepped out of the car. The security team knew her, and they wouldn't question her presence. All she had to do was convince Jonathan to come with her.

He was the first to exit the hotel, and she moved in beside him swiftly. She wrapped her arm through Jonathan's and drew him in the opposite direction of the open bus door.

"It's okay, Vinny," she assured the bodyguard over her shoulder. "Uncle Jonathan is going to ride with me tonight. We have a lot of catching up to do." She flashed him her sweetest smile and hustled Jonathan toward the waiting limo. She opened the back door herself and practically shoved him into the back seat. Climbing in after him, she glanced back and locked eyes with Hank. He frowned and shook his head.

She pressed the intercom button.

"Take us to the Garden."

The car moved out into the late afternoon traffic.

Jonathan settled into the seat. "I see you caught on. I'm sorry, luv. I felt sorry for the poor sod. He said you were going back to London after you talked to me, and he wanted me to buy him a few more days." He graced her with his most innocent smile.

"I figured it out all right. I can't believe you involved Miriam in his scheme, too."

He shrugged. "She wanted to help."

"Yeah, well… none of it matters. I need to ask you something important."

"What do you want to know?"

She pulled a copy of a news article from the folder on the seat beside her and handed it to him. "This report says the NTSB determined Daddy's plane went down because of water in the jet fuel, not because of the weather or pilot error. Is it true?"

Jonathan handed the copy back to her without reading it. "I don't like to remember those days. I've spent seventeen years trying to forget."

"I know, and I wouldn't be asking you if it wasn't important."

He pursed his lips and stared out the window.

"Please, Uncle Jonathan. I'm trying to make sense of everything. I need to know what happened so I can move on. I need to put this behind me."

"I know you do. You were so young, and you were so upset we thought it best not to upset you more…with details." He turned away from the window and took her hand in his. "You're a big girl, and I guess it's time to tell you the whole story."

"I'm listening."

"We were in Denver for a week. We came in on buses all the way from Atlanta, and we were sick of being on the road. None of us wanted to spend another day winding through the Rocky Mountains, so we chartered a plane to fly us to Los Angeles. It was a way to buy ourselves an extra day or two in the sun. It sounded like heaven at the time.

"Anyway, the plane was fueled and the pilot was waiting for us at a small airport outside of Denver. Milton decided he wanted to make it to your party, which would mean leaving right after the concert. The rest of us wanted to wait until the next day. Someone said something about wanting to see the snow covered mountains in daylight. We told Milton to go ahead. The pilot could fly him to San Diego and come back to pick us up the next day.

"The airport wasn't convenient for the ski areas, so it didn't have much traffic, especially that time of year. Our plane was the only one scheduled to fly out the next morning, and it was the only one to fuel up and leave that evening." He squeezed her hand, and she looked into his eyes.

They glistened with unshed tears.

"If Milton hadn't left when he did we all would have been on the plane with him the next morning. We all would have died on that mountainside." Tears flowed freely down his cheeks. "When the plane went down, an investigation was launched, and of course, we stayed in Denver for several days. When we did leave, we flew out of Denver International. The investigation turned up the fuel problem. We had all had a close call, and it was Milton who paid the price for our lives."

Tears clogged her throat and filled her eyes.

Oh God.

Silence cloaked the back seat of the limo like a funeral pall. Jonathan spoke. "Now you know why I quit the business. The guilt was eating me up inside. We all should have been on the plane with him. We shouldn't have let him go alone."

Melody let the tears flow unchecked. They were for her father, for Jonathan, for all the band members who must have felt the same way.

"You see, luv, it doesn't matter when the plane left, he would have been on it either way. There were no other planes leaving, so no one could have known about the fuel problem until our plane took off. I'm sorry, luv. I keep thinking if we had all gone with him maybe something would have been different. Or if we had used the main airport. Made different choices. I don't know."

She wiped her cheeks with the palm of her hand, relieved in a way she couldn't understand, yet saddened Jonathan had suffered with such a burden for so long. "You made the decisions you thought were right at the time. You couldn't have known what would happen."

"My brain comprehends, but it took my heart a lot longer to come to the same conclusion."

She hugged him. "Thanks for telling me. I love you, you know. I'm glad you weren't on the plane with Daddy. I don't know what I would have done if I'd lost both of you."

His lips curved at the corners. "I love you, too. I always have. I felt I owed it to Milton to take care of you after he died. He saved my life that night and taking care of you was the least I could do to repay him."

"I lost my Daddy and you lost your best friend. I guess we've been taking care of each other for a long time, haven't we?" She smiled at him in the growing darkness.

The limo pulled into the Garden and stopped behind the tour bus. Hank leaned against it in what appeared to be a leisurely manner. She knew differently. None of them moved for a long time.

"I just have one more question," she said.

"Ask me anything."

She swallowed hard. "Whose idea was it to charter the plane, and when did you decide to do it?"

"That's two questions." He smiled

at her. "As I recall, it was Milton's idea, but we all agreed."

"When? When did he come up with the idea?"

"Well...." He closed his eyes for a second. "Our original plan, when we were on the bus to Denver, was to fly commercial out of Denver International, but we changed to the charter service after we got to Denver. Milton came up with the idea. He said it would get us to the beach faster. You have to remember, it was a long time ago, and there weren't as many flights out of Denver as there are these days."

"Was that the only reason he gave?"

"It's the only one I remember, why?"

"Nothing. It's nothing, just something I was wondering about." She glanced out the window again. With her eyes locked on Hank, she said, "You should go, Uncle Jonathan. I'm sorry I had to kidnap you." She gave his hand a squeeze in silent communication of the bond they shared and turned to him. "I'll be okay. Go on. Get ready to wow them again tonight."

He moved to the door, hesitating before he opened it. "He's a good man, Melody. I don't know where you're going with this digging up of the past, but don't make him wait too long."

He stepped out of the car, and when he came abreast of Hank, he placed a hand on his shoulder. She could tell he was saying something to Hank by the expression on the younger man's face, but she couldn't imagine what it could be. He moved on, and Hank continued to lean against the bus, his arms folded across his chest, legs crossed at the ankles.

Cold February chill poured through the open limo door. She shivered, whether from the cold air or the expression on Hank's face she didn't know. He pushed away from the bus, and her pulse faltered.

She wasn't ready to face him, but it appeared she had little choice. It was too late to run.

He ducked inside and pulled the door closed. He sat across from her and, without taking his eyes from her, pushed the intercom button, and gave his instructions to the driver. A moment later, she was alone with Hank.

She waited, breathless for him to speak.

"Jonathan says I should let you go back to London. Is that what you want?"

Was it? She didn't know anymore. She needed time to think about what Jonathan had just told her. Like Alice, nothing was as it seemed. Should she confront her mother or search for another explanation? Her suspicions were too much to wrap her head around knowing Hank was growing impatient with her.

"I don't know," she whispered. She took a deep breath and let it out. "I know all I do is ask you for more time, but please be patient with me a little longer. I love you. You can't think otherwise."

A tiny flicker of emotion crossed his face, but it was gone as quickly as it appeared.

"Time." A muscle twitched in his jaw. "How much more time, Melody? Are we going to spend the rest of our lives stealing a few minutes together in the back of a limousine or a hotel room? I want more. I want it all."

"I do, too."

"Do you?" Skepticism colored his words. "We'll be in Boston for a week. After that, we go to Philadelphia. I'll give you until we leave Philly to make up your mind. If you can't make a commitment to us by then...."

His words knifed into her heart. He reached for the door handle, and she put her hand on his arm, stopping him.

"What about the gold key?" She pressed her other hand against her chest where the precious metal was cradled against her heart—a promise she clung to. "You said I could use it anytime. You said you would be waiting for me. Was that a lie?"

His voice was cold as the raw New York winter. "Not at the time. I thought once I couldn't go on living without you in my life. I was wrong. It will be hell, but I can do it. It can't be any worse than the living hell I'm in now, waiting for you to decide how much you love me. Two weeks, Melody. We'll be leaving Philly in two weeks." He opened the door and slid out. The soft thud of the closing door reverberated through her body and sucked the air from the car.

She gasped for breath and fisted her hands over her stomach.

Two weeks.

Two weeks or she would lose him for good.

I won't lose him. I can't.

CHAPTER THIRTY-NINE

Hank had given her no choice. She couldn't put off the confrontation with her mother any longer. Melody screwed up her courage and headed west.

It was early when she landed at the small airport near her mother's home in Encinitas. A rental car awaited her at the general aviation center, and within minutes of landing, she was on her way.

She hardly noticed the beautiful spring-like day, the blooming flowers, and green lawns, so different from the barren winter landscape she had left behind in New York. She focused on the conversation ahead. So much depended on what she found out today.

She hoped it would be the final piece that, once in place, would allow her to see the entire picture clearly. Only then would she be able to go to Hank free of the guilt she had carried most of her life.

Her mother was surprised to see her but invited Melody in with a hug, fussing over her the way she used to do when Mel had come home on college breaks. She allowed her the indulgence, dreading the confrontation now that she was face-to-face with her mother.

"What brings you all the way from New York? I can't believe you came all the way here just to have tea with me."

She squared her shoulders. *Get it over with. You already know the answer. Let her try and deny it. Justify what she did.* "You knew there was water in the jet fuel, didn't you?"

Her mother flinched. "Yes, I knew. It doesn't matter what happened. The result is the same. Your father died when that plane crashed."

She stared across the table at her mother. *No denial. No apology.* Her stomach cramped. "It matters to me. Why didn't you tell me?"

"Like I said, I didn't think it mattered why the plane crashed. It did, and that was the important part."

Her blood ran cold. "You don't think it mattered that because he died, three other people lived? You didn't think it would matter to *me*? He was coming to *my* birthday party." She stabbed a finger at her own chest. "Do you have any idea how much guilt I've carried around all these years?" She shook her head. "Now I find out he would have died the next day anyway? And the rest of the band would have died with him? I don't understand how you can say it doesn't matter."

"It doesn't change anything. He's dead, Melody. What does it matter which day he died?"

Who are you? She couldn't believe her mother's callousness. "It doesn't mean anything to you that

Uncle Jonathan, Archer and Nathan are alive because Daddy left a day early? I've lived with the guilt all these years for nothing. His death saved their lives, Mother." She choked back tears of rage. "I'm sorry he died. Of course I am. But don't you see? He was going to die anyway. The plane would have gone down the next day with all of them on it."

She stood and paced across the small kitchen. It was all crystal clear.

"He loved you, Melody, and it killed him. That's what I see."

There it was—the unspoken blame she had sensed her entire life. Disgust roiled in her gut.

"Oh really, mother?" She crossed back to her bag and pulled out a file folder. She sifted through the news articles her mother had so carefully archived and pulled out a yellowed envelope. "Tell me, *Mother*. Whose fault is it Daddy was on that plane?"

She slid the envelope across the bar. Her mother paled.

"What are you saying?"

"Don't you remember, Mom?"

Her mother shook her head, refusing to meet Melody's gaze.

She snatched the envelope back, opened it, and slid the contents across the counter.

"It's a plane ticket to Denver. With my name on it." She held the envelope up. "Daddy sent it. There's a note inside. Do you need me to read it to you, too?"

Her mother turned her face away.

"Daddy sent me a plane ticket for my birthday. He wanted me to come to the concert where he was going to record my song. What did you do, Mother? Did you tell him I couldn't come? Is that why he was on that plane, because you refused to let me go to the concert?"

"You were only ten…."

She froze.

"I told him you had no business at a rock concert. It wasn't the kind of place a ten-year-old girl should be."

She thought she might be sick.

She'd thought she had known the truth, but this…. Her mother became someone else right before her eyes—a pathetic creature she couldn't fathom.

"He said he'd come to see you instead. He said he had a special present for you. I knew he would come if I didn't let you go to the concert."

A new, disturbing insight took shape. "You used me as a pawn to keep him, didn't you? Why didn't you stay with him? Why didn't we live at Ravenswood like a real family?"

"Milton loved you, and he loved his music. I thought if I took you away, he would forget about the music, and we could be a family. But he wouldn't quit touring, not even for you. I couldn't stand competing with the music, the fans, and the adrenaline highs. I couldn't live that way. I wanted to be a family. He wanted his music more than he wanted you…or me."

"You pushed him away, Mother.

You could have had it all, but you laid out an ultimatum he couldn't accept. Don't you see? You could have had at least ten more years with him? Instead, you used me as the bait to get scraps of time with the man you loved." She wiped tears from her cheeks with the back of her hand. "I feel sorry for you, Mom. He might still be alive if we had been together as a family. He wouldn't have even been on a plane if we had been in Denver with him or waiting for him at Ravenswood." She slid the plane ticket back into the envelope.

"You would have been on the plane with him the next day," her mother said.

"No. We would have been on a commercial flight out of Denver International. Uncle Jonathan said Daddy changed the plans to a charter flight after they got to Denver. He didn't know why. He didn't know it was because you were using me as a pawn in your pathetic life."

She knew what she needed to do.

Half running down the short hallway to the bedrooms, she opened the door to the room she had grown up in. It was just as she'd left it when she went to college at seventeen.

She had been running away from the guilt then. Sweet Briar College had been a perfect place for her to hide. The beautiful, sprawling campus at the edge of the Blue Ridge Mountains was quiet and easily missed unless one knew it was there. She had known no curious reporters would think to look for her there, and she had been right.

She'd chosen Willowbrook for the same reason.

Hank was right. She'd been running and hiding. It was time to stop.

Suddenly, her mother's obsession with staying out of the media spotlight made more sense. Her mother was afraid someone would find out about the plane ticket, and then the world would know what she had done. Some nosy reporter would piece together the puzzle, and everyone would know.

That's why she'd insisted they live almost like fugitives. Uncle Jonathan never coming to the house, always meeting her mother and Melody in out of the way places for his twice-yearly visits.

Her mother had drilled it into her. *"Don't draw attention to yourself. Don't tell anyone your real name. Mel Harper. Remember, you're just Mel Harper from San Diego."*

Melody glanced around the room.

I'm tired of being Mel Harper. I'm Melody Ravenswood, and I'm going to be Melody Travis.

On the shelf in the small closet, she found the shoebox where she'd stashed her childhood keepsakes.

Her mother came into the room. "What are you doing?"

Melody spread the contents over the bedspread. "I know it's here." She sifted through the old photos, broken charms, and assorted ribbons. At last she found it—the key to

Ravenswood.

Her father had given it to her when she was seven or eight—she couldn't remember which. It wasn't important. The old skeleton key fit the lock on the front door to Ravenswood. No one used the door anymore. Sometime in the late nineteenth century, a new door on the side of the house had become the most used entrance to the manor house, but the key would still open the real front door.

She wrapped her fist around the key and faced her mother. "I've already wasted too much time I could have spent with Hank. I don't care if we have five days or fifty years together. I want to spend every minute of it with him." She swept past her mother.

"You're leaving?"

"Yes. You made your choices, and I'm making mine. I choose to be Melody Ravenswood. I choose Hank. He loves me. He's offering me a life and a family, and I'm going to go get it and hang on to it with both fists for as long as I can."

She left her mother standing slack-jawed in the doorway.

From the moment her hand closed around the key to Ravenswood, she began to formulate her plan. Her heart was light for the first time she could remember. The guilt she'd harbored for so long vanished in the light of the truth about her father's plane crash. Her mother's part in setting the whole thing into motion and perpetuating Melody's misery brought only pity for the woman whose choices resulted in a lifetime of bitterness and loneliness.

Her mother would have to live with her choices, but Melody didn't have to suffer along with her. There was something bright and shiny waiting for her—a life with Hank, and she had the key to it. All she had to do was use it.

She had plenty of time on the flight back to the East Coast to think about what she had learned in the last few days. No one thing had led to her father's death, but rather a series of choices and decisions shaped fate. At long last, Melody decided blame was best placed on the tragic mistake, which resulted in water leaking into the airport's underground fuel tanks.

She took small comfort in knowing her father's decision to leave early had surely spared the lives of his friends and fellow band members. As for her mother's part in it, she tried to hate her, but when Melody peered in her heart, she found only pity for the woman who raised her. Her mother had let jealousy, pride, and her own selfishness cheat her out of time spent with a man who had loved her.

Hamilton Earl Ravenswood left behind a legacy of music, not the least of which was "Melody", the song that inspired young Henry Travis Jr. to focus his life on music. A new legacy was forming from the association—a legacy and legend

Melody wanted to be a part of.

Hank had put his own stamp on the song, molded the lyrics to tell a story close to his heart. Thanks to him, the song no longer haunted her sleep. In her dreams, she heard Hank's voice singing of a love so deep and passionate it claimed her soul.

She no longer cared if the media circus followed them to the ends of the earth. It was a price she was willing to pay to be with the man she loved. She wanted to be with him on the road, at the farm, or Ravenswood. Their children would have the best of all the different worlds their family would live in. It was a glimpse of Heaven, and she wanted it.

Sunny met her at the airport in Philadelphia. She had booked rooms in her name at the hotel where the band was staying, so no one would know Melody was there until she wanted them to.

"I need to find a good jeweler. Do

you know any in Philadelphia?" she asked.

Sunny put her considerable contacts into action, and before long, they were at a recommended jeweler. Melody interrogated him before she was convinced to part with the key to Ravenswood. Assured the job would be complete and delivered to her in less than twenty-four hours, she returned to the hotel to work on the next part of her plan.

The band arrived by bus a few hours later. She called Jonathan's suite and asked him to come to hers. A few minutes later, Miriam engulfed her in a warm, motherly hug then passed her to Jonathan for more of the same.

"How are you dear?" Miriam asked. "We've been so worried about you."

"I'm fine. Better than fine actually, but I need your help." She filled them in on her plan.

She had to ask, "How is Hank?"

"He's holding up, I guess," Miriam answered.

"He's been writing a lot of music on the bus," Jonathan added. "At least, I think he has. He sits at his computer surrounded by a bunch of newfangled electronic stuff and barely acknowledges our existence. I'll be glad when he finds out you're here. Maybe he'll be more social again."

"I'm sorry, Uncle Jonathan. I didn't want to hurt him and I promise to spend the rest of my life making it up to him."

He hugged her tight. "I think you're headed in the right direction. He's going to be so surprised. I can't wait to see the expression on his face."

"You'll talk to the rest of the band for me?"

"Consider it done," Jonathan said.

"Make sure they don't breathe a word to Hank. I want it to be a surprise."

"I promise, luv. The man won't

know a thing until you're ready for him to."

"You've heard Hank's first version of 'Melody' haven't you?"

He nodded. "Once."

"Good." She pinched his sleeve and tugged him over to the suite's grand piano. She pulled him onto the bench beside her. "I think I remember it, but it has to be perfect."

Jonathan helped her through a few measures she wasn't sure of and listened while she played it through on her own.

"Excellent! You're as scary as your father with that play it by ear thing, but Hank isn't going to know what hit him."

"Tomorrow night then?"

"Everything will be ready," Jonathan promised.

Miriam hugged her before she and Jonathan returned to their suite. "I'm so happy for you and Hank. I've known him all his life, and I think you're everything he's been waiting for."

"Thank you, Miriam. I hope I can live up to his expectations."

Miriam came by the next morning to see how Melody was doing.

"Listen to this," Melody said. She played the song through for Miriam. When she was through, she asked, "What do you think?"

"It's beautiful," Miriam said. "I can't believe you have such a natural talent. It must be wonderful to have such a gift."

"I haven't thought of it as a gift. My first thought when I discovered I could play by ear was horror. I felt like a freak of nature. But I find it's a great stress reducer. Over the last few months, playing has helped me get past the insomnia I've struggled with since Daddy died.

When I was at Ravenswood, I would go to the music room in the evening and play Hank's version of 'Melody' over and over. Eventually, I was able to sleep."

"It's certainly a gift. A gift from your father to help you cope."

She hadn't considered her ability in that light. "Thank you, Miriam. I like your view of the situation. Maybe it *is* a gift from Daddy to help me get through life. I sure hope so because I'm relying on it to get myself a husband and a family."

Jonathan arrived in time to overhear her last comment. "Oh, I have no doubt this stunt of yours is going to get you what you want." He crossed the room to place a soft kiss on Miriam's temple. "If Hank doesn't fall at your feet tonight, I'll beat him with his own sticks."

"Thanks, Uncle Jonathan. I'll hold you to that."

"It won't be necessary. He'll be a blithering fool the moment he sees you."

CHAPTER FORTY

Hank went through the final concert at Madison Square Garden like a zombie. He had lied to Melody—again. He'd told her he could go on without her.

Yeah, right.

Just the thought of continuing on without her was enough to bring him to his knees. Even though she wasn't in the arena to hear it, "Melody" came from the depth of his soul and wrenched his gut into a tight knot of pain.

He choked down a few bites of each meal with Rick standing over him like a trainer with his prizefighter. Each day with no word from Melody brought him a day closer to being alone for the rest of his life, and he had no one to blame but himself. Forcing her to confront her demons on his schedule and choose them or a life with him had to be the stupidest thing he had ever done.

She still had the key, and he clung to the hope she would know in her heart that he'd lied about that, too. If she came to him in ten years, key in hand, he would fall on his knees and beg her to stay.

Too many lies.

He'd been a fool, and he knew it.

Boston passed in a blur of pain and routine. If his friends found his on-stage performance deficient, they said nothing. He attributed it to the deep friendship they shared, not to his performances. He knew they lacked enthusiasm, but he couldn't find it within himself to care.

He spent his free time with his music. Most of what he'd composed was crap, just a mindless distraction and nothing more. The band and crew didn't know it, though, and they left him alone.

The trip to Philadelphia was excruciating. Melody didn't call. She hadn't been at any of the Boston concerts. He didn't know whether she'd returned to London or Willowbrook or if she had blasted off to Mars. He tortured himself, devising ways to find out what she was doing and then tossing them aside.

The clock was ticking but there was still time.

When he stepped off the bus in Philly, he had a plan. If she didn't show in the next four days he was going after her—the tour be damned. He would quit, no matter the consequences. He had lost interest in continuing without her anyway.

Groveling and begging were no longer out of the question. He would do anything, promise anything to have Melody in his life.

The day of BlackWing's opening in Philadelphia dawned brilliant. Hank stood at the window of his suite, absently counting the cars driving on the street below. The previous night, unable to sleep, he'd sat in front of the window and waited for dawn.

When the band left for Atlanta, he wouldn't be with them.

He watched the sun slant between buildings and slowly bathe the skyline in gold. It was time to face reality. She wasn't coming back. After the things he said to her in New York, he only had one choice. He had to go after her and beg.

Melody didn't want to live the kind of life he had offered her. She wanted to hide from the world in a small town, and that's what he was going to give her. He didn't have to work ever again if he didn't want to. They could live anywhere she wanted—even Ravenswood. He would miss Willowbrook, but without Melody, it wouldn't be home anyway.

Numb. It was the only word he could find to describe the way he felt. Turning his back on the sun's warmth, he crossed the room and fell face first onto the bed. Exhaustion eventually won out over depression, and he slept.

**

He surveyed the sold-out crowd. Tonight he would play the last set of his career and he felt nothing. No regret. No sadness. *Nothing.* He dug deep to find the strength to make it through each subsequent song.

She isn't coming.

He cursed himself at every turn for giving her such a highhanded ultimatum. His only excuse was the desperation he'd felt when she'd cornered Jonathan and he knew she would be leaving.

He would find her, make her listen.

She loves me.

That one hopeful thought became a mantra he repeated over and over to the rhythm of each song. It was the only thought he held on to as he faded out of the jam session and stepped off the riser. If he allowed any other thoughts to intrude, he wouldn't make it through "Melody" this final time.

Rick handed him a water bottle and towel just as he did every night. With his back to the stage, he drank down the water and wiped sweat from his brow and hands. He unconsciously registered the instruments bowing out one at a time. Soon, they would be silent, and it would be his turn.

He tried to summon the energy to cross the stage and sing her song one more time. He would do it because his love for Melody came from his soul and he couldn't deny it. He would sing of it one more time, and then he was done.

He closed his eyes and waited for the loss of his music to register. He searched his heart and found only the pain of losing Melody. It swamped all other emotions, all other feelings. He was doing the right thing—the only thing he could do.

The last guitar grew silent, and his heart skipped into a wild rhythm. He lifted his head and took a deep breath.

He handed the towel to Rick, and a cultured British voice he knew well spoke into the silence. "Ladies and gentlemen, please welcome our special guest…Ms. Melody Ravenswood."

The roar of the crowd echoed the blood rushing through his head. Hank whirled to face the stage. The grand piano sat in the darkness of center stage and striding toward it from the opposite side, bathed in a circle of white light, was Melody.

It crossed his mind he might be hallucinating. The scene was a study in black-and-white. Her slim legs were encased in black, and she wore a white shirt that could have come from his closet, only it fit her too well. Her raven black hair hung to her shoulders in soft waves. And gleaming in the spotlight against the stark white of her shirt dangled the key—the only hint of color in his surreal dream.

She took a seat at the piano with all the grace of a concert pianist. Someone shoved him from behind. "Go on. You have a song to do, buddy," Rick said.

Melody sat carefully on the bench. Her heart threatened to leap out of her chest as the seconds ticked by in suspended time.

Come on Hank. Don't leave me out here alone.

The audience was on their feet. She sensed movement across the stage. He approached slowly, as if he was afraid she would vanish if he moved too quickly. Her fist tightened, and the gift she had brought him dug into her palm.

She stood to face him. Her legs quaked.

He stopped close enough she could see the question in his green eyes. She held out her trembling hand. The gold skeleton key lay across her palm, the heavy gold chain spilled through her fingers. His gaze darted to her hand and back to her eyes.

"It's the key to Ravenswood. It's yours. *I'm* yours," she corrected, "if you want me."

"You came."

"I came. I couldn't stay away. I love you, Hank. I want to be your wife." She thrust her hand a fraction closer. "It's the key to everything I am. The key to my heart. I want you to have it."

He closed his hand over hers and slid the key from her palm. Ducking his head, he slipped the chain over. The key fell against his sweat-soaked shirt.

She was vaguely aware of people, and cameras and lights, but all she could see was Hank. She sensed the unspoken words passing between them—as binding as any spoken vows could ever be.

She reached up and placed her

palm over the key. His heart beat steady against her palm. "Sing with me?"

She took his hand and coaxed him down beside her on the piano bench. Her skin felt real against his.

Not a dream.

Nothing else existed outside the bright spot of light where he sat next to Melody. Her eyes sparked with mischief, and he wanted to take her in his arms and kiss her senseless.

"Sing what?"

She smiled.

"'Melody,' of course. In the key of love."

She played the intro and glanced his way. With one raised eyebrow, he questioned the arrangement. Her simple nod confirmed what he had heard. It wasn't a mistake. She would play his original version—the one she had given him permission to record. It spoke of a boy's love of music. It spoke of how the melody reflected his soul and inspired him. That she played it tonight—here—spoke of her acceptance of everything he was.

The gesture brought him low. He didn't deserve her. Not after the way he had pushed her.

He adjusted the microphone. She repeated the intro, and his voice joined the notes flowing from the piano.

Needing to touch her, he slid his arm around her waist and pulled her closer so they sat hip to hip. The physical contact grounded him in reality, and the essence of his soul gave voice to the melody.

"Sing with me," he whispered in her ear.

On the next chorus, Melody added her voice to his. Together, she sensed, they held the audience spellbound.

The last note faded away, and he raised his hands to cradle her face. With infinite tenderness, he brought his lips down to cover hers.

The audience, released from the spell, went wild. But Melody remained focused on Hank.

The band surrounded them, congratulating them both and reminding Hank they had one last song to do. He hoisted her up to sit on the piano, so she faced the drum kit with her back to the audience.

"Stay here where I can see you," he ordered.

The band took the stage as though Melody sitting atop a grand piano center stage was a regular occurrence. He took his place on the drum riser, his eyes locked on hers.

"One. Two. Three. Four." He counted out the beat, and Chad stepped to the mic.

The seductive lyrics of "One Night" filled the auditorium.

He remembered the day he played it for Melody. It was the day he knew music flowed through her veins as surely as it flowed through his. He would never forget the way her body had moved to the beat, recognized it for the erotic metaphor it was.

He never wanted a song to be

over more in his life. She was here. She was his, and he couldn't wait to get his hands on her.

He launched into the drum solo at the end of the song. Melody slid off the piano and headed toward him. He played the final note, jumped off the riser, and pulled her into his arms.

Rick led them through the backstage clutter. At the stage door, Hank shoved his sticks in Rick's hand and yelled over the roar of the audience. "Fill in for me for the next few days?"

Rick smiled and nodded. "No problem. When are you coming back?"

"Tell the guys I'll meet them in Atlanta."

EPILOGUE

<u>Fourteen months later</u>.
Melody stood on the back porch, watching Hank with their daughter. He was so relaxed, she hated to disturb him. The day was mild, not a cloud marred the crystal blue Texas sky. Betty Boop lounged beside Hank's chair, dreaming of chasing squirrels no doubt. Her paws twitched as she chased her imaginary quarry.

Hank made ridiculous noises and faces, laughing at the smiles and adoring looks he earned from Gloria. Melody wasn't too sure how much three-month-old Gloria was actually seeing of her father's face, but she wasn't going to tell Hank. He was having too much fun to disappoint him with details regarding an infant's developmental stages.

She called out to him. "You'd better bring her in. She's going to need her nap before everyone gets here." She didn't need an alarm clock to tell her Gloria would be hungry soon either. Her full breasts sent the message, loud and clear.

"Coming," he said, adjusting the baby in his arms. He'd always wanted a family of his own, but he hadn't expected the overwhelming love he felt for his tiny daughter. He wanted to hold her every minute of the day and never tired of just looking at her. She was so perfect. Named after his mother, she would be the spitting image of Melody. He was more than okay with that. His wife was the most beautiful woman on the planet, inside and out.

He crossed the lawn, carrying his precious cargo into the kitchen where her mother leaned one hip against the counter, a glass of chocolate milk in her hand. He faced her, his stance mirroring hers.

"I think I'm going to have to get a heavier chain. She's strong," he said, pride lacing his voice.

Gloria's tiny fist curled around the gold skeleton key he never removed. Her hand waved back and forth, yanking hard against the chain.

"I'll check into it the next time I'm in town." Melody sipped her chocolate milk. "Your dad called. Jonathan and Miriam are here. They're coming out for dinner. Stacy called. She, Stephen, and the kids will be here this evening. Chad and his gang are coming in tonight, too. Everyone else will arrive tomorrow."

"It's going to be a full house. Are you sure you want to have them all here?"

"I can't wait. This house was meant to be full of people."

"We could find somewhere else to put them all up. They don't have to stay here," he offered.

"Yes, they do. With the kids doing

some of the backup vocals on the new CD, having everyone in the same place will be easier on all of us.

BlackWing's new project was an album of children's songs. The idea had been born when Melody suggested Jonathan, with his British accent, record "Melody" as the a cappella lullaby it originally was. From there came the idea to do an entire album of original children's songs, using their own children for the backup vocals. Soon everyone in the band admitted to having silly songs they'd created for their own kids. From there, the idea took on a life of its own. Melody, with Jonathan's help, had unearthed a few of the songs her father had written and sang for her at Ravenswood. He had committed them to paper, after all.

He was excited that the project would involve their families, and children everywhere would enjoy the songs. All the proceeds from the sale of the CD would go to the Hamilton

Earl Ravenswood Foundation, which had given out its first musical scholarships a few weeks earlier to five deserving students. The new CD would allow the foundation to grow and double the number of recipients next year.

"If they get to be too much, just say so. I'll kick them to the curb," Hank said.

Melody finished her milk and set the glass in the sink. She held out her hands. "Hand her over. It's feeding time."

Hank passed Gloria to Melody's outstretched arms and followed mother and daughter out of the kitchen. He paused in the nursery doorway. "Can I watch?"

Melody settled into the rocking chair and unbuttoned her blouse. "You can watch." She freed her breast and guided Gloria to the distended nipple. "Just don't get any ideas. We have company coming, remember?"

Hank lounged against the

doorjamb, his fingers jammed in his pockets and his legs crossed at the ankle. "Too late," He glanced down at the evidence of his desire. "I get ideas every time I see you like this. It's the only time I'm jealous of Gloria."

Melody blushed and turned her attention to their daughter. God, they were beautiful together. Perfect. He had everything he wanted in life in this one room.

Melody placed the baby in the cradle and crossed the room to Hank. She tugged one of his hands from his pocket and laced her fingers with his. He smiled and followed her into their bedroom, kicking the door closed behind him.

ABOUT THE AUTHOR

USA Today Best-Selling author Roz Lee is the author of over thirty romances. The first, The Lust Boat, was born of an idea acquired while on a Caribbean cruise and soon blossomed into a five-book series originally published by Red Sage. Following her love of baseball, Roz turned her attention to sexy athletes in tight pants, writing the critically acclaimed Mustangs Baseball series.

Roz has been married to her best friend, and high school sweetheart, for over four decades. They have two daughters and are the proud grandparents of three adorable grandkids. Roz and her husband live in the wilds of New Jersey with their Labrador Retriever, Bud which is code for Big Unruly Dog.

Even though Roz has lived on both coasts, her heart lies in between, in Texas. A Texan by birth, she can trace her family back to the Republic of Texas. With roots that deep, she says, "You can't ever really leave."

When Roz isn't writing, she's reading or traipsing around the country on one adventure or another. No trip is too small, no tourist trap too cheesy, and no road unworthy of travel.

Roz Lee

Learn more at: www.RozLee.net